THIS
MAGIC
MOMENT

D0848400

THIS MAGIC MOMENT

A Love Story for People Who Want the World to Make Sense

GREGG EASTERBROOK

ST. MARTIN'S PRESS/NEW YORK

Design by Giorgetta Bell McRee

Library of Congress Cataloging in Publication Data

Easterbrook, Gregg.
This magic moment.

I. Title.
PS3555.A6965T46   1986   813'.54   86-13807
ISBN 0-312-80054-1

First Edition
10 9 8 7 6 5 4 3 2 1

For Nan
Who puts imagination to shame

Special thanks are due to my friends, colleagues, and masters Dominique Browning, Holly Brubach, Michael Carlisle, Thomas Dunne, James Fallows, Nicholas Lemann, Deborah McGill, Charles Peters, Paul and Sally Taylor, and William Whitworth; and to my brother Neil.

Miracles are not frauds just because they are sometimes—I do not say always—innocent contrivances by which the priest fortifies the faith of his flock.

If they confirm or create faith, they are true miracles.

—The archbishop of Rheims
in Shaw's *Saint Joan*

This magic moment
So different and so new
Was like any other . . .

—Jay and the Americans

—1—

AVERAGE WAIT 4 HOURS 45 MINUTES, said a monitor strung up over the museum entrance, blinking incessantly, as if trying to knock something from its eye. USE THESE FIGURES FOR COMPARISON ONLY, the device would add on each third blink. YOUR WAIT MAY VARY.

All up and down the grand stone foyer of the gallery people were waiting, suburbanites with kids mostly; the line folded snakelike, occupying every square foot of floor space. Though admission to the exhibit itself was being granted at a drip, those barely through the main door kept their stares fixed straight ahead with vigilance. HAVE YOUR TICKET READY, a monitor stationed hours to the rear advised.

Such crowds had taken over the Newbury Gallery of Modernized Art several times in recent years. First there had been "Treasures of Tutankhamen," followed by the Vatican exhibit, then "Treasure Houses of Britain," then the most popular of all, the two-part show of Lady Diana's dresses. Flashy traveling shows had brought Broadway flair to the museum business and with it Broadway standards: chief among them that appreciation of art is heightened by great expense and inconvenience.

Old man Newbury would have been much perplexed. He had endowed the museum for the very reason that a panel of academic advisers had assured him modern art would never be popular. After making a killing in turn-of-the-century Chilean copper concessions, Newbury had thought himself obliged, as do certain of the privileged who would have it that magnanimity in the administration of wealth excuses ferocity in its acquisition, to give a portion of his holdings over to activities that everyone admires but no one attends. His choices thus narrowed to opera, modern art, and international goodwill societies, Newbury chose art; establishing a large and soon venerable institution dedicated

3

to images its benefactor did not understand and concepts he was better off not understanding. Fortunately for the gallery, Newbury left a trust well insulated from his offspring, who inherited their father's avidity but not his business sense. After climbing aboard the Jamaican bauxite bandwagon roughly on the day the smart money started getting off, they devoted what remained of the family fortune to suing each other.

Drawing the present crowd was "Wind From the Winter Palace," an exhibition of czarist artifacts underwritten by a consortium of defense contractors. It represented an important advance in the state of the art: the first major touring show to come complete with theme music. A title track called "Till They Want Us Back" sung by musical sensation Suzanne-Suzanne was repeated continuously over the museum's loudspeakers, while a dreamlike music video depicting Suzanne-Suzanne and a regal man walking out of a castle and across the heads of an angry mob could be watched, over and over again, on wide-screen projectors near the ticket booths. The song went,

> *You—you, you you.*
> *They only saw your robes and feasts.*
> *They didn't know what was in your heart.*
> *The nice things you said to your wolfhounds.*
> *The wars you didn't start.*

> *Someday they'll want us back, us back,*
> *I'll be yours till they want us back.*

Whether repetition of "Till They Want Us Back" made patrons eager to buy the records and video cassettes available in the museum gift shop, or to strangle Suzanne-Suzanne, perhaps only a market analyst could say. But though the song was stupefying, it was not without virtue.

One paradox of life is that enterprises can be repugnant at some levels while profound at others. Disasters kill the innocent but also forge heroism and loyalty. Religions cause intolerance and then soothe it with love. Old man Newbury was all but legally a thief—just because you've been indicted in sixteen states, he never failed to remind dinner guests, doesn't mean you're guilty—yet distribution of his gains had made it possible for artists who otherwise might have been impoverished to enjoy the fruits of commerce and still consider themselves highly principled, through the magic of accepting money rather than acquiring it.

For its part the czar song caused Nora Jocelyn, a record company publicist, to meet a civil engineer named Warren Gifford. And that was more than enough to justify everything about it.

Warren Gifford came from an indeterminate location under inexact circumstances and considered the past, even his own, to be of fugitive significance; which is to say, he was an American. When his parents were living he had occasionally asked about the family heritage and history. His father would always fidget inconclusively as though he had been asked one of those high school civics questions whose answer no one seriously expected you to remember, like,

(D) What was the Hanseatic League?

There was nothing to hide or forget, just no sense that recollection was relevant, for Americans live entirely in the now moment, forgiving grudges and forgetting dangers. An American who is aware that when his grandparents were born there was no such thing as reading at night, or that Alaska was once part of Russia, or of any such item—even from recent social experience, not antiquity—is thought as quaint as a monk who writes with a quill.

Nor can it be said that Warren's place of origin was particularly distinctive. Nearly everywhere in present-day America life is basically the same, unless you are very poor or rich. People who live farther apart in this country than Paris is from Moscow eat in restaurants with the same names. In the Arizona desert they string up Christmas lights. And always there are screens showing images of everywhere else.

Most Americans are unimpressed to hear of their judges being led away in handcuffs, their professional athletes being addled by drugs, their journalists inventing stories, their congressmen making it with young boys. But when they find out that McDonald's prices are slightly different in different parts of the country, *that* amazes them. Things change in America, but they change for everyone at once, leaving no basis for comparison. Even the previous moment is reduced to a curiosity.

Because Warren Gifford thought of his own past indifferently, he was often surprised to hear life described as a progression of traumas and tumult: *American* life, not life in destitution or under tyranny. Late at night in college he would sit through long soliloquies about offhand slights or forgotten fifth birthdays, and how it had all been downhill from there. One woman he knew was fond of recounting in psychological lingo the day she stumbled on her mother and her high school biology teacher embracing next to a plastic skull. Generally, she would start this tale whenever in danger of being in a good mood. The number of people he met who seemed to live well, and yet insistently described themselves as miserable, made Warren doubly reluctant to reflect on his own life for fear that he would realize he had been scarred for life and not even known it.

As it happened, thinking up new things to feel bad about turned out to be one of the growth industries of the eighties. Had Warren anticipated this development and gotten in on the ground floor, he might have made a nice career out of being shocked and outraged. People getting worked up over minor issues is in truth healthy, a sign that the number of things really worth worrying about is on the decline.

Life—at least the part that was interesting to know about— began not in childhood, Warren felt, but when one was free to chose one's own mistakes. For example, one of Warren's first adult acts had been to vote for Richard Nixon.

Warren had voted for Nixon in 1972 because Nixon had promised to end the draft, a magnanimous gesture on Warren's part, since he had already been drafted earlier that year. At least he had gone in a lottery year when selection was random, an improvement over the drafts of the sixties with their many student deferments, which were in effect deferments based on wealth. During the sixties, applications to places like Yale Divinity School rose to record levels, as sons of investment bankers and movie producers suddenly remembered their lifelong commitment to serve His name, then fell off during the seventies, as by the strangest and most amazing coincidence their commitment wavered. Warren knew this because his regimental chaplain in Vietnam had been a Yale Divinity graduate who went to the extreme of actually believing some of the philosophy he had been taught, and enlisted feeling that in Southeast Asia he would find a high concentration of troubled souls.

By the time Warren had arrived in Vietnam, ground fighting involving U.S. troops was nearly at an end. There was little to do, except feel discontent. A bunkmate, a grinning white kid from Sarasota, told anyone who would listen that it was the ideal time to be in Vietnam, because a man could get wartime military service on his record for future political purposes without really having to fight. Assigned to the garrison of Tonsonhut, the big airfield, Warren's company spent most of its time on stand down, playing basketball in the hot thick air wearing fatigue pants and boots but no shirts, watching movies, or reading magazines. (By 1972, *Time* had better circulation demographics in Saigon than in most U.S. cities.)

During this period Warren, a mediocre student in early schooling, discovered reading. Besides vaccinations, it was the only good thing the Army ever did for him.

Though Warren's company never fought, fighting was not far away; and might have reached them, but never did. Few of the draftees seemed to worry about dying. Somehow it made you feel safer to be called near to death and dismissed, the way a motorist passing a bad wreck smiles secretly to himself because somebody else's number has come up. Warren sometimes entertained the notion that circulates among young soldiers that being near death makes the survivor invincible.

During his tour Warren never fired a gun, but twice felt mortality immediately at hand. The first instance came when a company basketball game was nearly hit by a falling helicopter. They heard an odd hissing noise and looked up to see a Huey Slick corkscrewing straight down toward them. At first the machine did not seem to be falling or moving at all, merely expanding in size. Blue smoke poured from the tail rotor bearing, making a pattern in the sky like stunt pilots make at air shows. They stood still and watched for a time before breaking to run. Looking back as he ran, Warren saw a body fly out of the left side of the Huey, where the troop door had been removed—maybe thrown by centrifugal force, or maybe the guy was trying to jump for it. Then the helicopter was flat against the field, as flat as ink on paper.

Aircraft using rotors for lift must be light and as a result are made of aluminum and magnesium, combustible metals that burn with a white heat. The only metal more dangerous when burning is uranium. As an engineer, Warren would one day find himself asked to critique a technical paper that advocated mining bauxite from the crust of the moon, where it is plentiful, for use as a sort of lunar coal to power ships to the stars. He would also get a government contract to study a proposal from the same source suggesting that entire nuclear power plants be placed in orbit around the earth: so that if they melted down, the radiation would be too far away to cause harm. Warren would cost his firm a significant sum of money by writing the words "what bullshit" across the document's executive summary.

Because aluminum and magnesium burn, it was well known to soldiers that when helicopters caught fire there was little hope of saving those inside them. The fire exhausted itself quickly, leaving only ash; a layer, hardly even a pile. Plus an outline. Between the intense heat, impurities in the alloys, and the porousness of concrete, burning helicopters often drew death sketches of themselves on runways—outlines, recognizable, which no amount of hosing down could remove. Sandblasting was required.

Now according to the television networks every Vietnam veteran returned to his ungrateful country with a vision of hideous import burned into his tormented mind, such that he could never again look upon a can of shaving cream without wanting to slaughter a church full of old women. This was not the case with Warren. He did not see the crash happening again in slow motion whenever a corporate helicopter passed overhead, bearing executives to some incredibly important meeting, the outline before his eyes. Thinking of the soldier thrown from the Huey just before impact made Warren sorrowful, but no more so than thinking of the pilot and the five other passengers who stayed inside and died too, whose bodies he never saw and whose death existed in his mind only as an increment of information. That one man had died in a strange way, while several others died deaths more prosaic, seemed inconsequential compared to the questions of whether any of them deserved to die and, considering that they all did, what happened to them next?

The same evening as the helicopter crash, Warren took the sense of invincibility that accompanies proximity to another's death and put it to good use.

Some cargo planes were due for night landings. There had been reports of activity near the base, so combat approach rules were in effect. Runway lights were turned off, and planes had to come in fast and low, wings tipped down until they raked toward the ground like plowshares, to present smaller targets. Only at the last instant would the plane level off, then cut its engines in order to lose speed before it overshot the field. This maneuver was more difficult than it might sound—the Air Force's equivalent of a carrier landing. Occasionally, pilots lost their nerve.

The first plane due, a C-130, made its first approach too fast and had to go around, bolting straight back up into the sky on full throttles. It lined up for a second approach and was again too fast, the pilot holding over the runway noticeably beyond the point at which he should have known there was not enough space left to land. Again he went around, and again was wrong, this time pulling the nose up with just a few hundred feet to spare.

Something was playing on the pilot's mind. By now a number of men had come out to watch the strip, both fearing a crash and fearing there would be no crash to satisfy their curiosities. There was talk of sending the plane to the Philippines, where it could make a standard landing. Too little fuel. An Army brigadier appeared in the tower and attempted to order the pilot, an Air Force lieutenant colonel, to let his first officer land the plane. But pilots on planes are like captains on ships; their internal authority is absolute. This one refused to relinquish the controls. He was on the verge of making full colonel, the jump to flag rank, and knew that "relieved in flight" would be the end of his service record.

Once more the C-130 slanted in, too fast again but not as badly. Warren began to pray for it to rise safely away. Suddenly the shadow snapped level, the engines coughed, and the plane dropped to the ground in a twisting motion, striking at an angle to its forward travel. All the right-side tires blew together. The C-130 slid diagonally along the concrete, heaving up sparks like spray from a speedboat. Then some gear struts buckled and the plane pitched over into the grass, snapping open its right wing and spilling fuel. Flames appeared immediately; it would only be a matter of time, probably not long, till fire touched the fuel.

As Warren and a dozen or so others ran forward, a hatch followed by an escape cord dropped from beneath the cockpit and down popped the airmen, none badly injured. The pilot, however, did not follow. According to the crew chief he was alive but refused to leave; he had ordered them off. Nobody knew what to do.

A pair of young captains arrived, one Army and one Air Force, peevish types because they had come to Vietnam too late to punch their tickets with combat rotations. They fell to arguing over who had the authority to supervise a rescue of the pilot.

"It's my airplane. I have control here," said the Air Force officer.

"It's my runway," the Army captain countered. "I will make the command judgment."

"The plane is off the runway."

"Roles and missions under FM102 gives field perimeters to the Army."

"High-skill personnel are priority assets."

By now the flames had grown hot enough to create a furnace effect, pushing clothing against the skin. Several of the soldiers were inching backward. The captains kept arguing, oblivious, one of them demanding a walkie-talkie with which to consult his superiors. Warren thought to himself, If I go now I've got a fair chance. Whereas if I wait for these two lunatics to finish their disputation and then they choose me, I'm dead for sure. He felt no fear, only urgency. Grabbing the cord, he hoisted himself up into the hold of the burning plane.

Passing through the hatchway Warren staggered for a moment as if he had been hit by someone he couldn't see. More to the point, as if someone he couldn't see had shoved a fist down his throat, except it was the reverse—there was nothing in his throat, no air. Warren, like most people, had never been in a situation where there was nothing to breathe, as opposed to where the breath must be held. Like many sensations that precede death, the effect cannot be imagined. Working his lungs produced only confusion and disorientation.

Forward in the cockpit sat the pilot, unharmed as far as Warren could tell. He had put his mask on and was sitting with his back to the controls, looking down the length of the plane into the cargo hold.

"Sir!" Warren cried, except he didn't cry that at all. The muscles of his face and esophagus contracted, but no sound emerged. Trying to yell without air is as hard as trying to rouse yourself to wakefulness from a bad dream. The pilot gave no sign that he was aware of Warren or the situation. His attention was fixed, the cargo hold his only concern.

Warren turned to look, but saw nothing. No article of value —in fact, nothing at all. All Warren could discern were cargo straps and jump seats serving as wicks for the busy flames, which were spouting up the way lawn sprinklers do when turned on without warning.

"Sir!" Warren attempted to call again. The top of the fuselage was beginning to parch where rising flames spilled against it. From outside on the ground Warren heard shouts and the sounds of still more bickering. Finally, looking backward, he realized what was holding the pilot transfixed. *The cargo hold was empty.* The plane wasn't carrying anything.

With difficulty Warren made his way forward to the cockpit. Wrapping his arms around the pilot, he lifted and accomplished nothing; the man seemed to weigh an infinite amount. Then he pushed from the side and the officer toppled over, out of his seat. In order to roll the pilot toward the hatch Warren had to tear his mask free. This broke the pilot's trance.

"He knew full well," the pilot said, "full well . . ." His lips formed a few more words, but no sound emerged.

Warren didn't think to breathe from the mask while it was near. He grappled and shoved until he had pushed the pilot near the hatch, and with an effort that took his last bit of breath, heaved him out. Suddenly, Warren felt total exhaustion. He tried to make his muscles propel his own body out the hatch, but nothing happened.

A piece of the aircraft broke off and fell with a crash, causing the fuselage to shift. Warren was thrown across the hold, away from the hatch. Catching himself against a bulkhead, he burnt his hands. Warren heard a series of rapid bursts near the middle of the plane, and, as the sides of his head seemed to collapse inward for a moment, felt a pleasant tingle spread through his nose. As this happened, flames in the hold brightened and the heat surrounding Warren became liquid. Oxygen bottles were exploding.

As the flames swirled and turned a pretty shade, he tried again to move toward the hatch but could not. Warren became aware he was passing out. He dropped to the hot metal floor and tried to gasp, drawing into his lungs only heat and the toxic sear of burning plastic. By reflex Warren closed his eyes against the fumes, then found he couldn't reopen them, no matter how hard he tried. The explosions from the hold grew louder. Then the fuselage lurched again and dipped nearly ninety degrees. Warren was sent rolling toward the hatch, which, following the latest shift, had become a hole in the floor. His body rolled across the opening, and fell into cold space.

Warren saw the face of the pilot bending to attend him. The

two captains and the other soldiers had withdrawn, figuring the C-130 would explode. Returned to his senses by the fall from the hatch, the pilot quickly bent down, circled Warren's arm over his shoulder, and began to drag him away. Warren would later think this the one time in his life he was glad to see someone assume a military bearing.

Fire equipment had arrived but was keeping a secure distance. The trucks' sirens blared, as if anyone could be watching a blazing plane wreck and not be aware there was a problem. As the pilot dragged Warren toward the line of pulsing lights an eruption of sound and yellow put them both into a nice cozy sleep. When he awoke in the infirmary, Warren knew he had been roughly five seconds and a random lurch of the plane away from dying.

"Your lucky day," said one of the base commander's adjutants, who came to call on Warren with a stack of papers. Seeing that Warren thought he was referring to the escape, the officer added, "I mean about the plane blowing. That should make it good for a Medal of Valor. If it had just burned down the best you could have hoped for would be a Distinguished."

Oddly, Warren had never felt fear during the incident, though he was not an unusually brave person. He had felt a mild sense of familiarity—perhaps from being in C-130s—coupled with a tremendous sense of urgency, a sense that every step had to be exactly right or *somebody else* would pay a horrible price. Who? Warren had continued to feel that somebody else was the one in true peril even after he had pushed the pilot through the hatch and only his life remained at risk. For a while he wondered if he had subconsciously assumed he was going to die, and if that feeling had generated some kind of disassociative reaction to ease the final moment. Then, thinking back, Warren realized he had felt this way from the instant he hoisted himself into the fuselage. Not being able to comprehend this perception, he set it aside.

Warren later heard through the grapevine that the Air Force flyer, who was revived on the scene, had spent half an hour by the wreck cursing and stomping the ground. When the brigadier hauled up in a jeep, a fistfight nearly broke out. Five more C-130s landed that night without incident, all using combat approaches and all equally empty. The planes had been ordered in not because they were needed but because it was the thirty-first and the base commander was five landings short of being able to report that Tonsonhut had handled a record number of sorties during the month. Following the crash the commander had frantically called in one more plane, because there was a bureaucratic dispute over whether crashes counted as sorties or not.

In the morning Warren went back to look at the remains of the plane. It had burned down to a black shell of hoop-shaped fuselage support rings. Lying about the wreckage were some oddments that appeared unscathed—a Thermos bottle, a flashlight, a pulley with its grease still lumpy and moist. There was an officer's .45, which Warren took as a souvenir.

The burned-out hoops suggested the ribbed carcass of a dinosaur. Warren was not fully convinced that man was the first advanced creature to inhabit the earth, given the vastness of time. After all, the fossil records were limited to lower animals that had died in fields and swamps. A future archaeologist finding only the remnants of contemporary animals that did not make arrangements for their own interments might not be too impressed with our epoch, either. Warren wondered what kind of conclusions future archaeologists would draw from the airbase itself—long easels formed of synthetic rock, decorated with pagan symbols like 34R and faint renderings of ancient flying beasts affixed to the surface in an unknown fashion.

After his discharge from the service Warren got a scholarship to UCLA. No human experience has inspired a more voluminous literature than university life, so there is no need to expand here. Suffice it to say that Warren, whose knowledge of the monied life came mainly from television, was immensely amused by the sight of Porsches and Corvettes parked in front of dormitories where their owners had to wait in line to use the bathroom.

Graduating with a degree in engineering, Warren took temporary jobs with small consultants and contractors in central California towns before finding a salaried position with a mid-sized architectural and engineering firm called Kessey, Denning & Hobard. The firm was hiring because it had been awarded a multiyear contract to refurbish the pump-generating section of a hydroelectric power plant.

Civil engineering proved to be slow, satisfying work. For decades it had been the province of government employees who labored in damp basements painted that special shade of revolting dull mint reserved for grade schools and city halls—a paint, it occurred to Warren, that must come from somewhere; perhaps a swatch on the Sherwin-Williams color wheel labeled Municipal Puke Green. By the time Warren joined the profession, the important government jobs were being handled not by civil servants but by private firms under contract. He learned that in contemporary technical affairs, like elsewhere in society, advice is respected only if it comes from strangers.

A government-employed engineer is fortunate if he has a map of the state to call his own. In the KD&H office Warren found every electronic convenience that could be imagined among the law-firm–style upholstered luxury. Some new piece of computer hardware arrived every week, often going directly into storage. The office was decorated in tasteful earth tones, with plants and art in the reception lobby; the air conditioning ran cold enough to hang meat. Each time the city wanted a new box of pencils it had to go through months of competitive bids, but when a contractor like KD&H placed a purchase order, the amount was simply added on to the master contract, already awarded, along with overhead and a standard markup for the company—which meant the fancier the company's office became, the more KD&H made.

In the reproductions room there sat a beautiful new Minolta four-color lithographic separator costing $39,000. Doug Denning, Warren's supervisor, had bought the separator at city expense in order to generate graphics that would adorn a proposal KD&H was compiling at city expense for running bicycle trails through a foundry put out of business by the Japanese. Every six months or so Denning would make a colorful, fuzzy line sketch of the trails and old slag towers as seen from a great distance; print an absolutely perfect brochure with the help of the Minolta; and then mail the brochures to the city council. About ten days later he would send a certified letter saying specific plans were behind schedule because his "impact assessment team" was devoting such time to obtaining community, minority, environmental, educational, and legal input that a cost overrun was regrettably unavoidable.

It occurred to Warren after a few months on the job that the impact assessment team was so busy obtaining community input that no one in the office had ever seen any of its members. Checking the project file he learned that the city council so far had paid nearly $260,000 for half a dozen contract extensions and received nothing more than colorful brochures. The impact assessment team itself didn't exist. Warren asked Denning if it wasn't time to start producing a few blueprints and site elevations.

"Upholding the highest standards of professional conduct is always our foremost concern," Denning answered, speaking in an oddly formal tone, as though someone was taking down his words. "Your comments and suggestions are encouraged."

When Warren continued to inquire periodically about the whereabouts of the impact assessment team, Denning would take him aside for a little speech about the real world. After a while Denning began referring not to "your comments and suggestions" but "your charges." Thus did Warren learn to hold his peace. The pump-generating project to which he was assigned was serious work, and by mutual consent Denning steered him clear of the fishy contracts. As Warren began to rise in the firm he would occasionally corner Denning at social events where drink had been served and try to convince him that without moral responsibility all else was supposition. Denning would always agree wholeheartedly, and the following morning be up to his usual tricks.

Talking to the base commander at Tonsonhut probably would have been the same. The situation at KD&H bothered Warren, but not so much that he couldn't go on. There were compensations. Being just slightly corrupt gave him an entrée into respectable society, where he quickly made friends. Able to afford suits and tickets, he developed an interest in culture. The Newbury Gallery became one of his favorites.

"This started only three weeks ago?" Lil Albritton asked.

She and her husband, Tommy Camero, had arranged to meet Warren in the foyer of the Newbury, forgetting there would be crowds. The three of them had to push through the lines, Lil repeating "Excuse us. Excuse us." Tommy was annoyed.

"I belong to this museum. Members shouldn't have to deal with this," he said. "I get the newsletter, for chrissakes." He cleared a path for Lil, a frail person of the sort others fear for. She often said "Excuse me" when it wasn't really necessary, and seemed always about to catch a cold.

It was said that Lil came from an old East Coast family and had an uncle who was prominent in something, although Warren was never quite clear as to what; their wedding had been announced in the *New York Times* even though neither had ever lived in New York. Lil and Tommy kept their own last names; there was an ongoing debate about what to name a child. (Those of you looking ahead for new frontiers of worry should consider this: Suppose Tommy and Lil have a child, Doreen Albritton-Camero, and Doreen marries the offspring of another union of young professionals, David Massey-Ritcher. Their child will be surnamed Camero-Ritcher-Albritton-Massey. And that child marries . . .) Tommy, whom they were following, was adept at slipping through crowds. He gave the impression of being firmly built, though dressed for the beach he was revealed to be almost as frail as his wife, arms straight as the bones beneath them. Working for a money-management firm that specialized in trading commodity and stock options, Tommy was in the business of testing his ideas on other people's money. He never bet the markets himself, though. Often he made fun of the idea.

"I'll bet the cafeteria is already jammed. It always is," Tommy complained.

In the cafeteria—where Nora Jocelyn was to join them—

Tommy spotted a table piled with paper and the Styrofoam residue of the last meal. The table took a moment to clear, fast-food-packaging theory dictating five pieces of wrapping for each consumable item. Tommy went to get cups of coffee. Lil picked up her conversation.

"You're going to propose to someone you met three weeks ago?"

She was almost afraid to ask for details, fearing that no matter what Warren said, each new piece of information would add to her impression of a drastic mistake in progress. Yet the thought made her giddy, like a librarian who feels professionally obligated to read a dirty book which has won literary acclaim. Lil and Tommy had cohabited for eight years before their marriage, and during that time had analyzed every conceivable aspect of the decision in great depth. They had consulted family members, friends, former teachers and co-workers, two professors of contract law, and a woman with a Ph.D. in relational interaction.

On her advice they had drawn up a chart of pros and cons, which they placed on the refrigerator door and amended day by day. When the "Cons" column grew considerably longer than the "Pros," Lil became depressed, so Tommy devised a complicated point-value system for weighing each entry. He stored the formula in his desktop computer and used it to produce periodic updates of their marriage prospects that resembled a football poll. The computer determined that an overall rating of 6.7 would justify marriage. When their rating hovered around 5.5 for several months, and once dipped to a low of 4.7, Lil grew further depressed. Eventually Tommy resolved the dilemma by changing the criteria, assigning, for example, fewer points to "flexible travel plans" and more to "not lonely." Another full year passed before they finally took the leap. Now along had come their friend Warren proposing marriage to a woman he'd known three weeks. To Lil it was as if he'd said, "By the way, I've decided to become an abbot."

"And this woman is a—a publicist?" Lil was reaching for a delicate word. She worked at a consumer-rights foundation and was deeply suspicious of anyone who spoke in favor of anything.

"A PR person, a flak. For Loco Gringo Records, Suzanne-Suzanne's new label. Besides she only flaks part time, to pay the rent. She's a singer and she writes her own compositions. She lives in Los Angeles, and being associated with the record company improves her chances of being discovered. Right now she's traveling with the czar show to make sure people play the record."

"Must be good at her work." Tommy had returned with Styrofoam cups of coffee. He grimaced. Even in the cafeteria strains of "Till They Want Us Back" were ubiquitous.

Warren explained that he had been in line on opening day and noticed a woman standing at the door to one of the museum staff offices. He was struck by her, captivated, and tried to take in as much of her as he could before she disappeared behind the door. But she didn't disappear; rather, she stood fast, as though waiting. For half an hour the line snaked in her direction.

"I thought I had plenty of time to think of something clever to say, but all of a sudden I was standing right next to her and my mind was blank," Warren said. "So I said, 'Would I ever like to get my hands on the person responsible for this song.' She said, 'Yes, I bet you would.' First thing she said, I swear it. From there on it was all formalities. I knew."

Tommy rolled his eyes. "You saw her the moment you walked into the room, even though there were two thousand people in the way."

"Yes. In fact that's exactly what happened. And I believe she saw me."

"Did you hear strings?"

"Well suppose I did? Suppose it did happen just like everybody wishes it would happen to them, but has to make fun of, because it hasn't?" Tommy shrank back. The tone of Warren's voice was forceful. "What if something jumped directly from your dreams into life and it was right and true?"

"Sounds to me like a moot question . . ."

"You'd be scared, that's what. Any disaster I can name, any fuck-up or failure, you'd believe in a minute without question

and without proof. When I tell you something good, you doubt.
It's not rotten enough to pass for real."

"Tell me something good," Lil said, her voice soothing.

"I know everything Nora's going to say before she says it, yet
it still comes as a surprise." Warren went on to present an impres-
sively synchronous inventory of likes and dislikes, shared ideas
and values. Only friends and immediate family members can
bear to listen to such touchy-feely talk, so the specifics will not
be repeated. The point is, it mattered to Warren. As passion
always rusts, romantic love stands or falls on its ability to transform the terrene—the mundane assignments and errands of living—into sources of mutual satisfaction.

"We've been together every hour since, except nine to five,"
Warren concluded. "She has to go back to L.A. this afternoon.
I'm going to ask her just as I drop her at the airport, and tell her
she can phone me with her answer when she lands."

As the obvious objections were raised, he insisted, "No, three
weeks is plenty of time. People think that one lunch date, one
moment at the bar—that a few *minutes*—is enough to tell when
it *won't* be right. Nobody finds it strange if you completely
dismiss someone's existence after the briefest encounter. Why
can it not work the other way around? We walk down the street
psychologically prepared to be robbed at any minute. Suppose
instead we found a sack of money with a note attached saying,
'This is for you. Please enjoy it.' We'd be scared and upset,
probably run in the opposite direction."

"But that doesn't happen," Tommy said.

"Prove to me it doesn't happen."

For a beat Tommy was flustered. "You mean prove that no
one ever finds a sack of money addressed to him lying on the
street?" He crushed out his cigarette. "Of course I can't prove
that."

"Then prove to me that people don't see each other across
crowded rooms."

There was a pause. "I just don't want you to waste your life
on an illusion."

"Now, Tommy," Lil said. "Everybody has to waste his life on

something." She began a maternal lecture on the deceptive power of infatuation. Warren stopped her.

"I've never been infatuated before. I'm thirty-four years old and never even felt the pang, if I understand it properly. Doesn't it strike you as odd that I haven't found someone by now to be infatuated with?"

"Not a bit." Lil was serious. "I think the chances of two good people meeting each other are very small, and the chances of them meeting when both are eligible and interested are infinitesimal. And considering how easy it is today to back out of a romance if something goes wrong, what amazes me is that any successful relationships exist."

"That's because people have gotten too smart to fall in love," Warren said. "Makes you sound a little soft in the head. Like joining a Moose Lodge."

"People have gotten smart? Come on down to the trading floor sometime if you want to see how far civilization has progressed." Tommy laughed to himself and turned as though about to signal for a waiter, then remembered he was in a cafeteria.

"No, too smart, or at least too educated. Too thoroughly schooled in the ways of disappointment. Everything is tainted, and above it all is the only safe place to be—that's the underpinning theme of the smart set. If you're not aware of how unworthy the world is, then you simply don't know what's going on." Lil had an Ivy League education, including law school, and Warren expected her to protest. She did not, so he continued. "Even regarding yourself. If you're really smart you know how unworthy you yourself are. A package deal of hypocrisies, self-obsessions, genetic predilections, and Freudian compulsions. Although, of course, your astonishing IQ compensates. Who in his right mind could love you?" Warren had seemed to direct the question at Lil. "I don't mean you personally. It's just—you can't use terms like *love* today around serious people without putting on surgical gloves and holding the specimen far away from your body for your fellow scientists to observe."

Schoolchildren on a field trip passed the table, momentarily drowning out the conversation. Lil was vaguely disturbed in the way people are unsettled by news of tragedies in foreign countries whose locations they aren't sure of.

After an interval filled with the clatter of crashing trays, Lil began a limited defense of smart-set bias. Intellectuals will always be uncomfortable with the idea of romance, she said, because intellectuals practice logical analysis, and romance, being nonlogical, is beyond their powers. At least, Lil said, the onset of romance—when the positive passions like intimacy and loyalty seem to spring from nothing—defies logical analysis, except at a cynical level. ("Liked her legs." "Reminded me of my first boyfriend." "I was drunk at the time.") Worse, the words spoken during the delirious early phase of romance always sound ridiculous except to those directly involved. If Andrew Marvell had courted Emily Dickinson, their cooing noises nevertheless would have made strong men wince. And above *all* else, Lil noted, intellectuals fear sounding silly.

On the other hand, the decay of romance, driven as it generally is by conflict or false expectations, and leaving as it does a painful psychological wake, can be subjected to abstraction. So, Lil concluded, it is only to be expected that intellectual analysis of love concentrates on the harm done. Serious works of art concerning romance usually begin at the breakup, skipping over the pleasure (the non-logical part) and emphasizing the pain (we warned you!). In this manner even flashbacks to happy days can be made to seem ominous. After love fails, Lil said, it is possible to impose a rational structure. Broken promise (a) led to seething bitterness (b) which unmasked sexual incompatibility (c) and so on. While romance is full and lulling, just try explaining it.

Furthermore, she continued, porpoise hides are used by gravel worship cults in Senegal to insulate their primitive huts from the fierce soap storms that sweep across the frozen veldt, producing golf balls the size of hail. Or so she might have been saying as far as Warren was concerned. He was staring up across the condiment cart at Nora Jocelyn, who stood under the arch of the cafeteria entrance unmoving. Customers milling in and out meekly parted to avoid her, for some reason not pushing or grumbling that she was in the way.

* * *

Now a word about describing women: don't. All that crap about creamy breasts and languid thighs—even literary types can't resist. We read the length of *The Great Gatsby*, for instance, without ever learning about Nick Carraway's physical appearance. But by the third reference to Jordan Baker we know her chest size.

Of course, physical appearance is a quicksand in everyone's path. On first inspection all that can be learned of a person is physical appearance. Those who are not kind or true may conceal their faults in ways that take years to detect. Appearance, however, is a test that may be graded quickly and reliably. The kind may turn cruel and the trusted betray, but a creamy breast will always be a creamy breast.

Children, as they learn the power of voluntary exclusion, organize themselves into a hierarchy of looks that in many ways is more enduring than the social strictures their parents and teachers impose. Attractive, average, and unattractive children group together without being told to: the cliques at any given high school have in common mainly looks, or lack of same.

By adulthood most people have been conditioned to search out, when thrown into unfamiliar surroundings, others with approximately the same looks-value as themselves. An unattractive man at a business convention is not only unlikely to try to make polite small talk with a tall blonde dish, he probably won't introduce himself to a dapper man, either. Often it is easier for strangers to mix with other strangers of different race or class than with those with noticeably better or worse looks.

Because first impressions cannot help but be physical, it is neither surprising nor discouraging that romance begins at this verge. Only when physical appearance remains the dominant consideration does it become objectionable, in the same way that love of money, rather than money itself, is the root of evil. Consider how society admires an ugly man who marries a gorgeous woman: he must be brilliant or powerful or loaded to land such a prize. The woman in the same partnership is disdained by society, including other women: she must be dippy or dizzy or greedy. The idea that love may be behind a mismatch of looks is scoffed at altogether.

At its most tyrannical, the hierarchy of looks holds that only a beautiful woman (Helen, Guinevere, Lara) may inspire great love, because visage and sensuality are the greatest qualities woman can offer. Whereas only a hideous man (Cyrano or Lancelot—who lived as an ascetic knight in the original Camelot legends to conceal his misformed face, and who became Hot Stuff only when Robert Goulet played him) may cause a woman to love with greatness; because the profound male qualities, namely courage, prosody, and vision, are found strictly in the otherwise wretched.

So to sum up about Nora Jocelyn's looks: she has them. Specifics are not important.

Warren jumped up and ran toward Nora, who did not move. She stood her ground in the midst of the mob filing into the cafeteria, seeming perplexed, as though Warren were someone she had been introduced to long ago who was embarrassing her by making a show of remembering her name when she could not recall his. Warren moved to embrace Nora, then stopped. She didn't say "Don't," but he had heard the word as plainly as if it had been announced over the public address system.

Nora did say, "I can't."

Rather than reply Warren shook his head, as if to say *I don't know what you're talking about,* but he knew perfectly well.

"I can't marry you. I know what you're going to ask. I've led you on and I apologize for my behavior." The words were clipped and businesslike. Nora avoided eye contact. "Now, please excuse me. I've got to go."

What happens when a skydiver grabs the ring on his emergency chute and it comes off in his hand? Or when an injured doctor in a wilderness cabin diagnoses himself and realizes he will die before his rescuers arrive? We would like to think that the condemned in such situations experience moments of sublime clarity offering at least partial compensation for their suffering. Then again, maybe the central nervous system insists on dragging them through panic, fright, and despair even though it can't possibly do any good. In Warren's case it was the latter. He was not only shaken and frightened but aware of himself as shaken and frightened. He could think of no response except to stand mute and appear well worth leaving.

A section of his mind was insisting there had to be words that would make it right: if only he could hit on them. There weren't, in truth, not at that moment. Words can easily turn the heart away, but rarely toward.

As the two of them stood dumbly, an older man with a tremulous West Indian accent bumped into Warren from behind.

"Apologies," he said. "Could you point me to the pre-Columbian daggers? Too long for the main exhibit, you know. And that song. Do you know if there are any wings where they aren't playing it?"

To be rid of the distraction, Warren, who had no idea where the daggers were, began making up directions that would have led the visitor a merry chase through the steam plant, past the loading dock, and, if followed precisely, into the city sewer. Nora interrupted and substituted the correct directions; apparently her three weeks at the museum had not been entirely wasted. While she was speaking, Warren was bumped again, this time by a young woman with shoulder-length hair who was handing out flyers. He took one and shoved it in his pocket, thankful that she moved along, not stopping to deliver a sermon on blessed Vishnu or the need to build anti-matter shields before the Russians did. When both of the intruders had departed, Nora spoke first.

"I can't marry you because I'm already married. I've been married a long time. I lied to you, and won't insult you by asking for forgiveness. You can think anything of me you want. Now I'm sorry, I really have to go." She stopped, out of rehearsed words, and seemed close to saying something she hadn't planned. Then, recovering her poise, said only, "Take care."

"Last night you said—"

"I said what I *wished* I could say."

"How can you just walk away from—"

"Warren, don't make it hard. There was a moment between us but it rose up like steam and it's gone."

"I'll call—"

"You don't even know where I live."

"In Los—"

"I lied about that, too. And about being a singer? Forming my own band? Lies." Some of the energy left her voice. "In PR they teach you to believe your own lies. If I was going to lie for a living I should have been a lawyer. But I wanted you to think highly of me. And look what I got. I'm sorry I took advantage of someone who deserves better."

"I'll find you—"

"You don't even know my married name." Nora looked Warren up and down in the manner of an aunt who has not seen a growing nephew in some years and is trying to determine exactly what, this time, is different about him. "I had a—I suppose you would call it a fantasy that we— No, it's crazy to say anything. Please just let me say good-bye."

Momentum was about to carry her away. Warren knew he could only manage one more sentence. He said, "This is wrong, and you know it."

She listened without reacting, then spun and disappeared. Warren stood watching her form recede and even after she was gone from sight stood for a long time watching. As soon as Nora had left, people began pushing Warren and grumbling that he was in the way. His mind went into overload like that of a man running toward an accident and trying to recall first-aid principles. Raise the legs for shock? Or is it lower the legs and raise the head? Eventually Warren became aware of Lil Albritton by his side, rubbing her hand back and forth across his shoulder blades, the only form of physical contact he had ever seen between her and Tommy in public, and one reserved for emergencies.

"She didn't seem very friendly to me," Lil said.

"Won't marry."

"I'm so sorry." In fact Lil was immensely relieved, thinking in years to come her friend would count himself fortunate for having escaped from a dreadful mistake at the bargain price of perhaps a few weeks of hangovers and self-pity.

"Already married."

"What a bitch!"

"Not from L.A."

Lil withheld an urge to say, "Maybe she's not all bad." She led Warren back to their plastic table, where, for the next hour, he blurted out every trite detail of the previous three weeks, every seemingly transcendent event now revealed as fraud. His listeners, being true friends, did their best to feign shock and indignation again and again. Finally, Warren wound down into exhaustion, but not before making one last extravagant claim.

"This is not just a feeling. It's more. It's something I *know.*"

Neither Lil nor Tommy could think what to say. A pretty woman walked past the table unaccompanied and Lil, snapping at an opportunity to change the subject, said, "Why don't you ask her out? She could take your mind off anything."

"Lil, don't pressure him. That's the last thing he wants to mess with right now."

But Tommy's wife was insistent. "You could tell her you knew her in a former life. That's my absolute favorite opening line."

"If you really want to get her attention, tell her you owed her money in a former life," Tommy suggested, nodding to himself with a glint of *I must remember that.*

It was decided that Lil and Tommy would get their friend drunk and then put him to bed on their couch. Warren decided that first he wanted to take a slow walk through the less popular corridors of the museum, where the hush and cool stone would be calming. So they wandered from room to room, past the guards with their clickers, past the machine-made placards commemorating that which is made by hand. To Warren's mild amazement one of the exhibit halls actually was lined with pre-Columbian ceremonial daggers.

Next was a hall of paintings from the late Italian Renaissance —Tintoretto and the like. Warren slid his gaze across the frames until one portrait caught his attention. He looked more closely, and what he saw struck him cold.

The canvas was Lo Spagna's *Saint Catherine of Siena*, painted, the placard said, around 1510. Catherine, in the Renaissance, had held something like the social standing of a rock star. She was the patron saint of unmarried women and, according to legend, an enchantress. Beauty was vital to her purpose, which was to inspire young women to restrain themselves. For if Catherine, who could have any man she wanted, could remain forever chaste, surely they could hold off another year or so.

Saint Catherine as Lo Spagna portrayed her would not strike the modern viewer as a looker, at least according to the current fashion in female beauty, which favors lips eager for unnatural acts, bodies better suited for marathon running, and clothing sure to cause instant death in an electrical storm. Catherine's figure was utterly lost under her habit, though her shoulders appeared unusually wide. Her eyes were dubious of whatever they beheld. Warren found they appeared to focus on him no matter where he stood in relation to the picture, a common illusion in skilled portraiture. The total effect was one of delicacy on a large scale, of a woman who would be easy to misunderstand but who would endlessly surprise.

Saint Catherine, in the painting, was also all but the twin of Nora Jocelyn.

She was plumper, the face suggested. And her expression was less anxious. Close to serene, if Warren understood that condition well enough to recognize its manifestation. Saint Catherine was on her way to heaven—with what hard care did she have to grapple? But otherwise Nora, all Nora.

Tommy and Lil had caught up with Warren, and joined him in marveling at the resemblance.

"See, there's a million like her," Tommy said, meaning to console. "Common type, common as buses."

The woman in Lo Spagna's painting, Lil pointed out, was not actually Saint Catherine: she had been dead and seated by the hand of God a century before Lo Spagna was born. The woman was rather a model from the painter's own milieu. Daughter of a local merchant perhaps, or possibly of lower station, as artists then could not always be choosy about who consented to pose for them. This explained her healthful appearance, for the historical Catherine was anorectic, starving herself as part of her worldly self-denial. By the time Lo Spagna arrived on the scene in the sixteenth century, the most-sought-after women were slightly padded—for eating lavishly was one mark of status that could not be faked (just as today refusing food confers a status that cannot be purchased).

Warren found it somehow comforting that he was looking at an image of a woman from the 1500s, not Saint Catherine herself. Nora didn't look like a saint. She looked like some slut off the streets of a filthy village full of superstitious half-wits.

Having sighed once or twice and taken his fill of the painting, Warren turned to leave. He glanced at the next wall.

What he saw there nailed him motionless. Then his eyes grew wild and he slammed his hands together into a clasp. He held this single fist together against his forehead as if a wind from the Arctic had begun to blow on him alone.

Some of the patrons edged uneasily out of the room. A museum guard approached, trying to appear stern in his comic opera uniform. Suddenly Warren shouted, *"Nora!"* The cry echoed down halls unaccustomed to any bright sound. He called out again, then shoved the guard aside and bolted from the room.

Warren ran into the cooling twilight of the street still crying *"Nora,"* though the woman was long since gone. His cry mixed with the hot clamor from a subway vent and jive blaring from a record and tapes discount store, three unnecessary sounds blending and reverberating into oblivion.

Inside the building Tommy and Lil remained motionless before what their friend had seen. Harmless little Lil was trembling violently.

On the wall hung another Lo Spagna of the same period, an untitled portrait of a young burgher or shopkeeper. Warren had recognized this face, too, and it had not been difficult. It was his own.

2

IS LOVE CURVED?

Composing himself, Warren could think of no constructive course. So he walked away from the museum and simply kept walking. Some number of hours passed before he remembered Lillian and Tommy; he called from a pay phone to assure them he was fine. Most of the old downtown and the industrial section to the south was deserted at night, nobody around to menace or be menaced. A few of the neighborhoods he passed through were less than elegant, but he didn't worry, feeling invincible or just numb. He reached a factory area. Abandoned mechanical palaces with iron spider-webs for windows; hand-laid masonry smokestacks that were worthless but would cost millions to duplicate; scrap yards whose dusty avenues were deeply rutted by the passing weight of machines.

Somehow Warren felt safety amid the residue of industrial production, as certain people are reassured by the sight and sensation of a freight train passing in the distance. It helped him believe that the society in which he lived really had been made, not just uncovered: a turn-of-the-century factory shell was more interesting to Warren, more vital, than all the legal briefs and government studies in the world combined. In the emptiest of them he could hear the dunning of presses, the cries of labor; feel the injuries. Of course Warren knew that the factory age was a mixed blessing for those who had lived it. Yet its products—bridges, freighters, tunnels, steel, rubber, cement—served him still. When Warren looked at pieces of paper, the major product of his day, he felt shamed.

Around dawn, seated on the loading dock of a sewing machine plant that had been shut down and was worth so little it no longer even merited a barbed-wire fence, Warren noticed the flyer he had been handed at the Newbury, still in his back pocket. It turned out to be a sample copy of *I Am He of Whom I Speak,* a newsletter published by the Azimuth Collective, which listed its address as a post office box in Vermont. The newsletter promised, for twelve dollars a year, to reveal the secrets of destiny, the tao, high-energy particle physics, and weight loss. Subscribers sending payment with their orders would also receive a valuable premium, a special edition called "Flatten Your Karma in 30 Days."

The newsletter itself was a smudged photocopy of a sort of essay, typed on plain paper. Comments were scribbled in the margins and some words underlined by hand. Whole sentences had been coated with white-out and typed over. Warren began to read:

HEAR NOW THE MANIFESTO OF THE AZIMUTH COLLECTIVE:
IF GOD DOES NOT PLAY DICE WITH THE UNIVERSE, NEITHER DOES HE PLAY VIDEO GAMES. WE ARE NOT HERE MERELY TO RUN UP THE SCORE. THERE HAS GOT TO BE SOMETHING MORE.

More than can be seen, perhaps as much as can be felt. More that can be realized and made to be. Imagination is the laboratory, but reality is the only test.

Let's warm up with a few amazing facts to upset your assumptions and astound your friends.

*Autolytic enzymes, present in living cells and dormant during life, activate after death and cause corpses to decay. This keeps the forest floor clean. But why should evolution have cared about the forest floor?

*When left alone, termites circle purposelessly and refuse to eat: they die of starvation even when food is present. Placed in groups, termites commence a complex social interaction in which individuals assume specialized roles, the purpose being to build fortresses of considerable geometric sophistication. Yet no detectable communication signals are exchanged among the insects. How did knowledge of geometry become stored in their genes, and what calls it forth?

*Human beings possess inner ear canals that enable the organ to adjust for changes in barometric pressure. Yet our ancestors did not fly or climb mountains for sport. What could have caused a primate with an ear canal to be more likely to survive than one without?

*Astronomers using new equipment sensitive to gamma radiation are finding very brief, extremely bright sources of such rays, called gamma ray bursters, in some parts of the galaxy. These bursts occur randomly and do not appear to be associated with any known phenomenon. At present there is no scientific explanation for their existence or magnitude.

Gamma rays are a primary product of atomic explosions. Are these new heavenly lights the muzzle flashes from a breakdown of diplomacy on a catastrophic scale?

*If they are, the combatants have been dead and perhaps extinct for a very long time. Because of the vastness of galactic distances, even transmissions moving at the speed of light may not reach us for immense periods of time. The unaided eye can see starlight up to two billion years old; telescopes can see fourteen-billion-year-old light. Thus "the past" still surrounds us today. The cosmos must be full of information that is very ancient. Some of it may be about us.

There must be so much more to existence than we are aware.

Think, for example, how much more there must be to a fact of cosmology that would seem too rudimentary even for comment—the predominance of the light element hydrogen. In the early hours of genesis, almost all the matter in the universe, more than 99 percent of it, condensed into hydrogen. It is presently thought this happened because the Big Bang, whatever its process might have been, favored the production of electrons over other subatomic particles. Hydrogen, the simplest and most electron-rich element, soaked up this surplus. Very well. But what *caused* the mysterious process of the Big Bang to order itself in such a manner that hydrogen would prosper?

Could it have been, as many seekers of knowledge have suggested, a coincidence? A COINCIDENCE! How is it college-educated adults observe that random chance cannot be relied on to produce so much as a bank lobby without teller lines and then proffer that, of course, random chance created and organized the entire universe?

Friends, your existence may be a pointless coincidence, but not mine.

We do not need to look to entangled issues like evolution to find fantastic webs predicated on events that are hard to accept as pure luck. A lucky break of empyreal magnitude occurred in the first millionth of a second of existence—for the most abundant element, hydrogen, turns out to be the most important element by far. Hydrogen is the fuel of stars. Without heat from hydrogen-powered stars the universe would be a warehouse of lifeless rock, and God, as curator, would be one bored Being.

Someone appears to have known in advance, or to have guessed accurately, that the firmament would require relatively small proportions of heavy elements to form planets and living things, and a vast supply of element one, hydrogen, to keep these dense points warm throughout the eons. Had the formula of the Big Bang been altered to favor element two, helium, the universe would have been dark, as helium does not ignite. Had the Bang process favored the third element, lithium, the universe would have announced itself with a spectacular strobe flash and expired unnoticed, as stars made of lithium, a highly reactive metal, would have consumed themselves very rapidly. Other elements, had they been favored, would have led to similar cosmic fiascos. Only one of the 103 known fundamental molecules would have done the trick, and lo and behold, that's the one we got. No doubt it's a coincidence!

Adherents of the "life is a coincidence" ethos will argue that hydrogen was favored merely because whatever process occurred during the Big Bang could function only in a way that generated electrons—that is, the outcome was dictated by physical law. This is a wondrous tautology. We don't need God because everything in the universe can be accounted for by physical laws, which just happen to be magnificently reasoned and symmetrical; no need, however, to account for where the physical laws come from. They are "assumed."

Suppose we observe an interstate highway with traffic flowing along smoothly, thousands of cars only a few feet apart going seventy miles an hour with collisions rare. We might ask, Why aren't they all ramming into each other like crazy? How did it happen that everyone going north is on one side of the road and everyone going south is on the other? Saying "people drive on the right side of the road because of traffic laws" is no explanation. Where did the laws come from?

There's more than one way to set up a road system, as we know from the example of nations where people drive on the left. For that matter, no law of nature compels roads to be split into sides at all. Imagine a highway where there's just one huge lane, people going where they will and each driver expected to dodge and veer like mad to avoid oncoming traffic. This wouldn't be a particularly effective way to organize highways, but nothing prohibits it. It's no "coincidence" that we all drive on one side of the road instead of playing bumper cars.

Many of the physical laws of the universe are set up in ways which favor life: hydrogen is plentiful, planets stay in orbit, the atmosphere shields against solar and cosmic radiation, our sun burns consistently rather than sporadically, and so on. For technical reasons we can skip over here, had gravity turned out to be only slightly more powerful, stars would have burned much hotter and the universe would already be out of fuel; had gravity been only slightly weaker, our sun would burn too cool for Earth at least to flower. To the extent that natural laws favor life, we tend to assume these organizational principles, being "natural," could not have been different. Wherever do we get off making such an assumption—especially when we are ignorant of what caused the genesis, and what preceded it?

Perhaps there are tens or hundreds or thousands of possible organizational principles for natural law, some good and some bad. Perhaps our universe functions under a physics administered through some good offices a little more involved than random chance.

Perhaps there is so much more. Matter and energy were

shown by the work of a well-known German high school dropout to be equivalent. Yet, though examples of matter being converted into energy are frequent in everyday life, no scientist has observed energy being converted into matter. At this young stage of our existence humans have a reasonable store of knowledge concerning how physical laws can be employed for destruction; to make explosions, toxins, and so on. We know little about how the same laws can be applied to creation. Perhaps when we learn what process was operating at the genesis, we will learn to take energy and make matter, and then shape the universe to our liking, just as God once shaped it to His.

Other shapes will change, too, when we learn the full process by which creatures evolve. Present evolutionary theory has been oversold. It covers only some of the changes living things undergo. Evolutionary mechanics as they now stand explains how organisms that *already exist* alter their forms in minor ways: the moth colonies that were observed changing color in response to changes in their environment confirm the lesser aspects of Darwinian theory. But Darwin cannot account for where moths come from in the first place.

Darwin supposed, for example, that constructive genetic mutations must take place bit by bit over many multitudes of generations. Further, he supposed that each new genetic proclivity, in order to be assisted by the genetic math, must make its bearer more likely to survive. No fish was ever simply "born" with a lung, enabling it to move to land. Lungs are too complex to spring from any one mutation; thousands of generations of proto-amphibians mutating toward proto-lungs are required. In a similar vein, as it were, eyes, brains, opposable thumbs, wings, and all other complex organs developed very slowly, according to Darwinian mechanics. In one view, the slowness of evolution explains why Earth has had life-supporting conditions for nearly three billion years, but societies of intelligent beings only for around 10,000 years.

This element of evolutionary theory contains its own negation, however. What could have made millions of proto-amphibians—born with incomplete, useless genetic precursors of lungs—more likely to survive in water than pure fish? They should have been more likely to die, since their competitors' bodies were tuned entirely to aquatic functioning. Proto-birds born with non-functioning wings should have been gobbled for lunch many millennia sooner than evolution made them safely airborne. And so on.

The "missing link," the intermediate primate that would show how our ancestors branched into the direction of humans while apes branched off in the other direction, is hardly the only important gap in biology. *Every* link is missing for every species. No fossil evidence of a transitional creature existing with incomplete prototypes of organs has been found. Bats, for example, have a complicated sonar locater system, which probably would have been worse than useless—making its carriers stumblebums more likely to die—in their early evolutionary development. Fossil records dating back to about 50 million B.C. show bats almost exactly in their present form; nothing like a transitional proto-sonar creature has been cataloged.

Darwin attributed this gap to the incomplete state of the fossil record. Transitional creatures, he said, have not been found solely because (here it comes again) of chance: paleontologists haven't blundered across them yet. A century later they still haven't, although they have found considerable evidence of creatures seeming to pop out of the air in finished form. A new modification of evolutionary theory says that Darwin was wrong about speed. Changes do not occur gradually, but spasmodically, in "punctuations." This idea still begs the issue, however, of what causes the change, just as the Big Bang theories beg the issue of what came before.

Once the more of evolution is known, man will begin to alter his form to his liking. Genetically, human beings are only one percent different from apes; the remainder of our DNA material is, roughly speaking, interchangeable. What will a being one percent improved over man be like?

God is not angered by inquiries into these, His personal

secrets. On the contrary, He is pleased. Like a parent to a child, He longs for us to grow enough that we may converse with Him. Children when young speak their own infantile languages; as they mature they learn the tongues of their parents. Someday, when we have learned to speak to God in His language rather than ours, He will ask us to explain ourselves. And on that day we had better be ready to do some pretty fast talking.

There will be so much more when the two great mystery forces are revealed. One is gravity. Every schoolchild knows that gravity exists, and can see its evidence. Undergraduate astronomy students can predict its effects with nearly absolute precision. Yet no one, certainly no scientist, knows what gravity *is*.

No gravity-thing has ever been found—no particle (like matter), no wave (like light), no field (like magnetism). When you drop a rock something obviously causes it to fall, but no one knows what. Technically, when you walk across a room every iota in the entire expanse of the cosmos shifts imperceptibly to accommodate the new locus of your gravitational output. Instruments sensitive enough could detect a shudder in the moon if a pickup truck were pushed into the Grand Canyon. (WARNING! DO NOT TRY THIS WITH YOUR TRUCK.)

Another fun fact about gravity is that it exerts itself instantaneously: not just fast, but without any passage of time. When the truck goes over the cliff several seconds pass before it hits the canyon floor. But gravity requires zero time to grab the truck and initiate its fall. Stars that are billions of light years apart can touch each other through gravity faster than the eye can be blinked. This means that at least one physical force which is all around us operates in a way entirely independent of our understanding of time and causation.

Einstein, who ultimately threw up his hands on the question of what gravity is, believed that the projection of this mystery force defined the very essence of space-time. Try first to visualize the shapeless, timeless snowball of the pre-Bang plenum. (Avoid trying to visualize what the substance was, because you'll give up.) Surrounding this snowball was not-anything. If you had been in a pre-creation spaceship you could not have flown to the vicinity of the snowball in order to inspect it, because there was no vicinity. The not-anything was neither small nor large; terms of measurement did not apply. The not-anything did not stretch across what is now the void; there wasn't a void, and it couldn't have been empty because it didn't exist. What a scene! Not even a television sportscaster could have made it sound interesting.

When the snowball detonated, its contents began to transmute into matter and energy. Both flew outward at tremendous speed. Running well ahead of them, however, was the gravity effect, which blew away from the Big Bang instantaneously. The moment the Big Bang was lit—after the passage of zero time—the entire universe felt gravity, endless billions of light years from the explosion site. The not-anything around the exploding snowball became a void, still empty and cold but now real: your spaceship could now fly into it. This was an extremely important and subtle consideration, another of those "mere" physical laws it is now fashionable to ascribe to the same process that governs roulette wheels. Gravity spread itself instantaneously in order to transform the not-anything zone into a real nothingness which the matter and energy of the Big Bang could explode into. Without this transformation even light from the blast would have had no place to go, and would have ceased to exist.

Currently there is scientific debate regarding whether gravity is a restricted effect—whether it expires over distance, which would mean the universe has boundaries—or is infinite, which would mean that reality has no limits. Einstein wasn't sure about that one, either. He did say that the conversion of not-anything into real nothingness took place by means of making the void "curved," whatever that means. It seemed to mean something to him.

The second great mystery force, known to every schoolchild but enigmatic in operation, is love. Like gravity, it can hold us together and expand boundaries; like gravity, it can cheerfully crush the clumsy.

It is vitally important that we find out if love is real. Does it function only in the laboratory of the imagination, failing the test of reality? Can we even call it curved?

Love, for example, should have been stamped out by evolution. In Darwinian mechanics bearers of love should have been less likely to survive—spending their time in unproductive mooning, heads in the clouds, oblivious to predators. And recent cultural developments have conclusively established that love is not necessary for the activities of reproduction.

Many of the thoughtful today would say that love is not a real force, or that it is a pleasant veneer we paint over various psychological needs and deficiencies which are best kept at a controllable level. But there may be so much more. In every age the most wise of the previous age have been proven wrong, and sometimes grossly wrong, on matters of importance.

For centuries, even in the face of contradictory evidence, leading scholars believed that the universe literally revolved around them. (Though 450 years after Copernicus, this is still the case at most major faculty clubs.) As recently as a century ago, doctors didn't scrub before surgery, being ignorant of the very existence of infectious microbes—a cause of disease now understood by kindergartners. Medical students were taught that malaria was caused by "bad air," the name coming from the Italian *mal aria*.

There exists no fulfillment in understanding science without understanding human emotions. Nor is there satisfaction in mastering the heart while shunning the technical issues of the world that nurtures it. Thus does the Azimuth Collective ask, Where fits love into the complete picture?

Is it like gravity—real, powerful, but so far ill understood? Or is it like malaria?

—3—

The discovery of the portraits had taken place on a Saturday afternoon. Warren found his way back to his apartment by ten o'clock Sunday morning. He spent that day wavering between the fear that he had lost his senses, and the delirious hope that he above others had been singled out for an experience that would give his life meaning.

Try as he might—and he had tried, mightily, during his aimless night's wandering through the old downtown, the late hour and the moderate danger heightening his senses—Warren could not locate in his mind any glint of Siena, or Italian village life, or Caesar's legions, or the moon over Mesopotamia, or any suchlike.

He tried to approach the problem analytically, as an engineer. If something happens but leaves no trace and cannot be recalled, then for practical purposes it did not happen; or at least, its happening is not relevant. During surgery intense pain "happens" in the sense that nerve synapses are triggered and signals are sent to the brain, instructing the mouth to scream. But anesthesia interrupts transmissions of the signals, which the brain never receives. The pain becomes a non-event.

At least, so we presume. Twice Warren had submitted to surgery for a knee ruined covering a kickoff in a college football game. Each time before going under he had wondered, What if drugs only block the *memory* of pain? If the subconscious is enduring the full agony of each cut, but failing to make an imprint on the consciousness?

Or suppose we are subjected to terrifying fright in our dreams —not just to nightmares but full psychological torment—and don't remember when the light breaks? Each night we settle onto the pillow looking forward to rest and release, little suspecting that hours of torture lie ahead. Only when some unexpected noise wakes the sleeper prematurely does he retain brief recognition of what a dark horror is this menace called sleep. But as the memory quickly sublimates, the wakened sleeper dismisses it and dives right back in for more torture.

Should this be true, Warren felt, then better not to know, since we must have sleep and surgery. In these cases ignorance would be bliss. Next, suppose that people did lead multiple lives. And suppose that instead of just catching an aroma of a previous manifestation, which tantalizes but fails to enlighten, in the manner of a fragment from a dream—as some people claim to have glimpsed past lives, fleetingly and inconclusively—one were to stumble upon a proof? A documentary proof, as the television commentators like to say. What good would it do you, Warren wondered.

Knowing you had lived before would be like knowing it was going to snow tomorrow. This knowledge would not prevent the snow from falling, nor stop your car from getting stuck in it. If there had been some good or ill between him and Nora on some previous plane, what possible benefit was it to find out now? After all, even knowledge of their present lives gave him little hope. Nora was already married. The snow had fallen.

A past life could not have occurred without reincarnation. *Reincarnation* is one of those words no educated person is supposed to let pass his lips without snickering. To Warren, reincarnation, taken either as a question of religion or of metaphysics, seemed no more or less improbable than the main competing propositions: oblivion and afterlife.

The notion of oblivion following death is favored by the evil, who would do what they please without facing an ultimate judge; by the anti-religious, who for a variety of reasons (Warren could think of several) hate established churches so much they cannot bear to agree with anything a church believes; and by the vain of intellect, who for purposes of self-flattery find it necessary to consider their own fleeting appearance on this planet the sole noteworthy event in creation.

Meanwhile, the notion of a higher state after life finds its support with the Western religions; with some agnostics, who don't know if an afterlife exists but also know that they don't know; and with the pragmatic non-religious, who find value in any belief that gives people an incentive to behave responsibly.

In the West, proponents of oblivion and afterlife tend to argue fiercely with each other but agree on dismissing the third possibility out of hand. They treat multiple lives as either too preposterous to dignify with comment (savages believe it!) or pooh-pooh it with the charming suggestion that reincarnation poses some kind of cosmic logistical problem—that God could never keep the records straight. Like many partners in theoretical combat, they fear that if an outside concept were to carry the day, each would be denied the satisfaction of seeing the other side humiliated.

Warren thought it hubris to reject the possibility of multiple lives. Since, after all, there exists no scrap of evidence, documentary or otherwise, giving any indication of what transpires before or after death, all thinking on the subject is pure conjecture or conviction—the former being a matter of taste and the latter, of faith, neither having or able to have the standing of fact.

The height of intellectual smugness occurs when Western philosophers look down on reincarnation as somehow physically impossible. Who is to say what is possible in the incorporeal realm? Everyone accepts that there are limits to petroleum, gold, stellar hydrogen, and other commodities. Could not souls, more difficult to make than these mere chemicals, be sufficiently precious that God conserves them? Warren recalled the line of thought in contemporary astronomy holding that the universe itself is perpetually reborn. From a singular point it Big-Bangs into existence, expanding for eons. Eventually the expansion runs out of steam and the universe begins to collapse. Over many billions of years gravity pulls all matter and energy back to a singularity, where the plenum explodes again, repeating the genesis anew.

Introduction of this theory of cosmic destiny had called forth no uproarious rejection among Western intellectuals, just debate regarding fine points of the physics involved. So rebirth could happen to the entire universe, but not one individual? Warren supposed that respectable scientists and writers who backed the recycled-universe theory would laugh out loud if it were suggested that reincarnation would be a natural component of such a cosmos. Perhaps the idea would fare better with the establishment if it was given some new name with the proper ring, like "conservation of ectoplasm."

What interested Warren for the moment was one element of the universe-reincarnation theory. It was assumed that during each Big Bang all knowledge of the previous universe—all "information," as scientists liked to say—would be annihilated, wholly and irrevocably. No form of record keeping could survive from one universe to the next, because even thoughts would be crushed out of existence by the infinite super-gravity preceding detonation.

So if through some fluke one universe—ours, let's say—were to figure out that it had sprung from the plenum of a previous universe, that would be quite interesting but otherwise irrelevant. There could never be any knowing what the previous universe had been like: whether there had been creatures, art, travel, wars, happiness, or desolation; whether they had found a solution to the broken heart.

On the day after losing Nora Jocelyn, Warren felt despondency, but not despair. He fought through that Sunday to keep despair—the abandonment of hope—from entering his feelings, focusing instead on the small but attainable goal of staying sane until the next day, a business day, when he might be able to track Nora down.

When Monday morning came it didn't take Warren long to get the name of the publicity company for Loco Gringo Records. He called the number and told the receptionist he was returning a message left by someone named Nora but couldn't make out the last name "scribbled on this pink note here."

"Nora McConaughty? At this number? She doesn't use this number. Who did you say was calling?"

"Doesn't—of course, this isn't where I usually call her. But I've misplaced her other number."

"I thought you said you didn't know her."

"I didn't know where—where she would be today."

"Why would she call you and leave the wrong number?"

"No, she left the right number. I just lost it."

"If you lost the number how did you know to call here?"

After several transformations of his cover story, Warren learned that Nora McConaughty, wife of Ford McConaughty, worked out of her home in Seattle; rarely traveled on business, but in this instance the client had specifically requested her; was due in Kansas City, next stop on the czar exhibit tour, within the hour; and would be staying at the Crown Center Hotel. Warren called in sick to KD&H, and by afternoon was on a flight to Kansas City.

As the plane took off Warren opened the ventilation spout to full, hoping to blow off his perspiration. When troubled he would sometimes try to ease his mind by focusing his thoughts on the absurdities of mechanized living. Outside the airplane wind was rushing by at six hundred miles per hour. Inside the airplane was a system designed to simulate wind. An electric power generating station consists of millions of dollars' worth of equipment to turn water to steam, followed by millions of dollars' worth of cooling towers to turn steam back to water so that it can be turned to steam again. Half the job of technology lies in compensating for the other half.

Another tactic Warren employed to soothe his thoughts was to think about technological developments that had happened in the wrong order. For instance, the rocket engine was invented before the jet engine. (Robert Goddard, 1926, versus Frank Whittle, 1937.) The speed of light had been measured before anyone knew to pasteurize milk. (Armand Fizeau, 1849, versus Louis Pasteur, 1864.) Max Planck had formulated quantum theory, which describes reality on a level much smaller than atoms, half a century before it was possible to direct dial a long distance call. Such facts were to Warren, as an engineer, what koans were to the taoist: logic breakers.

During the flight a couple seated across the aisle from Warren argued intensely but inaudibly. They would hush and sit up

straight—eighth-graders trying to fool a substitute teacher—
whenever a flight attendant passed. Not that many flight attendants would have noticed, lost in their own sullen contempla-
tions. Surely it was a boon to society that female flight attendants
had stopped being caricatures of Miss America contestants. But
now with job descriptions, grievance committees, and freedom
from the word *stewardess,* they had also stopped trying to make
people feel comfortable on planes, adopting instead the perpet-
ual scowl of the professional class.

Miss America: Hello, my name is Billie Sue Jean Bob. My
favorite person is Mother Teresa. My ideal evening is tap dancing in front of a fireplace. I would now like to recite a selection
from *Spoon River Anthology* while wearing a swimsuit. And I'm
going to stand with my crotch directly in front of your face, but
you wouldn't look, would you? The genius of calling it a "swimsuit competition"—as though it had something to do with athlet-
ics, or the emphasis was on the suits—was hard to deny.

Then again, was the marketing notion of male sexuality any
less real? A consensus has developed in pop culture that men can
be objects of romantic appeal either by being unorthodox street-
wise detectives who don't play by the rules, or by being sensitive
eccentrics who live in converted warehouse lofts. Men in the
former category are supposed to own their own ground-attack
aircraft; in the latter, to celebrate birthdays of obscure seven-
teenth-century Portuguese libretto writers and to be searching
the world for the last dinosaur egg. No room in this panoply for
office workers who ask women to the movies.

The high proportion of male romantic leads in pop culture
who did nothing of value with their lives made Warren suspect
that male screenwriters secretly viewed themselves as without
purpose—and felt their best chance of getting laid was to promote the concept of unconnected indulgence. This troubled
Warren because, though even rubes know movies and television
aren't true, the screen tugs at them nonetheless, making it seem
as though anything short of slow motion and evening gowns
leaves you a failure at love.

Warren took a pillow from the overhead rack—he wouldn't

have dreamed of asking a flight attendant for one—and laid it against the bulkhead, which hummed with the electric whirl of engines. The couple across the way who had been arguing were now both asleep, propped against each other, exhausted by their contentions. The drone from the motors made Warren drowsy too, and it wasn't long before he fell into a daydream of Nora.

He was thinking back to their fourth day together, a cool day with leaves in prospect. Every day with Nora was clearly ordered in Warren's mind and preserved in every particular: every day had lasted long into the night, and he had been willing to sleep only because he was so anxious for morning. Warren first took his ability to remember every detail as a sign of true feeling, until he realized it was not much of a trick when a grand total of three weeks was involved.

On the fourth day Warren and Nora had met for lunch in a turn-of-the-century hotel and sat holding hands, palm to palm. After coffee Warren pulled a key out of his overcoat, and they had gone upstairs to a room with dark wooden floors. Who made the first move was the only particular he couldn't remember.

Now you may be thinking that Warren got this flourish from reading the "Tips for Men" column of a woman's magazine. As it happened, he thought up the idea himself. But even if he hadn't it would not have mattered. So few *good* things happen that *why* they happen, when they do, is a consideration beyond trivial. Bernard Shaw once wrote that he did not care whether Joan of Arc had faked her divine voices, and couldn't imagine why anybody else would care either. Joan won the battle and multiplied the faithful. These were in themselves miracles; whether or not they began from a false premise, they ended up real, and that, according to Shaw, was all that mattered.

Afterward, lying together, Warren and Nora had questioned each other, as lovers do, about the little things, passing over the large, which in a proper lover is sensed and need not be stated.

"Don't say pizza."

"Sorry, pizza."

"You're saying pizza because everybody says it."

"But it's true. Pizza is my favorite food."

"I was going to say pizza."

"I have considered starting a religion based on the worship of this form of nourishment. Or moving to the forests of Italy, where I could trap wild pizzas and devour them in their native state."

"Have you heard the Pizza Principle? When a boy asks you out, if you don't like him make sure he takes you someplace expensive, so at least you get your money's worth while you listen to him talk about how important he is. If you do like him, go for pizza."

"I can't believe you say 'boy.' You're twenty-nine years old. Have teenagers been asking you out?"

"Men say 'girl' when they mean woman."

"Okay, but women say 'woman' when they mean female. 'Woman' is the noun, 'female' is the adjective. Would a woman who says 'woman executive' also say 'man executive'?"

" 'Boy' is an affectionate term."

"It sounds so sheltered."

"I'll talk dirty if you want."

"Not just now. Favorite season?"

"Fall."

"Another universal answer. Reason?"

"Everybody looks better in sweaters."

"I like fall for the colors, and because it gets cold."

"You *like* cold?"

"Forces you indoors, where you talk. When I was in California the sun was always out, people were always busy driving places, and I always felt like I was the one person in the state who wasn't doing something that would make everybody else jealous. Weather is an equalizer, since the beautiful people are stuck in it, too. Plus, when it's cold, you get a feeling of accomplishment just by walking in the door."

"I like the cold because it kills things."

"God, Nora. You must be a million laughs at parties."

"No, minor things. Plants. The important things survive, which reminds you what they are."

"Dogs or cats?"

"Dogs, definitely. Large and goofy. Must be male."

"There's a difference?"

"Darling, there's quite a difference."

"I mean in pets. Is gender behavior really that different?"

"All dogs should be male, and all cats female. Cats are aware of so much that they become confused, which is very female. Dogs have not the slightest doubt even when they ought to, which is male. Also dogs are masters of exaggeration, another male trait."

"At least we won't have cat books in the house."

"In between writing press releases I sometimes think about striking it rich with the ultimate how-to book. My original ultimate how-to book was going to be *How to Make a Million Dollars While Losing Weight in Bed With the Right Man.* Then the cat fad came along and I decided it would have to be *How to Make a Million Dollars While Losing Weight in Bed With the Right Man's Cat.* That was too kinky even for me."

"Now it would be *Eat Your Way to Excellence While Lifting Weights With a Lesbian Nun.*"

"Watch it, mister. How do you know I don't have a lesbian nun in my past?"

"I guess I don't. Why do you like dogs?"

"Dumb loyalty. The only kind of devotion that really counts is the kind that makes no sense. If you stop to think about a commitment, you will always talk yourself out of it. Suppose your dog could speak and you asked him why he was loyal. He'd say, 'Because I am.' If you pressed him for specific reasons he would become agitated and go hide behind the sofa. Your dog would stay with you in a burning building, even if he could get away, and even if staying accomplished nothing other than a final moment of companionship. That's the kind of love that counts, the dumb kind."

"What if I love you in that way? In a dumb, unstoppable way?"

Nora was slow to answer. "That would be very—admirable," she said. "Let's keep going with questions."

Warren was afraid to ask what she was holding back. Nora

seemed relieved when he came up with a neutral category. "Sports?"

"I like anything you can do outside. Hate all organized sport. I trust you're not one of those macho, perpetually injured types."

"I played football at UCLA. I mean, I made the squad. I only played in the closing moments of routs. There was a kind of reverse quota system where one or two guys on academic scholarship, not NCAA scholarship, would always make it, so the coach could talk about 'student athletes' at the annual alumni banquet. Anyway, I like the sport."

"Did you like the Spanish Inquisition, too? That was great organized violence."

"Now you've gone too far. Injuries do occur, but that's not the point of football. They occur by accident. I'll grant you that boxing is barbaric because the point is to do harm. But in most sports injuries are an unavoidable complication."

"Any so-called entertainment that leaves people crippled is sick."

"Dancers ruin their bodies."

"That's different!"

"Aha! Surrender, Dorothy. Whenever you have reduced your opponent to crying 'That's different,' you have a winning argument. 'That's different' really means 'That's exactly the same and I don't want to talk about it.' "

"Okay, but the world is full of aggression. At least dance is beauty. Why create a sport that celebrates aggression?"

"You have wisely shifted the conversation away from your original complaint, physical harm, but you will still lose. There are two reasons. First, because you will never get eighty thousand people to come to a ballet. Second, because it's better to exorcise your aggressions in a game, which has no lasting significance, than in reality. Think how much better our relations with the Soviets would be if we let them into the NFL. A little pregame hype would do more good than any summit meeting. And think of the team names they could have. The Moscow Molotovs. The Uzbek Ivans."

"The Kiev Chickens."

"You're pretty clever for a girl."

"Noticed you. What's your favorite position?"

"I played strong safety, but I always wanted to be a halfback."

"I mean sex. I'm changing the subject to the one thing which will take a male mind off football."

"You're putting me on the spot."

"It is you, dearest, who puts me on the spot. Now answer the question."

"I don't know how to say. It's that—there's no good word for a woman's—privates. 'Cunt' sounds too nasty. 'Pussy' sounds too silly. 'Vagina' sounds like medicine."

"Not like 'cock,' a nice manly word. Answer the question."

"From behind. I mean, the regular way but from behind."

"Why?"

"Most erotic. I can see you. You wouldn't know, but a naked back is the most powerful erotic stimulant of them all. The way the lines work and the way you know there's all this good stuff on the other side, but you can't quite see it. Naked women are sexy from the front, erotic from behind."

"Looks like we have another mutual favorite, Warren. I like it that way because it's a position you have to get into. You don't just wind up that way by lying down; some care and mutual effort are involved. Lovemaking is only about half the physical part. The remaining half is knowing the other person wants to do it with you. I wish I could think of an example, but you know what I mean."

"An example is, the moment in adolescence when your date reaches around to unhook her bra for you because you can't get it. I think that can be the most exciting moment of your life. Not because of what you are about to touch, but because it's when you know that she *wants* you to touch. That will always mean so much, even after you've gotten into hundreds of bras."

"'Hundreds of bras'? A typical weekend?"

"I meant—figure of speech. But it's why being with a prostitute doesn't work. The physical sensation is there, but the important part, the being wanted, isn't."

"What's your favorite time?"

"Like on a clock?"

"To fool around."

"Give me another five minutes."

"Seriously."

"Morning is pretty good. You're sober and you can see what you're doing. Somehow at night it seems to mean least. Often you're making it just because that's what two people do at night."

"Doesn't sound so bad to me."

"But you know what I mean. Yours?"

"Afternoon. For my favorite reason again, that you have to go out of your way. You're not already in bed, you have to arrange to get there. And you're not sleepy like at night, or in a hurry like in the morning, so you can talk afterward."

"Women always like to talk after."

"And men always resist. You think it's some kind of test. You should be glad when a woman wants to talk afterward. She's telling you she wants to make it again."

"What's your favorite thing of all things?"

"Dessert. What's your favorite quote?"

"Nora, that's not—"

"If you're going to come on to me like an educated man, you must prove yourself with a literate reference."

"You have just dropped a ten-ton weight on this conversation."

"No stalling."

"Okay, I quote Groucho Marx. He was playing a businessman and he said something like, 'This comes with my personal unconditional guarantee. If anything goes wrong, there is absolutely nothing you can do about it.' I believe that summarizes my philosophy of life. Or at least it summarizes my philosophy of business. Now what's *your* favorite quote?"

"In First Corinthians—"

"This is totally unfair. You had your answer in advance."

"—there's the famous chapter with all the greeting card lines about how love runs faster than the shortest mountain and so on. One of the lines is, 'Love does not insist on its own way.' Warren, this is one of the least understood lines in the Bible, and that's saying a lot. Think about the sentence carefully, because it may not mean what it appears to mean—whether you will accept not getting your wish in romance or with family members or that kind of stuff. 'Love does not insist on its own way.' Love's way would be love, right? But if you've truly reached the level of loving you have surpassed concern over the love itself. You want love but you don't *insist* on it. You realize you can only really possess it if you're willing to face life without it. In my opinion this one verse contains about ninety percent of what you need to know to understand what's become of God."

There was a pause. Then Warren said, "Is it too soon to say I love you?"

"No—maybe. I want you to think about what I just said."

"Of course I'll think about it."

"I mean really think. It could be important."

"You changed the subject when I said I loved you."

"Don't be sad. Do you really think that if something goes wrong, there is absolutely nothing you can do about it?"

"No. It just seems like when things go wrong they stay wrong. It's so much easier to misunderstand than to understand."

"Maybe for the moment. Let me ask one more question. What was the best time of your life?"

"Besides being discharged?"

"Besides that."

"Summer between my junior and senior years of college. I was a lifeguard at one of the beaches north of L.A. Had a tan for the first and only time. I rode my bicycle to get around, so I was in great shape. I didn't have to think about a thing, just looked at girls all day long."

"Sounds pretty good."

"What was the best time of your life?"

"Right now."

The chalk-slap of wheels broke Warren's reverie. He had slept through the landing. Being in the service had cured him of a childhood fear of airplanes: during the flight to Saigon he had been so preoccupied with more pressing fears that he forgot to dread the plane. On the way home the aircraft had seemed like a portable capsule of America. Now, to Warren, flying machines represented rescue and escape.

He waited for the downtown bus, knowing from his experience with an irate KD&H auditor that a cab ride from the airport to downtown Kansas City cost thirty-five dollars. The bus took him directly to Crown Center, a hotel and civic complex that had been built to great fanfare in the mid-seventies. Crown Center was a creature of subsidized loans, tax breaks, zoning exemptions, insider deals, and political muscle—just the sort of project Kessey, Denning & Hobard dreamed of getting. It was also a creature of modernist architecture, whose fundamental principle is, Offend Your Host. The Crown Center complex consisted of square concrete box after square concrete box, with pastures of concrete between. Not a curved surface nor a brushstroke—to say nothing of a living thing—for several city blocks. In Warren's mind, the complex possessed all the warm human appeal of an underground missile silo.

Crown Center, like so many modern "civic" developments—Renaissance Center in Detroit, L'Enfant Plaza in Washington, Century City in Los Angeles, Rockefeller Mall in Albany, the entire city of Stamford, Connecticut—employed blast-bunker design mainly to discourage the public it was ostensibly meant to serve. Looking at the Crown Center layout, Warren noted that the only really practical way to approach it was to be dropped off from a taxi or a limousine. The overall effect seemed calculated not to attract customers but to repel the pitchforks of the Jacquerie.

Despite the planners' best efforts to insure that facilities like Crown Center would be used only by the expense-account class, the place was mobbed anyway. Although rooms started at eighty dollars a night, the hotel lobbies and restaurants were alive with people dressed like shoe salesmen, beauty parlor operators, and Okies from Muskogee. The only sure defense against discrimination is money; putting money in the hands of the average man through economics seemed to Warren a far greater threat to the class system than taking it away from the rich.

It was a continuing puzzlement to Warren how easily the art of architecture had been converted, during the twentieth century, from a quest for grandeur erring on the side of the ornate to a worship of conformity erring on the side of repulsion. In recent years that trend finally seemed to have wound itself out. Yet the ascent of modernist boring-box design continued to have repercussions in architecture, as well as in related technical fields. Primarily, it had made laziness respectable. For whatever aesthetic merits modernist architecture may or may not have had, Warren was certain of one thing: it was easy to design.

Long nights of soul searching are not required to conceive of a single rectangle with flat surfaces, nor are tormented hours at the drafting table necessary to prepare flat rectangles for construction. Long after the Bauhaus abandoned its crusade for starkness as an aesthetic, the desire of succeeding generations of architects and architecture professors to knock off work at three P.M. seemed to remain. Hiding behind the modernist dogma, the big firms threw up highly profitable buildings that were neither creative nor comfortable because no one expected them to be; the hot architects pulled big fees for "ideas" that required little or no imagination.

Modernism in design, Warren felt, had been born as an aesthetic breakthrough, matured into a cult of indoctrination, and grown senile as it became an excuse for long lunches. How else could you explain the design community's decades-long struggle against the desire of human beings to be comfortable in homes, offices, and chairs? Warren knew several architects who made their living designing concrete boxes. Not one of them had his offices in a building that had been built after the First World War —all were in renovated brownstones or lofts. They wouldn't be caught dead in their own creations.

The year before, Doug Denning had landed KD&H a hefty Department of Public Works contract to generate ideas for greenspace. Confronted with a plot of city land, Warren's colleagues would speak wistfully of Versailles or Kew—and then sketch out ten interlocking flat square terraces with square lamp posts, low concrete benches only a robot could sit on, a million-dollar drainage system to compensate for the lack of soil, and a single piece of twisted scrap-metal sculpture symbolizing man's inhumanity to man. Nearly all the civic improvement proposals floating around KD&H followed the same pattern: right angles, featureless concrete, tetragons and tetrahedrons. *Impact* and *verticality* were the type of buzzwords used in accompanying promotional copy in places where *ugliness* and *straight line* should have appeared. As in, "The impact of the verticality between the flush portals makes a powerful statement to those versed in contemporary aesthetic standards." *Single* was another favorite, as in single design element, single departure from convention, single departure from the last proposal we did. Single something-or-other was supposed to reflect elegant simplicity, but what it reflected to Warren was that single design ideas were easier to conceive than multiple ones.

Unintended consequences of modernism, Warren thought, could be found in art as well as engineering. Whatever the visual merits of cubism, Pollack splash, solid color, or other new forms, there was no denying that art produced in the twentieth century required significantly less work than the art of centuries before.

Warren had looked at some contemporary smashed-plate art once and been interested. The part that had interested him, however, was the inlays on the fragments of the plates themselves, with which the artist had had nothing to do. On another occasion he had visited the Hirshhorn Museum in Washington, where there was an outdoor sculpture garden. At one end of the garden sat a work by the contemporary sculptor Mark di Suvero, a ship's bow. Not a representation of a ship's bow but an actual ship's bow, cut off the scrapped freighter *Westage.* The bow was hung by thick chains from a tripod made of I-beams, and had been spray-painted white. That's it. A ship's bow on a chain and spray-painted white.

At the opposite end of the Hirshhorn garden sat a cast of Rodin's *The Burghers of Calais.* The figures in this work were so nearly human, so brilliantly composed, that they conveyed to the beholder as much of Rodin's time as might an entire history book. Comparing the two, Warren wondered just what ineluctable message about our age a ship's bow painted white would pass on to future generations. Then setting aside the aesthetics he simply asked himself, Between Rodin and di Suvero, who spent the afternoon watching television?

Of course, art and architecture boil down to taste. Even when the standards in vogue are lacking, the sun continues to rise; no one is harmed. For engineers it is different. Across from Crown Center where Nora was staying stood a Hyatt Regency. It was there, in 1981, that a concrete skywalk had slipped its moorings and fallen into a crowd of tea dancers, killing 114 people. The skywalk's weight had been suspended from single pins, rather than distributed. This represented what the courts later called a "grossly negligent" design error. On the day of the tragedy the main topic of conversation at KD&H had not been how soon the sons of bitches who drew the blueprints would go to jail, but whether the event afforded Kessey, Denning & Hobard an opportunity to branch out into Kansas City.

"This is a great day for KD and H," Ernest Hobard, the third partner, had declared, holding up the morning paper. "Going to be a year, maybe two, before any of the firms involved can bid on local business again. Somebody's going to jump in. The race will go to the swift."

And indeed a race was on. Tort lawyers from across the country descended on Kansas City. A procedural dispute soon arose as to whether Kansas and Missouri lawyers would get the profits by trying cases of the victims individually in state courts, or a Washington, D.C., firm would get the profits by trying the cases together in federal court as a class action. Since the class-action course would have confined the windfall to just one set of attorneys, local lawyers tied up the case with motions for years. Justice was so well served that the widow of one victim, John Dixon—who was crushed under the spiked debris but not immediately killed, and suffered pain for four months before finally dying—got less than an unscratched bystander named Deborah Jackson who happened to be in another part of the hotel at the time of the incident. Dixon and Jackson had different lawyers and settled at different stages in the procedural jousting. The lawyers themselves pulled down an estimated $30 million in fees—Dixon's widow got less than $100,000—while the state took five years to revoke the licenses of the engineers responsible.

Just looking at the Hyatt, bustling again and brightly lighted, filled Warren with anger. Avoidable technological failures could not be forgiven. The Tacoma Narrows Bridge in Washington State, which snapped in 1946; the Silver Bridge over the Ohio River at Point Pleasant, West Virginia, which collapsed in 1969, killing forty-six motorists—Warren was of the opinion that those who kill through direct negligence should hold their own lives forfeit.

After the Hyatt Regency killings, managers sent a team of workers into the hotel in the middle of the night to dismantle one skywalk that hadn't collapsed, hoping, it appeared, to keep its defects from being used as evidence. Warren assumed that every executive involved in this maneuver was given a bonus and promoted.

Contemplating corporate responsibility was not Warren Gifford's idea of a good time. But seeing the Hyatt, a shrine to indifference, and being full of feeling toward Nora, caused him to focus his thoughts on the subject rather than Nora herself. Warren might not have been able to articulate it, but subconsciously he knew that moral worth must accompany the worthiness to give and receive love. And he wanted to be worthy of Nora's. Arriving at the Crown Center Hotel, Warren was surprised to find himself calm, not enervated. He was glad he had kept his mind on other things.

Going to the front desk to ask for her room number seemed like a bad idea. Instead he walked to the house phone a few feet away. Certain questions seem suspicious when asked in person but pleasantly neuter when mediated through impersonal electronic devices; asking a woman's room number is one. Warren got the number and started to write it down when a sensation he hadn't felt since completely forgetting about a term paper during high school infiltrated his mind—Nora had just walked right past him.

Not being able to think of any charming or disarming comment, Warren simply stepped into view. There was a brief registration of a smile in Nora's expression. Well, at least she's flattered, Warren thought. Then a harder expression replaced it.

"I can't," she said. "I told you I can't."

Foolishly, Warren jumped directly to the question he had planned to pose after lengthy and artful coaxing: "Do you love him?"

Nora seemed offended, and for a moment Warren worried he had given her cause to walk away. She was clearly trying to summon up righteous indignation. But she failed, and in a moment had succumbed to his request that they at least have a drink before he left.

They went into the hotel bar, one of those too-dark and too-done establishments that seem calculated to drive lonely travelers to drink. Nora let Warren hold the chair for her. This gave him a start. Any minor sex-role pleasantry permitted by a post-feminist woman can cause an instant of confusion on both sides. Only a few short years ago, Warren recalled, you could almost affront a woman by sending her flowers.

On the tables in the lounge were little placards, printed thousands of miles away, announcing the hotel's personal touch. Guests were invited to feel at home on Grandma's Porch Café, in Barney Bill's Pub, at Cadillac Jack's Steak Ranch. Barney Bill himself urged them to try his own original Blue Hawaiian Blaster, made with blue curaçao and frozen blueberry yogurt. Warren felt it troubling that, from Uncle Sam to Betty Crocker, promoters found fake people more compelling than real ones; and that the public so often agreed.

Trying to avoid the subject of his presence, Warren and Nora made polite talk. The czar show, she explained, was to open at Kansas City's Nelson Gallery in a week.

"I won't have to stay long, though. 'Till They Want Us Back' just made *Billboard* magazine's top forty. Once that happens, getting air time on radio stations ceases to be such an issue. People are buying the record like mad. Suzanne-Suzanne already says she wants to play the Czarina Alexandra in the new TV situation comedy based on those zany, madcap nights in the Winter Palace."

"It must be fun for you to travel so much."

"I *hate* to travel. This is my first time on the road for Harvey —that's my boss—and it is going to be my last. The arrangements have been impossible."

"Arrangements?"

"It's such a dumb situation. I'll tell you all about it some other time."

Some other time? We're never supposed to see each other again, Warren thought, but she'll tell me about it some other time. He was looking at her closely, and she caught him; or maybe she was looking closely at him. They both turned away. Warren tried to resume the small talk by asking Nora what she did at work.

"I write press releases mostly, and sometimes liner notes for albums. If I take all week to write one release Harvey thinks that's terrific. It must be the recording industry influence. To them two consecutive grammatically coherent sentences constitute literature. Since I work out of my home they never know how little time it actually takes."

"This—Harvey—doesn't object?"

"He's billing me by the hour. What's crazy is that the clients don't complain, either. Suzanne-Suzanne requested me. I mean she personally didn't request me, it was her agent. I did a bio sheet for her press kit and wrote it in such a way that it seems as if about four years of her life never existed. Apparently she was pleased by that. Los Angeles people in general, they're dumbfounded when they get any finished product at all."

They fell into discussing the parallels between public relations work and civil engineering. Make-work was also a more profitable line for technologists than real work. Warren noted that Doug Denning, the second partner in KD&H, had a gift for landing study contracts, the most lucrative ones of all because the real work quotient was close to zero.

"When I started at KD and H most of the study contracts were from government agencies. We would take months 'assessing options' or 'reviewing data' and the agencies didn't mind, because the more delay the better. The reason they gave us study contracts in the first place was to provide themselves with an excuse to put off a decision. There'll be some trendy crisis and whatever government agency sounds like it's supposed to act will say to reporters, 'We can't act until the consultant finishes his study.' And there's this understanding—you know, a nod and a wink—that we won't finish until the press has forgotten all about whatever the original crisis was and is jumping up and down about a new threat to civilization. Then we get a contract to study that.''

"If they didn't waste the money on you they'd only throw it away on somebody else," Nora said.

"What's spooky is that it's no longer just government agencies. Now we get corporate study contracts—big corporations—on the same terms. You'd be amazed how much they pay to have their own data rearranged in an inconclusive form. It's like they don't trust their own eyes; they only believe the obvious when told by someone else."

Nora shot an unhappy glance at the corner of the bar, where a lounge-act band was setting up. "Much of what we take most dearly to heart comes from strangers," she said. "Without sounding too clichéd, aren't we all? I think it would take many years, hundreds of years, to really know a person, to really be certain."

Warren was startled and began to speak, but the waitress interrupted, arriving with another round and a computerized tab noting date, time, price codes, everything but the relative humidity. The waitress put Nora's second glass of white wine off to the side, for she drank sparingly and had not yet finished the first. Warren felt slightly light-headed, and decided to steer the conversation back to a safe area. He spoke of the Hyatt Regency skywalk collapse and the other outrages; how he feared his own company, KD&H, could slip into the same behavior.

"About the only real-work project we've got right now is retrofitting some new unducted turbines into the pump generating station of a municipal . . ."

Nora's attention had vanished by the second syllable of the

word *turbine*. She was keenly interested in any matter that dealt with human nature, but could not stand technical topics; she did not inquire as to what a pump-generating station was, and Warren realized she never would. He got off the topic quickly and then asked her about writing press releases.

"I use what I call my 'Press Agent's Thesaurus,' " she said. The band had begun to play velour-trimmed music, forcing her to speak up. "It's a list of synonyms for *great*. *Astonishing, awesome, extraordinary, landmark, legendary, momentous, stupendous, superlative,* and so on. You have to get at least one of these words into the first paragraph. When you can't make any of them apply you can always use *provocative*, or at last resort, *unconventional*. In art, *unconventional* is code for *awful*. Usually the more fawning the better, because you're not really writing a press release for the press. You're writing it for the client. He's the one who pays your salary, and he's the only one who's sure to read the release."

"I would think that journalists would see through that sort of thing."

"Well, of course they see through it. Most forms of professional success are predicated on the ability to pronounce with total conviction words that would make any five-year-old burst out laughing. Lawyers who sweat when they tell lies, you know, don't go very far. It's the ones who lie with abandon who win the admiration of society. Most of my releases go to the entertainment publications, and they want to be snowed."

She took a sip of her wine. "Now I must tell you about my other reference work, my 'Critic's Thesaurus.' This one contains every antonym for *great*. *Abysmal, asinine, horrible, pointless, putrid, repulsive, tedious, vapid, worthless,* and so on. The fall-back word is *predictable* and the emergency word is *derivative*. *Derivative* is a fine all-purpose put-down because it applies in some sense to virtually everything, including every review ever written. I suppose my point is that publicists and critics are mirror images. I exaggerate how good something is, they exaggerate how bad it is. The only significant difference is I get paid more."

"Every review but the first one," Warren said. He had been

waiting for the chance to show that he could match words with Nora.

"The what?"

"Every review but the first one was derivative. And the first review, I happen to know, was by an *Australopithecus* who, upon seeing that the tribe's hunters had brought home only nine mastodon carcasses—rather than ten, the number that he had determined in advance would be suitable—rose from his reclining position just long enough to cry 'Ugh!' An inspiration to critics down through the ages."

Looking at the table, Warren noticed that he and Nora were holding hands, palm to palm. He wasn't sure for how long. They were embarrassed by the discovery. Both looked away. Nora had on her wedding ring. She hadn't worn it when they were—were what? Only in recent years had Warren learned that it was standard practice for the sexes to inspect each other for rings. His married friends, products of the sixties, seemed more like steady dates than husbands and wives—as though they still checked with each other about weekends.

During this awkward moment a man walked into the bar whom Nora recognized. Tall, hairy, with a mustache and meticulously pressed clothes, he was handsome in the manner of the Marlboro Man. He gave the two of them a salute, and a moment later more drinks arrived at their table. Now there were two cool glasses gathering dew and refracting the candlelight by Nora's side.

"Some guy running success seminars at the trade show across the street in the convention center," Nora said, trying hard, it seemed, to sound disdainful. "This morning he insisted on buying me breakfast. At least he claimed to be from the trade show. I'm not sure I believe him. For one thing he's too handsome. And he kept asking me these crazy questions about cell subdivision and the mystical relationships among prime numbers."

"Differentiation. Cells differentiate, property subdivides."

"Whatever. How people can put the moves on at that time of the morning is beyond me."

"Probably depends on how he did the night before," Warren

said, attempting in turn to sound unimpressed.

"I imagine he does all right."

"Then he asked you out."

"No, he didn't. I told him not to ask because I would not accept. He didn't try to twist my arm—some sales expert. In fact, he stared at me a little queerly as though he was remembering something and then became extremely apologetic about the whole situation."

"You were probably the first woman who ever shut him down," Warren said, feeling confident again. "Funny he should go for you in the first place."

"Thanks."

A major error. "No, I mean, he looks like the slit-skirt type." Warren knew that Nora took perverse pride in being a plain dresser, wearing clothes that fit neither current style nor her figure, and had meant to confer a backhanded compliment. Nora was the sort of woman who would have looked better in a 1963 Impala convertible than in a Mercedes coupe. This, for some reason, Warren found powerfully attractive. At a time when extremes of dress were socially acceptable, the woman in jeans and flannel shirt took on an appeal nothing short of see-through could match. As a faithful woman could win your affection even though you would never get to sleep with her—because you could imagine that, were she yours, she would be faithful to you —a shyly dressed woman could win Warren's attention even though he couldn't really get a look at the goods. The first time Nora had taken off her clothes in front of him, Warren scarcely believed his good fortune, for she looked much better naked than he would have guessed. Nora seemed to treat this as her own little secret.

"Don't you start on me, too," she said. "Harvey says that if I am going to represent the firm I must dress accordingly. Aside from the fact that I don't *want* to represent the firm, the thought of spending hard-earned money on office clothes, when the reason you're at the office in the first place is to get the money, just doesn't make sense to me. Really, with all this dress-for-success nonsense, they might as well reenact the sumptuary laws."

Warren didn't know what the sumptuary laws were, so Nora explained—rules dating to the late Middle Ages that regulated how members of the various social classes could dress.

"Didn't you take history in college?" she asked. Warren hadn't. "Well, it was my favorite subject." She spoke the last few words carefully and seemed to search his face for some sign as she did. Warren had come into the meeting determined at all costs not to make any mention of the Lo Spagnas or his suspicions. The last thing he wanted to appear was obsessed. Nora, he assumed, would simply think he was making it up. When he seemed blasé on the subject of history, she went back to explaining sumptuary laws.

"It was really caused by economics. As commerce among different places began, it started being possible for peasants to get money, and that threatened the social structure. The nobles were noble mainly on the basis of inherited property, right? If anybody could acquire property, then how could the nobles maintain the illusion that they were special and more deserving? So one of the futile laws they passed said that only noble classes could wear certain colors and fabrics. That way, walking down the street you could tell a noble from a merchant. Hoping to keep people in uniform, sort of."

The band had begun to play loudly enough that it was a wonder people seated by the speaker columns weren't vibrating. The arrangement was so standardized that Warren could not tell if they were doing new wave rock or a medley of show tunes.

"For instance in the fourteen hundreds, bright green dyes from the Orient became available in Europe. It was quickly decided that only the highborn could wear bright green, and for a lady to attend a ball decked out completely in apple green, well, that was the cat's meow." She made a face. "Can you imagine? People fighting over the right to look like the Jolly Green Giant? No wonder the nobles fell."

"This went on all over Europe?"

"Not everywhere. Mainly in the trading centers, like Florence and Siena, where money was changing hands. When people are going up and down the economic elevator it's very important to devise some system for keeping track of who has status—that's sort of what the high-class gossip publications do today. Bright green. Really, there are few humiliations to which people will not subject themselves in order to preserve fictions involving status.''

Warren hadn't heard a word after Nora said *Siena.* "Places—places like—"

"Like Florence and Siena. Naples was the biggest. There were others, too, of course, but I know the most about Italy. Trade was not so much a consideration in Rome. Rome then was wholly a papal state, except for the odd period when the Pope moved to France.'' She paused to see if Warren was still following along. "Now there's a subject, the Pope in France. That drove us to distraction.''

"*Us?*"

"You know I'm Roman Catholic," Nora said, "although I don't practice. I'm one of those millions of Catholics who claim to love the ceremony but can't stand to actually sit through it.''

"The Pope—moved to France?"

"Catholic bureaucracy went into a frenzy. The city fell on hard times. Through the thirteen hundreds, Rome staged jubilees and indulgence-selling festivals, to draw penitents and their pocket-books. For a price, you could sin with official impunity. Like being a construction contractor in New Jersey. It was worst for the Sisters. Their symbolic husband, the Pope, had left them for a symbolic French floozy. What stress there must have been on the nuns.''

Warren felt dizzy. She was about to say it was all true. Rather than beautiful, the prospect seemed frightening, too much to contemplate. He would have no choice but to believe.

"How do you know all this?" he demanded.

"I went to *college.* I know it wasn't the best school, but I did learn a few things.'' She hesitated. "My major was art history. The period we are talking about was among the most important in the development of art. It would have been a fascinating time to be alive.'' Nora paused again. By now Warren felt faint.

"There were several major painters in rapid succession. Can you imagine it? Botticelli, Tintoretto—"

"Stop!"

"What?"

"Stop," he repeated. "Don't say another word. Not another word. Please don't say any more about it."

Nora was taken aback, and considered him cautiously. What could Warren say? "An Italian Renaissance masterpiece was dropped on my head when I was very young. I don't like to talk about it." Or, "It's nothing, really, just that I once knew a woman in an Italian Renaissance painting."

"You know, Warren, I should tell you that—" Before Nora could finish he cut her off. Warren felt terror at the thought of mentioning the paintings. He insisted that they leave the bar and walk for a while, hoping this would give him a chance to think through the next move. Instead it seemed to dampen Nora's mood, and as they entered the lobby Warren realized he had made a tactical blunder. Now it was natural for them to part.

"It's gotten late, and I have to call on people in the morning," Nora said. "It think it's time to say good night."

"Can't we just talk some—"

"I don't think we should. The later it gets, the harder it gets to go to separate rooms. I'm *married,* Warren. I thought before — I don't know what I thought. Maybe I thought you could have an affair out of town without complications—"

Nora heard how these words sounded and corrected herself. "I'm only trying to explain my own poor behavior toward you. Maybe I thought a lot more. But for now, it feels wrong." She looked around. "What hotel are you staying at?"

"The Hyatt," Warren quickly fibbed. He had not rented a room, or thought of logistics at all—he hadn't even brought an overnight bag with him.

"Then you've got only a short walk. Sleep well."

"In the morning we could—"

"Don't make it harder. This was very sweet of you, to come here like this. I will always be touched. But now, good night."

Warren tried to kiss her; Nora turned, deftly, so that he only got her cheek. It was the sort of gesture that would have been an insult under other circumstances. Then, as if he had decided to start a wrestling match, Warren got a clumsy grip on her hand, turned it over, and kissed it. For a moment Nora became bewildered and discomfitted, glancing at her hand as though to confirm it was still there. She seemed to think Warren had done something totally unexpected. Then Nora leaned forward and lightly touched his lips with her own, whirled, and was gone.

To think about rooms and toothbrushes at that moment seemed too much to Warren, and possibly an offense, although against what he couldn't be sure. He couldn't run after Nora, yet he couldn't leave. Remotely he walked back into the bar. The waitress greeted him as though he were a lost friend. Hotel staff are supposed to do that, he understood, but this type of false intimacy seemed to Warren worse than distance, the way it is worse for politicians and preachers to pretend that they know you personally. One of Lillian Albritton's friends was a staff assistant to the governor. Warren had only a superficial acquaintance with her. Whenever they met at social functions she would chat for a moment, look him directly in the eye and say "We *must* get together soon," then walk away. Warren always thought, But we're together now. This happened several times, befuddling him completely, until he realized the woman simply said this all day long. Warren found the regularity of certain types of lies, not the magnitude, most distressing. Preachers and politicians lied so frequently that when they did tell the truth no one believed them.

In the bar Warren drank a brandy but ordered no more, knowing it would only make him slurred. He had seldom been able to take more than a few drinks without falling asleep. And he had seldom seen other people do it, either. Warren felt that most tales of heroic drinking were heavily embroidered; especially those in literature and theater, where whiskey flows in impossible quantities even assuming the worst about an author. Noël Coward's characters didn't drink martinis, they showered in them.

Too much drinking in theater isn't entirely the playwright's doing. Actors fall into the habit of drinking unreal quantities of whiskey when in character because what they're really consuming is tea, the stage substitute. Television actors commonly pour themselves what ought to be scalding coffee, right off the stove, then slug the whole cup down in a gulp, because they are actually drinking cola, the stage substitute for coffee. At some point during rehearsal the drinks become to the actors merely tea or cola, just as to playwrights whiskey becomes bottles of Gloom, and is dispensed accordingly. Warren thought of the bar game in which you challenge an opponent to match shots of vodka or tequila, having arranged in advance with the bartender that your shots will actually be water. After six or seven, as the opponent begins to stagger, you say, "You mean you can feel that?" Warren liked to imagine playing this trick on Eugene O'Neill.

Leaving the bar and its deafening dimness, Warren wandered about the hotel and then out across a concrete promenade. Beyond it was the convention center. Though the hour was late, the lights were still on inside. No one was checking the door, so Warren slipped in.

The hall was filled nearly to its high corrugated ceiling with machinery: bulldozers, road graders, self-propelled conveyers, prime movers. Banners proclaimed the annual convention of the NATIONAL ASSOCIATION OF EARTH MOVERS. Muck and fumes must have filled the hall as so many heavy engines were moved into place, but now every piece of equipment was spotless. The big fans in the ceiling, he presumed, were for blowing out stale air and carbon monoxide. The convention hall floor was divided by thin curtains on movable steel standards into what promoters generously called booths. All the curtains were exactly the same; exhibitors were forbidden to bring their own, in order to force them to rent from the hall and pay several hours' wage for a three-minute installation job.

Most of the booths, decorated with company logos and various attention grabbers, were empty. A few dedicated salesmen were making last-minute pitches. At major events like the petroleum show in Houston and the military aviation conventions in Paris and Farnborough, England, high rollers competed for the most elaborate booth. Chorus lines complete with special effects were not unheard-of. The year's reigning TV bubblehead blonde sign- ing autographs and occasionally leaning forward was a perennial. Trade shows for less well-heeled industries usually featured magicians, lounge acts, and local babes.

By one exhibit Warren caught sight of a card-trick specialist folding up his table, which had been set in the bucket of a giant Kumatsu front-end loader. "Sorry, guy, the next show's not till eleven A.M.," he was told. Warren shrugged to indicate he had not expected a show. "Well then, why don't you give me my cards back so I can go home for the night?" the sharp asked as he drew a run of jacks from Warren's breast pocket and artfully spread them into a fan. Then, with a nervous grin, he indicated the machine and added, "You look like you understand these things. They swear to me it's been rigged so the bucket can't empty while I'm in it. I don't believe them."

Trying to appear authoritative, Warren climbed up the ladder and into the cab of the loader. A temporary electric power source had been hooked on to the hydraulic system, so that the bucket could be demonstrated without having to start the huge diesel engine. After a while Warren found the safety device that was supposed to prevent accidents—a single strip of duct tape over a PTO interlock toggle switch. Dumping the bucket would be easy as pie. Warren laid on his back underneath the dash, cut several wires that he guessed controlled the bucket motions, pushed them back through the firewall, and removed several fuses. On a whim he took a piece of paper from his pocket, wrote *GET OUT OF THE U.S. MARKET!* [*signed*] *International Har- vester,* and stuck the paper into the fusebox. Climbing down, he assured the card sharp that the bucket would not move at all now.

Many of the exhibits had audio-visual gimmicks. One, a fully articulated mechanical figurine of Thomas Jefferson, was dili- gently pointing out the improved features of a rock crusher. The robot machine would move its hands this way and that, cock its head and smile at no one, then speak a Jefferson quotation about self-reliance. Warren assumed that when the exhibit was staffed, a salesman would stand next to the figurine and talk to it, throwing out questions that the machine would appear to answer. Apparently Thomas Jefferson had been left on by mistake and was going to repeat his spiel throughout the night.

At the Caterpillar Tractor booth farther down the row two local babes were packing up their belongings. Having been to trade shows before, Warren felt that "babes" was the only appropriate term for women, usually models or out-of-work actresses, who stood next to air compressors or schematic diagrams of electrostatic precipitators while dressed in evening gowns. Usually, babes were required to pretend they were present for some reason other than the obvious one. This pretense might be satisfied by having a babe participate in some banter with an emcee type—low-grade sex innuendos that the babe would pretend not to understand—then launch into a short technical speech about the product. The emcee would then react with chagrined amazement and make some crack about how the body had a brain, too, all of which was supposed to give this leer session a surprise antisexist twist and thereby make it all right.

Only by seeing a young woman in a Spandex body suit and four-inch strap-up heels stand on a rotating platform surrounded by middle-aged men in a fully lit convention hall in the middle of the afternoon, and giggle through a dissertation on adiabatic exchange coefficients, could one truly appreciate this scene. Yet it was the gratuitous cracks, not so much the revealing outfits, or the absurdity of it all, that Warren found grating. Why not simply have a little dignity and let the emcee announce, "Fellow Earth Movers, the Cummins Engine Company is pleased to present one fine babe. Look closely at her top. Owing to the sheerness of the material, both nipples are clearly visible. We invite you to inspect the babes at the Detroit Diesel Allison booth and judge for yourselves whether their nipples are fully displayed. Just another in a series of performance comparisons we hope you will keep in mind when specifying diesel engine components."

Nora had told Warren that in her kinder moments she found it charming that men placed themselves in such thrall to women's body forms. The most powerful or wealthy male, the most lofty and self-important, would come totally unglued over what was, after all, merely an accentuation. Even philosophers and deep thinkers, whose powers of detached reasoning were supposed to qualify them to struggle with the very meaning of existence, would go all to pieces over the difference between thirty-three- and thirty-five-inch boobs. "It's crude," Nora had said, "but at least there's one thing men like that's human."

Stopping at the booth, Warren looked up at a Caterpillar D-10, largest bulldozer in the world. These machines were so big they had to be shipped to construction sites on railroad cars in sections, then assembled. A Caterpillar salesman materialized and, before Warren could stop him, started into his routine. Though the two babes were getting ready to leave, they participated in the sales talk out of habit, calling their lines out as they zipped up shoulder bags.

"Do you realize that this machine has the highest power to weight ratio in its class?" the salesman asked.

"And the torque peak is achieved at 1,720 RPM, nearly 14.5 percent lower than any outsized competitor," one babe declared. She made the word *achieved* sound immensely prurient.

Finishing his presentation, the salesman gave Warren an admission pass to the Caterpillar hospitality suite back at the hotel. He went, welcoming any delay in deciding what to do. Even people who have sought each other for years can't necessarily say whether they are driven by infatuation, illusion, chemistry, or love proper; nor can they say what mix of the first three factors, in what dilution, is needed to produce the fourth. How could Warren know whether his feelings were genuine? Or just, he thought unhappily, impulses?

Leaving the convention hall Warren noticed a name tag that had been dropped on a folding table. HELLO, MY NAME IS JERRY MELROD, the tag said. Warren put it on, deciding that for the moment he would rather be Jerry Melrod of A-OK Equipment Sales-Lease, Front Royal, Virginia, than himself.

In the suite, Caterpillar officials greeted Warren with lively calls of "Hi, Jerry!" and inquired about the business climate in Front Royal.

"Too soon to tell," Warren answered to thoughtful nods, "too soon to tell." Having read his share of presidential speeches and syndicated columnists, Warren knew that business was always recovering, but never recovered. The one thing no Western economy seemed capable of producing was a conclusion.

The reception, like most drinking functions, offered the appearance and motion of gaiety under a pall of morose obligation. Warren watched out of the corners of his eyes and couldn't help feeling a little superior. Earth movers living it up, he thought. To his left stood a clutch of garishly dressed middle-aged men sporting name tags. He could overhear them talking about how a cab driver would know where to find an after-hours club for some oh-la-la. First time away from the wives this decade, boys? Warren wondered. Aware that your cab driver is likely to have just arrived from Bhutan?

As the reception drew to a close Warren wandered back down to the hotel lobby. He thought of simply sitting there through the night, to demonstrate to Nora by his unshaven presence that he was willing to be tested. Considering the lateness of the hour, the lobby was still busy with guests and staff. Sharing the floor with these small people and their passing concerns annoyed Warren. He wanted to believe that because the circumstances of his feelings for Nora were dramatic, he knew something others didn't know. Having to look, act, and be just as lonely as the earth movers did not help. Warren slumped down onto a bench near a bank of pay phones, his mind faltering.

The middle-aged thrill seekers he had seen in the hospitality suite passed by on their way to find a cab and, it was safe to predict, more drinks but no action. Warren laughed to himself. One pudgy man broke off from his comrades to stop at the phone next to Warren. He was calling his wife—to report where they were headed, that he was only going to be part of the gang, and that she shouldn't worry if she had to call his room and no one answered. From the tenor of his comments Warren could tell this was not the first time he had talked with his wife that day, and would not be the last. He could also tell the call was being placed not out of deception or from fear, but because home was where the pudgy man really wanted to be, and his wife's voice was the voice he really wanted to hear.

Warren felt abashed. This man, he thought, knows more about love than most poets. Routine love has a drama all its own, a drama of patience and small attempts. People don't think much about it or make art about it because no one particular moment is memorable. But that, he realized, is the whole point. How many thousands of phone calls like this one are made every day, not one of them worth preserving and yet every one priceless? Every one a tiny jewel for the crown that will someday be placed on mankind's head.

Not suddenly, but in a quiet way, Warren found himself filled with resolve. Where does love begin? he had asked himself. It doesn't matter, he now answered. All that matters is what you know, and I cannot leave this place now, knowing what I know.

Warren stepped over to the bank of elevators, pressing the Up button repeatedly. The control panel showed all the cars fluttering frivolously about the top floors of the hotel. He found the stairs and ran up the six flights.

At the door to Nora's room he hesitated just long enough for panic to overcome his palpitations and supply the final impetus. He knocked, first softly. Then moderately; then as loudly as he could. There was no answer.

Nora was a light sleeper, Warren knew. He knocked again, calling out her name. Still no answer.

Oh God, he thought, she's with the Marlboro Man. They've just finished and they're smoking free samples.

Warren pounded against the door. He stepped back to inspect it, wondering if he possessed the strength to kick it down. The door appeared secure. Given the unreal but widely believed Hollywood protocol of doors that pop like corks, it would have been something of a low point in life for a former college football player to hurl himself against the door to his one true love and bounce off.

A hotel security guard, hazy and half awake, appeared at the far end of the corridor, summoned by a guest in one of the adjacent rooms. Warren checked to make sure he was still wearing the Jerry Melrod tag. Then he approached the guard, pretended to stumble like a drunk, and feigned pleasant surprise at seeing a uniform. He started a patter about losing his keys.

"Been over to see the show yet?" Warren said, speaking in an accelerated mumble he hoped would make the guard anxious to get it over with. "Come by booth number seventy-four and see my D-10, world's largest bulldozer. Torque peak achieved a full five minutes later than the nearest outsized competitor. I'll never say a thing if you'd just let me in my room here. Don't happen to need an earth mover, do you? Only $338,000, and we're offering a hell of a financing package. If you could—"

Waving a hand for relief, the guard pulled out his master key and slid it into the lock on Nora's door. Warren became aware that he had no idea what he was going to do or say, not the slightest notion of how to explain himself or this intrusion. He wanted to cry out that he'd changed his mind. The door swung open and the guard stepped in first, flipping the light switch. Light spread irrevocably, paint from a kicked bucket.

The room was empty. No Nora, no suitcases, nothing. A few towels had been used and tossed around. The bed was mussed as though it had been napped in but not slept in; there was a single dollar bill on the nightstand and a piece of hotel stationery on which was written *thank you.*

The security guard surveyed the scene with foggy interest. "You sure travel light," he said.

Then Warren saw the note on the dresser. The presence of a piece of paper seemed to set matters right in the guard's mind, and he left after favoring Warren with a few words about proper procedures.

Warren sat down on the bed, contemplating the note and its existence for some time before opening it. Written words within. The simple possession of written words from Nora would be his first physical confirmation that their affair was happening in the actual world, not in his mind. He opened the note and read:

Warren Dear,

I'm assuming you will get this note one way or the other. In fact I have little doubt. I hope you didn't hurt your leg breaking down the door.

I have gone home to Ford. (That's my husband.) What you may think I feel for you, I do feel. But in this time and place I cannot be with you. There's more to this than you know— that I cannot just walk away from. If you have love, you will not insist on your own way.

Truly,
N.J.

For a time Warren didn't move, reading the note over and over. He stared particularly at the "Dear." *Dear* is among the group of words, like *cherish* and *patriot,* that are almost always embarrassing but which, when used with precision, can ensorcell the listener. Properly employed by a post-feminist like Nora, a daughter of the semi-revolution, old-fashioned diminutives melt the heart away. The first time Nora had spoken to Warren like this—it was in some neutral context such as "Well, sweetheart, looks like we're in for some rain"—his eyes had nearly watered.

At length Warren put down the note and fell into a dreamless sleep on Nora's bed. Her bed, because *she* had touched it, never mind the thousands of others. Light was intruding through the hotel curtains when the telephone rang. Warren leapt off the bed, thinking, in sleepy confusion, that it would be she. Instead a voice said, "Good morning, Mrs. McConaughty. It's seven A.M."

Afraid of answering in his male voice—not wanting even an anonymous hotel operator to make rude assumptions—Warren said with portent, "I will inform my wife."

He wondered what it felt like to be the person who could honestly say that. Was it a sublime sensation—or did Ford McConaughty daydream about cocktail waitresses and centerfolds, oblivious to his fortune? Later Warren went downstairs to pay Nora's bill, which, it turned out, had already been charged to

Loco Gringo Records. Warren felt better for attempting this minor defense of her good name; the stabilization of society having greatly reduced the number of opportunities for chivalry.

There, at the cashier's desk, Warren was once again obliged to pretend to be Nora's husband. Just saying the words made him feel rudderless. It also made him wonder: If sorcery made it possible would I exchange places with Ford McConaughty? Before Nora, Warren would never have considered a divorced or widowed woman, insisting on a first time for both. Now he felt he would surrender his identity entirely to be with her. He would be happy to cease being himself and become the man she had already chosen, were it possible. Loss of ideal circumstances, errors, or misspent time didn't seem to matter; only the achievement of what should be.

Returning the key, Warren asked to inspect the bill. Listed under long-distance calls were several short calls to Los Angeles and one lengthy call to Seattle. That, of course, was clearly either a good sign or a bad sign. And at the top of the bill was Nora's home address. The cashier did not appear to find it curious when Warren copied his own address down.

The following day a bunch of roses, eleven yellow and one red, arrived at a comfortable suburban home in Seattle. Unluckily it was Ford who answered the door.

"Honey, I believe there's something we need to discuss," he said as he sat down carefully on the edge of the couch. "Who's this Jerry Melrod?"

4
NOW THEY ARE

When Warren returned home from Kansas City, he found a second Azimuth Collective newsletter already in his mailbox. This one arrived in a brown buff envelope stamped with the return address of the Vermont Department of Motor Vehicles, Montpelier, Vermont. Imprinted in block letters on the front of the envelope was the motto REGISTER NOW—AVOID THE RUSH! Someone had drawn a line through these words and written over them *December Issue.* Warren opened the newsletter and began to read:

THE MANY PHILIPS OF MEDIEVAL FRANCE HAD NOTHING ON THE ST. LOUIS SUBURBANITE OF TODAY.

Compared to 99 percent of all human beings who have ever existed, the typical middle-class American lives like a prince in splendor. Roman tetrarchs, Turkish viziers, Ottoman caliphs, and Saxon dukes would look with envy on the material circumstance of the resident of a Utah trailer park.

Don't want to believe this, do you? You want to think yourself the victim of harsh circumstance and unfair demand. Join the crowd. Even the rich and the beautiful spend most of their time complaining. *Especially* the rich and the beautiful.

But if you read this and are American and don't know how good you have it, you insult your ancestors. And sell your own life short to boot.

The wealthiest and most privileged of the past, for example, had to struggle with the simple physical necessity of keeping warm. Kings wore all those robes because they were *cold.* They shivered in their castles, sealing their intrigues in dank passageways. A century ago no one, not even the affluent, had central heating, which now in the U.S. almost everyone has.

During the energy shortages of the 1970s it was fashionable

for Americans to *talk* about shivering in their homes, but few ever actually did. Commentators spoke of cool building interiors as though they represented a shocking threat to humanity. They represented, in fact, the condition that almost everyone who has ever lived considered perfectly normal.

Nor can many in today's America appreciate that until this century not even tycoons and presidents could escape the summer heat. Constantine, George Washington, and J. Pierpont Morgan regularly sweltered through temperatures the typical American would complain bitterly about if asked to endure for a single day. One reason the rich bought country houses was to flee someplace a few degrees cooler than the city; today nine out of ten new *cars* have air conditioning, to say nothing of almost all buildings.

Our forebears would not have to see the moon rocket to be dazzled by the material superfluity of contemporary life. That night is treated as day would be sufficient to amaze them. The cycles of day length, varying with the seasons, were controlling elements in the lives of our grandparents. When Abraham Lincoln ran for president, political speeches and rallies were held in mid-afternoon—before it got dark. Most social events were held in summer, in the orange eves. Technologically advanced London boasted of streets lit by lime: limelights produced enough mild glow to keep two people strolling on the same sidewalk from ramming into each other, and this was considered luxury.

Sons of royal houses through history have fallen victim to diseases most Americans have never heard of. One hundred years ago, a cholera outbreak in France killed 15,000 in a single year; more than have been killed so far by AIDS. The biggest causes of death at the turn of the century, outranking heart disease and cancer, were (1) pneumonia; (2) influenza; (3) tuberculosis; (4) diarrhea and enteritis. All are now defeated. A prize to any reader who even knows what enteritis is!

No amount of money, fame, or family connections could till this century have secured cures for typhoid, tetanus, polio, lockjaw, diphtheria, syphilis, malaria, rickets, yellow fever, or an infected wound. How many young Americans are aware that complications from a small cut can kill? Most of the historical health threats against mankind have been reduced to the status of inconveniences *within the lifetimes of our parents*, with the developments of vaccines (polio and tetanus in the 1950s), sulfonamides (1932), and antibiotics (discovered in 1928, but not commonly available until the 1940s).

We live in the trough of the first penicillin generation, for whom bacterial diseases mean nothing. Goethe or Peter the Great might have given their possessions for a hypo of benzathine; today the poorest American can obtain one in minutes. We are now so blasé about diseases that terrified almost everyone else who ever lived that we don't even remember, much less celebrate, the man who gave society penicillin—Alexander Fleming. (A second prize for any reader who knew that!) During World War II several million people died of infection. Today it's rare for a house pet to go that way.

The very concept of hospitals as places of healing is new to this century. Till around 1900, what we now call hospitals were strictly places where the very old or hopelessly ill went to die. Sick people were better off staying home and taking their chances. What we now call doctors were then more like what we now call funeral directors—their primary role was to preside over death, not recovery.

How does the idea of surgery without sleep or painkillers strike you? That's all that was available to Prince Metternich or the Duke of Wellington, anesthesia having first been used in 1842. Mind if I cut your stomach open while you watch? Mind if I don't wash my hands? Antiseptic surgery was first tried in 1865. The related notion of having routine procedures like births and tonsillectomies done in hospital safety is newer even than our parents. Jimmy Carter, elected in November 1976, was the first American president not born at home.

We neglect to bear in mind that travel has only just stopped being an undertaking associated with sickness, huge wastes of time, and exhaustion. Two hundred years ago a trip from Copenhagen to Atlanta would have been a physical challenge and a danger even for ambassadors and archbishops. How would you like to spend a month on a small wooden ship being tossed from side to side, followed by a month on horseback? Today this trip can be accomplished at a moment's notice for a price within most budgets, with a brief spell of drowsiness the main side effect. Automobiles—a flexible, convenient means of rapid transportation which the robber barons in their private railroad coaches would have envied—are now available to most teenagers. Every kind of device that moves with an internal combustion engine made possible by gasoline is a recent arrival. No one even knew petroleum *existed* until 1857.

Think of a subject as basic as your dinner plate. No American can dream of not being able to obtain any amount of food desired regardless of season, his budget allowing. This luxury was beyond the imagination of almost all the admirals, landholders, duchesses, and popes who ever lived. Canning is a mere 150 years young, refrigeration a phenomenon of this century; before it neither the Mellons nor the Rockefellers could store food in fresh form. In America pensioners serve tomatoes and strawberries in February, which Henry the Eighth could not have done. College students drink the brandy of Napoleon, and feel sorry for themselves. Hot chocolate, the royal liqueur of the Aztec courts, is sold in gas stations.

Americans also now have, in great abundance, a luxury unknown on a historical scale—the luxury of loneliness.

Until this century, even families of means usually lived together. Three generations to a house, no matter how grand the house, were the norm. Four were not exceptional. For children, there was no escaping from the ravings of senile grandparents; for grandparents, no relief from the screeching of kids. When young people married, they often went directly from living with their families to living with their in-laws, never experiencing what privacy might be like.

Now it has become rare for grandparents to live with children, rarer still for young couples not to have homes of their own. Whatever the merits of this development, it must be counted in the calculus of social wealth. Having older

Americans live separately from younger Americans has required the construction of an entirely new infrastructure layer. Extra housing, extra sewers, extra cars, extra dishwashers and vacuum cleaners, larger power plants and landfills. They all make possible the luxury of loneliness.

Similarly, single adults now often live alone, bathing themselves in the jasmine of privacy, and extra material goods have been made for them, too. Until roughly this century, young members of the middle class usually could not live alone simply because enough housing and appliances were not available for this purpose. Those who managed to live by themselves usually did so in circumstances we would consider minimal—as boarders, with only a room to call their own, instead of a full set of bath, kitchen, and other facilities. The current availability of true single living is a solitary luxury, a ring hidden in a box, but a luxury indeed by historical standards.

Of course, though the poor today may enjoy advances that the rich of preceding generations would have envied, they are still poor by today's standards and that is all that matters. Let's set aside the question of wealth versus poverty for the moment, and also the question of whether today's material blessings can be sustained. Consider instead a pattern that lies beneath fluctuations in living standards, and how it affects something entirely different—standards of the heart.

Very roughly, from the onset of organized societies in the later millennia B.C., to the European Dark Ages, the rich have been different from everyone else in a sense much larger than having more money. The rich lived entirely *unlike* their poorer fellow beings. Having a dwelling with walls, and eating regular meals, was enough to set a person fundamentally apart from common people who lived in hovels or with no shelter at all. Through this first period the ruling classes also had access to items that, for all intents and purposes, the general population did not even know existed: art, philosophy, writing, staged entertainment. Generally, the privileged did not have to fight in wars or perform the backbreaking manual labor that was the

lot of the common man. Their legal rights were in no way
comparable. The privileged could do almost anything to
commoners, including kill them; commoners had almost no
recourse.

And during this first phase there was little personal contact
between the rich and poor. What did occur had little meaning.
Romantic love, to the extent that it was sought after (in earlier
ages love had only a fraction of the standing it holds today),
was available mainly to the upper classes; the masses had no
material opportunity, or freedom of choice, to experience
romance as we use the word.

Sometime during the Dark Ages, this relationship changed.
The collapse of progress and the unceasing, inconclusive
warfare among city-states and local tyrants had the curious
effect of blending the classes together.

Since there was a shortage of physical structures in this
period, and new ones could be raised only at stupendous cost—
the darkness having spread over production, commerce, and
specialized labor as well as science—and as there was great
need for mutual protection against disorder, classes tended to
compress. Noblemen and peasants often lived together in
crowded common rooms. When the community was attacked,
noblemen fought alongside peasants, and with equal
desperation. As there was no central authority to call on for aid,
defeat meant death or abjection for all classes.

Under these conditions, the rich led lives that were in
structure not too much different from the lives of the poor.
Nobles wore a nicer cut of fabric and did not have to bend over
so much, but their daily routines were largely the same as the
routines of the poor, their diets similar, and, since everyone
lived together, their dwellings identical. Contact among upper
and lower classes was frequent; elite luxuries such as
education, travel, and art were rare for all. Meals were taken in
the common room. The thought of retiring to privacy was alien
even to some lords.

Privacy was, itself, an abstraction. The Norman Privy Council
of the thirteenth century was so named because it met in one of

the few truly private chambers in the Isles. Outhouses were
dubbed "privies" for the same reason, and were perhaps the
only private place many people of the Dark Ages ever entered.
(And when they did, be assured, they were very eager to get
back out.)

Linked to the general misery of this period was the very low
significance of romantic love. One must sympathize. It is not
surprising that men and women lacked the energy to pursue
transcendent emotions when nearly every moment of the day
was given over to eking out subsistence, while plagues and
pointless wars regularly mocked the perseverance of those who
did manage to survive. During this time, with travel rare, most
people lived out their lives within the confines of small villages,
where the potential choice of partners was slim and the chance
of finding a partner who moved the heart perhaps slimmer,
given the degree of inbreeding. Lovers didn't have too much to
whisper about except rats and rain. You could get your life's
story over with in a few minutes.

An impediment to romantic love during this middle period was
the simple lack of places for lovers to be lovers. Sex was
snatched in the fields—try an actual roll in the hay sometime, if
you think the notion sporty, and remember to bring your
tweezers—or in the common room after dark, with everyone
else listening. Being semi-public, lovemaking became lewd
rather than erotic, more laughable than beautiful. Literature
from this period treats sex as bawdy and embarrassing because
that was the way most people experienced it.

Making love in the fields or common room entailed a
complication: clothes were loosened but usually not removed.
The sensual pleasure of nakedness, and the intimacy it builds
between partners, was rarely known. The idea of being naked
during sex was very nearly considered a perversion.

As the Dark Ages passed, the structural relationship of rich
to poor changed back to roughly what it had been before.
Science, trade, and rationalism caused material wealth to begin
to flow, bringing with it schooling, art, and leisure for the
privileged. Nobles and successful merchants found they could

send their children to universities, away from contact with peasants. The rich began to favor frilled, foppy fashions because such impractical clothing would show at a glance that they performed no manual labor. Laws, revived by the end of disorder, gave vast advantages to property holders. National governments confined the war of all against all to discrete flurries of destruction; and as knighthood deflowered, it became the better part of valor to hire or conscript armies, allowing the upper classes to avoid having to fight.

Most importantly for our purposes, as the Dark Ages ended the privileged moved back into private rooms and shut their doors. Contact among the classes diminished again.

The Dark Ages had been so dark that architects lacked the sense (or perhaps the supplies) to build chimneys. Dwellings were heated, to the extent that the term applies, by open fires at the centers of the common rooms, smoke venting directly up a hole in the roof. Needless to say, this made the structure too hot near the fire and frosty everywhere else. Once masonry chimneys became typical, houses could have several small rooms rather than one large room, each heated by its own small fire without choking the occupants.

The growing number of doors that locked was an immense boon to romantic love. Revival of travel made it more possible to meet an inspiring romantic partner; arranged marriages were put on the defensive and eventually defeated. Even the Catholic Church, after its customary period of attempting to deny the obvious, decided to embrace romantic love as an enforcer of the marriage contract and a metaphor for spiritual love. Romantic indulgence remained, however, primarily a pleasure for those classes possessing means and leisure.

Finally, we come to the American century, in which relationships among classes have taken on a new pattern.

Today there are dramatic differences in *degree* of wealth, but the average and the privileged lead lives that are *structurally* similar. The pattern is approximately the same as it was during the Dark Ages—except it is now repeating during a period of prosperity and freedom.

Just about everybody today has his own place to live in, drives a car, wears a suit or dress, travels at least occasionally, uses the phone system. Just about everybody has some education: there are very few schools to which only the rich are admitted. Laws treat everyone the same in theory, and nearly the same in practice. The rich have higher-quality possessions, and more of them—but few basic *types* of possessions are denied to the public at large.

The test here is that almost any poor American could walk into the home of a rich American and immediately recognize, understand, and use almost anything within it. A rich man's car is snazzier than a poor man's car but it can't really do anything the poor man's car can't do. (And if the rich man's car is a Jaguar, the poor man's car is more likely to start.) The most influential cultural forms—television and cinema—are exactly the same for rich and poor alike, a historic first.

And today romantic love is a goal universal among the classes. Marriage is based on love; men and women have many opportunities to meet and court at leisure; bad partnerships can be revoked; lovers are rarely subjected to intolerance for their partner choices.

As every age is in some ways different from the previous age, it is easy to proclaim epochs. Yet in one essential aspect such a claim now seems fair:

Since time immemorial, philosophers have been predicting that if only mankind could cast off the yoke of subservience to physical sustenance, magnificent awakenings of the heart and spirit would be made possible.

Well, guess what?

Now they are.

—5—

The romance between Nora Jocelyn and Warren Gifford had begun in a fury. But following Warren's return from Kansas City, months of inaction passed. There was no reply to the flowers he sent. Warren became afraid to contact Nora, fearing he would only make matters worse. He never so much as said the first word to anyone about the two Lo Spagnas, telling Lil and Tommy to forget the incident had occurred. When they asked what had become of Nora, Warren said she had joined the Peace Corps.

Often, through these months, Warren was unable to account for his time. The paintings haunted him as a problem that he did not know how to solve. If the resemblances were just coincidence, then he was a fool for taking them seriously. If they were more, he was fated to a life of lonely misery, crazy from what he knew and couldn't act on, boring strangers in bars with unsubstantiated claims of having been present at an epiphany. There didn't seem to be any possible happy ending.

At the office, Warren would browse through trade journals or old files, rarely sitting at a drafting table or otherwise trying to look busy. Fortunately for him, this was not considered unusual behavior at KD&H. Avoiding business, Warren worked on his list of "befores," which grew longer:

• Air conditioning was invented before the light bulb. (John Gorrie, 1850; Edison and the forgotten J. W. Swan, independently, in 1880.)

• The Declaration of Independence was written before anyone knew that oxygen is necessary for fire. (Oxygen itself not discovered till 1794, by Joseph Priestley.)

• Michelson and Morley accurately predicted the nature of intergalactic space 25 years before the Model T. (1883, 1908.)

97

- J. J. Thompson measured the radius of an electron, less than 3×10^{-15} meters, almost two decades before the first farm tractor was assembled. (1897, 1915.)
- Saccharin was used before rubber gloves in surgery. (1879, 1890.)
- The principle of the atom bomb was known in scientific circles twenty years before the principle of radar.
- Atom bombs themselves were built before the invention of transistor radios.
- The hydrogen bomb, capable of destroying the world, was exploded before cars had automatic transmissions.
- An American spacecraft landed on the moon before pocket calculators had percentage keys.

Contemplating his silent telephone, Warren decided his favorite "before" was this: teenage girls understood the electronics revolution before IBM.

When telephone ownership became widespread in the fifties, teenage girls instinctively grasped that the telephone's role would not be confined to what its inventors anticipated, namely brief factual communication. (In the beginning telephone conversation was clipped and highly formal, like a radio exchange.) Rather, they knew, the machines themselves would become a form of social interaction—and a significantly more amenable form than those they supplanted. Teenage girls were decades ahead of computer hackers in recognizing that a substitute for human contact could be preferable to the real thing.

Using phones, it would be possible to summon the electronic essence of someone's personality: to exchange thoughts without having to make arrangements or plans, without having to see or touch the person, and with the promise of quickly terminating the encounter without inconvenience. And there would of course be no need to look your best. A similar form of restricted interaction had always been available through letter writing. This new form, however, would require notably less effort, and leave no permanent record. The exact contents of electronic interactions would be forgotten almost immediately.

One coming change in telecommunications gave Warren an uneasy feeling. Since their invention, phones have functioned on the electromechanical principle devised by Alexander Graham Bell. The mouthpiece converts spoken sound into an electric wave, which travels along the wires and is converted back to sound by an earpiece. Sound is a wave to begin with; therefore all the phone network really does (besides switching the calls around from place to place) is amplify sound across distance, by adding energy to the wave so it doesn't fade out as it travels.

If I spoke to Nora on the phone, Warren thought, what I would hear would be *her voice;* not a representation of her voice, but her voice itself. At every point along thousands of miles of cable her voice would exist. Having cables carry the wave might seem at first to make the process unnatural. It's no more unnatural than having air carry the wave. Or a wall carry the wave, as sometimes happens when people shout from room to room. Metaphysically, it is the human voice that emanates from a standard phone.

Not for much longer. Sound waves, Warren knew, are good for voices but bad for computers. The modems people attach to computers are there to translate digital sequences into waves —so phone lines can carry them—and then back into digital at the other end. But waves cannot carry as much electronic detail as digital codes, making computers connected by phone run slowly.

In order to speed up computers, phone companies are in the process of changing their technical standard to transmission of digits rather than waves. This means, in turn, that phones will no longer be able to carry voices. Sound waves entering the mouthpiece will be converted by a reverse-modem device into a string of digital pulses. The device would scan Nora's voice, break it down into something like very short musical notes, and then assign each note a digital code value. The codes would be transmitted to Warren's phone, where they would be reinterpreted as sound waves for the earpiece speaker. In the process, Nora's voice would be lost. Warren would hear an electronic emulation of her speech: he would talk, not to her, but to a machine that was telling him what she had said and was trying to imitate her inflections when she said it.

As the months passed, Warren kept to his apartment, spending many hours in make-work tasks like cleaning up (no company was expected, but his place had never looked better) or reading the ingredients labels on packaged foods and even shampoos. Warren was rational enough to know that preventing the waste and expense of spoiled food was a thousand times more valuable to mankind than whatever minor complication trace amounts of preservatives like BHA could cause. But he looked at labels just the same.

While living in Los Angeles, Warren had traveled back and forth to San Francisco to date a Stanford student named Jewel Wonigan, who read food labels more carefully than textbooks. Once, she purchased containers of every brand of yogurt in the local grocery store (seven) and took them home to make a comparison study. Determining that a yogurt made from mountain goat's milk in eastern Oregon had one gram less fat than the other brands, Jewel would eat only that cup, although she would have been hard pressed to say exactly how much of anything a gram represented.

Jewel came from a monied background but never took material blessings for granted: she insisted that Warren consume the contents of the other six containers. Every aspect of consumer culture seemed to vex her, a handicap Warren attributed to her being raised in New York. When Jewel decided to make Warren dinner, going out for the provisions entailed half a dozen stops or more—one specialty shop for fish, another for Devon cream, a third for whole coffee beans, a liquor store for wine, a bakery for bread and dessert, a K-Mart for paper towels for use as napkins. Jewel knew every specialty store in San Francisco and every subtle gradation in their wares. To Warren the stores seemed interchangeable, all run by ex-Silicon Valley executives who described themselves as having dropped out (how can you drop out by opening a place of business?) and all having names like Cheese 'N' Choke.

When Warren took Jewel Wonigan to a King Soopers in the L.A. suburbs—a many-acred monument to consumption where brioches and bulk teas could be found under the same roof along with Hamburger Helper, medicines, laundry detergent, and fourteen brands of motor oil—Jewel was startled into disbelief, like a Russian who refused to accept that an entire town wasn't being staged to trick him. How could such luxuries be available to the workers?! How could people who shop at supermarkets know about brioches?!

Jewel didn't seem to enjoy shopping in the King Soopers, though, because it was too well-ordered. In New York, her home, order is so unusual as to be viewed with suspicion. Warren practically had to bribe Jewel to get her into a 7-Eleven. She wanted to wait in the car, thinking the place would smell of white bread, Crisco, and John Birch Society tracts. Once she was coaxed in, however, Jewel bought two Big Wheels and a lime Slurpee and became a convert, always wanting to stop and sample the latest cellophane confection.

When college ended, Jewel returned to Manhattan. She often called or wrote to say that she had finally met the love of her life. Usually there was a declaration that she had found total human perfection on the hoof, followed by a nasty falling out that she never wanted to discuss, followed in very short order by a new romantic object.

Twice Jewel moved in with a new man the same week she moved out on an old one. Not someone she had been quietly seeing on the side, but someone she had met the week the previous escapade ended. Another time she moved in with a woman who wrote revolutionary copy for poster artists, teasing with hints that they were more than roommates (once calling Warren to report that her analyst said she had "at last been set free from the male myth of biological determinism"). That affair had ended too, and the woman published a lengthy article in *The Village Voice* expressing deep outrage that her lover "whom I'll call June" could have orgasms only in "heterosexually derived positions."

Finally Jewel's luck turned. Taking graduate history courses at

Columbia, she met an assistant professor of revisionism. Their wedding followed shortly thereafter. The bridegroom came from money, too. Perhaps it was like marrying within the faith.

Over the months when Warren was afraid to pick up the phone, he sent many letters to Nora. All went unanswered. To avoid interception by her husband he sent them without return addresses. So technically, Warren would tell himself, if they haven't been delivered I would have no way of knowing it. But he felt certain they had.

On a desperate Saturday morning Warren returned to the museum to look at the paintings again, only to find they were gone. The display had been rotated with an exhibition of Peruvian religious pottery. The curator told him they weren't scheduled for another showing until 1992, and would he mind coming back then? Warren made certain that the curator got a good long look at his face, and though she seemed to raise an eyebrow, she said nothing.

Warren also bought gifts for Nora, but never sent them. Sending the flowers had been dumb enough. Warren felt it would be dishonorable to attempt to create strife within the McConaughty household. Besides, it probably wouldn't work.

Shamefully, for a few weeks Warren hoped that the fruits of modern technology had failed and that he had gotten Nora pregnant. Perhaps her Catholic upbringing would drive her duty-bound to the real father. What misery all around would be in store! After Warren managed to purge himself of this wish he felt reprieved—as though he had stolen something, not been caught, and then returned the goods before they were missed. He was quite pleased to be able to waste several days in contemplation of the metaphysical question, If you take something and then return it without the owner ever knowing it was gone, are you guilty of a crime? Warren decided his answer was, Only if you don't think so.

Next he began to fear that Nora would have a child by her husband in order to settle matters. The very idea! His sixth sense told him the McConaughtys had been debating and postponing

children; why, he didn't know, but this afforded him hope that
a chink existed somewhere in the marriage. Nora was twenty-
nine. Warren found himself thinking about biological clocks,
which are supposed to worry only women. If they were going to
have each other's children, they had to get the ball rolling soon.
Warren presumed that even under ideal circumstances it would
take Nora a year to get over Ford; then they would want several
years together, unfettered, to be lovers exploring; and that
would pretty much put Nora up against the boundary line for
starting a family.

Things diminished to the point where Warren sat down with
pen and paper to draw a chart, which reminded him, in turn, of
a young medical student he once knew who had plotted out
college, residency, marriage, and an alternating cycle of practice
and maternity leaves right down to the month for the next thirty
years, though she wasn't even going out with anybody at the
time.

"So you're having an affair with a married woman, but not per
se. That is, not an affair per se in the cheating sense?" Doug
Denning asked.

Gradually, Warren came to feel obligated to tell Denning why
his work was suffering, although of course he left out the interesting particulars. They were sitting in the second partner's office.

"What you have is an innovative relational concept," Denning
concluded. "Very innovative. I wonder if it might start a trend?"

Denning was more than a little excited by proximity to a
possible trend. His life would have been made complete if he
were quoted in a newsmagazine about the day a trend that was
sweeping the country had begun in the offices of Kessey, Denning & Hobard. A future-oriented company, he would have
pointed out.

They shot the breeze most of the morning. After all, Denning
noted, Warren's mental state was a legitimate company personnel matter. Denning was always grateful for a legitimate excuse
to put off work.

He had a window-wall office, the best in the firm, looking out over an artificial pond that the developers called a lake. Once in a while Denning remarked that it would make a perfect backdrop for filming a television interview. Now, as Denning talked on, gazing out over the pond, Warren suspected that his boss was imagining himself being interviewed by Phil Donahue about the incredible affairs-without-per-se-cheating phenomenon. *"Phil, I knew immediately this was no isolated instance, but the beginning of a trend that would sweep the country. It's very now, very eighties, don't you think? No commitments but no sex, either. Yes, this is where he was sitting when he told me. Of course it looks like a normal chair."*

So despite his flagging performance, Warren's stature rose within the firm. Later that day, Denning posted a new work-distribution chart that took Warren off some minor projects and elevated him to second in authority over the pump-generating station redesign. The senior engineer, Alvin Rademacher, grabbed the new chart off the board excitedly.

"Jesus, Warren, this is excellent," said Rademacher, whom everyone called Max. Max was the only person in the firm Warren truly liked. "It's going to look great in your file. You'll be at the head of the line for next associate. Or a time-stressed project. You're sure to get slotted if they put us on a core overload or a missile launch."

"Max, we're never going to do a missile launch," Warren answered. "The city council doesn't have any missiles. If they did, they'd probably use them against each other. We do pumps, water mains, and landfill berms. And that's all we'll ever do."

This comment hurt Max Rademacher's feelings, and Warren regretted it. From a professional standpoint Max was the most accomplished engineer KD&H had ever had, but his manner did not reflect self-confidence.

Max had come to Kessey, Denning & Hobard from the government services division of Westinghouse, where he'd done work on the breeder reactor—work that was considered breathtakingly original. Since the Westinghouse government services shop did most of its projects on contract to federal agencies, it was enough like a federal agency that internal politics ranked higher than work output: Max brought those biases along with him. Anything concerning bureaucratic gamesmanship called forth his worst qualities. Max spent an amazing amount of time in pursuits like measuring the square footage of floor space or firing off memos about who could assume what acting title when one of the principals went out of town. In the evenings, Max would pour over the work of the younger engineers, trying to find out which ones were most promising and thus the greatest threat to his own prospects for becoming a partner. Invariably, and perhaps against his will, Max would make design improvements in the process, to the point where Warren felt that ninety percent of the company's worthwhile production originated in Max's brain.

A good conversationalist, Max was given to the sort of grand statements newspaper columnists make—the kind that sound tempting only when you are certain they stand no chance of being taken seriously. For instance, Max would say that the solution to Northern Ireland would be for the British to pull out unannounced, let the hotheads finish each other off, and then declare the ruins the Palestinian homeland. This type of talk endeared him to Warren. The younger engineers at KD&H, who spoke only about their possessions and their careers, seemed as interchangeable as tape cassettes.

Rademacher invited Warren into his office. As senior engineer he merited an outside wall, although his window was only 29.4 percent as large as Denning's—something Max had been meaning to take up with the management committee.

The firm was headquartered in a new industrial park located just outside the city limits for tax purposes. Kessey, Denning & Hobard had been careful to elude the city taxes that provided most of its revenues. This location made Warren a reverse commuter, driving out from the city in the morning and back in from the suburbs at night; he and the maids.

Beyond the office complex was a frontage road, and then an eight-lane freeway. From Max's window you could see the freeway breathing cars in and out of the city, most of them carrying only a driver, as Americans acquire dignity through displays of mutual loneliness.

From Max's office window you could also see where Max lived. He owned a condominium apartment in a new high rise across the frontage road, one of those skinny buildings with suspended concrete-mold porches just big enough to turn around on. At first Max had lived in an apartment on the opposite side, facing the city skyline. After a few months he went through all the paperwork and expense of selling his city-side condo in order to move across the hall to a unit facing KD&H. Old man Kessey, the company patriarch, was losing the battle with his wits, and talked increasingly of security. Max saw this as an important opening. After moving across the hall, he circulated a memo saying he was now in a position to watch the office twenty-four hours a day and "provide an additional tier of deterrence." Precious little was known of Max's personal life, except that he had been widowed young and had remained alone since. But few doubted his claim to pass evenings sitting by the sliding glass door to his concrete porch, eyes on the entrance to KD&H. When Kessey presented him with a complete set of door and alarm keys, Max was triumphant.

On the wall of Max's office was a framed photograph of him shaking hands with President Ford. They stood before a vast, seemingly endless contraption of pipes and plumbing. Two other, very somber men looked on. Though the picture had been taken more than a decade ago, Max appeared to be exactly the same age.

The contraption in the photograph was a mock-up of a breeder reactor. Max had worked on breeders most of his adult life, and had never gotten over their failure. As a young engineer he had found the premise of the breeder irresistible: a controlled crisis machine whose very goal was to come as close to the line as man dared. Breeders would run two thousand degrees hotter than conventional nuclear reactors and, unlike them, explode if mishandled. When it began to appear that breeders could never be made safe enough—to say nothing of cheap enough—Max, like most of the project insiders, insisted on plunging ahead, making increasingly improbable claims about future performance and spending money as fast as possible, hoping to sink so much cash into the ground that Congress would be compelled to spend more in order to rationalize the previous spending.

Max had been head of the team developing the emergency feedwater system, which was supposed to extinguish a runaway atomic fire by dousing it with coolant. It was a prime technical challenge. Tens of thousands of gallons had to be moved in a few seconds without warning, and with no possibility of breakdown —no chance that complications from failure in primary systems that could cause the emergency cooling to fail, too. Feedwater systems possessed a drawback, however, that could not be engineered out: if successful, they destroyed the reactor in the process. This would be better than letting the reactor explode, but that was about all you could say for it. Coolant boiling off the nuclear fuel and reacting with the normal liquid sodium bath would reduce delicate interior components of the machine to radioactive rubble. Breeder optimists, particularly chairmen of certain congressional subcommittees and vice presidents of certain companies, said not to worry. It would be possible to run right up to the line without ever slipping across.

Westinghouse let Max go when the breeder project was terminated, even though, as Max missed no opportunity to point out, his picture shaking hands with President Ford had once run in the company's annual report. "Third in my class at MIT, picture in the annual report, back on the street faster than a vacuum cleaner salesman," he would say.

Dismissal hit hard at Max because he had lost his savings the year before in a foolish attempt to work the stock options market using a technical-indicators system of his own design. He had made bad plays on margin—the polite world's equivalent of bookie loans—and incurred sizable debts. About the only thing Max had saved was a set of conceptual drawings from the feedwater system, and he tried to force them like slides of Mexico onto the younger engineers. Warren won Max's loyalty when, looking for ways to divert his mind from Nora, he became the first volunteer. Many of the copies were worn and heavily creased—difficult to read along the fold lines—suggesting an old love letter that is often taken out and reread to see if it really says what memory thinks it said.

A set of engineering plans cannot be glanced at. The pages must be studied, the reviewer backtracking and rethinking each option the designer pondered and discarded before it can be determined if the plan is elegant. Intermittent study over a few weeks' time had persuaded Warren that the design was, in fact, brilliant. This did not change Warren's conviction that the world was better off without breeders. In moments of candor Max would admit as much.

After Warren finished telling Max how highly he thought of the drawings, Max asked him to throw them away—he didn't want to see them again. Warren, confused, moved to throw them into Max's wastebasket.

"Not here! On your way home from work." Max vaguely knew that Warren was worried about some far-off love. He tried to sound avuncular. This sort of talk sometimes rang hollow coming from Max, who had no family, though it was nowhere near as bad as when he lectured on The Proper Way to Raise Children, a subject on which no childless person should be allowed by law to speak.

"The breeder reactor was a failure as technology, but a masterpiece of social commentary," Max said. "It teaches us not to try for that which is theoretically possible but bound to fail in practice. Between people the same obtains. This idea that violins will play in the background—such love exists only in abstraction, like mathematics. We can discuss it but we cannot actually experience it. We can even make up rules about what it might be like if we could do it, as in academia, and applaud each other for breakthroughs. But we cannot actually enter a hypothetical world. Do not torment yourself for failing to do what cannot be done."

Trying to rejoin without giving away too much, Warren started to say something along the lines of better to have loved and lost. He did not get far.

"Better to lose!" Max bellowed, tearing a sheet from his desk blotter and starting to draw side elevations, a nervous habit.

"You think it is poetic to float around being in love. I say, the floater is the cynic. A little kiss here, a little help with the gardening there—the love you might actually get—is never enough. Only if you leap out of bed each morning singing a duet does it count. The great poets, who carve their initials in the ages—how many of them had happy love lives, hmm? How many experienced one percent of what they said other people are supposed to experience?" The drawing he was making resembled a giant gantry for lifting whole skyscrapers. "Demanding what no one can have—tell me what's romantic about that."

It was almost noon. Warren asked Max to go out for lunch, which he never did. Max had a brown bag in the office refrigerator containing a tunafish sandwich and celery stalks, which he planned, in accordance with his daily habit, to eat in the drafting room where everyone could see him. When Warren persisted Max replied, "We can't go *now*. It's only eleven fifty-four."

So they waited until exactly noon. Passing the reception desk, Max loudly announced, "Mr. Gifford and I are meeting a client for lunch." Then he wrote down the name of Denning's favorite restaurant on the In/Out board, so that if Denning looked while they were gone, he would approve.

Denning's favorite restaurant was The Eatery, a flat suburban shoebox kind of place with no exterior features, a parking lot five times larger than the restaurant itself, and big roof-mounted air conditioners that mischievously seemed to be running regardless of the season.

The Eatery was a little odd even by the standards of a business where mason jars and chrome railings are placed side by side. Entering, one first saw an unusually large cocktail lounge done in red velvet so plush it would have sent Freud racing to his typewriter. Only guests with sharp eyesight could see inside the lounge, for the lighting was better suited to developing film. There were attractive young waitresses in slinky evening gowns, and a fake-fire pit at the center. Patrons sat on velvet-covered benches sunk slightly into the floor; the waitresses knelt to take orders and serve drinks.

Beyond the cocktail lounge was a brightly lit dining area featuring booths with uncomfortable orange plastic seats designed to make the diners move along smartly. Service in the eating area was provided by middle-aged waitresses of the hi-ya-honey truck-stop variety, dressed in traditional black and white. This nutty combination was designed to combat the anti-drinking fad by giving businessmen incentive to linger in the lounge but not the dining area; alcohol has a higher markup than food, and its diminished consumption has been as bad for restaurateurs as good for everybody else. The Eatery's owners had decided it was time to counterattack.

Warren knew all this because KD&H had done an analysis of zoning regulations for The Eatery in exchange for holding Denning's birthday party there. Backing the restaurant was a company that test-marketed eating concepts. It had grown prosperous during the late seventies franchising singles-bar treatments that employed the letter *J*—T. J. Pendleton's, P. J. O'Rourke's, L. J. Simpson's, J. J. Houlihan's, Santa J. Barbara's, Henry J. Boulder's. Then it scored another hit with a software program that matched dessert menus to local demographics. Since The Eatery concept was intended for sale as a franchise, Warren expected that thousands of dollars in legal fees had been invested in the question of how to ensure the lounges would be staffed with good-looking women while avoiding sex discrimination suits.

Although Max left The Eatery phone number at the office, they actually went to Max's apartment. Max thought it was silly to spend money for lunch; for his part, Warren was happy to be spared The Eatery. Women in slit skirts stumbling in semi-darkness when the sun was shining outside seemed to him a parody of sex appeal.

Nora had once said that there were a few ideas for appreciating the aesthetic beauty of the female form that had been invented by women, but most had clearly been invented by men. Male ideas for looking at women's bodies, Nora reasoned, centered on making women reveal themselves as a routine matter, in circumstances unrelated to intimacy. Slit skirts in public restaurants, bikinis, *Playboy,* beauty contests, and so on pushed the notion that showing skin is *nothing personal*—done with detachment and quite respectable. "Men want taking off your clothes to be just a social convention, you know, like neckties," Nora had said. On the other hand, she continued, the negligee must have been a woman's idea, since its purpose was personal—designed for use in private, and to lead directly to making love.

It probably wouldn't be long, Warren thought, before there were hunk restaurants catering to female executives. Assuming that the hunk fad is genuinely rooted in women's minds; to him it sounded suspiciously like a male idea. Guys on Madison Avenue and Sunset Boulevard hyping the notion of a national outburst of uncontrolled female lust, in hopes of making it so.

Max's condominium was Spartan, having little more than a recliner chair in the living room and long folding tables of the type found in church basements, which substituted for a desk. There were locked metal filing cabinets, some unopened mover's boxes, and no rugs. Their footsteps echoed through the place.

"Max, a triumph of minimalism," Warren said.

"I don't like being cluttered," Max replied. He had not finished paying off debts from his stock losses, and was embarrassed by being a senior professional without the means to live comfortably. He went to the kitchen, where he made tunafish sandwiches and, after grumbling about being out of celery, cut carrot sticks. Conducting a furtive inspection of the apartment, Warren spotted only one artifact of sentimental value. It was a framed photograph of Max in his youth, grinning, hair slick as though he had just gone for a quick dip in an oil refinery. His arm was around a happy young woman.

Seating himself at one of the folding tables, Max said, "The significant thing about your generation is that you have lowered the temperature of human events. You had your nineteen-sixties, got it all out of your systems, and now nothing excites you. Your generation is so burned out emotionally you have to pay money to go to courses where people explain to you how to be interested in yourself."

"Thanks."

"No insult, I mean this as a compliment."

"You're not supposed to mention the sixties anymore," Warren said. "They're overanalyzed."

"They are overanalyzed wrong," Max replied. "Changes happen all the time, so to understand the full picture you look for changes that become permanent. Vietnam War? Ended. Civil rights? Laws passed. Hippies? Extinct. Now what's something that happened during the sixties that has kept on happening and probably always will keep happening?"

"The Pill. Or the equivalent."

"Not bad. That's one. But the answer I was thinking of is college. Your generation is the first one ever, any time or place, with more people going to college than not going." Max seemed to be able to speak and eat simultaneously; his sandwich was already gone. "College will be the end of passion, and this I assure you is an excellent development."

Warren had to bite his tongue to keep from saying that it was easy for a fifty-year-old man who hadn't asked a woman out in two decades to assert that the world was better off without passion.

"I'm not talking about degrees," Max continued. "I'm talking about what happens to you personally at college. Before the postwar generation, for most people the first test of human relations came very young. People married in their late teens, early twenties. When you get married three things can happen: happy marriage, unhappy marriage, divorce. Some other day we can argue what constitutes each one. My point is, each of these outcomes is *significant.* Loads of complications, personal and legal. Straight from childhood to adult woes.

"The pattern now," Max said, "is for later marriage following an interim period of college—away from the parents and their expectations, neither child nor adult. Free to make all manner of mischief, to try experiments with people that *don't matter* because the results will automatically be cancelled at the end of the year. So you fool around, here and there. A few steady dates, a little sleeping around, this type of thing. You fall into thinking that no particular act of attachment or passion really counts. It's all part of the syllabus. And consider whose influence you are under!

There is not one college professor in the United States—believe me I know, I speak as a lecturer for five years in physics at Johns Hopkins—who believes that love is real. Easier to find one who believes in bringing back the Hapsburgs, or raising Atlantis."

"That's defeatism."

"No, optimism. The less passion, the better. As people get smarter and better educated, they cool off. Okay, fewer poets and saints. But fewer broken hearts. Believe me, it's a small price to pay."

Warren thought his own situation was being discussed. He tried to think of an evasive reply. "There are some elements of this I can't tell you, Max."

"Oh boy, secrets. The young always have secrets." Some fuel source expired in Max and he fell silent.

Warren considered the notion that people were actually better off if they felt less. You could construct a nice edifice of logic to support an abolition of passion. The bad marriages, rushed into, could be disbanded with less pain; the good ones would be preserved by the absence of impetuous affairs; the ritualistic frictions among races, countries, and classes would lessen; many fights and sneerings, much envy and pettiness could be avoided, were emotions not taken so seriously. These benefits in return for giving up the outside chance that a small number of people would run through autumn leaves together in slow motion. Warren let his eyes rest on the row of glass-box office buildings outside the kitchen window, all with names like Data-Tron or Accu-Tech, looking cool and harmless.

Later that afternoon, after quitting time, Warren stopped by Max's office. Max had the day's company correspondence spread out on his desk. He covered the papers up in a flurry.

Warren took a shot in the dark and asked, "How did she die, Max?"

"None of your damn business."

As Warren cajoled and the evening light faded, Max grew weary and told the story, speaking succinctly for once. Married at age twenty, hometown sweethearts. Together for seven years.

Trying to work "our" way through MIT, in the library at all hours, apartment in the slums of Somerville. She takes a lover but Max isn't aware, too busy trying for distinction. She confesses all, asking forgiveness, but Max walks. Says he'll be back the next morning and she better be gone. Next morning Max returns, has come to his senses, wants to work it out. She is gone, left town with the lover. Very smooth and handsome, minor record, check forging and such: carpet salesman. Has left note saying their life together is over. Max can't find her. Parents don't know where she's gone, either. She never contacts them.

"Five months later I get the call," Max said. "Sergeant something of the Kentucky State Police. It's four-thirty in the morning. He asks for Mr. Rademacher and I'm groggy from dreams, I think he means my father. I say, I am sorry, my father has passed on. The policeman says, 'Lord have mercy, it's a double tragedy.'"

The second-shift watchman passed by in the hall, popping his head in the door to offer a perfunctory nod at Max. "We get the names straightened out, then the cop spills it," Max continued. "With a shotgun the bum has killed her, then shot himself. A neighbor tells police that my Betty has wanted to come back but has been afraid because he threatens. Second-degree murder is the charge. Hot-blooded act, not premeditated, they say. Killing someone because you are in a bad mood is only a no-no to the courts, not a mortal sin.

"And can you believe it, the bum doesn't even die. Imagine not being able to kill yourself with a shotgun. Only the French are so incompetent. Twice he is put on trial and each time gets a mistrial when he must be returned to the hospital. A year later he kicks off, without ever being convicted. So technically the bum dies a free man. Just like the rest of us, eh?"

Warren did what he could to console, but the older man had become morose. He started to offer to drive Max home, then remembered that Max lived two hundred yards away. After sitting with him for a while Warren said, "I hope it will be a small consolation to you that your story has helped me immensely. I'm going to be gone for a week. Tell Denning I'm taking my personal leave."

"Going?" Max caught on quickly. "To this woman? What's the point?"

"Suppose you'd come back that same night, Max, instead of the following morning. Think of the millions of consequences that seem inevitable to us later but really turn on tiny failures of timing. Suppose I've had a failure of timing before, Max. I can't take that chance again."

"Jesus. You can't just take off. Denning will fire you like that." Max snapped his fingers.

"One week personal leave per five years invoked at the employee's discretion. No entry may be made in employee's file. It's in the contract, Max. You probably wrote in the clause yourself before the forms were sent to the printer."

"We start diverting water at the generator site in two days."

"So? I'm not supposed to be there anyway. The prime contractor handles supervision."

"You give in to your passions after what I just told you!"

"Just because something hasn't worked before doesn't mean it can't work now. Or later."

Max stuttered and his demeanor transformed. "I will not be party to this," he said. "I am management. I will not be tainted by association with unauthorized action."

Back at his apartment Warren made reservations for the morning flight to Seattle, planning to call Denning after he was on the ground there and it was too late to change his mind.

Missing a connection, Warren didn't arrive in Seattle until late afternoon. He had assumed he would go directly to Nora's house and—and—and what? Ask her to a movie? The truth was, Warren had no plan; he could not think of anything to do in the hours ahead that would make matters better rather than worse. He knew only that he had to try.

How much more amiable life must have been in centuries past, when possibilities were constrained! A frustrated lover in Renaissance Siena, Warren thought, could not have picked up the phone and had the object of his affections on the line in seconds. Or stepped on a plane and gone to find out for himself the hard way. Unpleasant confrontations were harder to create because it was significantly harder to arrange to see or speak to someone; someone of the opposite sex especially. If you did manage to arrange a meeting, it probably wouldn't be private. And if it was private there would be severe restrictions on what you might propose—a lifetime of social conditioning holding you back. How comforting to crouch behind the bourns of social convention and not be *allowed* to say the dangerous words in your heart, as opposed to today, when anybody can say anything to anyone, and any number of misguided arrangements are possible.

It made Warren think of those English novels where heartsick lovers spent their entire lives bewailing the pitiless social strictures that left them no hope for joy due to one complication or another. In a perverse sense, many cultures of the past had considered misery induced by idiotic social conventions to be a mark of distinction. The English admired futility, and the Japanese positively idolized it.

Warren rented a car and drove north toward Seattle, winter sun breaking in stripes across Interstate 5. In winter the low sun plays hit-and-run, warming a chosen spot for an instant and then retreating. Seattle, as a city, also plays tricks on those who approach from the south. Cresting a foothill they discover a vast complex of light and activity that they falsely assume to be their destination. It's the Boeing plant, miles long, with an airfield busier than Boston's. Passing this expanse of factory Warren could see dozens of aircraft parked on the taxiways, including 747s painted in the colors of state-owned airways from the poorest African and South American countries. The Third World, he thought, might be mired in poverty but it had no shortage of in-flight movies. The elite of the hungry nations spared no expense creating the means to get themselves out.

No matter how many times Warren observed runways or planes, they never made him think of Tonsonhut. Once, on a company assignment, he had spent a week at an airport taking decibel readings. The city council had given KD&H a contract whose objective boiled down to determining whether jetliners are loud; people who had built homes near the airport because the property costs there were low were now complaining about the noise, although it was the noise that had driven down the property costs in the first place. During that week no potent memory of Vietnam, or the transport plane fire in which his life was nearly lost, had forced itself into Warren's consciousness.

Examples of convenient forgetfulness in history and politics are too many to mention. Warren thought instead of the lesser examples from daily life. He thought of the child who, misunderstood by his parents, once a parent does not strive to understand his own child; of the businessman who, once impoverished, now holds in contempt those without resources; of the lover who, once trusting and left brokenhearted, now lies to another. How very hard is it to imagine a second life lived in ignorance of the first, when so many people seem to forget their present lives within their own lifetimes?

Nearing the city limits, Warren became lost. It was a welcome practical problem. Somehow he had missed the turn for Mercer Island, where Nora lived, a green paradise with a realtor's perfect combination of physical beauty, proximity to a wealthy city, and distance from the smokestacks that made the city's luxury possible.

Getting off the highway, he found a gas station selling an independent local brand. Warren got out of his car and walked inside to ask directions. Having worked in gas stations he felt it the height of rudeness for someone who wasn't buying anything to roll over the ringer wire or blast the horn and expect the poor gas jockey to come trotting out like a servant. On occasion, when Warren had had car horns blasted at him repeatedly by drivers for whom he was not trotting fast enough, he responded by aping a shuffling Stepin Fetchit act of exaggerated deference and then giving out directions calculated to take the drivers many miles from their destination. This, Warren knew, had been a clumsy revenge. The drivers, when it finally dawned on them that they had been sent on a wild goose chase, would affix the blame not on their own lack of manners but on the inherent worthlessness of menials such as gas station attendants, and would treat the next one all the more rudely. But such is revenge. Inherently, an inefficient process.

Inside the gas station Warren found the owner, a hard-faced man in coveralls. Bright white lighting washed his features out, prosecutorial. The walls of the station were papered with automotive supply calendars. On one a model whose multiple-tier hairstyle seemed to be held in place by the earth's magnetic field wore a teddy nightgown and cradled a torque converter between her breasts, grinning as though the device had just asked her to dinner.

As he stood, the gas station owner was revealed to be wearing a small revolver in a hip holster—a .25, the kind of gun so thin and delicate it almost seems silly, until used. "It's only a deterrent if the bastards can see it," he explained. "I'd like to carry something with more balls but I don't want to deter the customers, too."

Referring to a wall map, he gave Warren directions. "Go as far as you can this way," the owner said, pointing to a road, "keep going till the government takes away your right to drive." There was a highway temporarily blocked by monorail construction. "When the government forces you to turn right, go two miles . . ."

After finishing his directions the owner walked Warren to the car. Noting the rental plates, he asked, "You from back East? Never been there. Hate the place."

Warren pointed out that compared to Seattle, every place was back East.

"You really need one of these back East," the owner said, patting the baby gun. "When the Russians invade it's going to be every man for himself. You better get yourself a handgun."

If the Russians invade, Warren thought, the last thing that will save you is a handgun. What you'll need will be automatics and anti-tank rockets. Warren found it transparent that even the National Rifle Association opposed general training in automatics, the weapons best suited for the "well-regulated militia . . . necessary to the security of a free state" by which the Second Amendment right to arms is justified, while the NRA favored a free market in handguns, the only type of firearm useful mainly for crime.

"When you rented that car did you freely negotiate the price?"

"Pardon?"

"Did you freely negotiate the price? Or did you just sign a preprinted contract prepared by some big New York law firm without negotiating the terms?"

"I guess I signed."

"Just as I thought!" the gas station owner declared, pulling an oil-mottled pamphlet from the pocket of his coveralls. "Take this and read it sometime when you're ready to think for yourself. Now let me ask you another question. Why do you suppose there are so many blacks in this country?"

"Slave ships, as I recall."

"Sure, sure. But who financed those ships? The big New York banks. Now ask yourself. Why did Henry Kissinger and his New York banker pals create slavery in the first place? In order to help blacks take over the country."

Warren was happy to get clear of this armed lunatic. Try as he might to feel superior, though, he could not. He was a handgun owner too, still having the .45 he had found in Vietnam. Often, Warren reminded himself that it was illogical to keep pistols. Rifles were better for hunting and shotguns the best weapon for self-defense of a home; handguns were in civilian life more likely to be stolen and turned against you than to do anyone any good. Yet somehow, Warren couldn't make himself part with the .45. He hated to admit it, but he was drawn by the glory of the engineering. Hard to believe that the .45 Colt semi, which looked sleek and ominously modern, had been designed in 1911, when single-action Winchesters were still common.

As insurance against accident, Warren stored the gun in one part of his apartment and the magazine in another, with the first round in the clip being a blank. It was false security, he knew, but better than nothing. In the service Warren had developed a

knack for snapping the clip out of an M-16 with the same motion
he took it; combat weapons, designed for rapid reloading, are
equally prone to rapid unloading. When Warren noticed rifles
stacked or lying unattended he would sometimes remove all
their magazines and leave them in a pile, having developed a
healthy fear of their ability to fire with the most nominal human
encouragement. The first and only rule of guns is, They Go Off.
Designed to go off, they tirelessly await the chance. Something
willful about a gun seems to *make* it fire.

Once, in the fraternity house at UCLA, one of the brothers had
found his .45 and, after making only an idiot's cursory check for
a clip and not looking to see if there was a round in the chamber,
began pointing it at the other brothers and yelling *Pow! Pow!*
Next, the gun was tossed back and forth to great laughter around
the house dining room, each brother heaving it just out of Warren's reach. When he finally got hold of the .45 again, Warren,
furious and frightened, held it up to the temple of the brother
who had stolen it and said, "Fool. Don't you know how many
people I've killed with this gun?"

After that Warren was treated with considerably more respect
around the frat house. But he sat alone in his room for hours
afterward, trembling at the thought of the damage that might
have been done, and how easy it had been to lie to his own
advantage when the opportunity presented itself.

Finally crossing the bridge to Mercer Island, Warren could
sense its beauty through the darkness. Green as Sherwood Forest, mountains out one window and ocean out the other, surrounded by freshwater lakes—he had never known such a place.
Not far to the east were the Cascade Mountains, the Alps of
North America; south, the rumored Mount Rainier, landmark
and dominant feature of the Seattle skyline despite being visible
only a few days a year owing to the persistent cloud cover.

There are some who do not object to gloomy weather, and
Nora was one. Sun, she had said, gave her the nagging sensation
that there was somebody important she ought to know but

didn't. Or a party to which everyone had been invited but her. Rain, she maintained, builds character.

It was past eight in the evening when Warren found the McConaughty home, in the middle of a shaded, hilly street. The house was dark. A blue Toyota was parked in the driveway.

No one answered the bell. Clearly this was either a good sign or a bad sign.

The house was smaller than Warren had expected, not remarkable or noticeable, just a house on a block of houses. Warren found it hard to think of Nora as limited to any one place, or lowering herself to the point of requiring physical arrangements. Nora in a cramped apartment in a bad part of town, using footlockers covered with shawls for tables as she concentrated on a great act of art or humanitarianism—that Warren could picture. Too busy with her cause to trifle with curtains. Or Nora in any of a wide variety of palace configurations—that he could imagine, too. But a plain stucco house sold by a realtor in a striped jacket, a house she was merely living in toward no special end . . .

. . . and a house full of plumbing and laundry and dishes where, Warren found himself thinking, even a man and a woman who cared for each other would have trouble staying interested in sex. In romance movies you only see the couples sipping champagne as they row across ponds. You never see them scouring bathroom tile. Keeping the house satisfied, all its pipes and fuses, must be more demanding than satisfying a lover.

For a while Warren sat in his car in front of the house. Then he began to think that, strange as it would be to walk up to her door unannounced, it would be stranger still for Nora and her husband to come home and find him casing the joint. So he drove around the block, looking for a hiding place. Finding a small rise of property unbuilt upon that was diagonal to the McConaughty home and about a hundred yards away, he parked the car. By standing at the far end of the rise, Warren could see the outline of the house and watch for Nora and Ford's return without, he felt certain, their seeing him.

So he stood, hands in his pockets. An hour passed; then another. Warren walked up and down the block to break the monotony, but always when he reached the rise again he could see that the McConaughty home remained dark. It occurred to him it might remain dark for days or weeks. They might be on vacation; out of town on business; staying with friends while the place was sprayed for termites.

Warren also became aware that pacing up and down the same block for hours would not go unnoticed in a quiet residential neighborhood. If someone called the police, he would need a plausible explanation at the ready. *Sorry, officer, thought the bus stopped here.* Or, *Meeting friends here, officer, right here at this vacant lot.* Or, *Used to be a burgher in sixteenth-century Italy, officer. I met this woman in an artist's studio and I've been after her ever since. . . .*

No policeman came. A few people from the neighborhood walked by and he greeted them cheerfully, as though he expected to be recognized. That seemed to help. As the hour approached eleven, Warren grew cold and got back into the car, starting up the engine.

The car was a new Dodge jammed with digital gimmicks that told the time, day, engine temperature down to the degree, and whether it was A.M. or P.M.—for those who were merrily driving along the interstates unable to determine on their own whether it was day or night. The car told you everything but the atmospheric pressure in Bolivia. It was also equipped with an electronic voicebox that made routine announcements of the obvious, for instance that the door was open. When the Dodge was started, the voicebox would clear its throat by declaring, "All monitored systems functioning."

All *monitored* systems. A legalistic hedge. Not even your car would give you a straight answer anymore. Warren found himself imagining a team of Chrysler lawyers locked in earnest debate over what the car would be allowed to say. When the interior of the Dodge had been sufficiently heated he shut the motor off and, dulled, feel asleep.

With a snap of the head Warren awoke to discover it was one

in the morning. Groggy, he stood up on the doorsill of the car to get a view of the McConaughty house. It was ablaze with light —a different house now, spacious and inviting. There were several cars parked in front; a group of people could be seen through the picture window.

They were moving about, holding drinks. Cigarettes were being smoked, red points dancing and seeming, as do fireflies, to become larger as they moved away. One cigarette was being passed. The group appeared to be boy-girl boy-girl, marrieds or long-time pairs. Couples were hovering near each other without colliding or looking expectant about whose place they would be going back to.

These, Warren realized, were Nora's friends. They seemed as undistinguished as the house. Not statesmen or athletes, actors or scholars. Just some people she had bumped into at work or in school. A bit dumpy, he began to think. Probably grinding bores. Nora was stuck in reality just like everyone else.

At that moment Nora came into view, framed in the yellow bath of the house lights. Concentrating on viewing the friends, Warren had momentarily forgotten his reason for being where he was.

Nora walked straight to the center of the bay window and looked out toward the street. Involuntarily, Warren ducked, though she could not have seen him, given that the bright interior lights of the house would have narrowed her eyes against the dark. Nora stood perfectly still. She appeared to be watching the point where Warren had been standing earlier in the evening, as if it were glowing. Shifting, she put one arm behind her back and locked the hand on the elbow of the opposite arm, as a nervous gangling kid will do waiting to be bawled out. It seemed a ridiculous posture for a woman grown and graceful. Nora kept looking at the spot just in front of her lawn. Then she turned and looked back over her shoulder, answering someone. Reaching outward with both hands, she drew the curtains shut. The yellow light shrank away.

Warren slipped down into the car: there she was, a hundred yards away. Whatever was going to happen was about to happen;

there could be no dreaming or speculation. Warren had thought this moment would be meta-empirical, but instead he found himself anxious to get it over with. Against a husband, friends, a house, habits—what chance did he have? He wanted the embarrassment done and to receive his consolation prize, the knowledge that he had tried. The digital clock in the Dodge read 1:08:44. That was what second it was.

Two right turns put the car onto Nora's street. Drawing close to the house Warren saw the front door unexpectedly swing open. Light spilled out, then people. The guests were departing, walking down the driveway. Warren slowed. Another car was approaching from behind, headlights insistent. Warren decided to circle the block and wait for the guests to leave. At the stop sign he looked back, straining to see which one of the men was staying. The car behind him flashed its high beams. Warren drove on, stopping around the block to recover his breath.

By the time he circled back to the intersection at the foot of Nora's street the parked cars were gone. Warren stopped the Dodge again, he thought, well out of sight. He saw Nora standing alone at the center of the driveway, hands clasped before her waist in a pose of nunnish patience. For a while she held the position.

Then she turned smartly in the direction of Warren's car; looked him right in the eye; gave a friendly wave; and walked back into her house. The downstairs light went out.

Warren drove back in the direction of the city, pulled off on a freeway ramp, and woke the snoozing night clerk of a Days Inn who took his credit card from the rotating bin underneath a Plexiglas shield. After sunrise he returned to Nora's house and knocked on the back door.

"It's open," she called.

A path along the side of the house led to the back door and Warren had taken it, not wanting to be seen at the front door. There was a small terrace with screen windows facing the backyard; the terrace contained no chairs but, rather, appeared to be used as a storage area. The paraphernalia of home ownership—

hose attachments, wrenches, an unopened croquet set—filled the space. An assortment of ratchet nubs were scattered on the floor like gravel.

On the inner wall of the vestibule was a smeary silkscreen poster advertising the Mercer Island Community Theater production of Brecht's *Mother Courage and Her Children.* Nearby were posters for Ibsen's *John Gabriel Borkman* and Sartre's *No Exit.* Mercer Island was an affluent locale made up of individuals who had enjoyed every advantage in life and risen to enviable positions. Apparently its community theater had produced three consecutive plays about how life was horrible beyond words. There was, Warren knew, a pessimism quotient in art whereby the better a given class of people has been treated, the more brooding becomes its self-expression. Perhaps some convoluted form of civic obligation was at work. Or perhaps, Warren thought, the favored wanted to have it that privilege is an even greater burden than poverty, and thereby make it seem that the poor were being done a service.

Opposite the theatrical posters was a framed advertisement for the Xerox 1048 copier. Adjacent to the back door hung a small blackboard, on which was written in thick green chalk:

> *Bulbs 75W 100W*
> *Masking Tape*
> *Half and Half*
> *Donuts*

Next to *Donuts* the word *No!* was inscribed in pink chalk in a flowing hand that Warren recognized. There were other scribblings, but he did not stop to read them. Opening the door, he found Nora standing in the kitchen. She wore a zippered warmup suit, though Warren was sure she never ran or engaged in any kind of formal exercise. As far as he could tell, she kept her figure by eating and drinking very little.

"It's about time you got here," Nora said with no inflection. "And of all the nights to pick, after one of those weeknight parties at Lou Ann's. Imagine hiring a male stripper and having him pretend to be one of the guests. Where does she get those ideas? He came on to Felicity Nash and she was about to agree to go home with him when, bam, he whips off his pants right in front of everybody. And then nightcaps here. I was exhausted. But then you couldn't have known about that, could you? Coffee?" She was chattering along as though his arrival was a routine event.

Wanting to win her attention, Warren stood his ground, not speaking. He knew that under certain circumstances, complete inaction can be mistaken for profundity. But Nora didn't fall for it.

"That was some stunt last night, staking out my house like the FBI," she said. Then, "Sorry to keep you waiting."

"How did you know I was there?"

"I knew you would be coming long before you arrived." She paused coyly and let the boast sink in. "Impressed? Don't be. I knew you were coming because your office called. Who else did you give my number to, a skywriting service?"

"I didn't give it to anybody," he said defensively. The conversation was taking a wrong turn.

"Well, your office called yesterday and said you were going to lose your job if you weren't back by tomorrow, which is now today. Are you in some kind of trouble?" She set a cup of coffee on the table between them, still nonchalant.

"It's just office politics. Don't worry about it."

Nora laughed a little to herself and looked up. "But then it's always today."

"What?"

"I said you'd lose your job if you didn't call by tomorrow, which is now today. But then it's always today." Nora was doing her best to sound serious. "Today is the only day it's ever been. And it's always now." She started to chuckle aloud. "Kinda makes you think, doesn't it?"

They laughed together. Finally she looked directly at Warren, fondness in her eyes. "Pretty dumb move to come all this way, lose your job, just for a cup of coffee."

"I know it was wrong"—Warren was struggling to regain the

initiative—"especially to your own house where your husband might walk in any minute, but I felt—"

"You're right about that. He will walk in any minute. About fifteen minutes." Warren practically jumped into the air. Nora smiled. "Because I asked him to. He's coming home for lunch. To meet you."

"You've got to be kidding."

"I told him you were a friend of the family from back home. There is a Gifford family in Escanaba, although I didn't know them. So it's only a little white lie."

"He's coming here?"

"Indeed. And now listen, Mr. James Bond, you stick to the cover story, understand? It took me months to smooth over that Jerry Melrod business as it was."

"Tell me why you asked him here."

"Because, dear heart"—Nora's speech slowed—"because I thought that if you saw Ford and me together, you would accept it. You may go away thinking how stupid I am to stay with him, if you like. And then you'll get over this."

"You think you're doing me a favor, don't you?"

"Yes, I do."

"If you want to do me a favor, kiss me."

Warren barely realized what he had said, blurting it out without thinking, like an answer on a quiz show. Realizing it sounded masterful, he tried to straighten up and feign confidence. Nora inspected him, then stepped forward. There is never any telling what people will do if asked, Warren thought.

"Only one," Nora said.

They kissed. She pressed up against him below the waist, the way men do automatically but women only do when they mean it.

"Okay, two."

To Warren the sensation of their embrace was total, as though all his body was surrounding all of hers and being surrounded in turn. He longed to make the sensation deeper, but knew he should take no further step. Then, saying nothing, Nora pulled the big zipper running down the front of her warmup jacket: she was bare beneath. Holding the edges of the jacket in her hands, she wrapped her arms around his back, so that the material, which was elastic, enclosed them. Warren pressed a hand against one of her breasts. Rather than fumbling for the best grip, as is traditional, he held his hand on the inward slope, where he could feel for her heart. It beat slowly.

A muffler scraped against the driveway approach outside. Warren and Nora jumped apart. The jacket of her warmup suit, though zipped again, had been stretched to twice its normal size and was conspicuously not right.

"Sit down at the table and look casual," Nora said. The prevailing winds were shifting much too quickly for Warren to keep pace, so he did as ordered. Nora hurried up the stairs and returned wearing a heavy sweater that corrected her appearance.

"Remember, don't you dare say anything to hurt him," she instructed, choosing words that seemed to carry a slightly different meaning from her earlier comments about Ford.

The back door opened. "On the track!" a solid male voice announced. Nora went quickly to her husband, and there followed a rapid exchange of happy comments only some of which could be overheard.

"Does it say how much?"

"Could be as much as eighty."

"Eighty!"

"Could be. Anyway it's got to be up, up, up!"

Nora and Ford entered the kitchen. Ford McConaughty was a handsome man with an adult man's haircut of the type one can obtain only by impressing the barber, and a properly tailored overcoat of the type only a man fully pleased with adulthood can wear. He shook hands firmly but just for a pump or two. Ford was taller than Warren—not that it matters, Warren told himself—and carried a paper shopping bag, which he set down on a counter in order to rub his hands together like a chilled huntsman approaching a fireplace.

"Carlos, the bastard, after years of telling me not to expect anything, is suddenly my best friend," Ford said. "He's invited us to his lodge."

"When?" Nora asked.

"Not for a month."

Nora seemed relieved. "Time to plan," she said.

"But not much time to eat, particularly when making new friends," Ford said, indicating Warren. He opened the shopping bag, which contained delicatessen food. "I wasn't sure what you'd want, so I got you roast beef. Is that okay, Warren?"

"Fine."

"Everybody likes roast beef," Ford said, unwrapping the sandwiches and putting them on china. There was a BLT, which Ford took, containers of coleslaw and potato salad, and a small cup of soup for Nora. Nora brought milk for Ford, coffee for Warren, and plain tap water for herself.

"Ford is with Xerox, and has just made the executive track," Nora explained.

"Not a formal thing, but everybody knows what it means," Ford said. His name would be placed on a list of those proposed for corporate-level posts—a large raise, a job with Xerox national rather than the regional office in Seattle, and a run at a top management position. The complex qualification process Ford described made it sound as if he had just been nominated for president. Listening to Ford talk caused Warren to feel like a child, even though, objectively, his own career accomplishments were as great as Ford's or greater.

"And it means I'm finally out of sales," Ford said. "Have you ever been in sales?" Warren shook his head. "Or the service? Well then, if you remember how it felt to get out of the service, you know how it feels to get out of sales."

"It's not like he sells door-to-door," Nora interjected.

"Industrial accounts," Ford said, "but no sense gilding the lily. Sales is sales. I was just doing cold calling on a grand scale." He looked at Warren closely. "Can I get you a drink? We don't drink around here during the day. But since you're on vacation I don't suppose the rules apply to you."

Warren again shook his head no, but Ford was insistent. "One man's opinion, but you need a drink," he said, walking to the icebox. "Have a rough flight?"

Ford brought Warren a can of Rainier Ale, which he poured into a stemware glass. When he sat back down at the table Nora pulled her chair close to his, resting her arm on it.

"This means moving to Rochester," Ford explained, continuing with the previous topic as though he were being interviewed. Rochester, where Xerox had been founded—a little on the snowy side, he said, but noted for its quality of life. Local symphony orchestra, Eastman School of Music, proximity to the Finger Lakes, Niagara Falls, the Chautauqua Festival, and professional sports in Buffalo.

Nora made an I'm-surrounded face. "I can't wait to see the Bills versus Peru or whatever it is."

"—Kodak headquarters is also in Rochester, so there will be lots of people like ourselves to meet. And according to the brochure from Mr. Kearns's office, there are more French restaurants per capita in Rochester than anywhere outside the financial district of New York. Excluding France, of course. Anyway, Carlos has been to them all."

"We've only been to the East Coast once, on a trip," Nora said. "It was a disaster."

This reference brought the conversation to a momentary halt. "Well, it wasn't perfect," Ford said. "But then what is?"

Nora explained that they had driven cross-country—with stops along the way in various cities—the ultimate objective being Broadway, where Ford had purchased tickets for five shows. But after the first show, Nora had refused to attend any others. "I threw a fit, a real girl fit. We ended up giving the tickets away. And then that endless drive back after nothing."

"Why did you refuse?"

"Jealousy. I was possessed. Those women up there, filling a whole theater with their little birdie voices. It made me so jealous."

"I told you they use hidden microphones," Ford said.

"And the audience. The women in gowns, the men in tuxedos. I know it's philistine. The show was *Oklahoma!*, for heaven's sake. But those people in their fancy clothes sitting there perfectly quiet listening to those women. It got to me."

"Between you and me I was just as glad not to have to go back to that filthy Times Square," Ford said. "Haven't those people in New York ever heard of garbage collection?"

"Now Ford, you're just saying that to make me feel better."

"I suppose."

Finishing her story, Nora said they decided to drive back via Rochester, to see if they might like the city someday. Not far out of Manhattan, driving north into upstate New York, she insisted on stopping to visit West Point. They ended up staying two days, and the time available to stop at Rochester ran out.

"Can you believe it?" Ford asked. "Here she is, former president of the Joan Baez fan club, with all her pot-smoking friends —that, by the way, will have to stop now, Nora—and we skip Greenwich Village to see a military academy."

"It reminded me of something. I suppose Mackinac Island— that's in U.P. Michigan, near my hometown—with all its formality and porches." Nora seemed a little distracted. "Anyway, the point is I ruined the entire trip."

"Honey, we don't have to tell somebody from Escanaba where Mackinac Island is," Ford said, using the matrimonial "we."

"Oh—of course."

"So, Warren. How long since you've seen Nora?"

"I—I knew her a long time ago."

"Well, that's great. I've never really met any of her childhood friends. She left them all in her wake."

"Ford."

"Left them behind. Did a little better in life, is all I mean. You'll have to forgive me if I don't have the best impression of Escanaba. What happened there was inexcusable, in my judgment. Not that I mean to insult your hometown. Did you enjoy that part of the country?"

Warren did not know where Escanaba was, let alone what had happened there. He knew only that Nora was from a small town in Michigan. He fudged, saying, "I liked it well enough. Though I was young at the time." Ford laughed a hearty salesman's laugh: he probably never failed to laugh at a joke. Then he looked at Warren, expectant of more.

"We took a lot of weekend trips to Detroit when I was a kid," Warren said, reaching for any comment. "That was pretty interesting. The auto industry and all."

"No kidding. To Detroit." Ford was impressed. "Your folks must have really had the get-up-and-go spirit. I would have sworn it was four hundred miles from Escanaba to Detroit."

"Tell us more about Rochester, dear," Nora said.

Ford was happy to return to that topic, explaining that although Rochester was an Eastern city, its cost of living was no higher than Seattle's. "So, combining salaries, we should be able to live well. Assuming you can keep at it part-time. Will Harvey care if you move?"

"Harvey doesn't know where I live now," Nora said. "His secretary dials all his calls. He likes to be announced—'Hold the line for Mr. Harvey Kaspian.' I've been thinking of quitting anyway."

"That would be the second piece of good news today," Ford said, and then to Warren, "Until I met Harvey I never believed people in California actually are the way they say. Open shirts, as if you wanted to see his chest. Shouts into the telephone. And an earring on a *bus*inessman! Probably belongs to one of those California self-worship cults. Not the ideal individual for someone in my position to be associated with, if you follow my drift."

Nora made a show of looking at the wall clock. "Ford, it's getting late. You promised to drop me off downtown. And Warren has a plane to catch."

"We'd love to give you a lift to the airport, but it's so far out of the way," Ford said.

"It's fine. I have a rental car."

"Right, I noticed the plates. One of those new Dodges. God, if I'd only bought Chrysler when it was down. Just hang on a second while I run upstairs and put on my bow tie."

"Not the one Mother gave you last Christmas . . ."

"You bet. Biggest, ugliest bow tie ever made. Never been out of the box. Going to wear it to celebrate." Ford turned to Warren and said, with sincerity, "I'm sorry we had so little opportunity to become acquainted. If you are ever in Rochester please come and stay with us. We'll always have an extra bed."

After Ford had gone upstairs, whistling, Warren rested his chin in his hands, a statuary of defeat.

"He's a nice guy," Warren said. "I was sort of hoping he'd be a jerk."

"Sorry."

"And he's smart. I was sort of hoping he'd be dumb."

"Too bad."

"And handsome. I sort of had in mind a bridge troll."

"Ford is a very good-looking man. I could lose him if I was careless."

"He seems to look after you."

"In certain ways he adores me. He still comes home for lunch almost every day, though we've been married ten years, and it's a long drive."

"What happened in Escanaba?"

Nora was obviously distressed the subject had come up. "I'll tell you all about it sometime," she said. "In brief, Ford did something very generous for my father. It cost him a lot of money. We're only just now starting to have money again, and I want Ford to enjoy it."

"He bought you."

"Quiet!" Her expression turned to anger. "I'm not going to dignify that remark. And let me tell you something else. You thought you would just come here, find me married to a monster, and say some magic word. It's never that easy. If Ford were not a decent man, I would not have married him. Or if he were a horrible man, the cause of my leaving would not be you. Do you remember the Jane Fonda movie about the woman who leaves her husband, an officer, for a disabled veteran in a wheelchair? It's played as if it were this huge awakening, you know, wow, Jane thinks for herself. But the husband she leaves is a psycho. *Everything* about him is wrong. What was she waiting for? It's just never that clear, Warren, who you belong with."

Warren held his tongue until he was sure she had finished. Then he asked again, "Do you love him?"

"That's such an unfair question. Ford is a sweet and attentive man. No woman in her right mind would walk away."

"Do you love him?"

"If I had it to do over again, he is not what I would have chosen. But I was hardly dragged into it. And I *don't* have it to do over again. This is where I am, at this time."

There were thumping sounds from the stairs, and Ford was back. Nora made several pointed references to what a hurry Warren was in to catch his plane, adding, without humor, that his office had called to say his presence was urgently required. This seemed to make a good impression on Ford.

"Good-bye," Nora said as she and her husband drove away. "I promise I'll write."

The following morning at nine A.M. Warren returned to the McConaughty house. This time Nora came to the door herself and opened it.

They got into her Toyota, Nora at the wheel. "Someone is watching over you, young man," she said. Ford was having lunch with Carlos that day to discuss his promotion, she told him, and would not be home at noon for the first time in a week.

Nora turned the car east. In an hour they were in the Cascades. They stopped at a small mountain cabin owned by the family of one of Nora's friends, and there made love. An important comment was also made. In the aftermath, Nora got back to her house only moments before Ford would have discovered her absence.

The following day was Saturday. Warren sat alone in the Days Inn. He did the same on Sunday. On Monday morning, though he and Nora had not specifically discussed it, Warren was back at the house. That morning, and again in the afternoon, they sat talking, rarely touching. Late that afternoon Warren was preparing to leave for the motel when the telephone rang.

"It's for you," Nora said, shrugging her shoulders as if to add, What's next.

On the line was Max. Except that he identified himself as Alvin Rademacher, enunciating precisely. Warren began to explain that he would be back at the office in a day or two and there was nothing—

"Don't you know? Haven't you heard? The retaining wall. Right down the middle it gave. The entire work area for the number two pump was flooded."

"Good God. Were there injuries?"

"Eighteen men in the hospital. No, seventeen men, one woman. Six in intensive care. Happened during shift change. Worst possible time. The bad injuries, they don't know. Some may not make it."

"I'll go straight to the airport."

"Airport! Airport!" Max repeated. "We are all going to jail!"

Drawings of the retaining wall flipped through Warren's mind in sequence. It couldn't collapse, just could not. At his insistence the wall had been rated for twice the anticipated load. Plus stress sensors wired independently. Hobard, the third partner at KD&H, had made fun of Warren for demanding needless redundancy.

Hurriedly, Warren tried to explain to Nora that he was compelled to leave. He did not tell her what the news was. Later Warren would realize this had been a serious mistake, but as so often is the case with folly, the decision seemed reasonable at the time. As he left, a sullen look of persecution came across Nora's face; the look, Warren thought, of an athlete reinjuring a knee that had just finished healing. Standing on the street in front of her house, the two stammered good-byes and took verbal half steps, both sensing errors being made that they were powerless to prevent.

Nora watched him drive off, cringing as he squealed the brakes on the Dodge to avoid another car as he merged with traffic at the intersection. That night she kept her promise to write, composing a lengthy letter certain passages of which she would later wish she could take back. But likewise, what Nora wrote seemed reasonable at the time.

All in all, it was a fiasco of a parting. But it would have to do. They would not see each other again for nearly three years.

6

MORE THAN MAN, LESS THAN NATURE

On the previous Saturday, while sitting in the Days Inn wondering what Nora and Ford were doing at that moment, Warren had taken note of the oil-mottled tract given him at the gas station. He expected Ku Klux Klan trash or worse. Instead it was a back issue of *I Am He of Whom I Speak.* Warren began to read:

GOD HAS A TERRIBLE PERFORMANCE RECORD. WE OUGHT TO FIRE HIM AND PUT SOMEBODY IN THERE WHO WILL GET THE JOB DONE RIGHT.

God has permitted—or failed to prevent, which is all the same to the victims—killing, cruelty, and torture on millions of occasions. How long would you last on your job if you made millions of mistakes? Not long, unless you were civil service.

There are those who accept God's silence regarding the atrocities and injustices that frame history on the theory that He wishes to give each mortal soul a test. Holders of this view generally proceed to argue that souls failing the test (on their first and only try) are assigned forever to dwell in a special zone of God's making; the distinguishing feature of this zone being savage physical and mental torment.

Some God you've got there, boys. Imposing suffering on all during temporal life, followed by an increased degree of suffering on almost all throughout eternal life.

If God really is this sadistic, we had better find a way to destroy Him while there's still time. Not destroy metaphorically, as in the God-Is-Dead intellectual movement. Destroy physically, as in, with bombs. There at last is a cause that might unite the fractious nations of our globe! Find out where God lives, and hit Him with everything we've got.

Religious institutions have been, shall we say, somewhat

139

inconvenienced by the fact that God suffers a gross degree of evil to exist. Bound to the premise that the Father is all-powerful and omniscient, church leaders tend to view discussion of His failure to use perfect power to protect earthly creatures as bad for business. So they attempt to divert attention elsewhere.

They say, for instance, that God has received an insufficient quantity of worship, which He greatly desires. Oh what trite and transparent motives do children ascribe to their elders! God wants to be *worshipped!* What a jerk. We might as well say God seeks publicity. If God is an egotist in addition to being a sadist, our troubles are deeper than we feared.

Should history teach nothing else, it teaches that trying to divert attention from a problem instead of addressing it leads invariably to greater woe. The woe of faith today is that we look for God where we have unilaterally decreed He should be —everywhere—and, not finding Him, suppose Him dead or a fraud from the start. We blame our Creator for not being all we expected, rather than ourselves for asking overmuch.

Perhaps there is a simple and less than sadistic reason why God has not stopped earthly atrocities. Perhaps He can't. The determinative flaw in our search for God may be the presumption that He is all-powerful.

First, think of the riddle with which Sunday-school pupils delight to foil their teachers: If God can do anything, can He make a mountain so big He can't move it?

Sunday-school teachers usually respond with comments like "What a silly question," which translates to "Please don't ask that." Yet they need not fear the question, for the answer is incipient and quite benign to the preservation of faith. Of course God can't make a mountain so big He can't move it. A mountain so big it cannot be moved is an impossibility—and even an omnipotent God could never perform a feat that is Not Possible. No force could not make a rope so long it had no end, a wall so high nothing could fly over it, and so on.

On the list of actions that may be Not Possible are prescience and time travel. Why should even an omniscient God be able to view events that have not yet happened? They don't exist, and the maximum possible amount of knowledge about something that does not exist is still nothing. If seeing forward in time is Not Possible, God could never be certain of the outcome of any action He might take. He could know only what was *possible to know:* He could know what is in your heart today, but not what will be in your heart tomorrow.

Western religions speak of a unitary, solitary God incapable of reproduction or calling forth into being an equal companion: which leaves Him short of all-powerful even by the preferred church description. If men and women, who make babies quite well thank you, do something God cannot, how is it God can do anything?

Nor might seeing forward in time, even if possible, necessarily engender perfection. Suppose, knowing everything you now know, you could be transported back in time to 1935 and given a position of authority in the government of your choice. Would you be able to stop World War II?

To pick a less stressful moment. Suppose you could gather up all the knowledge and information from the present in a super-computer; put together a collection of any amount of supplies and technological devices you please; and be teleported back to Chaldea, capital of Sumer, in 5000 B.C. You would be received as a god. You might well command total obedience. Would you be able to begin manipulating the flow of history so as to form a perfect world?

But, you say, I am me. I am not as smart as God. Maybe God in His wisdom could have touched Chaldea and made it perfect.

We know that He didn't. We also know that God, in tending the vastness of a universe, faces far more complicated problems than the Chaldean example. It would not be surprising if He found that even limitless power and total wisdom were insufficient to achieve social perfection. He would still be constrained by the boundaries of the possible.

Now let us suppose that God has limitations, imposed not just by the structure of reality, but by the particulars of His own nature within that structure. Suppose, for instance, that God can be in only one place at a time. His eyes can see all—all that is possible to see—but only in the direction He is facing.

This could be a breathtaking power, considering that our one place has billions of inhabitants, the fullness of whose thoughts and desires would be laid bare. But within the context of the universe, such a handicap would cause God major problems. There exist a hundred billion suns in our galaxy and at least a billion other galaxies, with many more galaxies believed to exist beyond the range of present detection instruments. This suggests there may be many millions of localities where creatures are possessed of immortal souls. If God is dashing madly back and forth among a billion blundering worlds, trying to instruct and preserve them from a billion kinds of ignorance —small wonder He has so little time for us! In fact, from a mathematical standpoint, considering that *Homo sapiens* has existed for less than a million years, it's a wonder He's gotten around to us at all.

If God were able to look in on each of His worlds only occasionally, He'd be in a tremendous hurry. God would attempt to explain His vision and leave principles that we could follow voluntarily in His absence. Persuasion is always preferable to force, because force is only effective when being applied, whereas the effects of persuasion linger after the source has vanished.

Not being able to know the future, however, and thus not certain what impact His words and deeds might ultimately have on mischievous creatures such as ourselves, God's message might well be halting; uplifting, but confusing or incomplete. Especially if He has to make a billion different attempts to explain Himself to a billion diverse cultures.

And if God's message were misinterpreted or misused, *He would not find out about it till much later.* The Bible brims over with admonitions for man to learn morality and faith on his own so that God, who is absent, will be well pleased when He returns. There may be more clues in these verses than have yet been recognized.

It is heinous conceit on the part of man to demand that God

be all-powerful. When we suppose this, what we are really saying is that the only sovereign who could sit above our magnificent selves would be a being of total perfection. What vanity! What colossal self-aggrandizement!

One can easily imagine beings which are superior to *Homo sapiens* yet inferior to the sum of the universe. Indeed, using genetic engineering and bioelectronics, man himself will soon be making such beings. This alone demonstrates how easy they are to imagine.

It is also easy to imagine that a sovereign master might be vastly more magnificent than his subjects, yet humble before the forces of nature. Suppose, for example, that God has at His disposal an energy output equal to that of our sun. This would be a fierce God, able to hurl our world into the freezing void should He choose. Yet this God would quake before the power of all the stars in the Milky Way combined. And would be fricasseed by the galaxy Arp 220, an astronomical system in which stars interact, producing 100 times the luminosity of our Milky Way.

Next suppose that God is greater still: available to Him is energy equivalent to the stellar output of a typical galaxy. This God would command magnitudes of strength our minds can barely guess at, yet still would shudder before a quasar. (Meaning quasi-stellar object, not television set. Although what is being shown on a television set would probably make God shudder, too.) Quasars, no bigger than our sun, continuously emit more energy than whole galaxies. The physical process employed by quasars to achieve such ferocity is, so far, a mystery to scientists. God may know it, but that does not necessarily mean He can defy it. We know the physical process of nuclear explosions and that knowledge is no defense.

Only if God's power exceeded that of all the engines of nature combined, might He be able to "do anything." And then we are back to where we started—there's no excuse for the mess He has made.

If God is strong and wise but not infinitely strong and wise, He may serve as an influence on nature, rather than its dictator. He would marvel, as we do, at the cosmos and the fruits of creation. He would strive, as we (sometimes) do, to improve them.

Why for instance can't God be the missing factor in evolution? He could account for the sudden leaps that Darwinian mechanics is at a loss to explain. Already in our century, man is close to knowing how to revise genetic outcomes—is it not astonishing conceit to think that even a flawed God *doesn't* know about genes?

Perhaps when visiting worlds, He examines their creatures with immense scientific skill and an all-embracing love of life, then adjusts their life codes for improvement and survival, hoping, but not certain, that He has guessed correctly. While God is absent, creatures continue to evolve on their own in lesser ways—in the ways Darwin observed—but rely on their sovereign for guidance into major new areas of development like lungs, eyes, and independent minds.

God could serve as a correcting influence over nature without necessarily having the might to control it, in the same way man serves that role on a modest plane.

Today doctors stand dumbstruck before the sophistication of the human body: they have no inkling of how to "make" one from scratch, as nature is clearly able to do. Yet this does not prevent them from being able to improve the body *in areas where nature failed.* Medical science has eliminated most of the diseases that nature failed to eliminate; compensated for natural biological design flaws like the self-poisoning appendix and the self-asphyxiating shock reaction; and sustained the body through a wide range of injuries and infections with which the body's own systems could not possibly cope.

Most Westerners would maintain that God's most recent attempt to explain Himself occurred 2,000 years ago. On the face of it, there is no way to describe the mission of Jesus as anything other than a failure. Jesus inspired the creation of a major religion, but that feat has been performed several times in human history, not always to good ends; so in and of itself it proves little. He succeeded in bringing many to faith and moral behavior, but at the same time created a vehicle used to subject millions of innocents to wars and persecutions. We cannot dismiss this consequence, as the hierarchies of Christian churches find it convenient to do, as somehow beyond anyone's control. For if Christ was not responsible for the results of his own actions, who is?

On the ultimate question of transforming the world, Jesus again failed. The numerical majority of those who have lived in the last 2,000 years have not followed Christ's teachings. (We speak here not of official religious affiliations, but of what is felt in the heart and practiced in daily life, concerns that Jesus said were more important than denomination.) Even should the world someday come to its senses and follow the gentle path to which Jesus pointed, his mission would still be classed a failure from the standpoint of divine perfection, because hundreds of millions would have suffered needlessly in the meantime.

Assuming Jesus was inspired of God, we are left with three possibilities.

First, Jesus was sent by an omniscient, all-powerful God who knew exactly what He was doing and wanted things to work out exactly the way they did. Next possibility, please!

Second, Jesus was sent by a God so fundamentally different from man that His wishes cannot be explained in terms we understand: whose interest in us is abstract, and who does not intervene on earth because He has concerns tangential to our suffering. In this scenario, the most we can expect from our sovereign is an occasional inconclusive brush. God will remain to us as eclipses were to the ancients, a source of wonder but not fulfillment.

Finally there is the possibility that Jesus was sent by a God who's doing the best He can. A God who doesn't have all the answers—*can't* have them—and isn't sure what to say. Who was bewildered and hurt that the manifest proclamations of good delivered by his prophets started being misunderstood and misused almost the moment they were uttered.

A God more than man yet less than nature would not be a cause for sadness. It would be grounds for unbounded joy! The human promise would increase a thousandfold. Evils and suffering would stand not as "natural" conditions or staged theological tribulations—but as mistakes to be corrected. Either by God when He returns His gaze to us, or by man as we increase our knowledge, or by man and God working in joyous partnership toward a joint goal of investing life with higher meaning.

Perhaps the thought of science joining forces with God sounds like a contradiction in terms. Through history the pursuit of science has been resisted by purveyors of religion who, for internal bureaucratic reasons, insist on promoting themselves as the sole repositories of knowing. Today, in turn, the pursuit of religion is resisted by science, which for internal bureaucratic reasons feels it must disprove God entirely, finding a random-chance explanation for everything. Scientists have come to direct the same intolerant glare at those who propose a role for the spirit as the Vatican once directed at Galileo for proposing a role for facts.

What a ridiculous restriction on thought! Why must the alternatives be confined to all-God or no-God?

It is difficult to believe that a world which in this century alone has endured the calculated slaughter of the Jews by the Germans; the Filipinos, Koreans, and Burmese by the Japanese; the Tibetans by the Chinese; the South Vietnamese, Cambodians, and Laotians by the North Vietnamese, Chinese, and Americans; the Poles by the Germans and Russians; the Ethiopians by the Italians; the Afghans and Hungarians by the Russians; the aborigines by the Australians; black South Africans by Afrikaners; the Tutsi by the Hutu, the Pondo by the Zulu, the Ibo by the Yoruba, the Oromo by the Amhara, and the Ndebele by the Shona; the Tamils by the Sinhalese; the Armenians by the Turks; the Sikhs by the Hindus; the Hindus by the Buddhists and the Buddhists by the Hindus; Moslems by Moslems; every faction in Northern Ireland and the Middle East by every other faction in Northern Ireland and the Middle East; the slaughter of Russians, Chinese, Chileans, Salvadorans, Greeks, Nicaraguans, Mexicans, Vietnamese, Cubans,

Ugandans, Haitians, Burundians, Rwandans, Nigerians, Dominicans, Sudanese, Indonesians, and Spaniards by their own countrymen during civil wars or repressions; the slaughter of tens of millions of soldiers and civilians from nearly all nations during the mass hysteria of combat; and which has seen the development of the nuclear slaughter system that if used only one percent as carelessly as slaughter systems of the past will end human life forever—is a world running smoothly under a plan of divine guidance.

It is equally difficult to believe that a world that includes the soaring eagle and the singing whale; the 1,000-year-old redwood tree and the 3,000-mile migration of the Ascension turtle; the lifelong mating of sunbirds and dolphins; the loyalty of the dog; the playfulness of the otter; the engineering skills of the beaver; the differentiation of a single invisible embryo cell into thousands of different types of cells and billions of total cells to make a human, with an error rate of roughly one in a trillion; and the indomitable pounding of the human heart, heard through all the travesties described above—is a world operating strictly by random chance.

Why can't existence on the cosmic scale be just as we perceive it here on the earthly scale? Subject to influence and improvement, but hard to understand and even harder to control.

And why can't God the cosmic creature be just like us? Hurt and confused by His failures, lonely and short of love, but still, in spite of it all, willing to press on.

—7—

When Nora had opened the back door on that second morning in Seattle she had sighed in the wistful way someone sighs when leaving a beloved old house to move into a larger new one. On that morning, as she sat Warren down in the passenger seat of her Toyota and started driving east, away from the city, Nora had needed to see the Cascades. They came up, crisp storybook mountains, in startlingly little time—making her wonder how objects so vast could be just around the corner without exerting some kind of palpable influence on daily affairs.

That morning Nora had stopped in front of a small A-frame cabin, which from its appearance was rarely used, situated at the end of a rutted dirt road whose switchbacks her car had had difficulty negotiating.

"Good, it's cold in here," Nora said as they entered the cabin, chill air brushing off their clothes. "The place belongs to Felicity Nash's father, and she won't say anything. Make a fire."

Warren built a fire while Nora removed a picnic basket from under the hatch of her Toyota. He hadn't seen her place the basket there. She must have packed it and set it in the car well before she knew he'd be coming back and not going home, as she had requested.

Nora laid some food from the basket on a wooden table and uncorked a bottle of wine by placing it on the floor and gripping it between her feet. Warren was huffing at the fire, trying to make it flame. "Can't get the fire lit. Bad sign," Nora teased.

Once the fire was on its own, Nora took Warren by the hand and led him to the table. They had held hands at every opportunity, even during the drive from Mercer Island, a clumsy business, with Nora's hand shuttling back and forth from the stick shift. Holding hands seemed to both of them important exactly

151

because it was physically awkward and slightly childish. Warren thought of the aggressively modern professional women he had known who were eager to have their most intimate parts licked but thought that holding hands was in poor taste.

Except for the glow from the fire, the cabin was dark. A winter overcast hung outside, opaque, hiding away the sun. They sat on a couch before the fire and drank a strong red wine. Nora asked Warren about his first time. He told her a typical story of youthful pressure.

"At least yours was with a girlfriend," Nora said when he had finished. "At least you had the right idea. Mine was with a guy I'd never met."

Warren felt a tingle of fear, a fear that there was something about Nora on which he had been far wrong.

"I went away to college as a virgin," she said. "One day I just told myself, This has to end. The first guy I find who's not an obvious psycho, he gets it. So I met a boy at a dorm party and went back to his room. I just had to get it over with."

"Have you always been so romantic?" Warren asked.

"Somehow I always thought there would be no romance for me," Nora said. "I know your question is facetious, but my answer isn't. I guess I did it that way with that boy because I knew it would be horrible and it would make me hate the idea of sex and men, which it did, for a time at least."

Nora looked off into the winter gray. "Ever since I was little I had this feeling that whatever love meant, it had already passed me by. You know how sometimes people's first loves at age sixteen don't work out and they spend the rest of their lives feeling defeated, like there's no point in trying again? I felt that way even before I had a first love—that the chance for me had gone long ago."

Warren did know people who had become old and weary while barely out of their teens, feeling that the possibilities for them had been foreclosed. They didn't seem to understand that the young years, when learning takes place with intense speed and disappointments are more keenly felt, can appear to consume more of the emotional self than they actually do. He asked, "Did you ever see this guy again?"

"God no," Nora said. "Or any of his friends he gave my number to. I feel bad for him, though. The poor boy has probably gone through life wondering why all the other girls don't hop into bed within an hour like the first one did."

"You have a generous view of male sensibilities."

"Now we're doing questions again. How many?"

"How many what?"

"Women. Have you made it with."

Warren wondered what number would make him sound desirable yet not a cad. "I really can't remember for sure."

"You *better* be able to remember."

"Maybe ten?" he finally said with the Southern inflection of the simultaneous interrogative and assertive. Then added quickly, "Most of them were pretty casual deals."

"Am I a deal?"

"For chrissakes, Nora, I've chased you halfway across the country."

"Well, how do I know? That could be your technique."

"And you?"

"Three. The frat boy, Ford, and you."

"I don't believe it."

"Then don't."

Warren couldn't believe it because he assumed that Nora could walk into a room, point at any man she wanted, and leave with him two minutes later. In fact, she could not do so. But most men believe the world works that way—that women can always get what they want sexually—and Warren was no exception. "You must have had so many men after you," he said.

"I wish," Nora answered, then reconsidered. "Actually, I don't wish."

She looked out, where a fuzzy snow had begun to fall. "Would you really want that kind of power? Maybe for one night, just to see what it's like. But to be that way all the time would be— like being a bully, a big teenager on an island full of eight-year-olds. Suppose I looked like a centerfold and wore sexy clothes. I could make almost any man I wanted sleep with me. But what happiness would such allure bring? I'd come a lot, but I can do that for myself. I wouldn't get satisfaction. If people wanted to sleep with me because they thought I had the best boobs, they would be the ones getting the satisfaction, not me."

"I think you have the best boobs."

Nora kissed him. "It makes me so happy you think that, because I know it isn't true. If I really did have the best boobs your wanting them would be a problem."

Warren laughed. "Did you take some kind of special course where they taught you to talk that way?"

"I hardly ever talk this way," Nora said. Then, resuming, she asked, "Do you understand? This is why kings and dictators cannot be happy. They force people to obey them yet get no pleasure out of it, so they force more people to do worse things, seeking the pleasure they can never find, and the whole business degenerates. Nobility of the Middle Ages often turned to perversions but even that didn't give them pleasure, because it was forced."

The fire had reached a roar punctuated by an occasional *pop!* And with it moods were shifting. "All this talk of breasts and perversion is making it hard to concentrate," Nora added.

"You're the one who mentioned perversion."

"So I did." Nora disengaged herself from under Warren's arm and wriggled to the opposite end of the couch. Kneeling, so that her head was above Warren's, she began to unbutton her shirt, a plain Oxford cloth too thick to show the outline of her bra. Nora tried to work the buttons like a seductress, pausing at the one that would reveal her chest. Then she fought with the snap on her jeans and began trying to push them over her hips while holding herself upright.

It didn't work. Getting the pants off is a step that has never been performed with dignity. Usually, attempts end with one impatient partner grabbing the cuffs and yanking. Nora had her pants halfway off when she lost her balance and toppled to the floor.

"I'm really sorry," she said. "I should have worn a skirt. Someday I promise I will."

Finishing the job with a perfunctory yank, Nora stood naked in the firelight, one side of her glowing bright, the other only dimly revealed. Though they had made love before, Warren felt as if this were the first time, and it renewed his hope that people could try again in life without being poisoned by prior disappointments.

After they had caressed, Nora asked Warren to tell her what it was like for a man to be inside. He said that it was like diving into a pond on a frying summer day and then standing up in the water. The first sensation, relief; the second, of two halves of the body far apart yet connected.

Late in the afternoon Nora began to cry and would not explain why. They were lying on their sides, her back to his chest. Warren had been saying how much he loved her and Nora had been saying they shouldn't talk about that. She attempted to distract him by taking one of his hands, locking it in hers, and pushing both hands as far as she could between her legs, where it was warm and alive, like it must feel if you could touch the ventricles of the heart.

But Warren kept insisting, and finally Nora said, "I was working in that museum for three weeks, you know. I saw, too."

For a long time they simply stared at each other, trying to remember. Then Nora looked out the window and comprehended the fact that the sky had gone black with evening. They almost ran from the cabin, leaving it a mess: furniture moved, food strewn, flue open. Warren prayed to himself that Ford had beaten them home and that a final confrontation would begin. But because of his promotion Ford had been taken out after work by friends from his office. When Nora's car reached the McConaughty house, it was lightless and silent.

8
FEAR OF SINCERITY

While Warren was flying back from Seattle on the night of the accident at the construction site, three identical copies of the Azimuth Collective newsletter arrived in his mailbox. Each contained an appeal for contributions to cover rising postal costs. The edition read:

IT HAS BEEN SAID THAT EVERYONE IS A CRITIC. THAT ADAGE IS IN THE PROCESS OF BEING TRANSFORMED INTO A FACT.

The careers most avidly sought today are those in which the thing a person does is criticize what other people do.

Law, journalism, consulting, academe, government regulation, even the misnamed "data management" industry—clerical workers know data cannot be managed, for numbers always get their way—are concerned not with doing, but commenting upon or analyzing that which has been done by others. Traditional critics who write on art and letters from cramped grottos pale in numbers when compared to the growing ranks of those who criticize from plush downtown offices. And certainly pale in income!

Law today represents the automatic career choice of the talented young. We think of lawyers as so many Perry Masons. Yet the majority of contemporary American lawyers do not participate in trials, or for that matter enter courtrooms. They seldom engage in active functions like sifting evidence. Mostly they sit by themselves commenting on what others have done—composing briefs that complain of another party's actions, analyzing government rules, analyzing errors in cases from the past, criticizing the actions of courts, criticizing the other party's briefs criticizing their briefs.

In the federal court system that is the exemplar of U.S. law, only the first level, the circuit courts, actually tries cases. The

159

other two levels, the appeals courts and the Supreme Court, exist to criticize what the lower courts have done. They are higher both in terms of legal organization and in terms of the accolades bestowed by society—passing judgment being viewed as more prestigious than taking action, and passing judgment on other judgments being a prestige most rarefied and pure.

High courts follow the modern imperative of always being willing to say when others have taken the wrong steps, but seldom being willing to specify what steps would have been right. In most cases they do not resolve issues. Rather, they cancel an earlier attempt at resolution, and send the case back down the chain. Consider the logical sequence that occurs when a higher court finds error by a lower court and remands the case for the lower court to try its luck again. First the higher court says, We find the lower court incompetent. Then the higher court says, We leave it to the incompetents to straighten this out.

Journalism is another profession oriented toward criticism. Wanting to barricade themselves against the snipes they direct at others, journalists employ a professional ethic which holds that they may condemn but never advocate. Officially this ethic is to insure objectivity, but its real purpose is to let journalists off the hook. Journalists may shower complaints on the solutions proposed by others but may not themselves propose solutions that would in turn be subject to criticism. Standard to this genre is the 47-part series exposing Congress as a den of corrupt, hypocritical, misinformed hacks—and then calling on Congress to do something about it.

In management consulting, a profession much in tune with the spirit of the times, the finest products of the best business schools float from company to company criticizing how others run businesses but not attempting to run a business themselves. Legislatures of the land resound with voices condemning in moral falsetto nearly everything suggested by nearly everyone —but few legislators will commit themselves on the question of what government *ought* to do. Single-issue pressure groups, which have replaced political parties as the core units of

American public activity, are oriented around hysterical attacks on other people's programs. The true purpose of most single-issue groups is to help make everyone a critic—by offering donors a convenient means of declaring someone else responsible for the general condition.

Academic life is mainly criticism: not a new condition, but an increasingly significant one as higher education expands. In academic circles the surest path to professional success is looking down on others. Entire disciplines exist for this purpose.

Professors of economics and of political science often decline to join political administrations, opportunities for which they would seem eager. But they do not wish their theories tainted by real world necessities; they would rather discourse on the blunders of others than hold power and become accountable themselves for its frailty. This in effect concedes government to those the professors consider duller-witted than themselves; guaranteeing lots to criticize.

Teaching at the university level often centers on showing students how to detect and criticize the mistakes of history, politics, and art. Heaven knows there are plenty to choose from. Yet from this approach students increasingly seem to learn the wrong lesson.

Rather than leaving college determined to improve on the mistakes of history, they leave determined to avoid doing anything for which they themselves might be criticized. In law, journalism, consulting, and similar professions they find havens. The very best students in the humanities may be encouraged by their professors to view the uttering of clever put-downs as an end in itself. Such people come to fear sincerity; to fear association with any belief or action that springs flawed from this flawed world. Then they cannot understand why, with every advantage in life, they feel empty and unhappy.

Though the traditional critics have fallen behind the new white-collar critics on the income scale, they continue to serve as models of achievement. From a career standpoint, artistic critics draw attention to themselves most easily through condemnation. In the vicious appraisal the persona of the critic rises to the fore, while in the neutral or affirmative review his persona recedes. This is not the only way to win career success as a critic, but it is the most obvious way.

Since every human action is to some extent flawed, the superficial aspect of criticism is deceptively easy. Through selective argument anything can be ridiculed—a theater critic might condemn a funny play by saying it lacks weight, and the following day condemn a weighty play by saying it lacks humor. One book may be attacked as dense, reliant on stock characters and driving toward a standard point; others in turn attacked as spare, reliant on fantastic characters, and failing to address a Great Theme. Anyone can play this game with any aspect of art, politics, invention, business, science, or anything else. The skilled critic keeps the fallibility of all things in proportion, and acknowledges an obligation to advance a coherent philosophy. But as the wrong lesson is the one most readily learned, it is rarely the skilled critic's example that is followed.

As more and more people attend college and then move into professions based on criticism, the nation will increasingly hold up commenting as more admirable than creating. This could apply not just in the upper class, where it has long been a problem, but in the middle class too, for average life is becoming more white-collar than blue.

To the extent that these forces are professional, they are sure to be extensively analyzed. But what about their personal effects?

Criticism, released from its cage, cannot be restrained. It runs amok and destroys the everyday. Nearly all daily actions when subjected to criticism seem trite and outwardly stipulated. Yet it is in the elevation of the everyday, the enrichment of those moments that do not have significance, that love finds its sustenance.

If, professionally, we wish foremost to become critics of others, how long before we become detached observers of our own lives as well? Before our sophisticated knowledge of each other's faults makes us unwilling to take the most failure-prone step of all—that of falling in love?

—9—

On the desk in Warren's office were three documents. One was a copy of the first amended brief in *The People vs. T. R. Berns and Sons Construction Co. et al,* a criminal negligence action concerning the collapse of a retaining wall. Kessey, Denning & Hobard, consulting engineers, numbered among the et al. The second was the letter Nora had written a few nights before, on the day Warren left Seattle. The third was a notice of intent to file a wrongful death liability suit. This notice was signed by a union lawyer representing the estate of Harriman D. Anzalone, Jr., a sheetmetal worker who had died in surgery at 3:18 A.M. on the morning after the accident.

The lawyer had clipped to his letter a newspaper story about the death, complete with an old family photo of Harriman Anzalone in a barbecue apron. Victim, the newspaper said, had been thrown against a concrete abutment by reservoir water advancing from a barrier that ruptured on the first day of renovation at the municipal pump-generating station. Victim suffered multiple internal injuries, hemorrhaging of the kidneys, and irreversible flooding of the lungs. Is survived by wife and seven children.

Scattered elsewhere on Warren's desk were charts, notes, coffee cups, a small bottle of Visine, and the .45.

It was well past midnight. The complex in which Kessey, Denning & Hobard's offices were located was deserted. Heat and light for the building normally shut down at seven P.M.— overtime work was as rare among the insurance-claim processors and title search firms that leased the rest of the complex as it was at KD&H. Warren had to file a written request with the building management company to keep the power on past seven. The management company, begrudging this, had left the lights on only in the wing where Warren worked: most of the office remained dark and seemed to Warren to have become very large. He had to transfer the coffeemaker from the company kitchenette to a table in the drafting room, near an electric outlet that had power.

Down the hall in a lightless closet hung Warren's high school football jacket, a gaudy arrangement of purple-and-yellow nylon with *Weasels* written across the back in swirling letters. On the left sleeve, like a naval rank bar, was a single yellow band, indicating the wearer had received a game ball. In the left inner pocket of the jacket was the .45 clip. Warren cleaved to his practice of keeping guns and ammunition separated.

Preliminary indictments in *The People vs. Berns et al* had been filed as soon as court opened the morning Harriman Anzalone, Jr., died. Warren's name had not been in the first filing, but it was added to the amended brief now on his desk. The charges were lodged with evident glee by the district attorney, a political foe of the mayor's. The mayor had sponsored the generating station renovation, pushed funding through the city council by promising a "new era of accountability," and then awarded the performance bonds to an agency run by his wife's brother.

The D.A. planned to run against the mayor in the next primary. As a result, KD&H had been warned to expect the case to be tried in the papers as much as the courts. Any evidence prosecutors might find that was suspicious but inconclusive—for example, that a key engineer had been absent without leave when the accident occurred—was sure to be leaked.

Spread out on the floor next to Warren's desk were elevations, blueprints, R.F.P. responses, and specification tables from the project file. Taped on the walls were some sketches Warren had made during a brief visit to the site itself. As soon as his plane landed Warren had gone there, hoping to arrive before lawsuits could be filed and named parties banned from the scene. A state trooper wearing a nineteenth-century-style cowboy hat with a chin strap had refused to let Warren take photographs or cross the police line formed with what appeared to be church pew cord. When Warren asked if he could make sketches, the trooper, who hadn't been prepped for this question, stammered a little and then agreed.

The security didn't seem to matter much. There was little to see. Mud lines on walls indicated that the water level had reached as high as fifteen feet. The first surge had thrown workers, tools, supplies, and a sizable diesel generator against the far end of the enclosure, where Anzalone had hit the sharp edge of a concrete column. Most of the workers had survived by swimming on top of the surge until an operator in the generating station control room, ignoring his supervisor's order to call the police but touch nothing, had started up the main turbine in its pump mode, which reversed the influx of water before the area filled. Had the operator not acted without hesitation, some forty men and women would have drowned.

As the water slid back in the direction of the ruptured wall, it deposited debris at random like a glacier. Silt was still ankle deep. Warren had watched a forensic team working in fishermen's rubber overalls, laboriously cataloging the exact location of every wrench and shoe dropped by the receding flood. Hangar lights had been set up, causing the scene to resemble a movie set. It was hard for Warren to believe a man had been killed in such a place, cool as it was with scientific detachment. Disaster aftermaths are usually that way: teams of experts use expensive devices and intricate theories to rationalize an instant of madness.

This was the fifth consecutive night Warren had stayed at the office studying files, looking for the answer. He kept all suppositions about what had happened in his head; even the most innocent notes might be subpoenaed. Should Warren discover that he himself was to blame, however, he intended to write everything down and then turn his thoughts to the .45.

The first round in the gun magazine was, as always, a blank. Warren felt that if he could make himself raise the weapon to his temple and fire the blank—hear the crack by his ear, an inch from the dwelling place of souls—without fainting or screaming in fright, then he would know one more pull was the right thing to do. His life would be forfeit if Anzalone's were on his conscience. He might be able to adjust, or make amends to the family, or even forget, but he could never again be worthy. To go on would be treason to his own beliefs and the greatest cruelty to Nora, considering the contents of her letter.

Perhaps, Warren thought, if there really were something to the startling images of the Lo Spagnas, there would be another chance in another time to find Nora once more. The prospect of having to start again—the learning over of what was now obvious, the stubbing up against what now came easily, the repetition of so many pains—made Warren feel deeply tired. But for Nora he would endure it as a trial, as an opportunity to regain his worth. Warren was certain that Nora would not have to accept the same cost too, to struggle dumb through adolescence again. He envisioned her materializing as a happy and finished adult, because it was the only way he could envision her.

Her letter, twenty-three pages long, had been with Warren since he received it. Proof at last, documentary proof, that Nora's feelings were not imagined. Much of it concerned Escanaba, a small town on Michigan's wooded Upper Peninsula near the junction of cold Canada and Lake Michigan, about as far from metropolitan life as any location in the Eastern Time Zone could be. It seemed, she wrote, "that Indians would jump out of the trees at any moment":

> I had four brothers but no sister, so there was always status attached to the mere fact of gender. Of course when I was little I took advantage, but as I grew I came to wish that gender would go away. In my earliest memories I hear my father saying that I would marry someone rich and that would be the salvation of the family. There was so much talk about me getting married that it became like a fable everyone knows but no one believes. Too much talk smothers romance. By the time I was old enough to have boyfriends I felt the subject had already been talked to death.
>
> I suppose this is why it scares me somewhat that you are so excited about my being a girl. I can imagine all

the clever replies to that statement you're composing. But would you love me as much if you couldn't get inside me? Would you become a queer in order to be my lover?

I say this only half kidding. The answer to that question must be yes if we are talking about love. When we were at Felicity's cabin I tried to imagine that you were a woman. It was too confusing and I had to give it up —even a scrawny man is so different to the touch than a woman that there's just no mistaking. (Don't mean to call you scrawny.)

The point is, the idea neither turned me on nor made me sick. It only made me think that, if you were a woman, we would go about things somewhat differently. I was sure I would have wanted to be your lover regardless, because I love what you are. Can you say the same about me? Would you wear tight jeans and swish around and swallow my come if whatever it is that makes me had been born into a boy? And don't say how disgusting. I swallowed your come, and I'm not disgusting.

Neither of us can know whether what we saw in the gallery had any significance. But whether you get one try or a hundred, it is always a roll of the dice regarding what gender your spirit is born into. I was fifty-fifty to be a boy. I can hear you now saying you don't want to think about that. You'd better. Next time around it might happen.

This portion of the letter, read many times, always brought Warren to a halt. He could not think of Nora as a man, though he could vaguely picture the both of them as female, since in that combination Nora would still be a woman.

Anyway, four brothers against one sister is the closest I can come to a psychological revelation from my youth. I don't believe a person's behavior can be traced to specific "big moments" except for those few people who endure genuine traumas in the common-sense meaning of the word, not the psychobabble sales-talk meaning. What you are is an accumulation of incidents and indications, none of which has relevance except in context: you have to be around someone for a very long time until you can be sure what the context is.

How many people actually experience big moments in which their lives are transformed? Expecting big moments is about as sensible as picking shoes for the Judgment Day. This, dearest, is what makes me not believe in the paintings. I'd *like* to believe. What a Big Moment that would be! We could both feel like something's happened to us that never happened to anyone before. And the rest of our lives, our choices, would be so clear. But, realistically, big moments just don't happen. It's amazing enough in the scheme of things that two compatible people ran into each other in a crowd and one of them spoke.

Another section of the letter read:

During my high school days I did a sort of teen-queen singing act in a restaurant called the Pheasant Room, which the manager insisted on calling a club—you know, so he could say, "Our policy here at the club . . ."—although the club served mainly Pabst Blue Ribbon and spaghetti. Part of the policy was to put a Nehi grape on prominent display near my microphone stand so that no one would suspect the underage girl was drinking.

My act was pop tunes and bee-ooo-tiful music, but occasionally I'd sneak in songs like "California Dreamin'" because I thought they made an incredible statement. Of course, I had no idea what that statement was. The club manager eventually fired me because, he said, when people were relaxing they didn't want to listen to "social commentary." The words that got us so excited then now seem so trite and trumped-up. "Stopped into a church/I passed along the way." Okay, so you stopped into a church. So what? Just saying "church" made it sound significant. When you're young the appearance of making a statement is in itself a statement.

I had a good voice, but only relative to the competition in a small town at the foot of Mt. Nowhere. I know my spirit badly wanted to be born into a woman with real singing talent, which it wasn't. If I had really been serious about it I would have gone to Los Angeles or New York, sung in a band, and waited tables. But I was too scared. I was certain I'd fail. So I kept telling myself I wasn't "ready."

There was no money for voice lessons, but I did teach myself basic piano and how to read sheet music. I liked to do arrangements of lyrics. Arrangements of what? you say. People will take a song and think nothing of re-arranging the harmony, beat, signature, orchestration, till it's transformed from rock to Muzak. Any change in the sound is fine. But then they sing the same old stupid lyrics as if they were a coda of revealed wisdom handed down from Aristotle to Erasmus to Leslie Gore. The worst part is that the melody is usually pretty good, while the lyrics, which everyone treats as sacred, are disasters. You can't imagine how embarrassing it is to stand up in front of mature adults and sing, "Why do birds suddenly appear/Every time you are near." Or these nonsense lyrics that are supposed to sound Deep with a capital D when you know they mean nothing at all! Have you caught the new David Bowie song: "I stumble into town/Just like a sacred cow/Visions of swastikas in my head." Must have chained Bob Dylan's monkeys to a word processor to come up with that.

So I wrote my own lyrics to popular songs. People

at the Pheasant Room treated me as though I had contracted meningitis. First they would glance around a
bit, wondering if maybe they'd forgotten the exact
words. But when they realized I was singing different
words, my own words, they would start to boo, even
if mine were better.

I suppose they wanted to lock their minds onto the
lyrics they already knew and drift along. Like when you
listen to a political speech, you want to be told what you
already believe and not have to think about why you
believe it. What I could never figure out is the relationship of bad lyrics to the musicians themselves. In rock
music, many performers are capable of writing music
that is creative and engaging. Then they add moron-
level lyrics. Is it that they don't know how to express
their thoughts, or that they have nothing to say?

You would think that any basically creative person
must have *something* to say. It's like the movie directors
who do brilliant photographic effects, which must require some form of creativity, then resort to the same
old predictable garbage for characters.

In another section she wrote:

My early life experiences never quite made sense to
me till I realized that I fall into the category of women
who possess enough looks to distort the circumstances
around them, but not enough to convert them to gain
by being an actress or a news personality or whatever.
If you are attractive, people make allowances and spoil
you in a manner that is diabolical because you think
everybody gets treated that way. My father wanted me
to enter beauty contests. Every father thinks his daughter a princess, but mine tried to pretend I actually was.
I didn't understand till long after that every unnecessary dress or pair of shoes he bought me represented
something one of my brothers needed and did not get.

I think parents want to believe their children are good-looking not just out of pride, but because looks ensure the child's place in life. What can make you safer and more secure than appearance, which every society glorifies, and which does not require work to achieve? (Unless you're a model and must starve yourself till your ribs show.)

If you are beautiful or handsome, someone will always look after you. The great convenience of superficial qualities is that, having so little meaning, they cannot be misunderstood.

I still have a few outrageous photos of myself trying to launch a modeling career. In one I'm about sixteen, wearing a swimsuit, walking between two rows of tables at a department store fashion luncheon. Forming the gauntlet are middle-aged ladies in gloves and ribbons, formal lunching attire, straining backward over folding chairs to get a look at me. Their faces are contorted into the maximum degree of disapproval that a matron can register in public, which is quite a bit. I have on skyscraper heels and *white,* if you can believe that, white nail polish.

During the show you wouldn't notice their expressions because you had to concentrate on poise and trying to look eleven feet tall. But I would see those photographs later, discover what had been on their faces, and it would make me cry. How could they think so harshly of someone they didn't even know?

At that time I thought the disapproval on the ladies' faces was personal. Only as I got older did I realize that some women go to shows and so on exactly for the purpose of disapproving of what they see. Women inspect each other closely for flaws in order to relieve their own anxieties. This is the secret appeal of fashion magazines like *Glamour.* You can flip through page after page making critical judgments—that's too flashy, she's too flat, that look's been done, that hair wouldn't stay in place from here to the door. It's relaxing. If you go looking for flaws you will always find one.

For a time I was resentful of my father's attempts to push me into a degrading pursuit. I thought, How can he put his only daughter on public display like a tea service at the same time my mother is telling me that to let a boy look at me in private would be a crime against nature?

What wonderfully flexible standards we have. To offer yourself to strangers in an unnatural setting is fine because someone else is dictating the terms; whereas, to offer yourself on terms of your own choosing in private is wrong because then you must take responsibility for your actions. For a lawyer to defend someone he knows full well to be a murderer is socially respectable because he's only doing it for money. If he did it on principle, that would be weird.

Doesn't that sum up the social distinction between professional and personal? People want to hide themselves away in occupations where they don't have to think about their actions because they "can't"—because there is some set of rules which conveniently prevents them from changing things. Those are also, by the most extraordinary coincidence, the occupations that pay best.

In my junior year of high school, Father prevailed on me to try for Miss Michigan. I told myself I'd do it for the scholarship. Brilliance on the part of the beauty pageant business to give scholarships—who could object to that? If they gave cash prizes the girls would be whores, so instead they strutted around holding roses for the advancement of science.

At the regional competition I sang my little heart out. At the finals in Lansing I wore an unpadded suit that was the least you could get away with at the time. And I lost. Not a runner-up or even mentioned, and in those local pageants they tried to say something nice about everybody who didn't fall off the ramp or advocate birth control. It was a shock. Somehow I had always thought this kind of thing—worldly approval, if you will—would come to me anytime I lowered myself to ask for it. Better to have this illusion shattered early than to carry it through life. The whole drive home, six hours, I didn't say a word.

In small towns everybody hears about your losing out to the big-city girls, and you know what? They like it. Makes you one of them, passed over and going nowhere. Before this Miss Michigan episode my high school guidance counselor had been encouraging me to go east to a good school for college. Afterward she started saying, "Why don't you think about Northern Michigan?" It was like somebody put an announcement in the newspaper. Boys who'd been afraid even to ask me to the movies suddenly wanted to go for drives to Rapid River Falls, the petting spot. I wanted out of Escanaba in a bad way.

The University of Washington gave me full financial aid, which is how I ended up in Seattle. It was sophomore year when I met Ford, who was then a first-year grad in business. (He's only thirty-four. I know you think he's much older. Ford is the sort of person who didn't fight growing up—he really looked forward to it.) We were married at the end of the school year. He seemed to me as much as anyone could ask in a man—smart, cosmopolitan, slow-moving. And marrying him meant I would never have to go back to Escanaba, not even for summers.

Ford is from Seattle. He knew all the restaurants and the perfect scenic turnouts on all the roads. For our first date he took me on the Anacortas ferry, winding up slowly through the impossible San Juan Islands—they're like a cross between Hawaii and Switzerland—toward Vancouver. The trip lasts almost a day. We sat on wooden benches watching the water slip away, eating hot dogs, and feeling the motors thrumming like they were circling each other. You'd go out on deck to get wet and cold, then come back into the warm, then go out to get cold again. I was hooked.

Later I learned that Ford had asked out half a dozen underclass women that year and every first date had been the Anacortas ferry. But if our starting circumstances were a little phony, so what? You have to start somewhere. In a way the thought that he would try a day-long ferry ride five times, get shut down five times, and still try again was kind of romantic. Maybe he was looking for the one who would understand. Anyway, it was enough for me. I'd never met a man who did anything more than talk about himself or try to get me drunk.

Before we were married I made Ford promise we would never leave Seattle, unless it was for someplace even more glorious. Seattle seemed like Paris with its lights to me. Plus you know I hate to travel; I would have been happy then to spend my entire life within King County. In high school my grades had been erratic, but I started getting straight A's in college. It was extremely gratifying, doing something right in the eyes of the world. And when marriage gave me a practical excuse to stop singing, I dropped it cold. Lately I've been doing community theater and imagining the heights I could have soared to. Sure. In a classic case of the blind leading the blind, I also do volunteer work with a group that counsels pregnant teenage girls. They call themselves a "center," but since they only have one location I don't know what they are the center of. Felicity's idea: I've gotten used to it more easily than I expected. The girls seem to need direction so desperately, and I'm supposed to pretend that I know a good direction when I see one.

Looking back from the standpoint of all the things you don't find out until you're better off not finding

out, Ford and I should not have married. Early in the
marriage our common interest was making a home.
Now that the home is done the divergence in our other
interests is beginning to show. I never talk to him as I
talk to you. Ten years from now, I fear, Ford and I will
have little to say to each other. He denigrates my
friends, who I admit are not the crown heads of
Europe, but I don't denigrate his friends. The number
of times he asks me about my job can be calculated by
the phases of the moon, though he expects to speak of
his unceasingly.

Ford acts possessive in a way that is hard to explain
without sounding like one of those overwrought femi-
nists who are only happy when presenting irrefutable
proof that the entire world is conspiring against them
personally. But you'd know what I mean if you could
observe us together. He *tells* me to do things he ought
to *convince* me to do, and probably could convince me
to do if he'd only try. Ford has yet to refer to me as "my
lovely wife," but I know it's coming. I've caught every
other man at those infernal Xerox pot-luck suppers
saying it. And we have a kind of impasse over the fact
that he wants children, but not sex. I mean no more
than once a month. Please don't think my interest in
you stems from my horniness; it does not. I could accept the notion of never making love again at all, if it
was for a purpose. But not because of lack of interest
on the part of my own husband.

Now look at the inventory of my complaints
weighed against the complaints of nearly every other
woman in the world today! Or for that matter, who has
ever lived. Women lost in loneliness, in economic or
tribal hopelessness; women tied to thoughtless, brutish,
awful men. Ford is gentle, considerate, and highly responsible. What possible right have I to complain?
Think of the centuries in which women lived out their
lives without a single moment of what you and I would

consider "meaningful" contact with the opposite sex, to say nothing of romantic or sexual satisfaction. Like respect, romance for women comes from our page of the calendar. If you read the literature of old you find that a woman who did experience even a few hours of meaningful romantic contact with a man might spend the rest of her life stewing about it and having flashbacks. Not just plot convention: when a theme recurs in literature, it is usually because it reflects life.

All my life I have wondered whether love is real—not just something felt but something *there,* a force. The conclusion I always come to is no. I think it's like soldiers who don't find out they've experienced "glory" until years later when the official war histories are released. Sometimes events happen in your life that resemble love; you should be thankful for them, but not be fooled.

Warren, you are an unusually logical person. What sense would it make for me to throw aside a life that is agreeable and pleasant with a man who is decent in return for the very long-shot chance that we will always feel toward each other as we do now?

These are matters I need time to ponder. Obviously I am thinking, or I would not be writing this letter. The greatest gift you could give me now would be patient silence. Not forever, but for long enough that I can sort this out. If there is truth to this Siena business, then what possible difference could a few extra months make? And if there is not, it is better to wait and let the fever pass.

I continue to think you would do well by yourself and your own future to assume this romance will fail. That is my advice to you as lover and friend: assume the worst. If history is any guide, it is surely what you will get.

Truly,
N.J.

PS: Sun now on horizon. Maybe we'll get to see the mountain! Please excuse late-night handwriting.

Actually, Warren kept re-reading the letter out of sequence, because there were passages he wished to avoid. They were the words that had frozen his heart:

My father is a bus driver. During my teen years he worked for a small charter company—taking the glee club on field trips, that kind of thing. The pay was poor and the work sporadic. With five kids he was strapped all the time. We lived in a county-subsidized housing project, a brick shoebox with four doors, one for each family, and four miniature porches. Only one person could stand on the porch at a time —I don't know why they even bothered to put them on. Probably for dignity. Across a courtyard ground down into brown cloud dirt there were two other structures exactly the same. I am not asking for sympathy, merely describing the conditions. We considered ourselves lucky.

Sometimes Father would take us out to Detour Point, where we would watch the dotted line of ore boats carrying taconite from the Mesabi Range in Minnesota down to the mills of Gary and Calumet City. It made him angry that there was a vast money-making machine passing right by his door and he couldn't make himself part of it.

Anyway, the year Ford and I were married, Father flipped a bus full of children. He was driving along a road with no shoulder when he glanced back to look at some commotion among the kids. School bus drivers are expected to keep their eyes on the road and be den mothers simultaneously. As he turned to look, he moved the steering wheel with him, causing the bus to veer. One of those peg-handle steering wheels—he was holding the peg. The right front tires went off the shoulder and when he jerked the wheel back sharply, the bus flipped.

Twenty-two of twenty-nine children were hurt, although, thank God, nothing permanent. You will be interested to know that by the end of the week sixty-five families had filed claims for compensation. There was no written record of who was or wasn't on the bus, so people with a child of the proper age tried to cash in. Rumor around town was that the charter company had a big insurance carrier in Chicago that was made of money. The truth turned out to be a little different. The company had no insurance at all. It had filed a bogus state certificate and paid off an inspector not to report it.

The company quickly fired my father, and for public consumption tried to fix all the blame on him. They said he was a drunk, although why if he was a drunk they would let him drive around a busload of kids they failed to explain. Father claimed that the bus was inadequately maintained, which in turn raised the same question about him: If the bus was unsafe why hadn't he reported it before? Father was afraid of losing his job.

For months this was the favored topic of debate around town—was Donald Jocelyn a drunk or a coward? Half the people in cold-weather towns like Escanaba are drunks themselves, but they always play at shock and amazement when one of their number is trapped into revealing his condition.

Many of those who sued the charter company also sued my father—legally, a futile gesture, since you can't get damages from someone with no money and no job. But lawyers insist on suing as many parties as they can. They want the world to live in fear of lawyers and when they get a chance to ruin someone's life they do so as an object lesson. These were local lawyers, too, not out-of-towners. They knew Father had nothing and they didn't care. It was good practice.

At this point I must admit one of the things that attracted me to Ford was the fact he had some money. I'd be lying if I said I didn't consider it.

We would go to an expensive restaurant and at the end of the meal he would simply pull out a card and sign his name. Then we would walk away. At the time this seemed as magical to me as though he had waived a wand of lignum vitae and made the entire restaurant (especially the snobby waiters!) disappear. And we would take cabs. When you are in college, plotting to steal chicken salad from the dining hall, the idea of riding in a cab is nearly beyond comprehension.

I did not know then how Ford came by his money. Ford grew up with an aunt. He lost both his parents when he was eight years old: his mother to emphysema, his father the same day in an auto crash, when he was driving late at night and blinded by grief. There was inheritance and life insurance money, double indemnity for the car accident. Ford did not get the money till he was twenty-one, and then handled it prudently, paying for his own education and all the costs of the wedding. When that was done he had $45,000 left. In the 1970s, $45,000 cash was a sizable sum.

You wonder what makes me loyal to Ford. I'll tell you. He hired two attorneys to defend my father. And after setting aside enough money for their fees, he decided, on his own, to give $1,000 to each of the families with injured children and $10,000 to one family whose little girl needed to see specialists. The attorneys begged him not to do it—said the court might consider it a tacit admission of culpability. Once a lawyer finishes twisting things around it can sound like the victim interfered with the civil rights of the bullet! But Ford knew those people were poor, that there was no insurance, that even if they won against the bus company it would be years before they saw the first dime.

So the money was immediately wiped out. Remember, this happened after we were married—winning me was not a factor. They all tried to thank him, and do you know what he said? He said, When somebody does a favor like this he doesn't want thanks. He just wants the next person to pass it along.

I think at heart Ford was glad to be rid of the money, because he wanted to make his own fortune so that he would be able to enjoy it. Yet his gift was an act of true kindness—a heroic act within the confines of what is possible today. I felt his character had been tested, a clear test of the type that hardly ever really happens, and he had passed.

After giving away this money we felt very noble, like anonymous benefactors. All we could afford for entertainment was to bring home a pizza and watch TV, but somehow it was more fun than the fancy restaurants we had patronized before. This was our best time together, our closest time—which suggests to me that there is some reward for virtue.

In recent years, as Ford has started to rise on the career ladder and money has started to come our way again, he has changed in ways that make me sad. He's more materialistic; I suppose that is inevitable and I should not complain. What stings is that money has taken away the closeness we once shared. Now he's very conscious of getting invited to the right party, of pleasing the right strangers, when before he only wanted to please me. And he has started to look down his nose at people who don't have money, which he never did when he was among their number. Ford says there is a distinction between those who lack money temporarily and those who are never going to get any. I don't know how to talk to him when he says things like that.

Father's legal problems took awfully long to solve, draining him. Had the drunken driving charge been proved he would have gone to jail. Eventually the at-

torneys beat every count and even got him his operator's permit back. Now he works part-time driving a
school bus for the township. Crummy work—you get
about five hours a day at $4 an hour for dragging
yourself in twice, morning and afternoon. But he can't
protest, being lucky to have any work at all.

When Father started driving again—the lawyers got
an injunction forbidding any employer from holding
against him the fact that he had been tried for an un-
proven offense—there was an ugly incident. Two of the
parents whose children had been on the crashed bus
refused to send their kids to school.

Strangely, it was parents of children who had not
been hurt at all. I think they were bitter because they
got no money. There is a common misconception that
anyone associated with an event that generates publicity automatically becomes rich. Celebrities and politicians seek publicity so avidly, and publicity is so
randomly distributed between the deserving and the
quacks, that I suppose it's unavoidable for people to
believe that getting on the air is like winning a sweep-
stakes. I admit this does not damage the financial status
of the public relations industry—we rely on people
believing that a few gossip-column mentions or a talk-
show appearance will elevate them to an exalted status.
Publicity is in our private desires the modern equivalent of a religious epiphany.

So we had these two parents whose faces had been
on the evening news for a fleeting instant and now
could not understand why they hadn't signed for a
mini-series. The day before my father started back to
work, one of them phoned Ford at the Xerox regional
office to demand money. When he said no, they called
a television station in Detroit.

This team of—I guess you'd call them—humans
wearing color-coordinated bush jackets flew all the way
up from Detroit in a helicopter. Must have landed to

refuel five times. The helicopter was painted camoufl-
age colors and on the side said in big letters CHANNEL
SEVEN NEWS COMMANDOS.

Bedlam. Cameramen were following children down
the halls of Lincoln Elementary School demanding in-
terviews. They asked Mrs. Rosen's eight-year-old if she
had a "statement for the press." With cameras rolling,
the woman who started all this threw herself in front of
a bus. Only it was a parked bus. And they had the
camera lens set wrong so she had to do it over. The
reporter kept telling her to emote. I think they did
about a dozen takes before they finally got a picture that
made it seem as though she were being menaced by an
approaching bus.

Then the reporter saw Father across the parking lot
and insisted on getting back into the helicopter and
flying over to him, even though he was no more than
a hundred yards away. He stuck a microphone in Father's face and said, "Is it true you killed twenty-two
children?" That night in Detroit they broadcast a report of the shocking, stunning scandal up in Escanaba,
including film of the station's helicopter circling over
the municipal garage while shining a searchlight on the
parked buses.

Now, in order that you understand, there is something I must tell you that I have never told anyone. Not
even Ford. I have never met or known anyone I would
trust this secret to. You must give me your word of
honor, spoken to yourself, that you will never tell a soul
or you may not read any further.

Father was in fact guilty. He had been drinking.
Father swears to me that liquor was not the cause and
that he has not had another drink since the day they
found him unconscious in that ditch. I call him every
week and make him swear it to me again—make him
swear on his own mother's grave that he will go to hell
if he touches alcohol again. Imagine making your own

father say that, again and again, like an infant.

My worry is ceaseless. If he should have another accident, Warren, I would be as much to blame as he. After all, I have only to say the word and they would take the bus away from him for good. But how can I do that? The driving is all he knows. Without it his life would wither away, and my mother's along with it.

Last year we went home to visit, drove across that North Dakota flatness for what seemed like weeks. I got everyone out of the house on a pretext and turned the place inside out, looking for any bottle he might have hidden. I didn't find one. But how can I be certain? He might be drinking in bars. Or what if he breaks down and goes on a bender—how will I know when that's coming? Father reaches mandatory retirement in two years and I hold my breath till then. The fear and the responsibility wear on me like I cannot express. Of all that has happened in my life this I would most wish to banish.

That night in Kansas City when you were telling me about what happened with the hotel skywalk and how furious it left you—I can't tell you what it meant to me to know that you feel exactly the same as I do about an issue that makes most people shrug. I am totally confident you would never allow yourself to be involved in any irresponsible act. I couldn't bear the thought of anything more like this. Really, I would sooner die. I would rather jump off one of those defective bridges than go through this again.

After folding the letter, Warren covered his face with his hands. Twenty-three pages of everything that made him love Nora. One paragraph that might make it impossible for him to see her again. How could he tell her he stood accused, possibly guilty, of the very offense they both dreaded?

Warren had no way of knowing that after Nora had written the last few lines she decided they were overstated. But, too tired to rewrite, she had let them stand. It was her habit when writing letters never to cross out inexact lines and replace them with better wording, because she did not want her correspondents, inspired by college introductory courses, holding up the pages to the light and trying to draw immense psychoanalytical insights from what she had initially said. Warren put the letter aside, and returned to studying the blueprints.

Several times as the early morning hours advanced, Warren jumped on what appeared to be errors in the plans. Each time close inspection showed the error was illusory or insignificant.

Around four A.M. he decided to make a set of photocopies of relevant documents. Should KD&H fire him, his access to the files would be cut off. After gathering together blueprints, spec sheets, purchase orders—everything his bleary mind could think of—he stacked them by the copier. When exhausted, simple tasks like making photocopies can become as difficult as walking uphill through a blizzard. First Warren had to rig three extension cords to the machine, then fumble with the instruction cards in semi-darkness. Soon he had succeeded in jamming the paper feed.

For a moment he wished Ford were at his side providing expert advice, and was surprised to find himself thinking of Ford in an almost affectionate way, as a fellow in common cause. How can you fail to feel for those who love what you love? Although Ford was not someone Warren would choose as a friend, there was nothing to belittle within his character. Warren reminded himself that even if he could win Nora, his victory would come at the expense of an admirable person; a person whose suffering would be keenly felt.

After burning his fingers on a hot surface within the feed mechanism, Warren finally got the Xerox running and had his copies made. He carried them down the dark corridor to the closet where his football jacket hung. Using duct tape, he secured the copies inside the back lining of the jacket so that, if necessary, he could walk out with them undetected. Warren then felt for the gun magazine in the inner pocket—the size of a cigarette pack, costing about fifteen dollars, good for killing about six people.

Deciding his brain was fried for the night, Warren got the .45 from his desk and put it in the jacket, too. Having both gun and clip together filled Warren with revulsion. He was tempted, then and there, to throw the gun out the window and be done with it forever. But the KD&H building, being contemporary, had no windows that opened (another invention of the modern architect who would not be caught dead in the kind of structure he lowered down on others). Sealed windows, droning ventilation, cold in the summer and hot in the winter. All the ambience of a chain motel, Warren thought. He stumbled back to his desk and fell asleep.

When the receptionist arrived to open the office she found Warren and woke him. Rather than fighting the inbound rush hour to get home and change clothes, he decided to force himself through the day as he was. There was a razor in the men's washroom that he used to shave. Watching himself shave, Warren wondered why Max Rademacher, with all his snooping, had not uncovered whatever caused the collapse—what should have been to his precise eye a glaring error.

The morning passed in a blur. Slightly before noon, Doug Denning buzzed Warren on the office intercom. Like most electronic devices the intercom had been designed to make the most unpleasant noise possible. Its buzz sounded like a loon in mortal agony. Telephone answering machines were the worst, pumping directly into your eardrum a sound only dogs ought to be able to hear. Why not a bell or chime? Warren supposed that such insidious devices were designed by a frustrated engineer whose heart had been broken by an unfaithful bassoonist—and who found his revenge by filling the world with grating, off-key squeals.

Denning asked Warren if he would "step in." Reclining in his high-backed chair, Denning gazed out the window toward the artificial pond and pressed his hands together in a V, elbows on the armrests.

"Warren, may I be totally frank and candid with you?" Denning asked, not looking at him. Totally frank and candid generally meant that the conversation would be even more circuitous than usual. Warren took a seat and prepared to doze off.

"In the science of business management there are certain overarching principles sublime in their defiance of detection by the layman," Denning began. "By layman I refer to the individual who naively views a business organization as people and/or persons involved in making a product for sale, rather than seeing the organization for what it really is, a matrix of throughput interactions. Are you following me so far?"

"Sure, Doug. Right with you." Whenever Denning started to ramble about management theories, even the other managers gazed out the window.

"I was confident you would, Warren. Let me preface myself by way of introduction. Last month my management horizons were considerably broadened when I attended a human resource potentiation seminar for top management personnel, held at the Aladdin Hotel in Las Vegas. Did you get a chance to read my summary memo?"

"I—I skimmed it. Mainly I remember—I thought the first paragraph was very good."

Denning perked up, turning back toward the room. "You really read it?" he asked. "I would be grateful if, when your schedule permits, you would critique it for me. Flow-counterflow conduits are the roaring rivers of throughput interaction, and even top-echelon mega-managers such as yourselves must—"

Denning stopped and reddened momentarily. "Sorry," he said. "I play the highlights of the seminar on my car tape deck while driving to work. Perhaps I have played the tape once too often and should resume my normal habit of listening to classical music or public affairs broadcasting. At any rate, what I meant to say is that even managers at the highest levels must not isolate themselves from feedback. Assuming feedback is properly structured, of course."

"Of course," Warren said.

Denning smiled. "You're following along so well. That

confirms my initial estimates of your management potential, and may I say how gratifying that is. Now then. Do you recall the principles of the Mega-Management Matrix?"

Luckily, Denning did not pause for an answer. He plunged ahead.

"Initialization, Activation, Co-Generation, and Elucidation. Each one scientifically quantified. Statistically, in the last month alone—" Denning held up his hand like a short-tempered traffic cop. An attractive woman in colored tights was jogging by the pond, and Denning appeared to enter a trance.

There were two glass jars on his desk, each containing polished glassy marbles. The proportions of the marbles varied daily, and Warren had never understood why the contents of these ornaments were in motion. When the vision of long legs disappeared, Denning took a marble from the right-hand jar and dropped it into the left. "A good day is about here," he said, indicating with his hand a third of a jar. Then, pointing almost to the top, "The all-time record. How I remember. It was a Thursday, and I was due downtown at a black-tie reception in honor of the mayor's nephew's parole. I knew I was close to the record but I had to leave by six and I thought, No way. Imagine my surprise when the aerobic dance class let out early and no fewer than—"

Denning caught himself. "But let's get directly to the point, shall we?" He cleared his throat. "I've been formulating the matrix of KD and H." Moving to the wall, Denning pulled the cord of a large roll-down chart. An incomprehensible jumble of boxes, lines, and arrows appeared, looking like the 1935 Pan American Airlines route structure map.

"The blue lines represent Initialization, the green lines Activation, the orange lines Co-Generation, and the yellow lines Elucidation," Denning explained, using a pointer. "You will note that there are no red lines on this chart. That is because the throughput process never stops." He rolled up the chart again before Warren had time to glean the slightest inkling of what he had been looking at.

"Do you realize," Denning said, "that when I first drew this matrix I was only able to assign myself eleven lines? After attending the seminar, I was able to find no fewer than thirty-seven. And the throughput transaction total for this office has risen sixteen-point-three percent in the last month alone. If that's not a productivity increase, I don't know what is."

Denning sat down again, satisfied. "My primary transactional responsibility within the management ultrastructure," he continued, "and one that I take great pride in, is interface actualization, as I think the chart clearly showed."

"You mean you talk with people," Warren said.

"Yes, exactly," Denning said, his face again lit with pleasure. "I talk with people. What a charming way to put it. I would venture that Dr. Ted Puissance, creator of the Mega-Management concept and author of the best-selling volume *Dominate Without Guilt*, would categorize you as having an advanced validator instinct. This is very key to success in large organizations."

Denning scribbled something on a legal pad, tore it off, and handed it across the desk. "If you haven't had a chance to read *Dominate Without Guilt*, here is a toll-free number you can call. It's also available on cassette. I'd loan you mine, but that would be a violation of copyright laws. Now, Warren." Denning paused. "May I be completely honest and open?"

This was going to take the entire lunch hour. Warren nodded in a drowsy haze. He might have thought that Denning was for some reason stalling on purpose had he not sat through such sessions before.

"I'll come straight to the point," Denning said. "While I am pleased to handle the interface throughputs for Kessey, Denning and Hobard, consulting engineers, that does not necessarily mean that every aspect of the job is to my liking. Nor should it be. As Dr. Puissance says, 'If you're happy in your work, what grounds do you have to demand a raise?' Sophisticated advice. Think about that, Warren, should you ever find yourself about to become happy."

Denning was fingering one of the marbles. "Some of the necessities of human resource potentiation are, to be utterly frank, less than ideal. For example, there is the backflow function for the non-actualized employee. Consider being a fifty-year-old man, or woman (should sex apply), and finding out after years of loyal service that you are non-actualized? It's hardly fun bearing that news, let me tell you. Then there is the shred function for your remnants of extralegal activities. . . ."

Denning's intercom light flashed once, then twice. He clicked the button without picking up the phone and his expression changed. "And then there is the offload function," he said. Denning looked directly at Warren, who, nearly asleep, groped to compose a comment.

"Well," Warren said. "I feel for you, Doug."

"Excellent!" Denning shot up out of his chair, visibly relieved. He came around the desk and began to shake Warren's hand with vigor. "The rational-empathy response you have shown is a very advanced one, very mature. Much more mature than the negative-outlash type response that is so common." He was walking Warren toward the door. "This again vindicates my confidence in you. As Dr. Puissance says, 'Invest in character. They aren't making any more of it.' " Denning opened the door and nearly shoved Warren through. "Do be sure to chat with Stacy on your way out. All the best."

Warren stood outside the door for a while, puzzled. Hobard appeared in the corridor, a dark man with enormous bushy eyebrows that seemed to cast his face in permanent shadow. Hobard apparently had not expected to see Warren still there. Stacy, Denning's secretary, was crouched behind her row of plastic plants.

After regarding the figure in his path Hobard said quickly, "You're a young man, Gifford. You'll land on your feet." With that he brushed past and into Denning's office, closing the door hard.

Stacy indicated a manila envelope on her desk. "Everybody feels just terrible about it," she said. "When this blows over we'll send you a big card or something."

Warren picked up the envelope. It was embossed with the logo of the company's law firm. Inside was severance pay and a notarized letter directing Warren to vacate the premises within ten minutes of being informed of his dismissal. KD&H had obtained a court order forbidding him to clean out his desk, or even re-enter his office. The letter promised that within seventy-two hours his office would be "inspected by a neutral third party acceptable to the courts" and that "personal effects of the afore-mentioned will be approved for returnment by the fastest available surface carrier." *Returnment?* In addition, there was a release that Warren was asked to read carefully and sign in the presence of a witness. Without looking at the release he tore it up.

Quickly walking to his office, Warren found the door padlocked from the outside. Installation of the lock must have begun the moment he "stepped in" with Denning. The drafting room was deserted: the other engineers had by the strangest coincidence all gone to lunch simultaneously. They must have known in advance. Max was not in his office, either, though normally he wouldn't leave the building during working hours unless it was on fire.

Warren ran to the coat closet. His jacket, taped full of photocopies, hung undisturbed. He put it on and zipped the front securely. The jacket felt heavy; Warren remembered there was a gun in the inner pocket. They certainly weren't expecting that, he thought. He was sorely tempted to burst back into Denning's office waving the .45 and shouting, "Call Dr. Puissance. I feel a negative-outlash type reaction coming on."

Instead he left the KD&H building quietly. Warren went back to his apartment and made several attempts to contact Max, dialing his direct number. Usually Max answered his own phone; this time a secretary picked up. By early evening Warren had grown weary. He turned on his answering machine and went to bed.

Only in his dreamy, pre-sleep state did Warren realize he had forgotten to make copies of the most carefully guarded documents at the office—the contract histories that Hobard insisted on storing in his personal safe.

In the morning Warren went to the district attorney and offered to cooperate in the investigation. The assistant D.A. to whom he spoke seemed puzzled, several times asking Warren if he had a lawyer and warning him against certain types of statements. Finally, he buzzed his secretary for a copy of the morning paper.

"I am now convinced you have not seen this," he said, handing Warren the front page.

A headline declaimed, COLLAPSE LAID TO DESIGN FLAW. Defendants Kessey, Denning & Hobard yesterday fired a project engineer allegedly responsible for the tragedy, the newspaper account stated. Defendants were claiming to have in their possession an unauthorized memo from the engineer directing that the pace of construction be accelerated "regardless of complications which may arise." This memo, the story said, was not actually signed by the engineer but, rather, initialed "for W.G." by a typist. Lawyers for KD&H told the paper the memo was unsigned because the engineer had dictated it over the telephone while being absent without leave.

In addition, the article said, KD&H had released to the press photocopies of memoranda from nationally known engineering expert Alvin Rademacher instructing the project engineer to employ a large safety factor in the design "no matter the delay or expense." Attempts to contact Gifford for comment were unsuccessful.

There had never been any such memos from Max. For the first time in his life Warren felt truly shocked. This was simple betrayal. Then, on a jump page inside the newspaper, he noticed a small box connected to the main story. It said:

> The civil engineering firm of Kessey, Denning & Hobard yesterday announced that it had changed its name to Kessey, Rademacher, Denning & Hobard. A spokesman for the firm said this change had been planned for some time and was unrelated to yesterday's developments. "This merely reflects our feeling that Alvin Rademacher is one of the country's most prominent engineers, and should be rewarded as such," said a statement issued by P. Emerson Kessey, the company's founder.

For weeks Warren did little more than pace. The company was refusing to say exactly what he was supposed to have done to cause the collapse; Warren poured over the blueprints and calculations almost obsessively, always failing to find any flaw. Actual litigation of the case would be months, more likely years, away. Warren did not know if he was guilty or innocent. And did not know when he would know.

Time and again he tried to summon the courage to contact Nora, as well as the wisdom to know what to say. In the fog of confusion, dead-end streets can seem like highways, and Warren went down one: he vowed not to contact her again unless and until his name was cleared, no matter how long that might take. Whatever current of coincidence or destiny, love or illusion, in which they were caught, it would have to carry them until then.

One day while Warren was out Nora called, leaving a message on his answering machine. "I know I asked for time, but this is ridiculous," she said. Her voice was chipper.

Hearing her voice and remembering Nora's father, Warren felt himself a greater traitor than Max. He became so fearful of answering the phone, discovering her on the other end, and having to tell her what had happened, that he began leaving the answering machine on even when he was at home.

A few days later another message came from Nora, this one wary. Then a third, tense. "I know you're in that box somewhere," she said. "Please call. I have news."

Finally, Warren sent a brief, ambiguously worded note saying there was a temporary difficulty he couldn't discuss and that he would be in touch. On the day the letter would have been delivered his phone rang repeatedly. Each time, when the recording began to whirl, the caller hung up.

After a while the messages from Nora stopped. Warren took the tape that had her voice on it out of the machine and kept it on the nightstand by his bed.

10

UP FROM PREGNANCY

For several months during the period in which Warren withdrew from contact with Nora, and nearly all human contact as well, the Azimuth newsletters stopped. Warren had come to enjoy these strange missives. Their unexplained cessation made him feel still further cut off from his fellow creatures.

One day a postcard arrived saying that publication had been suspended while the Collective formed a subsidiary to market software for financial management and inventory control. Later, another card came, announcing that the financial management subsidiary had gone bankrupt. Holistic spreadsheet programs were being offered for a closeout price of fifteen dollars per disk in order to clear the overstocked warehouse.

Then the newsletters resumed. The next one said:

THROUGH HISTORY MEN HAVE DOMINATED WOMEN BECAUSE MEN ARE PHYSICALLY SUPERIOR.
NOT IN STRENGTH, BUT IN NEVER BEING PREGNANT.
Until this 20th century, non-pregnancy has been the single most important physical asset an adult individual could possess. Height and strength, even in barbarian times, have been by comparison subordinate.
Since throughout the development of human social organization all men possessed the asset of non-pregnancy continuously, while only some women possessed it and then only on some occasions, it was inevitable that men would achieve a dominant position. Just as it is equally inevitable, now that non-pregnancy is accessible to women, that the favored position of the male will vanish.
How rapidly we forget even central facts of daily life! Some aspect of pregnancy—being pregnant, recovering from birth,

197

becoming pregnant again, caring for infants—had before our
turn of the page been the normal status for most of the world's
women from their late teens till late maturity. Today, in the
technological nations, the cycle of pregnancy has all but halted.
And though in the technological nations some poor girls *start*
the cycle by having babies in their teens, they don't *stay*
pregnant through their adult lives, an essential difference.

This new circumstance should not be ascribed mainly to birth
control, although that is an important influence. Nor is it due to
smaller families, though they matter, too. There is a greater
consideration. In the past, women were pregnant over and over
again because they had to make several attempts at a baby for
every one child who survived to adulthood.

Take note that painters during the Middle Ages seldom
depicted infants or little children, except the baby Jesus, who
was shown as a kind of miniaturized adult. In the rare portraits
from the Middle Ages that depict mother and infant together,
the subjects regard each other not lovingly but with an air of
remote abstraction. Writers of the same period had little to say
about rug rats. Even chroniclers of royal houses usually noted
the birth of children only if the child was an heir who would do
his part to perpetuate political strife. When youths appear in art
and literature of the Middle Ages, they seem to materialize in
their early teens, as though they just arrived on a train.

Yet babies, then, were a far more integral element of daily
life than they are today. Why are they *less* represented in art,
rather than more—today's art being full of complex thoughts
about the kids? Because intense emotional attachment to the
young is, in the scheme of things, a recent innovation.

The reason babies of yore were paid so little regard is that
few of them lived. Body chemistry might dictate protective
impulses, but many men and women thought it foolhardy to
invest the higher cultivated emotions in a creature that was
odds-on to die before it spoke.

As recently as 1900, 15 percent of the babies born in Western
Europe and North America died before the end of their first
year of life. The tenor Enrico Caruso, born 1873, was his

mother's eighteenth child—and her first to survive infancy. Statistics for the middle centuries are harder to come by, but it is believed fewer than half of those babies born live made it to adolescence; the incidence of miscarriage and stillbirth was also far higher.

Infant death underpinned the cycle of pregnancy. Many if not most women became pregnant as soon as they were capable of doing so, and stayed that way as long as they could, to increase their chances of having a few children reach adulthood. Since then, as now, the prime childbearing years coincided with the period during which people established their livelihoods and social positions, women were rendered physically disadvantaged just when it counted most. Even if social convention had allowed it, the majority of women could not have devoted themselves to what we now call careers—except part-time, in a weakened condition, which a non-pregnant man, other things being equal, could easily best.

How else could males have so effectively organized society to the detriment of half its members? Physical strength was hardly the deciding factor. The evidence of that is simple: from early on men who lacked physical strength played focal roles in society.

Socrates and Pythagoras did not pump iron. Alexander, a frail boy whose sickly body expired at age thirty-three, conquered the world. While most men are strong compared to most women, most men are weak compared to the minority of men with natural athletic talent.

So from the morning hours of history there was agitation—on the part of *men*, the majority of whom would be miserable if society were based solely on muscle and force—to create categories of life in which strength did not count. By the time of Socrates many such categories existed and were accorded importance: scholar, philosopher, priest, politician, mathematician. As human societies developed, inventors and engineers built machines which narrowed the gap between weak and strong.

Now if strength was never really essential to social

superiority, how did men enforce their claim? By not being pregnant.

Alexander and Pythagoras may have been weaklings, but neither was ever knocked up. It is often put forth that nothing physical made a man more likely than a woman to be a good scholar or scientist, and so the fact that most of the scholars and scientists through history have been male demonstrates sexist bias even in these supposedly rational callings. But until recently, something physical *did* in fact make males more likely than females to be good scholars or scientists. Males were not sidetracked by making babies.

Or by death. The velocity of medical advances has made us forget that even in our grandmothers' day, when a woman became pregnant she took her life into her hands. Victorian literature brims over with characters tormented by the death of wife, sister, or mother in childbirth. This is more than literary artifact: death caused by pregnancy was a common sorrow of the time. Today when contemplating pregnancy a woman thinks mainly of timing, comfort, and economics. She rarely wonders whether she will survive the experience—which was the foremost question on the minds of nearly all the women who have come before.

In many societies a woman's risk of death through pregnancy was greater than a man's risk of death through combat. Looking back on the red river of time it seems as though warfare has been constant, but numerically speaking, the majority of men who have lived have passed their lives without serving in an army. When peace prevailed, the danger to men ceased, but women continued to die for the cause of pregnancy. Some cultures allowed upper-class men to buy their way out of military service. Upper-class women could not buy their way out of pregnancy: nurses might do the rearing, but the bearing there was no evading.

During the prehistorical period of *Homo sapiens*, when incipient cultural dispositions were being forged among tribes, those who might have stood up for the interests of women were not physically able to do so. At that time the demands and health complications of childbearing were pitiless, rendering women indentured to men before the arguments on social organization even started. Considering that, as time progressed, almost every woman, poor or privileged, remained to some degree in thrall to the production of babies, it is not surprising that the notion of female inferiority came to permeate many cultures and lands.

And because, through the millennia, there was no alternative to the cycle of pregnancy if human life was to continue—usually even educated women endorsed some acceptance of childbearing duty—it is not surprising that men came to treat female inferiority as a proclamation of nature. Strictly speaking, it was.

Very early in the game men must have sensed that the advantages of big biceps simply were not going to last. Science wouldn't stand for it. But no development (or so they thought) could alter the relationship between pregnancy and non-pregnancy the way pulleys altered the relationship between arms and lifting. Women would always be stuck and men would always be exempt.

Imprisonment by pregnancy was complicated by the biological structure of *Homo sapiens.* Childbearing pains and responsibilities fall much more heavily on women than on females of other species. The female lion runs at full speed the day before birth, delivers without assistance, and lends only incidental care to the cub. In nature, females can be found as leaders of packs of socialized animals, such as chimpanzees, and some animals such as llamas organize their social structures as matriarchies. This occurs despite the fact that the female leaders almost always have less physical strength than their male followers, and it suggests two pertinent insights.

First, and disturbingly, the drive for dominance of one creature over another may be more deeply seated in the living psyche than sexual bias, and thus more difficult to eradicate. Second, because female animals were not subjected to the extended debilitation during pregnancy that afflicted female humans, their physical inferiority could more easily be compensated for by mental agility and leadership potential. Thus women seeking to influence human socialization, especially in the formative stages, were at a greater relative disadvantage than female chimps seeking peace from male chimps, and so on.

For a variety of reasons including the size of the human child in relation to the mother's size (the human fetus at birth is about five percent the pre-pregnancy weight of the mother, whereas in most animals the birth weight is less than one percent of the mother's pre-pregnancy weight) and the largeness of the infant head in relation to the birth canal, the degree of debilitation experienced by women during pregnancy, as well as the pain during labor, is unique in nature. And needless to say, the duration of care human females must give their children is without parallel in the animal kingdom, even discounting for our longer lifespans.

Babies, by the way, have more than one thing to do with sex. From an evolutionary standpoint, sex was made pleasant so that dumb animals would do it and thereby propagate their kind. We humans should be eternally thankful that this biological contrivance was passed along to us, since, unlike animals, we do not require it.

If lovemaking conveyed no sensual rewards, people, having intellect, would still force themselves to engage in it for reproductive reasons—as they force themselves to engage in many unpleasant activities, such as work, that are necessary to sustain the flow of life. A human physiology in which there is no pleasure or joy attached to sex is not impossible to imagine, especially for anyone who has ever dated an Ivy League coed. Of related interest here is that *Homo sapiens* is the only mammal adapted for lovemaking year round, or physically arranged for continuous sexual attraction. Women, unique among animals, have visible breasts even when not nursing, to remind males of their sexuality. And whether or not *Cosmopolitan* subscribers believe it, men have larger reproductive organs (relative to body size) than any other mammal, hence to remind females of the same consideration.

We must conclude from this that men and women were deliberately designed to savor frequent intimacy for reasons other than procreation—pleasure, and the incubation of human love. This bedevils the far-fundamentalist and far-feminist fringes, who see only the abuses of those trusts. What we ought to ask ourselves, though, is why we inherited such beautiful adjuncts to love, when biologically we did not require them. They are gifts. Gifts from a friend.

At last, today, the tyranny of female biology is broken. Birth control makes pregnancy itself subject to regulation. Medicine has rendered childbearing almost free of serious risk, and found ways to sustain nearly all babies. By the 1980s, only 1.3 percent of babies born live in the United States failed to reach their first year; in some countries the percentage was lower still. The death of a pink, breathing infant has taken on a sense of tragedy bordering on catastrophe. What was once typical now seems incomprehensible.

All of which raises a vital question. You knew it would!

Was the huge disparity in childbearing obligation between men and women, ultimate source of so much prejudice and repression, an inevitability? Or was it one of nature's errors left for us and God to correct?

Proclamations of nature have been repealed before. And more will be repealed in the future. With the cycle of pregnancy routed, all the prejudices that sprang from it have lost their foundations, and the illogic based on it lies exposed. It is not hard to foresee a future in which arguments over the status of women have been reduced to the category of historical footnotes.

In fact, it is not hard to foresee that woman's ability to create living beings, form families, and experience a range of empathetic maternal emotions denied to men will eventually lead to a general assumption that it is men who are physically inferior.

Laugh while you can. Azimuth Collective is giving 10 to 1 odds that this happens by the end of the third millennium A.D., perhaps sooner. Technology will see to it, as genetic engineering solves or at least alleviates the unpleasant side effects of pregnancy, such as labor pain.

Then, inevitably—unless true bliss is realized and society purges itself of prejudice entirely—women will come to dominate government, business, academe, and the rest. History will have performed another of its celebrated reversals. And the next task will be to correct *that* foul-up of nature by extending the power of childbearing to men.

These latter prospects are too remote to concern us here, although not as remote as might be presumed. Azimuth further offers a standing 5 to 1 wager that any prediction made in its newsletter will be realized in less than one-half the time estimated by Azimuth methodologists themselves. (Please, please, do not write in to remind us that we failed to short energy stocks after predicting that the oil shortage was a passing fad.) What is of concern here is that emancipation from pregnancy both expands women's possibilities and takes away their excuses.

No longer will women simply lose themselves in babies, regretting and then forgetting the things they will never be able to try.

Now there are twice as many people who have to figure out what the hell to do with their lives.

—11—

No further word came from Nora.

Just legal notifications, polite threats, and warnings. Several times per week Warren would have to meet the postman downstairs to sign for letters sent return receipt, officially informing him of things he already knew.

Warren tried calling Max without success; his home number had been changed and was unlisted. Warren studied the blueprints tirelessly and could find nothing. They seemed *fine.* He studied Nora's letter and each time felt less hope. Never, never could he come to her like this. If she still had an opening in her heart, he could approach her only as an innocent. And Warren did not know if he was.

There was a practical consideration Warren could not evade: he needed a lawyer. A friend of Tommy Camero's who practiced securities law gave Warren general legal advice for a time, and accompanied him during a few discussions with the district attorney's office. The D.A., whose ultimate target was the construction firm of Berns and Sons, which had ties to the mayor, offered to grant Warren immunity from prosecution in return for his cooperation. Warren refused. Immunity was accepted only by the guilty who were getting off.

"If I really am guilty I will admit it," he said, thinking, I will do more. "But I may be blameless. If so I want my innocence back."

"Don't we all," the D.A.'s assistant had said.

Fighting the case meant Warren would need a criminal defense attorney. Unemployed, he could not afford competent counsel. Without a good lawyer he might go to jail and would surely never achieve the proof of innocence—acquittal or dismissed charges—he felt he needed to approach Nora again.

Warren knew one person with money to burn: Jewel Wonigan. The only sensible thing to do was ask her. They had not
spoken since her wedding. Warren had been unable to attend
because the ceremony was in New York and at the time he was
in rural California, working as a walk-on hire for a consulting
company that was well into the fifth year of a planned ninety-day
study of a proposed irrigation canal. Arriving on the job he
discovered that for two years the company had done nothing but
study the need for further study. Its conclusion? Too soon to tell.

There were no hard feelings between Warren and Jewel because both had known from the start that their relationship, like
many youthful involvements, was based mainly on a mutual desire for good boffing. In the odd way that two people sometimes
do, Warren and Jewel had complemented each other physically,
and neither could resist the other's presence. Jewel was sex-
crazed in an endearing, almost goofy fashion; she wanted sex
constantly, and Warren was sure he was not the first man to
benefit. Or more precisely put, she wanted the action of sex
constantly, not necessarily the attainment. Jewel would suggest
forms of exotic play that Warren would never dream of letting
past the realm of abstract fantasy. Then, trussed up in straps and
buckles, she would suddenly burst out laughing, or want to talk
politics.

Steeling himself, Warren called Jewel. The call went too well:
she insisted he come visit, an added financial strain. On the
phone Warren made clear that his purpose was to ask for money,
and Jewel sounded enthusiastic nonetheless. She had, it occurred
to him in retrospect, always possessed a higher opinion of events
in the distance than of those within view. She would eagerly
propose a weekend trip and talk and talk about how wonderful
it was going to be, until the moment to leave actually came. Then
she would drag herself through it, her mood brightening only
when talk turned to what they might do some other weekend.

Her great-grandfather, Albert Wonigan, had made a fortune
during the Gilded Age with a patented coupler for railroad cars.
His children branched out into batch-iron casting. Their children
sold off the rail and foundry operations to start a diversified

holding company with interests in theme-park packaging, dairy-cow leasing, television character tie-ins, pension-fund management, rock-group-figurine licensing, grain speculation, logo test-marketing, airline menu development, real-estate-trust administration, Medicare claims processing, salvage consortiums, Japanese champagne distributorships, anti-terrorist training for corporate chauffeurs, and limited tax partnerships to help professional athletes depreciate their own lives. The firm, rechristened International Diversified, or ID/Corp., was considered a business-school success story.

This change in corporate identity had had the fortunate side effect of allowing Jewel to live her life in privacy, her last name unrecognizable except to the most dedicated students of accumulation. Warren himself had learned of her circumstances only after they had dated many times.

One morning after a date Jewel had been leafing through the paper. Normally she read only the news and lifestyle sections, but that day she had lingered over the sports and teased, "I could get us tickets to the Lakers game tonight." Then she disclosed that ID/Corp. owned fifty-eight percent of the Lakers' starting back court, plus the entire coaching staff of the visiting team.

Warren had had mixed feelings about this revelation. He distrusted wealth, yet was charmed that Jewel seemed more pleased by her access to free tickets than with the millions in assets available to her. Once Warren knew her secret, Jewel went out of her way, on many occasions, to condemn the repulsive nature of capitalism.

Over the phone, Warren learned that Jewel and her husband, Randall Levine, lived in upper Manhattan—close, but not too close, to Columbia University. He was surprised to hear Randall had recently quit his teaching post in Columbia's Department of Revisionism in order to enroll in law school. A professorship at Columbia sounded like the kind of job people killed for.

"Didn't he like teaching?" Warren asked.

"That had nothing to do with it," Jewel said. "He was insulted by the money. You can't live in New York on what they were paying."

Perhaps that was true, but Warren was puzzled as to why it should matter, recalling that, in addition to Jewel's inheritance, Randall Levine had family money too.

"It's a matter of self-respect," Jewel said. "This is the eighties. Randall needs to be able to call himself a lawyer."

New York. Where all the men act gay, and all the women act like normal men. The buzz of skyscrapers, artists, and ambition. If you were kidnapped and flown around the world blindfolded and then shoved out of the plane above New York, you would know where you were before you hit the ground.

To Warren the vibration of New York City was so palpable he thought it should be possible to build instruments to detect the city's pulse scientifically. Then New York buzz could be re-created under laboratory conditions and analyzed. Perhaps it had something to do with the arrangement of skyscrapers creating a tuning fork effect out of the echoes of obscenities shouted on Manhattan streets. Whatever the source, once mastered the vibration could be amplified and used as a weapon. Trained on Russian troops in the heat of battle, pure New York buzz would make them throw down their arms, overcome by a sudden desire to complain and eat.

Approaching New York from the air, Warren marveled at the sheer brown stretch of it: a machine so large that there was no point from which the whole—assembled over three hundred years by millions of persons using billions of pieces—could be seen. At any given moment there were more gears turning in New York, more valves opening and closing, more pistons slamming up and down at the insistence of exploding fuel, more electrical impulses coursing through wires and switches, than could, for all intents and purposes, be counted.

This was literally true, Warren thought, and it said something about the nature of knowledge. Though each individual mechanical device in New York City had a finite location and could be observed, it was simply not possible to produce an exact inventory of them, even if nearly unlimited resources and personnel were assigned to the task. By the time an army of canvassers starting at the top of Manhattan island reached midtown, all their information about the top would be obsolete.

If that was true of a single city, what chance was there to get an exact grasp of the universe, even if you had fantastic powers? And the people! Imagine trying to get a complete understanding of what every one of New York's seven million residents thought on just one topic. Devoting the entire Gross National Product to this task would be insufficient. To do the same for all the residents of the globe . . . plus who knows how many more globes . . .

New Yorkers harp on how poorly their city works, but to Warren it seemed a miracle that the city ran at all. The human body was the only device he knew of that rivaled New York in complexity. As the plane banked to land, Warren tried to pick out a single building and focus on it, visualizing how many parts were inside that part of New York (elevators, kitchen appliances, clothes); how many other parts functioning at a distance were necessary to sustain it (power plants, water filtration, sewage treatment, factories the world over, Home Box Office); and how many parts within the part were designed to neutralize the effects of other nearby parts. The effect was one of machines layered on machines to form a vast machine that was itself merely a cog. Gravity spread into the primordial void making it curve; America spread into the wilderness making it hum and whir.

At Kennedy Airport, Warren took the shuttle bus to the inbound subway. Several riders were attempting to converse, shouting through the din that enclosed the train. Paris made its subways quiet by equipping the cars with rubber wheels. As his train lurched from side to side Warren wondered if the wheels on New York subways were even round.

Suddenly, power in the line died, dropping the train into a silent glide. For a moment the conversations could be clearly heard.

In the darkness, words floated by about repairing a motorcycle; about Eddie goddamn it this is the hundredth time; about I always get my fish there; about you loved me once, why is it different now? When the power came on again and the train snapped back to full motion, Warren looked around, trying to connect the speakers with their words. Though he picked out Eddie sulking by the forward door, he could not locate the faltering lovers.

Getting off at the wrong stop, Warren walked for a while, became lost, and decided to hail a cab. He was hoping the driver would be a colorful, cigar-chomping, lifelong New Yorker who would make quotable remarks about life, politics, and entertainment, then wind up by telling a memorable anecdote. From the frequency with which cab drivers appear in the news about New York, Warren had thought that knowledge of anecdotes was a section of the medallion license exam. (4. Complete this sentence: Three Jewish mothers go into a deli _____.) The driver turned out to be a Nigerian who didn't speak at all.

Cabs, Warren knew, were the second most important topic of conversation among the professional classes of New York, trailing only the perennial debate over whose apartment was most overpriced. The papers ran five articles about the shocking inadequacy of cab service—the scandalous circumstance that drivers did not have graduate degrees in English literature; the appalling lack of inertial guidance systems—for each article about drug violence in the South Bronx. Cabs merited such concern because they were one of the few elements of city life that the Manhattan professional class could not control. No matter how highly a New Yorker regarded himself in comparison to mundane denizens of remote egg-farming regions, he still had to submit to the indignity of jumping about like a lunatic in order to get a cab.

Warren arrived at Jewel's building, a brownstone with soot-caked walls and smeary windows. Garbage was strewn around the steps. The elevator was coated a blinding shade of international orange—probably the color on sale the day it had been painted. Carpets in the halls showed stains and cigarette burns. Warren was surprised that Jewel, given her resources, would live in a tenement.

When Jewel finished disarming a series of security devices and opened the door to her apartment, Warren beheld an immaculately decorated modern home with brass spiral staircases, two fireplaces, walnut furniture, and entire walls hand painted in thick fountain strokes of primary color. There was also a bathroom with sauna and whirlpool and a library Theodore Roosevelt would have envied. Deflecting Warren's compliments, Jewel noted that many apartments in her building were similarly impressive. When he asked why they didn't spruce up the exterior, Jewel responded with a perplexed look, indicating she did not understand what he was talking about.

They sat awhile talking through old times. Jewel was a tall, sometimes clumsy woman who alternated between making a stunning impression and bumping into tables like a nitwit: she never seemed fully conscious of where her arms were. She had taken a job with Columbia's community services division, which she tried to explain her responsibilities in a burst of social-work jargon Warren could not follow—something to do with "facilitation." She was also auditing courses at several schools, and thinking of getting a degree in business administration.

Jewel went on to say that they were to meet Randall and some friends at ten P.M. for a late supper. Eyes alight with anticipation, she ran down the list: "I planned this all out myself. First there's Dennis Milton. He's in law school with Randall. He comes on as very gay, but he's not, really. He only pretends to be gay in order to seem better educated.

"Then there's LaSonia Trescott, also Columbia law. She's black, from Philadelphia, so I'm hoping to set her up with Corby Thompson. Corby is from Philadelphia, Main Line old money, blue eyes, a free-lance producer for PBS. Black women always go for straight Wasps with blue eyes.

"Corby will be coming with Janet Simpson. She's Jewish. They live together. Straight Wasps go for Jewish girls, at least up till marriage. For Janet I've invited Ken Morris. Ken is black. Jewish girls always go for a black man, especially one with a long"— Jewel paused and winked knowingly—"with a long view of the great issues of our day. Ken is very respectable. He just graduated Columbia law and got a job with Mudge, Rose, one of the best Wall Street firms. I can't tell you what a treat for womanhood a respectable, well-hung black man represents.

"Now don't worry about Corby and Janet arriving at the same time. They live together but date other people.

"Janet has a foundation grant to write a biography of a biographer, and Corby has another grant to make a documentary of her psychological responses to her own work. He films her taping other people for oral histories, and last week he filmed every minute of her day, all twenty-four hours, including filming the two of them while they slept, using an infrared lens. Corby may have his Minicam with him and insist on recording Janet's play for Ken. I forgot to tell him not to bring it.

"Also Paul Baxter will be there. He's a law professor at Columbia and nobody really knows anything about him, except that he's Jewish and has his shirts made in London. The only classic flirting combination we will not be observing tonight is Jewish man/Catholic woman. There wasn't time to find a Catholic for Paul. It's just as well. His shirts are the best thing about him."

This brought the guest list to a close. Supper being hours away, Warren started to explain the purpose of his visit. Jewel interrupted.

"We'll discuss that tomorrow at lunch. I only talk business when I'm eating. Let's go to a movie!"

Flipping through the paper, Jewel decided she wanted to see the Ingmar Bergman movie *Fanny and Alexander.* Warren thought it would be depressing, but she assured him it wasn't the usual Bergman: *"The New Yorker* called it 'festive,' " she said.

Truth be told, though, Jewel liked depressing movies, and violent movies best of all. During the slasher-movie fad Jewel had gone to see nearly every new release. Once she dragged Warren along. In the basic structure of a slasher movie the victim, usually a pretty young girl, is terrorized at length; reduced to whimpering and tears; stripped of her clothes; almost allowed to escape; then graphically butchered in stylized close-up. Jewel contended that this was a legitimate metaphor for the modern condition.

As they watched the film, *Slaughter Sorority,* a deliciously built coed, sobbing and pleading, was stalked in the basement of a field house. Through plot connivance, her blouse and bra were peeled off. Cutaway flashes of an open exit and happy people on the street were shown.

The camera swung forward to show the girl making her break for the exit and as it did, Warren heard Jewel exclaim under her breath, "Get her!" Then the mad slasher, his face hidden beneath a deep-sea diver's helmet, jumped out of a closet. He grabbed the screaming girl from behind, pressed a spear gun against her back, and fired it. In hideous slow motion the spear head burst through one naked breast as the slasher grabbed the other breast and twisted the nipple. Jewel let out a squeal. For no apparent reason, the sequence of grabbing and bursting bloody spear was replayed three times. That night, Jewel was insatiable.

For a long time Warren thought this incident meant there was something seriously wrong with Jewel. Yet she never showed any violent inclination in her own behavior. The thought of spanking a dog horrified her.

When pressed, Jewel would say that sadistic violence in film was merely "realism." She wouldn't go to horror movies—monsters from the deep, that sort of stuff—because monsters weren't "real." Realism is a favorite studio rationalization, although there is hardly a thing realistic about slasher movies—other than the willingness of people to do anything for money. A good working estimate is that more crazed serial killings are depicted on television and in the movies in any given year than have actually occurred during the last decade.

Warren suspected that Jewel liked violent movies because they were full of passions. Negative passions to be sure, passions of psychosis and agony, but passions nonetheless. In the elite world where Jewel dwelled, positive passions like love and loyalty were so sneered at that those longing to feel their hearts skip a beat had to seek their release in negative passions like voyeuristic sadism.

A clue to this was that Jewel also often accompanied her mother to matinees of weepers, those searing sagas of lost longing beloved by pubescent girls. They were full of passions too —silly passions in this case, but passions nonetheless. Jewel took her weepers on the sly. If any of her smart-set Manhattan friends found out, she used her mother as an excuse. On the other hand, Jewel freely admitted to being a fan of slasher movies, urging her friends to come along. Many did, delighting in the very worst manifestation of American pop culture.

They went to a midtown movie house where *Fanny and Alexander* was playing alongside a six-part French documentary and one of the *Stars Wars* episodes. Someday, Warren thought, children will think *Richard III* is a sequel in the *Richard* series.

People in the movie line were wearing hooded parkas or quilted down coats that extended to the knee, though the temperature was mild. Several were reading print-heavy publications Warren did not recognize. Making conversation, Jewel asked Warren if he had read *The New York Times Magazine* cover story about the vast changes sweeping over China. Then she laughed and apologized for being too provincial. By the time the line had begun moving she had scoffed at a *New York Review of Books* article, complained about a *Village Voice* theater review that wasn't negative enough, and protested a morally inexact position the city zoning commission had taken in its white paper on Central America.

After watching the movie for a while Warren went to get popcorn. He lingered at the door to one of the other theaters, refreshing himself with the sound of spaceships blowing up. *Star Wars*-type movies "killed" a hundred times more people than slasher flicks. They just died offstage, without the graphic glee. Warren wondered whether it was worse to depict violence as an art form or a team sport.

By the time he slipped back into the Bergman movie, the female lead was pacing around the bier of her dead husband, wailing at ear-splitting volume. Dim gray snowscapes followed. "I thought *The New Yorker* called this movie 'festive,'" he whispered to Jewel.

"Compared to *The New Yorker*, it is festive," she replied.

Soon the evil pastor was introduced into the movie's plot, and the mother and the two title characters imprisoned. This was the first really depressing development—the husband's death, though sad, had come at the end of a full life—and it increased Jewel's interest. Each time the evil pastor staged some depraved stunt the camera would zoom in on a cross. When Warren tried to make *sotto voce* comments, Jewel shushed him. After a while he fell into a daydream and Jewel, who saw his head dip forward, did not wake him, glad to be spared further distractions.

In his daydream Warren imagined that the *Star Wars* movie attacked the Ingmar Bergman movie. A spaceship flew into the reverend's castle stronghold. Luke Skywalker and Han Solo emerged to rescue the children, dispatch the pastor with buzzing laser swords, and set neutron detonators around the guilt-shield generator that protected psychological pretensions. They made the jump into hyperspace just as all of nineteenth-century Stockholm exploded in a dazzling fireball.

When the movie ended Jewel and Warren went to a café to meet Randall and the others. Jewel warned—in the fashion one warns not to pay attention to Aunt Pearl, who's fuzzy as a peach —that some of Randall's friends were conservatives. With the lawyer glut preventing a juris doctor degree from being an automatic ticket to affluence, she explained, even students at Establishment liberal institutions like Columbia were breathing fire in order to increase their chances of corporate employment.

"Don't take anything they say too seriously," Jewel advised. "The pendulum will swing back. Besides they don't believe it one way or the other. It's just debating points."

The Levine party had commandeered a back corner of the café, where they had pushed a number of tables together. They were all talking at once, gesturing in the air like semaphore officers. The waitress was not pleased when she saw Warren and Jewel arrive, making the party even larger. Large groups demand extra attention and then leave small tips, each member of the party finding it convenient to assume others will take care of the common problem, the way the rich view charity.

"We ate already," Randall called out in lieu of greeting. He was seated at the head of the table, a master of ceremonies. "What kept you? You walk or something?"

"It was a long movie. I would like you to meet—"

"Pleasure," he said, not waiting for the name, then went around the table giving names and identifications as fast as he could say them. There was an extra guest Jewel hadn't expected, a red-haired law clerk named Maureen. "What luck," Jewel whispered to Warren. "She's obviously Catholic. Watch Paul Baxter close in on her."

Randall cleared spaces at the table and motioned for Warren and Jewel to sit together as though they were dates. He paid little attention to either of them. The group was drinking Bass Ale from a pitcher; Randall waved impatiently for more glasses. Jewel, pouring, spilled ale all over her pants and on one of the law students, who continued arguing without interruption. They were debating whether McCarthy had been worse than the Rosenbergs.

"—couldn't happen in a truly free society—"

"—small price to pay for the preservation of—"

"—Alger Hiss was clearly—"

"—Whittaker Chambers was unquestionably—"

"—the most heinous, unconscionable, utterly contemptible —"

"—the vilest and most pervasive—"

Warren found it impossible to follow who was taking which side. To him, rehashing the McCarthy–Rosenberg question seemed about as useful as debating whether it was worse to die of pneumonia or influenza.

But here was the unslayable dragon of Left-Right mythology. As each side felt that Joe McCarthy or Julius Rosenberg proved the worst about the other side, the case was preserved with special affection by both. Besides, being locked in the past, it made perfect debate material—the issue could never be resolved. Estimating the present exposes the speaker to criticism, should his estimates be proved wrong; analyzing the past requires only criticism of others.

"—deliberate campaign of calculated—"

"—deceitful ploys and cynical manipulation of—"

Thinking it proper manners that he try to join the conversation, Warren asked if the sins of both sides during this period didn't roughly cancel each other out and wasn't it time to move on to other issues?

A wall of silence descended. For a moment the law students leaned forward and regarded Warren with amazement, as though he had burst into a rendition of the Yugoslavian national anthem. Then the debate picked up at full pitch where it had left off.

"—shocking abuse of public—"

"—outrageous appropriation of constitutional—"

It occurred to Warren that cases like McCarthy or the Rosenbergs refused to go away because they possessed an increasingly rare quality, a clear ideological spin.

America is a hybrid country, neither capitalist nor socialist, where corporations demand subsidies and Marxists gripe about taxes on the sale of their books. American voters want ringing speeches about self-reliance but also increased Social Security benefits; drastic budget cuts in everybody else's bloated programs, but more spending on theirs. Government officials accommodate them by changing stripes almost daily. Just as, Warren felt, they usually should. Pragmatism—the understanding that effective compromises are better than theoretical tirades —has been the American national trump card. But as usual, what's good for the country is bad for the ideologist. Pragmatism interrupts the assigning of blame, which is the ideologist's prime concern.

There was a cessation of the Left-Right debate, followed by a debate about apartments and cabs that Warren couldn't quite catch. Randall Levine, who had hardly spoken to his wife, seemed deep in conversation with Maureen, the Catholic. Ken Morris said loudly to someone, "All right then, what was *your* favorite war?"

Jewel was straining for a look at a distant blackboard on which the day's menu was written in eye-test-sized letters. Farther down the table someone was declaiming, "I see no reason why we should fund cancer research. If medical advances can't pay for themselves on a user-fee basis, then they fail the market test."

Jewel whispered, "Can you see which of the specials comes with French fries?"

"Parking places," Paul Baxter was saying intently. "Automobiles are being purchased at a rate of eleven million copies annually and retired at a rate of four million, a net increase of seven million automobiles per annum. Physically, where are they going to come to rest? Already it's impossible to park in New York, Chicago, Boston, and San Francisco. We've seen stress reactions on the part of the parkees, and incidence of parking-space violence. I'm telling you," he concluded, leaning forward, "the potential is there. Parking rights litigation. A growth field."

In the general direction of the menu blackboard Warren had noticed a woman sitting alone, her back to the café. She was reading a hardcover book. On her table was a bottle of red wine and a single glass, but no food. The opposite place setting and chair had been removed, apparently to discourage strangers from inviting themselves to join her. The woman was plainly dressed, slender if her back was any indication, and wore her hair exactly like Nora. Warren began to feel funny.

At the far end of the table, discussion had shifted to the space program. "It's not the money that bothers me, it's the environmental damage," Corby Thompson was saying. "Think of what we've done to a lunar ecosystem that was undisturbed for billions of years. Think of the footprints."

One of the other voices said, "I feel cheated that the energy crisis did not destroy capitalism. We finally had proof that the global reach of multinational corporate power was intolerable and now everything's *fine* again." It was Janet Simpson speaking, and she sounded heartbroken.

Warren heard Paul Baxter break in from the far end of the table. "Geography is a completely obsolescent concept." He was the sort of person who always leaned back and paused before he spoke, even if he was ordering a plate of nachos. "People don't live in cities anymore, they live in markets. Just yesterday I met a fellow from the Atlanta market. Surprisingly urbane. All politics will eventually be reduced to consumer preferences."

At that moment there was a stir by the entrance. Warren

looked up: the Marlboro Man had just walked through the front door of the café.

He seemed even more handsome than he had in Kansas City —mustache trimmed hair by hair; dressed in a perfectly creased black tuxedo with a white silk scarf; wearing a white cowboy hat. Every woman in the café, and about half of the men, looked up longingly.

Jewel let out an audible "oooh" and put her elbow down into a bowl of pretzels, causing it to flip over. LaSonia quickly touched both hands to her earlobes, to make sure she had earrings on. Only Janet paid no heed. She kept on speaking, her strident voice now easily heard throughout the room.

". . . in his lesser known and therefore better books," Janet was saying, "went beyond employing images to represent symbols, which in my thesis I call image imagery, and used image imagery itself as a metaphor of . . ."

The Marlboro Man surveyed the room, then sauntered up to the bar. People parted to make way. A bottle of champagne and two tulip glasses were placed before him by a fawning bartender without, as far as Warren could tell, any words being spoken. Cocking back his cowboy hat, the Marlboro Man began to walk forward. A shudder went through the crowd. Enough hormones were released to start a small pharmaceutical company.

The Marlboro Man had set his sights on—the woman with the book. It has to be Nora, Warren thought, only she could attract such a man by her bearing alone. The bastard has been looking for her ever since that morning in Kansas City, traced her somehow to this bar, and now he's making his move in full view of—

Warren jumped up, nearly causing the table to spill as his knees struck the bottom of it with a resounding crash. The Marlboro Man looked his way. He seemed taken aback and, then, delighted. He changed course and walked toward their table.

"You *know* that guy?" LaSonia asked, near to drooling.

"Sylvia Plath has always been my role model," Janet Simpson continued, oblivious. "She killed herself in 1956, the same year

I was born. People say it was depression over her work, but I think she used gas from a power monopoly deliberately, as a protest against the corporate state. Her death symbolizes an original sin inherited by our generation. Otherwise I reject everything that's been written in my lifetime."

The Marlboro Man arrived at the table, smiling a confident smile. There seemed to be a danger that LaSonia and Jewel would begin disrobing on the spot. He looked at Warren and spoke in an almost paternal voice. "I think you and I have things to discuss. Please call or visit." He handed Warren a calling card. "And don't worry," the Marlboro Man continued, indicating with a gesture of his head the woman with the book, who hadn't looked up or acknowledged the hubbub. "It's not. I wouldn't."

Then the Marlboro Man turned to LaSonia. He gallantly kissed her hand, took a flower from a vase on the table, and slipped it into her lapel. "My darling," the Marlboro Man said, "how I wish tonight were to be our night. When the poetess wrote, 'Were you not still my hunger's rarest food / And water ever to my wildest thirst,' it was you whose face of earthly perfection she saw. I shall come for you again, my darling, this I vow. And our desires shall be consummated." With that the Marlboro Man walked away, and LaSonia fainted.

Jewel and Dennis Milton moved to help her, though both were weak in the knees as well. The rest of the assembly could do naught but follow the Marlboro Man's progress as he drew up behind the woman with the book, tapped her shoulder, tipped his hat, and spoke briefly. She rose and was revealed as drop-dead gorgeous. How did he know that? Warren wondered. The couple left the café, she clutching her book and he still holding the bottle and glasses. It was some time before the drone of café conversation resumed.

"There's got to be *something* wrong with that guy," Ken Morris was saying, agitated. "What's it say on his card? He's got to have some weany name like Bernie Markowitz, right?"

Warren looked. The Marlboro Man's name was Ned Stryker.

While the rest of the table took up an enthusiastic discussion of the Marlboro Man's appearance, Warren dissolved away.

Nora had come over him: just the mistaken imagining of her presence was intoxicating. Often Warren felt her as though she were in the next room, slightly beyond reach, or behind him where he couldn't quite see. He would catch sight of a woman in the distance who bore some physical resemblance to Nora and would continue trembling long past the point when she came close enough for him to see that it was someone else. Those moments of imagined contact were the only times Warren felt his soul was traveling in the right direction.

When Warren was able to focus on the conversation again, Jewel and LaSonia were still talking about Ned Stryker.

"I think it was the tuxedo that got to me," LaSonia said. "Once I was auditing a class in post-feminist awareness at Sarah Lawrence and I made the mistake of saying the most powerful erotic image I could visualize was a four-star hotel room, champagne and roses, afternoon Paris rain in the distance, a man in a tuxedo, fully clothed, looking at a woman with absolutely nothing on but jewelry and heels. They told me I couldn't come back to the class. I think the correct answer was a woman alone with a jar of honey."

Without warning Randall Levine stood. "Time to call it a night," he announced. The rest of the table rose too, troops dismissed. As the group filed out, Randall passed Jewel near the doorway and said, "I'll call you," not looking at Warren. Then he slipped away, laughing with the others over an unheard joke. He left arm-in-arm with Maureen.

"I forgot to explain something," Jewel said, trying to match his degree of nonchalance. "We're separated. It's no big deal."

Jewel stuck her hands into the pockets of her coat. The reflection of police lights flickered red down the street, but they heard no siren. "He says being married limits his possibilities."

Warren had not been much impressed with Randall Levine and wanted to say, What possibilities? Jail on a morals charge? Instead he asked what Jewel meant.

"You know, possibilities." She fidgeted. "When we were dating, everything was fine. As soon as we were married he started getting nervous. He said having made a choice foreclosed too many options for him. I guess he wanted to be able to walk down the street imagining he would meet some starlet and they would go off to Copenhagen together." The police lights flashed insistently, although their source still could not be seen.

"Are you going to get divorced?"

Jewel shook her head no, weary of the question. "When you're young you have a thousand friends," she began to say. "Standards aren't so high, there's a lot going on, friends are easy to acquire and lose. In high school you have a hundred friends and in college you boil it down to maybe a dozen. By the time you grow up, you're lucky if you still have a few people you can count on. You look at all these friendships that you've put so much into and they've all gone awry and you think, they're not worth it. Or maybe *I'm* not worth it. Same difference."

"Don't be stupid."

"Not stupid," Jewel said, looking out into the street. "I know *I* wouldn't go through the effort to be my friend. Why should anybody else? As for marriage, one is my limit. Getting this far was hard enough. If it eventually works out with Randall that's fine. If it's doesn't that's fine, too."

The police lights had passed by, and the street returned to darkness, broken by orange vapors from the streetlamps. Warren tried to touch Jewel in a consoling way, but she brushed aside his arm. He started to ask, "But do you—"

"Oh God, Warren." Just the question made her angry. "Nobody loves anybody. Utopia has been exposed."

Jewel waved for a cab. One appeared instantly; for her they always did. Most of the ride they sat in silence.

As the cab passed the remains of a Westway construction site, Jewel asked a fairly esoteric question about the financing of large capital projects. Happy for a new topic, Warren delivered a long answer. Jewel asked follow-up questions that showed she had been listening closely. As the eldest of the present Wonigan clan, she had long been under pressure to come into management of the firm, but always claimed to be revulsed by the idea. Jewel went on to ask more questions about municipal finance, using technical terms she would not have picked up casually.

Back at her co-op, she gave Warren some towels and showed him to the guest room. Then, as if she had forgotten something minor like pointing out the bathroom, Jewel added, "Although you can sleep in my room if you want. It's okay. Randall and I have an agreement."

Warren did not know how to handle the situation.

"I've missed sleeping with you," Jewel said. "Separation has been great for my love life. Everybody wants to make it with a rich bitch. Women, too. You wouldn't believe these artistic types in leotards. So don't feel sorry for me. But I miss sleeping with somebody I like."

"I think it would be better if—"

"That's okay, too." Jewel simply walked to her room and closed the door, showing no emotion.

In the morning nothing was said about Jewel's offer. They went to lunch early, businesslike, to a stunningly decorated hip-Italian restaurant recessed below the street in a brownstone. The waiters were unusually handsome young men, probably unemployed actors, dressed to the very height of chic. They seemed to know Jewel by sight.

Warren first poured out much—not all—of the story of Nora, and then of his need for a lawyer. Jewel was mildly surprised. She had expected Warren to request a loan to start a business. That was the usual pretext under which people asked her for money, she explained. Sometimes they really meant it, other times they planned to say the money had vanished in a "business loss." Once Jewel understood the nature of the problem she agreed to help, and to postpone repayment of the loan indefinitely. She wasn't interested in thanks.

"You don't get anything out of this either," Jewel said. "Besides, if you never pay me back I'll just write it off as a bad debt. That way it will only cost me half of what it would cost you." Jewel wrote down the name of an accountant and instructed Warren to have his legal bills sent there.

"If the lawyer recognizes your last name he'll triple his fee," Warren said.

Crossly, Jewel lifted an eyebrow. "This accountant represents a blind trust. The lawyer will never hear my name." She was annoyed at being underestimated, but in the past never would have thought of such a detail.

As they worked their way through several attentively served courses—a tiny hi-tech pizza with no tomato sauce cost $18.50 —Jewel ate ravenously, as she always did, and twice as much as Warren. She seemed to be in no hurry to report to her job at the community services center, and indeed had not mentioned work all day. By early afternoon Jewel was drunk and Warren was hinting that the time had come for him to leave.

"You can't stand what I said last night," Jewel declared. "You don't understand how people are afraid of having to deserve each other."

She crooked one finger and another glass of wine appeared at her side, as quickly as had the cab. Probably a cab would drive straight into the restaurant if she signaled it to.

"I get this semi-crackpot newsletter," Jewel went on. "There was an interesting idea in one of the issues.

"It pointed out that once, people weren't expected to be desirable. The most that was expected of them was to stay alive— spending the whole day pitching corn or hoeing sheep, whatever rustics do. It was a hard existence but it also excused people, excused them for not being remarkable or notable."

Warren's interest was piqued. Jewel noticed. "I say one thing a little poignant and *now* you want to fuck me. Well, forget it. But listen. Century after century people worked the whole time. They were always tired, always hurting their backs or big with babies. Most of what we say makes life worth living—culture, leisure, eroticism, philosophy—the average person couldn't get no matter how hard he tried. The only people participating in what we consider the things that make life worth living were a tiny minority of high-born flaming hypocrites."

One of the waiters, a dashing sort named Wortham who treated Jewel with particular familiarity, brought a multilayered chocolate-and-raspberry dessert compliments of the house. Jewel, who could talk several days in advance of what sweet she would eat on what day, paid little heed. She did pause to explain that Wortham had recently been laid off from a television soap opera when his character—a molecular biologist searching the world for his long-lost twin brother who had been carried away by Canadian bilingual terrorists—disappeared in the Panjshir Valley until next season.

"Now it's all turned around," she continued. "The tyranny of circumstances has been replaced by a tyranny of possibilities. People have all kinds of time; too much. With time you should do something significant. All kinds of chances; too many. With chances you must prove your worth." Another glass appeared without her gesturing at all.

"People today can get closer than ever to whatever it is that's supposed to justify their existence in the first place. That's why they are so anxious, so afraid. Why people with good jobs, beautiful faces, every advantage in the world are lying on psychiatric couches trembling with a fear they can't explain. They know they are supposed to take the next step. And they're afraid they don't deserve it."

For some time Warren couldn't think of anything to say. After getting Jewel to drink some coffee, Warren went, not to the airport, but to Pennsylvania Station. He wanted to take the train to West Point, to see what had drawn Nora there when she, like he, was in Manhattan and anxious to leave. Telling Jewel he was headed for West Point, Warren expected a lecture about fascist death factories. Instead, Jewel just nodded. Later it occurred to Warren that, in her addled state, Jewel had probably thought West Point was a resort on Long Island.

Rolling north up the Hudson River, Warren pondered the level of invective he had heard in the café. Granted the speakers were lawyers and law students. Yet all had been describing complaints against the country, whether from a conservative or liberal perspective, in the most exaggerated terms imaginable. The conservative faction had been outraged, aghast, astonished, etc., about the fools, idiots, and imbeciles, etc., running the incompetent, confiscatory, repressive, etc., government. The liberal faction had been etc., etc., etc., about the greedy, dictatorial, repressive, etc.

America is constantly spoken of by Americans as though it were a society on the brink of abyss. What amazed Warren about America was that the bombs *didn't* go off. The fearful energies of the sixties had been dissipated painlessly, by historical standards. Bobby Seale, the sort of revolutionary who in other times would have instigated the deaths of thousands, was writing cookbooks and doing Nautilus. The FBI had collected twenty-six pounds of files on John Lennon and they *couldn't* get him. Some colossus.

Much of the social cooling could be attributed to rounding off the hard edges of complaints. After Vietnam had ended and the civil rights laws were passed, the number of issues with clear aspects of right and wrong—the kind of issues that sustain radical emotion—diminished. In the sixties, every thinking person could agree that travesties such as poll taxes against blacks had to be stopped; by the seventies, the ground had shifted to debatable issues like quota systems, where even blacks couldn't agree.

Still the level of invective remained, because America is the only country where revolution is a marketing device. It was no coincidence that Randall Levine's friends had a flair for condemnation; they aimed to succeed in a society where condemnation sells. When Americans hear of censorship overseas—films banned, newspapers shut down, *poets in jail*—they simply can't believe it, because they live in a society where anybody can condemn anything, and they observe that this strengthens rather than weakens the status quo.

Everything American government does, for example, is lampooned to the point at which criticism abdicates its significance. Americans are even accustomed to hearing government impugn government: almost every one of the multiple state, local, county, and federal branches hollers about almost everything done by every other branch. Politicians and editorialists describe themselves as being shocked or stunned so often, on such vanishing matters—it is not unusual to read a newspaper column expressing metaphysical horror over a matter like sugar import tariffs—that their words attenuate into vapor, impossible to grasp.

That this lesson was not obvious to the world's paranoid states, Warren could not believe. The way to quench political unrest was not to suppress it, but heap it upon the dissatisfied: mass-manufactured dissent. It was even good for the business climate. In America, government condemnation is a growth industry, creating jobs on the left and right alike. How many liberal journalists or conservative fund-raisers actually wanted government to do as they said? Not many; they'd be out of work.

The Amtrak train lurched and crunched northward toward West Point, swaying from starboard to port. Surely, Warren thought, the tracks at Promontory, Utah, were smoother. Europeans fantasized about encountering a mysterious beauty on a train and, after three incomplete sentences, embarking on a dazzling affair. This could never happen on Amtrak: It's impossible to think about sex when you are motion sick.

Warren could not say in logical terms why he was spending time and money stopping at West Point. Perhaps, since Nora had been drawn there, he would find some clue to her character.

At his destination Warren found himself less interested in the academy grounds—too monotone and fortified, gray Gothic buildings each one like the next—than in the nearby town of Highland Falls. A town of nineteenth-century charm and architecture just beyond the academy's gate, its rows of cordial houses proved a calming sight. After wandering among them most of the day, Warren concluded it was the houses of Highland Falls, not the military academy, which had drawn Nora.

When young, Nora had worked summers on Mackinac Island, a resort not far from Escanaba. Mackinac functioned as a closed society centered on a grand hotel of turn-of-the-century design; chambermaids wore period costumes and motor vehicles were banned. Nora had spent three summers there as a dining hall waitress, wearing layers of frills, and had enjoyed it. Highland Falls bore a similarity to Mackinac and had the same feeling of being thrown out of time, which Warren found appealing. That, it seemed, had to be the explanation. But no larger a clue to Nora's nature.

Late in the afternoon Warren walked to the academy proper and regarded the Plain. What a preserve of distinction West Point must have been a hundred years ago, he thought, when admission there meant approximately what admission to Harvard Medical School does today; when the gentle homes of Highland Park were lit with a sense of their own lore. It was not unknown, at the time, for entire families to move near West Point after a son was admitted, just to bask in its reflection.

Tired from walking the grounds, Warren stopped to rest at the visitor's center. A cadet in dress grays, who showed no evidence of having started shaving, was marching smartly up and down the length of the hall. Whether this tour was an honor or a punishment Warren could not tell—in the Army the two are often difficult to distinguish.

By a display of ceremonial swords stood an exhibit case of academy mementos from various conflicts. Warren's attention fell on the Spanish-American War section. Absentmindedly, he began to inspect the contents: binoculars; a field-length photograph of a graduating class being mustered out to serve; medals; maps of Cuba and Manila; various newspaper accounts. Most had to do with glorious victories. One, from an 1899 edition of the local paper, was personal. Headlined

FINGER OF FATE
POINTS TO TRAGEDY
IN SANTIAGO

it read in the lurid style of the time:

Tears streamed down the battle-hardened cheeks of grizzled soldiers today as Zeus's hand hurtled a thunderbolt of tragedy upon the garrison of this forsaken Cuban villa.

A United States Army Captain and Military Academy Graduate was carried to untimely rest when, without regard for life or limb, he thrust himself into a burning store house in an attempt to rescue an enlisted man imprisoned there by raging flame. Munitions that had been placed within the store house exploded seconds before the rescue could be completed.

Brute fate delivered a savage double blow as this Captain was scheduled not three short days hence to be given leave detail home and joined in Holy Matrimony to the daughter of a Poughkeepsie shopkeeper much respected for his honest prices and church-going ways.

Brig. General Barrington Mayes, commander of the garrison, said today he would recommend that the Medal Of Valor be conferred posthumously upon the officer, aged but twenty-three when he departed this earth, Captain Warren M. Gifford of the 9th Michigan Rifles. . . .

"Sir? Sir?" the cadet was asking.

Warren had dropped to the floor and was frozen in a crouch, hands together. After trying several times to bring Warren around, the cadet raced off toward the far end of the building, a dense booklet of regulations and procedures concerning stricken civilians shimmering in his head.

There was really no need to look at the article again. Warren was certain he knew what the rest would say. He was anxious to be gone before the cadet returned with nurses, triplicate forms, and a colonel.

Slowly Warren rose back up and looked. What he saw was as obvious and expected as if he were reading the results of a football game he had already seen:

In seclusion and accepting no visitors due to her burden of sorrow is his betrothed, Miss Nora Constance Jocelyn.

—12—

MORTAL
BUT
AGELESS

While Warren was at West Point, another issue of the Azimuth newsletter arrived. It was printed on computer paper, with the perforated borders still attached.

The issue was 190 pages long. Through some electronic snafu, 182 pages of inventory statistics from an office furniture warehouse had been included. There was also a pie chart depicting Irish immigration patterns of the 1820s; six bar graphs showing staffing levels at the Department of Commerce; and many columns of hexadecimal computer code. Printed in boldface in the midst of the code was the sentence: **Mike—there may be a glitch in this program.**

The relevant portion of the newsletter read:

AS SCIENCE CANNOT SAY WHY APPLES FALL FROM TREES, NEITHER CAN IT SAY WHY THE HUMAN BODY GROWS OLD.

The *what* of aging—the metabolic failures that occur—is, like the mathematics of gravity, well understood. The *why*, like the nature of gravity, remains a mystery.

When young the body is able to make itself: both structurally, by changing inorganic nutrients to living tissue and bone, and conceptually, by arranging those materials into human form. From an early point after conception, when its internal mechanisms are tiny and weak, the body can manufacture and properly organize an entire galaxy of cell types, including advanced cells such as neurons. What has taken hundreds of millions of years to design, the frail, ill-defined embryo makes with ease.

Then the ability to work this magic is lost! Actually not lost— deliberately thrown away. The genetic mechanisms that know to put an arm next to the shoulder, a subclavian artery under the collarbone, and so on down to the feet cease functioning in the early months of womb life. The genes that know about making female eggs become dumb shortly before birth; the genes that know about making nerve cells fall silent shortly after. The body seems to commence a process of slowly sabotaging itself. As the years pass its ability to perform even simple tasks such as tissue growth—tasks the body could easily manage when new and struggling—dwindles away.

Yet the body's knowledge of how to do these things does not vanish. It remains encoded in every person throughout the whole of one's life.

The DNA strand in each human cell contains a complete set of plans for a fresh, vigorous person. The body of an 80-year-old, for instance, knows full well how to make a brand-new kidney or heart, just as it knew eight decades before when it was a plasmic lump. But the 80-year-old body, unlike the lump, refuses to act on its knowledge. Why?

It is not enough to say that people (or any living creatures) age because they wear out. Cars and hair dryers wear out. Living organisms have the power of self-generation— chemically, the ability to take molecules and re-arrange them into other forms. If automobiles could suck bits of steel and plastic in through their carburetors and re-arrange them into new valve gaskets or brake pads, then automobiles would never wear out. Living creatures possess the power to replace their own parts, yet in most cases decline to do so.

Compared to the breathtakingly ornate process of embryonic growth, making repairs in a finished body ought to be a parlor trick. To pick just one example, counteracting a cataract, which takes years to form, ought to be many orders of magnitude easier than creating an eye in the first place. Yet the typical body succeeds at the difficult task and fails at the easy one—all the while maintaining on file in each of its cells a complete genetic blueprint of what healthy eyes look like and how to manufacture them.

Perhaps the body ages not because it has to, but because it wants to.

Or more precisely, because it has been told to.

In the winding river of human DNA there are genes that act and genes that suppress other genes. What exactly each molecule does is far from certain; human DNA contains approximately six billion "points" of chemical information, and altering a single point may interactively alter many others. This is both a source of festival joy to the lovers of life—for it means there can, in effect, be a limitless number of people, with no two snowflakes alike—and a nightmare for cellular biologists.

Sometimes, as evolution adds new features to the body, it does not remove the genes for old features but, rather, switches them off by adding suppressors that work full-time. At other times the suppressor chains have only part-time authority, stopping actor genes when they reach a certain point. The part-time suppressors of interest to us here are the ones that switch off cell differentiation.

The entire human body grows from a single cell too small to see. That cell transforms itself not just through growth—if it merely grew the result would be a giant blob—but through differentiation, the change from one type of cell to another.

Some types of cells—for example, skin cells—reach their finished form relatively quickly, and then begin to multiply, their differentiation halted. Others cells are transitional phases on their way to transforming again; nearly fifty steps of differentiation are required to make advanced cells like neurons.

Genetic suppressor signals are needed to tell the various differentiating protoplasms when to stop. The signal's nature is, to put it mildly, enigmatic. While suppressor signals clearly occur—*something* must be telling the cells what to do—no test has ever detected them in action. Analysis of cells immediately before and after differentiation shows no trace of any chemical messenger that distributed the stop command.

As thousands of types of human cells emanate from the

single first cell, suppressor signals must be precise. During the rapid growth phases of embryonic life and infancy, the stop command is received and understood with majestic precision: even accounting for congenital defects, humans as a group produce millions of billions of correct cell changes for each flawed cell.

And once a normal cell has received the stop command, it stops differentiating for good. This—not "wearing out"—ultimately should be held responsible for aging.

Suppressor genes in effect make the body forget how it has just accomplished a task. Genetic blueprints for self-generation are rendered useless, locked in a file. Some parts of the body retain the ability to grow new tissue for replacement of damaged tissue. But after infancy only growth, or the duplication of cells, is permitted. Differentiation of one cell type into another is not.

Such genes that deny the body access to its own knowledge are not present in all creatures. Insects and a few types of reptiles can override their suppressors to grow new limbs; plants, as gardeners know, do so with enthusiasm. But none of the higher animals regenerate.

If we assume that the development of life was guided in some fashion by some purposeful influence, we must then ask what end the deliberate switching off of self-making knowledge is designed to serve.

Perhaps it is a programming requirement of the evolutionary computer. Evolution, being nourished by random mutations of very complex molecular structures, may require millions of tries to get a change right—and millions of survival tests to sift good changes from bad ones. If creatures did not age, they would be far less likely to die. (Agelessness must not be confused with immortality. A planet of ageless creatures would still know death from disease, violence, and so on.) Creatures regularly dying—clearing the way for new, slightly different versions—may have been a necessity for the evolutionary quest.

But why was aging chosen as the executioner? Evolution might have, instead, programmed the arteries leading to the brain to close after a given period: a quick death following a life of full vigor, rather than a slow disintegration.

Many animals have internal clocks sensitive to changes in the hour of the day, or even the season. Deer, for example, rut in the last weeks of November so that their young will be born to the warmth of spring. To program the body for suicide would have required, however, a means to count to seventy, or whatever number of years was chosen by whatever chose it. Clues from cyclical natural events, such as the shortening of daylight in the fall, probably would not have been enough to make the clock reliable. Where could an accurate metabolic time-piece be found? Aging is exactly such a clock. The cells themselves are the timers. Their running down, like springs, tells the body when to expire.

This is only one of several possible explanations. A vexing drawback is that it would seem evolution should have favored agelessness.

Darwin reasoned that whichever creature transmits the most genes to the most young gets the prize. Surely a longer lifespan would confer a tidy head start in Darwin's contest. Longer-lived creatures would have a longer period during which to transmit their genes: plus better odds of doing so, via remaining longer in the youthful state of strong muscles, sharp hearing, and so on. This suggests the possibility that ageless creatures would have won on Darwinian terms but been bad for creation in some way; so our Creator intervened to program genes for death and frustrate evolutionary mathematics.

God might have had a powerful bureaucratic incentive for doing so. Without aging, the ultimate fate of the soul would be reduced from the central question of all existence to a diverting topic of after-dinner conversation—since souls would leave the body only occasionally, by accident or murder. This, of course, would drastically reduce God's jurisdiction. And no self-respecting manager, not even a celestial one, voluntarily surrenders turf.

Alternately, when programming bodies to age, God might have been acting strictly in our best interests. Perhaps something happens after death that no one should miss.

A final possibility is that aging is simply another one of nature's foul-ups that God or man—whoever gets there first—will eventually correct.

Bear in mind that contemporary doctors can control cataracts, which nature forgot to enable the body to do, but cannot make eyes. Perhaps in the original plan, suppressor genes were supposed to have start-stop functions for emergencies, and along the way something got screwed up. The fact that some cells restart the differentiation in a destructive way—what the modern medical establishment calls cancer—indicates that a factor for restarting is present in some aspect of our metabolism.

If aging is a genetic mistake, will it be possible to correct? Figuring out all six billion points on a DNA strand, and computing their nearly unlimited permutations, would, until recently, have taken the querulous and distracted human mind countless centuries. This, however, is the sort of job ideally suited to computers. As the speed and power of computers increase, the exact nature of individual genes will be cataloged. Then it may become possible not only to slice genes up, but reprogram them.

True "agelessness" would involve such extensive re-engineering of the body that it might not be desirable. Merely reprogramming the suppressor genes to allow access to the plans for heart cell construction would not, for example, be sufficient to provide a person with the means to periodically build himself a fresh heart. Since the gene code describes an infant's heart, not an adult heart, it might be necessary to create a body cavity in which the new heart could be nurtured through years of growth; a means to plug it into the cardiovascular system when ready; and a means to dissolve the exhausted heart and carry it away. Add regeneration provisions of this nature for the other organs and you wind up with humans who resemble the eggplant that ate Chicago. Growing the new heart outside the chest and then emplacing it may be more imaginable, but not much more appealing when it comes to rejuvenating an entire body through constant major surgery.

Now let's bring in a related factor. One hundred years ago the average lifespan in the United States was forty-three years. Today it is seventy-four years and rising. Two thousand years ago, during the flowering of the Roman Empire, only twenty percent of the population lived to see age forty. Today, eighty percent of the population reaches seventy. It is now thought that arthritis, senility, and osteoporosis (brittle bones) will become curable, and that the "natural" lifespan will be doubled to about 140 years in a few generations. This might occur *without* cracking the gene code. Adding genetic improvements to the scheme will stretch lifespans even further.

Were it not for cigarette smoking, which became widespread only in this century, and the cure for which—not smoking—is being implemented demographically, longevity would already be greater still. Adjusting for cigarette smoking and longer lifespans, the cancer rate today is about the same as it was fifty years ago.

Obviously longer lives will cause social upheavals. If confined to Western society, agelessness would foster an even greater moral imbalance between rich and poor nations than exists today. Conversely, if spread to the Third World without reductions in birthrates, agelessness would cause the globe to spiral out of control. Even within Western countries the strain on political and economic arrangements would be severe— especially providing pensions for people who may be in retirement for many more years than they work, and vigorous enough to expect the funds for an active life.

These, however, are merely practical consequences. Somehow they will be worked out. Let us now ask the question that science and economics cannot answer: What on earth are people going to *DO* with all this new time?

With perhaps sixty total years of leisure in childhood and retirement—schooling till twemty-five, labor till sixty-five, retirement till one hundred—when, before this century, fifteen total years of leisure was considered fantastic?

Perhaps it will be possible to continue to rely on material

culture to amuse us. That has more or less worked so far. Perhaps we could turn to advanced development of the intellect —although the advent of computers is in the process of rendering several categories of intellectual prowess superfluous.

Or perhaps, to give our longer and much-favored lives purpose, we could turn to a type of development that mankind has always speculated would surpass all others.

—13—

By the following morning Warren had located a drafty corner room in the Pough- keepsie town hall from which a retired assistant tax assessor ran the local historical society. Scattered around the office were maps, card files, old photographs, and pages from a handwritten manuscript titled *A History of Dutchess County, Volume Four.* The walls were painted a revolting shade of green.

During the course of a conversation meandering across such topics as ice harvesting in '26 and John Nance Garner's opinion of the Bonus March, Warren collected enough tips on the county record-keeping system to be able to index references to the surname Jocelyn.

"Jocelyn . . . Jocelyn . . . let me think . . . ," the old historian, frail even in a bulky cable sweater, said aloud several times, squeezing up his brow and looking off to a place no one but he would ever again see.

"I remember Joseph, Ben Joseph. Moved to southern Illinois after the first war. Never got over Judith Bowden. Jocelyn . . ." He was dismayed, fearing he had lost something left with him for safekeeping. "There was an Annette Judson. Lived at 414 Mt. Vernon until the shooting at 418. I can't tell you for certain what she's up to now. Haven't spoken to her in about forty years."

Warren let himself out of the office gently, embarrassed to be a citizen of a society obsessed by news images of what was hap- pening just exactly that very instant, yet indifferent to the re- membrance and comprehension of what had happened only a few instants before.

In a microfiche file room, Warren found references to Preston Jocelyn, owner of a river goods supply store. The store had been demolished in 1919, and the deed to Preston Jocelyn's house transferred the same year. No subsequent deed mentioned the Jocelyn name, suggesting the family had left town.

The assessor's vault contained a set of floor plans for the Jocelyn house, which Warren photocopied. In the county recorder's office there was a birth certificate for a daughter Nora, born August 12, 1881, six pounds ten ounces, race Caucasian, religion Methodist. That was all. No marriage license; if she had ever wed, she did not do so in Dutchess County. Warren subtracted 1899, the date of the newspaper clipping, from 1881 and got eighteen years old. The rest of the day was wasted. Warren found no further references; this Jocelyn family had disappeared without a trace.

Just as well, Warren thought. What he had feared most was finding a death certificate dated 1955, the year of Nora's birth. That would have been it. Next stop, rubber room.

Even as it was, Warren continued to entertain a hope that the entire situation could be explained away. There were millions of newspaper articles—maybe billions—in which none of the names meant anything special to anybody; millions of paintings and photographs whose subjects didn't remind anyone of anybody at all. If the odds of running across an apparent historical link between your life and another life from the past were a million to one, it meant that it would happen occasionally. There was a saying that went, Since the odds of any given citizen being president are 235 million to one, no one is president. Suppose the billions of newspaper articles ever written could be computer-skimmed. The average person would probably find his own name dozens of times, right down to the correct middle initial, plus the names of acquaintances. This would be eerie but otherwise lack significance.

Warren kept trying to think that he and Nora were exceptional only in that, through a million-to-one chance, they had happened to look exactly where one of the statistical oddities happened to lie. Some people see shooting stars, others don't—it's all a matter of looking in the right place. Ergo, nothing about a second coincidence added on top of the first was conclusive in the slightest.

"Ergo?" the county historian asked. "You're also trying to find somebody named Ergo?"

Warren had been sitting in the microfiche room, talking to himself out loud, when the old man came up from behind to announce that the building was closing. Spread out before Warren on a hard walnut library table were the Jocelyn house plans, which he had been blearily studying, concentrating hard. Warren said something about what a strange vision from the past these plans represented.

"Past? Hardly," the historian said, pointing to the latest assessment stamp on the property survey, dated 1983. It took Warren a moment to realize this meant the house was still standing. He could go there.

Finding the Jocelyn house wasn't difficult. When built a hundred years before, it had been on the fringes of town, in a rural area reached by dirt road. Now it was on a main street. Warren found himself fascinated with the thought that a structure designed for heating by coal and service by horse carriage could later be heated by electricity and served by automobiles—and perhaps later still served by something else. The house itself was narrow and upright, three stories tall and cinched at the base. All four faces had porches, an indication that, when the house had been built, no other buildings blocked the view. The exterior was a muddy brown color, not, Warren thought, like the houses at West Point. Then how many times had it been painted since the century turned?

Not lately, that was for sure. Drawing close, Warren saw that the house was in shoddy repair. The paint was peeling, and several planks on the front porch were rotted through. Something about the design, however, began to seem hauntingly familiar.

Warren had come halfway up the front walk when off-pitch rock music burst from the structure like a clock radio turning on at full blast. He had to wait for the music to subside—it halted suddenly, in cacophony—before knocking on the plank door.

A teenaged boy, his stringy hair in a ponytail, answered after a considerable lapse. Warren said he thought an old friend had once lived in the house and could he come in to have a brief look around? The boy peered up and down the street. "That's really lame, man," he replied. "Let's see the warrant."

Inside there was commotion, people running up and down stairs, doors slamming. Warren tried to explain he was not the law. The ponytailed boy remained hostile, stalling for time. Warren handed over his driver's license in an attempt to prove he was from out of state. After inspecting the license as though it were a page from a Gutenberg original, the boy pronounced, "So what. Anybody can fake these things. I have three myself."

From inside a rich female voice called, "Mad Dog, invite the gentleman *in.*"

The boy's hostility promptly dissipated and he stood aside, acquiescent. Warren stepped past. The house was dim, most of the shades drawn. Two colors of light could be seen, yellow from candles mounted in brass holders of what appeared to be antique quality, and flickering red from the monitors of guitar amplifiers. In the air was a powerful and pleasant scent of incense. Warren had forgotten incense existed. The whole house felt like music.

A young woman wearing an old-fashioned fluffy gown of white lace and high-heeled leather boots that disappeared under her dress stepped toward Warren. As his eyes adjusted to the dimness, Warren realized that around the room were five or six more young men, each as dirty and torn-edged as Mad Dog, in contrast to the girl, whose appearance was spotless. "I am Melody," she announced.

Melody approached Warren as though she were rescuing him from a shipwreck. She embraced him and, smiling with beatitude, took his hands. "You are troubled," she said in a lulling voice. "Your troubles will pass. Sit here and let the music cleanse you." She indicated a pillow on the floor.

"Yamaha, bring some hot herb tea." Melody instructed a boy who sat indolently in a corner, but who rose quickly when ordered. Each of the boys proved as deferential as Mad Dog. They seemed to bend in whatever direction Melody's voice was flowing. "We cannot offer you alcoholic beverages because we have none here," she continued. "Nor do we have any substance that alters the mind. We wish to find our thoughts, not escape them. Now, we will play."

Before Warren could interrupt, Melody made some imperceptible signal that brought the band to attention. They began to play—terribly. Warren wanted to plug his ears. This was music that would make false teeth rattle.

As the band performed, Mad Dog and his friends jumped about and made rude faces, imitating what they had seen in music videos. The girl continued to smile at the center of the chaos, tilting her head sweetly. Her singing, or at least the portion that could be heard over three bass guitars and an unattended synthesizer that had been programmed to thump out the back beat, was compelling and clean. Melody, he thought, might have the real thing when it came to vocal talent. He wished he could hear it alone; it might indeed soothe his anguish.

What an endearing trick, to ask if he was troubled. She probably always said that on first meeting: she would gain confidences and seldom run the risk of contradiction, since nearly everyone was troubled or liked to think of himself that way.

Considering the band's appearance and volume, Warren expected their songs to be hard-core punk. But, instead, their lyrics, what he could catch, were bourgeois as could be—boyfriends, Saturday nights, driving down that lonesome highway. Rock musicians sell themselves by combining the most androgynous S&M appearances they can devise with predictable complaints about middle-class suburban concerns. Boy George, the "shocking" rock singer in woman's makeup, Japanese kimono, and Hasidic hat, sang songs whose lyrics could have been written by Billy Graham.

Inconsistent? The key to rock marketing appeal was making teenagers *feel* they had experienced something rebellious. It occurred to Warren that most of the true revolutionaries of history, who spoke at risk of their lives, otherwise dressed and behaved fairly normally. Even Marx's beard and George Washington's wooden teeth were considered typical at the time. But then the last thing a rock musician wanted to speak would be words of true rebellion, words which might place his own favored position in jeopardy. After the revolution, nobody would get royalty payments.

As the band played Warren continued to have the unsettling feeling that the house was more familiar than it should be. There was a wide wooden staircase barely beyond view down the main hall. To test himself, Warren tried to imagine exactly how rooms would be situated up the staircase. After about twenty minutes the band wound down. Performing his final whirling flourish, Yamaha jerked so hard the power cord came out of his amp and most of the rhythm phrase vanished prematurely. Melody flounced through several deep bows as though an entire stadium were cheering. Her hair billowed beautifully, so much so that Warren looked around the makeshift stage for a wind machine.

"That was our new single, 'More of Same,' Melody declared, speaking into her microphone although Warren was only a few feet away. "We've been trying to get it released for almost two months now! But we do not complain. Every communication is, in a way, a message. I believe the record has not been released because the spheres are saying we are not yet fully prepared for the responsibilities of international fame. Fame would make us misaligned if it came too soon. Wouldn't it, Daniel?" Daniel, the drummer, had not been paying attention, and Melody sensed it though Daniel was behind her back, well out of view. Daniel's pupils were glassy and the bones in his wrists visible. He answered, "Yes, ma'am."

Melody put down the microphone and drew Warren toward the hall, where the light was better. Now he could be certain she was a teenager, seventeen at most. She whispered with a young girl's private allure, "They're good boys, but in peril from the vices of the street. They need positive role models. You cannot make music unless you are conscious."

Then Melody took his hands again and pressed them intently. She asked, "Have your troubles left you now? Do you feel the peace the music brings?"

Warren, working himself loose from her charms, tried again to explain that he needed to look at the house. Melody listened with a perplexed expression and after several mentions of the town hall and the historical society said, "You mean you're not the man from Assault Records?"

Embarrassed, Warren explained further.

"There is no need to apologize," Melody interrupted. "You were sent here for a purpose. If you had not come, you could not be here. Perhaps you bear a message you yourself do not understand. I often feel that way about our songs. Follow me, I will show you everything."

Melody motioned for Mad Dog, their "business manager," who remained suspicious. After demanding assurance that Warren had not come about back taxes, he admitted only to renting the house from someone who had bought it at a county foreclosure auction and was always out of town. The deal rang of small-time drugs. As the band members began to switch on the electric lights, Warren saw that the interior of the house, too, was in decrepit condition. Floorboards were ajar and pock-marked with burns, wall moldings were missing.

Melody took Warren by the arm and began to lead him up the broad staircase. "Don't let him open anything!" Mad Dog called after them.

The feeling of familiarity increased. Three second-floor bedrooms were exactly where Warren expected to find them. Sleeping bags, peanut butter jars, copies of *Penthouse,* and empty cans of Genesee 12-Horse Ale were tossed about the rooms carelessly. There was one immaculate room with Hallmark posters on the walls, a Bible, and a baseball bat by the bedstand. Directly above the bed was a faded dime-store portrait of a woman in a halo.

On the top floor Warren said simply, "This is the study," and so it was.

"Oh my. You have been sent for a purpose," Melody observed, impressed and pleased. From the study windows they could see the tired channel of the Hudson, sewn together by rusting bridges.

Resting his thoughts on the river, Warren asked Melody how she had come to this place. "I dropped out of school when I was fourteen, to go to New York City and sing." She added quickly, "I am completing my GED by mail.

"I waited on tables and lived with a man who assured me he was a famous spontaneous visual performance artist. Then one day his parole officer called the restaurant and warned me not to go back to the loft until the forensic team had left. So I renounced the temptations of flesh. This was a revelation. Once I had experienced the revelation, I was drawn to a newspaper advertisement for a vocalist for our band. The owner of the house also owns our rights. I am not privy to the details, but he has said it helps keep his assets cleansed. He assures me he is a reputable businessman in the South American import-export trade.

"The first night I laid down in my bed in this house," Melody added, "I received my inspiration for my life's work."

"Which is?"

"To compose a rock opera celebrating the sexual restraint of the women saints."

Firing off questions in rapid succession, Warren grilled Melody about the source of this idea. She didn't seem aware of Catherine of Siena, or anything similar. Her knowledge of the female saints appeared to be limited to the haloed figure over her bed. She also knew nothing about West Point or the town of Highland Falls—didn't even seem to be aware of their existence, despite their proximity.

"Actually my brother suggested the topic to me," Melody finally let on. "He has promised to send me the historical information. My brother is extremely knowledgeable about subjects no one understands. He also contributes financial support to our work here, although I do not tell the boys, because I want them to learn to take responsibility for something other than the cable TV payments.

"Perhaps, if your interest is history, you should visit him," Melody concluded. "He is not far away, and would be happy to receive a fellow seeker such as yourself." She wrote a name and address on a sheet of paper with little purple flowers in the corners.

"Thank you," Warren said, accepting the paper without examining it. "Let me return the favor by saying that I know someone with connections in the music business who may know how to channel your singing talent. How would she get in touch with you?"

"Just tell her to write Melody Stryker in care of the Poughkeepsie post office," Melody said. "If the letter is meant to reach me, it will. There's no point trying to call because they're always taking back our phones."

Melody walked Warren to the door. As he drove off, she stood on the front porch and waved ardently, hand held far away from her body like a Southern cheerleader.

Warren drove out of Melody's sight and stopped the car. His mind was in turmoil. Melody was the Marlboro Man's sister. And the exact layout of her house had been clear to him. How could he possibly have known unless . . . unless . . .

Unless he had a complete set of floor plans lying on the front seat of his rental car. Warren smacked his forehead in disbelief. No wonder he'd recognized the house, after staring at the design for hours in the county microfiche room.

Melody was right. He had been drawn there for a purpose: to realize that absolutely nothing about the building or setting was familiar to him. It was just a disheveled old house, built for a time and a people who no longer existed. Preston Jocelyn had taken his family somewhere; no one knew where. They did something and ended up some way that no one remembered. He could call out to the Nora Jocelyn of this place forever, and she would never hear.

Only at first did the thought seem comforting.

During the days of the Apollo program, many complained that it was a misguided society that would send a man to the moon but would not end poverty.

If only that had been the choice. Traveling to the moon was a physical problem that could be solved by building the proper machine. Once solved, it stayed solved. But what machine would end poverty? What device "bring" peace? How ideals like this could be achieved was hard to describe even in theoretical terms, much less practical ones.

Warren often thought of this conflict when confronted by a choice between a safe course and taking his fate into his own hands. He had thought of it years before, the day his draft notice arrived. Should he flee to Canada or join a fight he couldn't support? Ultimately, Warren had chosen to join because he realized Canada was the safe course. The responsible person accepted his obligation to serve, made his arguments against bad policy, and tried to control his fate by changing the system from within. Today these sentiments ring saccharine, but they had meant a great deal to Warren at the time. He had thought likewise on several occasions since meeting Nora Jocelyn, and now thought it again: *Some questions can't be answered even under ideal circumstances. But that's no excuse for not trying to answer them. Flawed good intentions are a thousand times more valuable than indifference, because at least they accumulate.*

Given the difficulty of achieving ultimate ends, perhaps many people really were happier living a circumscribed existence. Warren had always found engineering, and the sciences generally, heavy with men and women who were drawn by the promise of being freed from the larger significance of their actions. The minstrel Tom Lehrer once sang of a certain German rocket scientist who maintained that his development of the V2 was magically unrelated to the Nazi war effort:

> *Vunce ze rockets go up*
> *Who cares where zhey come down*
> *Zhat's not my department*
> *Says Werner von Braun.*

Some Manhattan Project researchers, Warren recalled, had performed the skillful feat of gaining fame and money by helping invent the bomb, and then gaining moral sanctity by condemning their invention. Most, however, took no stand on subsequent use, preferring to view it as none of their affair. Perhaps where they would live if the weapons were exploded was none of their own business, too.

The sciences—hard science, military science, political science, others—have always been fields in which bad judgments are excused by claiming some other sector of society is responsible for setting priorities. Increasingly, it seemed to Warren, instead of pressuring the sciences to become accountable, the humanities were demanding the same exemption. Students aspired to be journalists chronicling mistakes, not leaders looking for solutions; to be critics, not artists. Young people were going into law not only for the salaries but for the pleasure of using their minds without being responsible for the outcome. Law had even fashioned an ethical gymnastic in which the distortion of truth and disruption of justice—attempting to win for a client who deserved to lose—was a professional obligation.

Ronald Reagan, the fortieth president, spent more than a decade and $100 million campaigning for office, then years declaring that he should not be blamed for the actions of the very government he had longed to head. That this claim called forth little public reaction indicated it struck a harmonic chord within the bulk of the population. Americans, like their president, wanted to be important but not responsible.

Originally, Warren had been drawn to engineering by a different but equally American reason: the desire to make something big. Big enough to be marked on maps, like Lake Mead above the Hoover Dam, or the fourteen-mile Hampton Road Bridge Tunnel that playfully leapt and dove across the mouth of Chesapeake Bay. Maybe even big enough to be seen from space. Like many others, Warren assumed that any alien species that accumulated the knowledge necessary for spacefaring would have to have learned benevolence in the process, and thus its arrival would be a cause for celebration. Watching the trends in American life as his country's knowledge accumulated, Warren increasingly feared that the first furry, talking cylinder or whatever to float off a flying saucer would immediately cry "No comment!" and refer all questions to his official spokesman.

Big projects had become scarce in the engineering business.

The British and French were talking about bridging the Channel again, and the Japanese were finishing up one last breathtaker, a thirty-mile tube under the ocean from Honshu to Hokkaido. But in America, nothing much was happening. There were ten lawyers ready to sue for every one worker ready to dig. This bothered many people, who took the safe path of believing that making and building were ends in themselves; somebody else should figure out what it all meant. It bothered Warren less and less, however, even though it signified that his own professional ambition would never be realized. Economists talked endlessly, religiously, about "growth." Warren always thought, Growth for what? At what point have we grown? Places and devices were of value only if serving a purpose. America was pretty much built. So the question became, Now that it's finished, what are we going to do with it?

The address Melody had given Warren corresponded with the address on Ned Stryker's calling card—a rural route number in Chittendon, Vermont, a hamlet in the heart of ski bunny country. On the map it appeared to be only a few hours' drive. Warren decided to keep the rental car he had picked up near West Point station and go. He could drop the car later at the Albany airport and fly home, kissing good-bye to his last discretionary dollar.

Backwoods Vermont, a maze of winding roads and foothills, suited Warren fine. A perfect place to retire, or in which to build an electronic cottage. Regular Vermonters were said to resent the vacation money flowing up from the Washington–Boston megalopolis, but they certainly were doing their best to make it feel welcome. Every other structure was either a charming barn selling antiques or a complex of time-sharing A-frames.

After several wrong turns down unmarked roads, Warren found his destination. It was an old farmhouse transplanted directly from a storybook to the end of a Vermont country lane, sugar maple trees lining the approach. Before a tool shed sat a banged-up pickup truck and a four-wheel-drive Subaru station wagon. Inside the shed, which was open, could be glimpsed a meticulously polished Alfa Romeo Montreal, a curvaceous two-seat sports car that was never sold in the United States. Smoke curled from the farmhouse chimney.

Warren approached. By the front door was mounted a gold plate of the type law firms and lobbyists use to announce their corporate identities. On the plate was etched:

NED STRYKER ENTERPRISES
INVESTMENT COUNSELING
SUCCESS SEMINARS
PERSONAL TUTORING FOR FEMALE EXECUTIVES
NO-LOAD DISCOUNT BROKERAGE SERVICES
MACROVIEW HOLISTIC SOFTWARE, INC.
WORLD HEADQUARTERS, AZIMUTH COLLECTIVE

14

INFORMATION VERSUS KNOWLEDGE

L ying by the gravel path to the farmhouse door was a shipping crate of newsletters that Ned had been meaning to take to the post office. The crate was emblazoned with a bold purple-and-red insigne declaring:

AZIMUTH EXPRESS.
WHEN IT ABSOLUTELY, POSITIVELY HAS TO GET
THERE EVENTUALLY.

There was also an old news rack, modified to accommodate small periodicals, which Ned had been meaning to put in the back of the pickup truck for one of his frequent trips to the local ski lodges. The rack's locking mechanism had been removed. A fresh strip of stenciled lettering across the top said: HONOR SYSTEM—LEAVE 25 CENTS OR MUCH MORE. Instinctively, Warren opened the rack and removed one of the issues, although he did not look at it until later. When he did, he read:

WHY DO WE CONSIDER THE GREEKS SO WISE, WHEN THEY BELIEVED SO MANY THINGS WE KNOW TO BE RUBBISH?
WHY DO WE CONSIDER THE TYPICAL 1980s HIGH SCHOOL STUDENT AN IGNORAMUS, WHEN AGAMEMNON AND AESCHYLUS WOULD HAVE TREATED HIM WITH REVERENCE?
The Greeks were drastically wrong on many basic matters of fact, for instance in believing that all matter was composed of earth, wind, water, and fire, or that the earth was a disc, covered by a dome of sky. Even the laziest contemporary public school student knows better. The difference is that the Greeks had knowledge. What we have today is information.

261

The typical American has at his ready disposal more information about science, geography, astronomy, technology, physics, mathematics, economics, biology, and a host of other fields, than Newton, Einstein, Farraday, Copernicus, Galileo and da Vinci combined. Yet he feels that he *knows* less—that he does not understand the mass of statements and figures swirling around him, or how they relate to each other, much less how they relate to him.

Facts intimidate. Figures oppress. Facts scream out as you walk down the street! The typical modern "in depth" newspaper story contains on average 653.7 facts, each neatly stated, yet any reader who makes it to the end of such an article feels that he knows less about the subject than when he started. He has been bombarded with facts, but offered no knowledge.

By contrast the typical American of 100 years ago was embarrassingly ill informed. He knew little of the rest of the world, of the cosmos, of why the crops in his field grew or the metal in his factory alloyed. He was entirely ignorant of flight, relativity, video, and a thousand other subjects now quite mundane. Yet he had, it is fair to say, greater knowledge of his own purpose in life.

A cruder knowledge to be sure—purpose in life was then more commonly confined to physical security, family, and food, a definition few people today would accept. But knowledge nonetheless. The typical American of a century ago may have been going to a more simplified place than the typical American of today, but at least he knew where he wanted to go. Today we don't. How else can it be that people still fall for cults and crackpot theories in an age when pure reason ought to rule? They see the ocean of information around them and, not able to make sense of it, impose a crazy order as preferable to no order at all.

We think that since our information changes day by day, our values must change as well. Folderol! Claptrap! Or that, since no "truth" of today—truth in the informational sense, a fact about politics or technology—may last till tomorrow, truth itself is relative. Diddle! Twaddle! The wonderful promise of truth when truly attained is that it is untouchable by fact.

The Greeks impress us still because they knew truth about the human spirit. Many Greek plays rife with 3,000-year-old anachronisms are more relevant to contemporary hi-tech life than an entire year of charts and graphs from *USA Today.*

Thus an Azimuth Collective law: Information drives out knowledge. Knowing facts in itself is not bad—neither is having money, in itself. But paying more attention to facts than to wisdom is very, very bad.

The ease with which this present generation surrounds itself with simulated reality has diminished the value of "real" reality. Once, if you wanted to hear the music of human speech, you had to seek out a fellow being and converse. Now any number of machines—television, radio, recorders, computers—will provide a facsimile of human interaction, and as time goes on, the quality of such electronic mimics will increase. Will real reality and the knowledge it confers be stolen out from under us and replaced with digital information?

It is one of the annoying coincidences of history that television, a medium devoted to the suppression of knowledge, was invented during the aftermath of the Depression. Possibly, had television entered our lives at a more appropriate point, it would have assumed a more appropriate role—as an occasional diversion rather than a fountainhead. But to those who had experienced the Depression, free entertainment was too much to pass up; it would have seemed like a crime to have famous celebrities floating freely in the air and waste them.

Think of how television is now used in the typical home to drown out thought and inhibit conversation. Once, if the typical person wanted to learn about the world, he read. He skipped over sections that didn't interest him, re-read those that did, and came to his own conclusions at his own pace. Now the person who wants to learn about the world watches television, passively. He must take information at the pace television dictates. We have so many more facts available to us than the reader of *Saturday Evening Post* of fifty years ago. But are we any the wiser? If not, our material accomplishments are puffs of smoke.

Changes in the practical sciences have, for centuries, served to increase the velocity with which information is accumulated and dispersed. First, there were only facts that could be remembered. Then information preserved in writing, but difficult to copy. Then mass distribution of printed information. Then radio transmission of words and sound. Then mass distribution of visual information. Now electronic storage and retrieval. It's reasonable to assume that within a (historically) short amount of time, everyone in the technological nations will have almost immediate access to almost all the information that exists—and will feel they know even less.

Is the answer a return to the simpler, less informed life of centuries past? No; that is neither possible nor desirable. The answer is finding the meaning in the complexity of today.

—15—

It wouldn't be quite right to say that Warren was surprised to discover the true identity of the Marlboro Man. Not to be surprised by something is a different sensation from expecting it, however. Warren certainly was not surprised by what he saw when Ned Stryker answered the door.

Stryker was wearing a smoking jacket with silk ascot and appeared to have just stepped out of a tanning booth. A rich-hued Danish-modern pipe in his mouth pumped intoxicating scents of fine tobacco into the air. Warren had heard of men dressing this way but never actually seen the effect, which was stunning. The Marlboro Man looked more handsome than ever.

"My sister called to say you were coming," Stryker said. "Collect, of course. I'm really rather honored. You'll want something warm to drink. May I give you the tour?"

The front room of the farmhouse resembled a mountain-lodge set from the movies—lavishly thick rugs before a fireplace, silver bucket for wine, picture window with an unobstructed view of a postcard mountain scene. In an Early American kitchen full of brass and wood sat a cappuccino machine and similar contrivances; Warren was confident the refrigerator contained champagne, croissants, chocolates, imported preserves. A spacious refinished bathroom was lined with mirrors, chrome, and glass shelves holding an apothecary of colognes and perfumes. A small wing off the bathroom contained a sauna, whirlpool for two, and a tanning booth. Stryker gestured in passing to a walk-in closet larger than most Manhattan apartments. Inside, Warren caught sight of rows of tailored suits, tuxedos, leather bomber jackets, and the like, as well as what appeared to be a selection of women's silk pajamas of different sizes thoughtfully aligned in sequence.

In short, the trappings of chasing tail were everywhere—except in Stryker's office, a room distinguished by the cool hum of computers.

The office, Warren was relieved to note, was a mess—boxes, papers, magazines, newspaper clippings piled high. An entire corner was dedicated to stacks of very gray and dense-looking U.S. census studies. Warren recognized some sheets of paper here and there in the chaos; they were old copies of the Azimuth newsletter. Current issues of at least ten newspapers—from New York, Washington, Chicago, L.A., Boston, Miami, Houston, Denver, plus *The Wall Street Journal* and the *Financial Times*— were tossed in a heap. Another heap contained specialized publications like *Aviation Week, Scientific American, American Lawyer, The New England Journal of Medicine, Advertising Age, Congressional Quarterly,* and several others. Plus encyclopedias, *Facts on File,* annual editions of the *Almanac of American Politics,* the *Economic Report of the President,* and too many other volumes for Warren to note.

"Isn't it amazing the sheer volume of information that can be delivered to your doorstep in a free society?" Stryker asked. "Quite literally more than you could digest even if you did nothing else. And all crap. Facts, not explanations."

In a packing crate near the pile of old Azimuth newsletters sat several dozen copies of a splashy-looking hardcover book with Ned's photograph on it, *The One-Night-Stand Diet.* "Best single moneymaker I've ever come up with," Ned explained when he saw Warren notice. "Published under an assumed name, of course." The cover line read, BY DR. LIONEL ELLIOTT, Ph.D.

Spanning the room's longest wall were two computers, a small one for writing and a larger machine hooked to a telephone modem and to numerous cables. Throughout their conversion lattices of numbers and wavy lines moved continuously across this second machine's screen. It seemed to be monitoring minute-by-minute changes in the Consumer Price Index.

"I suppose you've noticed that I have an eye for the ladies," Stryker said as he served Warren a perfect cappuccino with a snifter of cognac on the side. "Allow me to explain. I believe there is something sublime about women, something ineffable, which cannot be experienced in the company of men. It is something I crave."

"What's that?"

"Pussy," Stryker said. He did not seem to mean it as a joke. "God, I love pussy. I really can't get enough. The only thing I can say in my own defense is, you should have seen me before. I haven't always looked like this."

"How did you look before?" Warren was amazed that even the most dedicated regime of exercise and beauty aids could have produced such a specimen.

"Which time?"

"Which—"

"Oh, I see," Stryker said. "No, I always looked this way this time around. It's really been enjoyable and quite an advantage in life. Did you know I was able to grow a mustache when I was nine?

"I see no reason why genetic engineering won't eventually make everyone either handsome or beautiful," Stryker continued. "That would be more equitable and certainly a boon to the general aesthetics in places like the U.S. Congress. Once I feared that if everyone were beautiful, beauty would cease to be a source of inspiration. No longer. The mountain vista here, of which I never tire, has taught me better. Mountains are not beautiful compared to hills or plains, they are beautiful in and of themselves; each would inspire, even if all the world were mountains of equal magnitude. I say this so that you can properly classify me as a believer in the perfectibility of life.

"At any rate, what I meant before was that you should have seen the way I looked in other lives. Horrible several times running. Envied the gargoyles on castle cornices. So I've earned this. Now, how can I help you?"

That was a question Warren could not really answer, since he didn't know how anyone could help him. He had come seeking only any clue about Nora or his own possible fate. But instead of raising these questions he told Stryker about the Seattle gas station owner who had read his newsletter.

"An example of the fine line between genius and insanity," Stryker replied. "In another life the man you describe could easily have been a professor of philosophy, or one of the Hapsburgs."

"He had some crazy theory that Henry Kissinger had created slavery."

"Hmm. Probably a good thing we got him out before he had time to try. But your gas jockey may in fact have been entrusting you with a vital fragment of collective racial memory. Who knows what Kissinger was up to in his previous manifestations?"

Stryker turned to the large computer. "Don't happen to have the man's zip code, do you?" When Warren answered no, Stryker began typing in commands. "It's all right. I'll just run a sort for Seattle. I may not have too many subscribers out that way." The computer beeped and Stryker studied its screen for a moment, embarrassed. "It seems he is my only subscriber in the Pacific Northwest," he said. Then he punched in a few more commands.

"Are you cancelling his subscriptions?"

"Hell, no. Doubling his rate." Stryker looked around at some of the cartons stacked on the floor. "Couldn't interest you in some advanced data base management software, could I? Goes far beyond spreadsheets and cross foots. My software has more than twenty-five options for graphic display of an overdrawn checkbook, and will find mystic relationships among your data. For example, are you aware how many figures followed by exactly forty zeros there are in the federal budget? How many numbers divisible by the natural constant E occur in the average American Express bill?"

Warren began to sense there would be value in keeping Ned Stryker on the topic. "In fact I did come here to ask you something," he said. "I wanted to ask—"

Stryker's expression sobered. "I know. And the answer is, you must decide for yourself. To me, as an intellectual proposition, asserting you have walked this way before is no more or less credible than asserting, as millions do, that they have not—since no one can *know* one way or the other. I freely claim to have lived many lives. Of course, I admit this claim is extraordinarily effective with women. Should my claim be accepted? Only the individual can decide."

"That's not an answer. That's an evasion."

"No, it is the literal answer." Stryker seemed insistent. "I believe that people live many lives," he said, "but our spirits are designed in such a way as to preclude direct knowledge of this fact. Only inferential knowledge is permitted. This inferential knowledge is carried from life to life in the form of hopes, moral values, and respect for inalienable rights—principles that all thinking people agree have transcendent stature, yet which no one can 'prove' deserve to exist."

Stryker paused and punched some buttons on the large computer. Noise began to emanate from the kitchen. "What the ultimate purpose of this exercise is, I do not know," he continued. "The Hindus say the nurturing of a soul is such a complex task, it takes many attempts, and as lives accumulate, the quality of the soul increases. That sounds reasonable to me. On the other hand, the Hindus say some very weird things about cows and wives. So I would caution, as with all religious beliefs, to discount by half.

"Looking around the world we see some people who are good, some bad, and most at various stages in between. We observe good people from bad families and bad people from good. We Americans, accustomed to making our judgments in seconds, are uncomfortable with the concept of slow spiritual development. We're too impatient to find out how the story ends. Yet I am equally uncomfortable with the notion that values of right and wrong are instilled in people in a flash, or by random chance.

"So—" A chime sounded in Stryker's kitchen. "Excuse me," he said, and then returned a moment later with a platter holding an exceptional selection of gourmet foods—crab and lobster salad, breads and pâtés, snapper in sorrel, blackened turkey, quiches, fruits.

"Thought you might be hungry, so I slipped this in the microwave beforehand," Stryker explained. "As I was saying, I do not believe we are meant to know of our previous experiences, except indirectly, through the accumulation of moral worth. What I believe has happened in your case is that there has been an error. A celestial fuck-up.

"I am certain you and Nora were intended to meet, but not under the circumstances that you did, and certainly not within the very building containing evidence you were better not to see. It's a colossal blunder, and heads should roll. It may not have been the first blunder concerning you two, and may not be the last. But only what you and she decide within yourselves regarding this event carries any final significance. Anything else I could say about it would be strictly an opinion."

Stryker opened a wax-wrapped cheese and popped it in his mouth. "And opinions are being overproduced, just like farm products. That's why the prices for both are depressed."

Warren ate quietly for a while, turning these thoughts over in his head. "I read your edition that said there really could be a world without evil," he told Stryker. "You dodged the issue of free will."

"Free will." Stryker made a face indicating *not that again.* "The same people who tell us murder, repression, rape, and torture are necessary so that the survivors can pat themselves on the back for having free will, turn right around and say, 'But you must worship God.' Why? 'Because He is King.' If we must worship God because He exceeds us in rank, where's the 'free will' in that?"

Stryker shook his head. "Think about what God has to be like under this formulation. He not only tolerates torture and slaughter and terror—He *likes* people to get tortured and terrorized because it increases the pleasure He gets from those who worship Him despite the horror. This makes God despicable, repugnant, an egomaniac. And thus, logically, not worthy of our worship. We might as well say a rabbit should worship a fox."

"Without free will, we'd all be zombies," Warren said. "Maybe there would be no fighting or crime. But what would be the point of life as a zombie? Why live at all?"

"Adam in the Garden was no zombie," Stryker replied.

His attention shifted as the large computer began to beep stridently and, for about ten seconds, display a dramatically rising sine curve. Then the curve dropped back down.

"Damn," Stryker said. "An opening for spread puts on Standard and Poors index options. But the market's already reacted. Anyway, Adam. Adam was free to do anything he wanted—so long as it wasn't wrong.

"Adam could build things, change the Garden around, devise technology, create art. His life wasn't risk-free—he might have gotten hurt or sick, tried to move away, done any number of unpredictable things. He might have shown courage; might have suffered too, for example, if Eve had left him. Beyond the truly sick notion that God introduced the snake and thereby Abel's murder in order to make things 'interesting,' the Garden was plenty interesting before sin.

"There is no reason, no conceptual reason whatsoever, that we could not be denied freedom in matters of right and wrong and granted freedom in all other matters. Something as little as a gene-code command making it impossible for one human being to physically injure another would take us most of the way toward eliminating evil in the world.

"Such a code is not so hard to imagine; most animals have a precursor of it, in that they are loathe to attack their own species. Perhaps God tried to invent this code and—since humans are so much more complex than animals—in the time available to Him, failed to figure it out. The challenge of allowing good while stopping bad is extremely complex, as the complexity of our own legal systems would indicate.

"If people were physically incapable of making themselves harm one another, the net amount of 'free will' in the world would *increase,* not decline—because crime, repressions, wars and tyrannies, which inhibit the very thing you say you want to increase, would be eliminated. Really, Warren, try not to put yourself in the position of defending evil, okay? If no killing or fighting were possible, God would be overjoyed. Only dictators, lunatics, and producers of television shows would suffer."

"Guess that's an okay answer," Warren said.

"What church were you raised in?"

"Episcopal."

"Great, because I have a good example from Episcopal," Stryker said happily. "If we are flawed—and clearly we are—it's ridiculous to think we should be held responsible for the frailties we were born with. We are only responsible for wrong moral behavior we engage in out of our own choosing."

Stryker sifted through the pile of books in one corner of his office, producing a worn pew copy of the Episcopal *Book of Common Prayer,* old version.

"Listen to this," he said. "Worshippers are supposed to repeat,

> Although we are unworthy through our manifold sins
> to offer unto Thee any sacrifice . . .

> We acknowledge and bewail our sins and wickedness
> by thought, word and deed against Thy divine majesty,
> provoking most justly Thy wrath against us. . . .

"Now really. A murderer or tyrant should plead thus to God. But the average person? If the average person in his average attempt to cope with life is really that contemptible, then God must be to blame for willfully delivering us into an impossible world.

"But I don't think He did. I think He made the best world He could under the circumstances, and He wants our help to make it better."

For his part, Warren was having trouble coming to grips with the fact that his mountaintop was turning out to be a bachelor pad in Vermont, and his guru, a man whose fondest wish was an evening with three Swedish models chained together at the ankles. "This idea about man helping God, that goes too far," Warren said.

"Not at all," Stryker replied. "It is well known that man's ability to make technological devices runs considerably ahead of his ability to manage the implications of his own creations. We are told that we dwell in God's image. Why should it be any different for Him? Perhaps God, like us, can create things much more readily than He can make sense of them. Then He would need our help, as we have already been able to help Him correct many flaws in the human body which—"

"You used that example already."

"Right. So I did." Stryker paused. "Could I interest you in some chocolate-marble cheesecake topped with raspberries flown in fresh yesterday?"

Stryker took away the tray of food and returned with dessert, plus the bottle of cognac, a dusty vessel the family name on which Warren didn't recognize, though he caught the French for *grand reserve.*

"You are staying the night—I insist—so don't worry about drinking and driving," Stryker said.

"I hardly mean to sound ungrateful for such hospitality," Warren said, "but you would stand a better chance of convincing me if you could produce another example."

"A bigger example? On God's scale?" Stryker asked.

"Yes."

"Okay. You're an engineer. So let's look at the ultimate question of engineering."

Stryker offered a box of cigars to Warren while refilling his pipe. Warren had not had a cigar in many years, and never tasted one the likes of this.

"In the going theory of the Big Bang," Stryker said, "it appears that the universe recycles—begins with an explosion, expands into stars and planets, later contracts back into a point of non-nothing, only to explode anew. If this turns out to be correct, there is no reason to assume we are universe Number One. We may be Number Two, Number Five, Number Eighty-eight, or Number 536,144,090 in a cosmology of unfathomable age."

"Or we could be Number One. We wouldn't know," Warren said.

"Correct. The least complicated assumption, though in some ways the most uncomfortable, because if we are Number One then it is our lot to face the question of where-did-the-beginning-begin—a subject which unnerves me because I've never so much as heard a *theory* about that one. But let's assume for the moment that we are not first. I want to pose an ultimate question which would have to be faced by every universe except the first.

"If we are not universe Number One, we must assume that all occupants of previous universes have been unable to prevent their own annihilation in the Bangs that created subsequent cosmic structures. We must further acknowledge that God either did not or could not block these catastrophes. Perhaps the collapse mechanism is so powerful that stopping it is Not Possible. Sort of a moot question for the next seventy billion years or so, but containing a point of immediate interest. When the universe detonates, is God destroyed, too?"

"That sounds to me more like a debater's flourish than a real issue," Warren said.

"Oh no, very pertinent. It may be that God can transcend the annihilation of reality and hang around in the non-nothing phase in order to guide the next universe. That makes sense to me, because I think He would need the rest.

"But suppose He can't. Suppose God cannot save Himself. Then He would be as vexed as we are, as perplexed and anxious, about His ultimate purpose."

Stryker took a good pull on his pipe and exhaled, filling the room with hot aroma. He seemed perfectly at peace. "An all-knowing God, realizing this, might become cynical and give up. A lesser sovereign might remain determined to muddle ahead, hoping for a breakthrough. This is by and large the way man responds, pressing on in spite of the evidence."

The two men spoke well into the evening hours. At one point Warren related the story of the newspaper clipping at West Point. Stryker became somber, and said little more afterward.

In the morning the Marlboro Man laid out a breakfast as fine as could be ordered in any Swiss hotel. He hardly touched the food himself, while urging his guest to partake freely. Warren had the eerie sensation of being fed a last meal.

When Warren was ready to leave, Stryker presented him with the box of cigars, plus a bundle of back issues of the newsletter and some floppy discs. He conferred these gifts cheerlessly.

"Two more things I want to tell you," Stryker said as they walked down the farmhouse lane to Warren's car. "First, I envy you. Second, I fear for you."

This comment chilled Warren, who thought Stryker was referring to the death of Harriman Anzalone, Jr. His own guilt or innocence in that affair was an issue that travel had, for a moment, put out of his mind. But it seemed Stryker was thinking of something entirely different.

"I want you to understand that if we do have many fates, they may not all be good," Stryker said, his magnificent features momentarily grown pallid, as though he'd forgotten to put on his makeup.

"It's a habit of man to think of whatever condition that comes into existence as somehow inevitable all along. In truth a wide range of outcomes are possible from only the tiniest variations of events. As the dozens of major forms of social organization and thousands of subsets that exist in our world and at our point in time alone, descended from the same root, do, I think, prove."

Stryker held the door of Warren's rental car for him, respectfully. "In one sense this is comforting. If the accomplishment of just ends takes many tries, then any individual failure should be no cause for disheartenment. But in another sense it means that nice guys lose. Things can go one way or another. If they go the wrong way for you, be grateful for what you have been allowed to know."

Returning home was for Warren like falling into freezing water. The negligence case, still in discovery, remained at least a year away from trial; the various civil tort suits might not be settled for much longer. Warren obtained a lawyer with Jewel Wonigan's backing. But he found getting another engineering job impossible. As long as the charges and suits were pending, no firm would hire him.

Unemployed, Warren withdrew into himself. At first he skipped social events, seeking to avoid the expense they entailed. As time progressed, personal contact itself became something he feared. Warren even began to avoid Lil and Tommy, who lived on the same block—always walking in the opposite direction so as not to pass their house.

Warren had had no news from Nora in many months, and could not bring himself to seek any. He had lost his courage, and was close to losing his faith. He was close to wishing they had never met.

In the summer, Warren found a temporary job framing houses —outdoor work where somebody else made all the decisions and a tangible product could be viewed at the end of the day—which lifted his spirits slightly. He nursed a hope of being hired on as a draftsman. But nothing came of it. When the seasonal laborers were let go he was jobless again.

At a particularly low juncture, Warren answered an ad for management trainees at the Hardees hamburger chain. He expected to be laughed out of the applications line, a thirty-five-year-old white-collar worker with a printed resume and "salary history." Instead, Warren found other older men there too, family men dressed in suits and speaking of their children. Warren felt ashamed to have considered himself too good for the job. When it was offered he took it eagerly, excited about $4.55-an-hour night work surrounded by adolescents.

Flipping bacon burgers from eleven P.M. to seven A.M. turned out to be harder than he ever would have guessed. It left Warren more drained than sitting behind a desk at KD&H, where his salary equated to four times as much per hour. It wasn't the physical labor—not being able to let his mind wander was the taxing part. Hour after hour of focusing his attention on the fryer bell, the stock levels, endless repetitions of the same requests; no opportunities to daydream about football or sex, as office workers can the day long.

There was a card in the back of the Hardees, by the walk-in

cooler, specifying what phrases could be used in addressing customers while on counter duty. "May I help you this evening?" was okay; "Hi, how are you?" was out. Anyone overheard taking an order without asking "Would you care for some French fries this evening?" was in jeopardy.

The night when Warren's crew worked through an entire shift somehow forgetting to put pickles on the Big Deluxe, the regional office went into a tizzy. Forms had to be filled out; a district supervisor came down to "follow up" and questioned each employee who had been working the grill as if he had witnessed the landing of a UFO.

After a few months, Warren quit Hardees, and the branch manager seemed relieved. Warren had considered goofing off so that Hardees would be forced to fire him, thus renewing his unemployment eligibility. But he restrained himself and left on honest terms. Once, later, he even went back for dinner, thinking it would give him cheer to be reminded that he was no longer trapped there. When there wasn't anyone on duty that he recognized, Warren felt strange. The place had transformed so quickly, and here he was, missing the company of teenagers.

Many more months of lonely withdrawal followed. Money shortages became serious. Warren sold his car and then began thinking of moving to a smaller apartment—but without a car or money for movers how could he do that? Such problems would consume him for days on end. Other days were taken up giving discovery at the office of lawyer after lawyer representing different parties in the case. One day he looked at the calendar and realized that it had been two years since he last saw Nora Jocelyn.

Around that time the telephone rang. The caller was B. T. Carpenter, a young engineer Warren had met years before on the irrigation canal project in California who had said he was moving back to Los Angeles to enter defense consulting. Warren could not remember what the *B* stood for, although he did remember a Trans Am with California vanity plates that read BT ME.

B. T. Carpenter explained that his firm had prospered and was within sight of two hefty contracts, but was taking static from the Pentagon because it did not employ anyone with actual military experience.

"I've got to be able to call my contract officer on C Ring by Monday morning and tell him there's a Vietnam vet on the team," Carpenter said. "Otherwise the little wimp is going to flake us to the tune of $675,000, not to mention a foot in the door for God knows how much in overruns. How about it?"

Warren had always told himself he would refuse defense work, not for philosophical reasons but professional ones: if patriotism was the last refuge of scoundrels, the Pentagon was the last refuge of consultants. Thinking of his bank account, though, he suddenly found himself more open-minded about the need to keep America strong.

"I only served two years in the infantry, and it wasn't exactly my idea," Warren cautioned.

"It'll do," Carpenter answered quickly. "We'll give your life to our enhancer, the guy who writes our contract proposals. He'll make it sound like you were with Patton when he crossed the Delaware. Ever wounded or anything? Go on any lightning commando raids?"

Warren mentioned that he had received a Medal of Valor.

"Holy Christ!" Carpenter said. "That's boss! Did you get it from Nixon personally? Or was he already dead then?"

Warren started to say that the distinction had not really been deserved; that he had been submitted for a medal mainly to salvage the base commander's reputation by recasting the general's idiocy as supervision of heroism. Then he decided to drop this subject and reveal worse news, his legal troubles.

"It's only an indictment?" B.T. asked.

"At the moment. To be honest, I don't know myself whether I'm guilty."

"Oh, I don't care about that," B.T. said. "Whether you're guilty of anything is your own private affair. Half the people who work here have been indicted for conflict of interest. So long as it's only an indictment, we can use you."

By the end of the conversation Warren and B.T. were bantering like old drinking buddies. And by Monday morning Warren was in coat and tie again, with an office and group insurance. The company won both contracts and Warren was given his choice of which to work on: a fire-suppression system for an experimental tank that would be able to submerge in rivers and fire torpedoes at other submerged tanks, or an earth-orbiting neutron projector designed to shoot down intercontinental ballistic missiles. Warren chose the tank.

"Suit yourself, but SDI is the wave of the future," B.T. said. "There's just no limit to what it might cost."

Now Warren was not opposed to the thought of shooting down nuclear missiles. In fact, as a potential target, he was rather fond of the idea. But he had looked over the concepts for beam weapons and couldn't imagine them actually working.

"Not a requirement of the contract," B.T. assured him. "Functionality is strictly a frill. What's important is that we demonstrate our national resolve by spending whatever it takes to get these weapons up there whether they work or not."

Closing his office door snugly, Warren sat alone and began leafing through the folder on the fire-suppression project. The design was hopelessly complex, more likely to start a fire than quench one. Yet Warren found it blissful to have an office again, a secretary willing to pretend he was important; to know that somewhere out there money was working its way in his direction.

The space defense group, situated down the hall, took itself quite seriously and was forever scurrying back and forth to international conferences and hush-hush meetings. For a while Warren wondered if they were actually on to something. Then he talked his way into one of the sessions. It was like Saturday morning science club.

"Suppose we built satellites that used super-cooled magnets so powerful they could pull the warheads off course during post-boost phase?" one of the participants was saying. There was a rapid buzz of excitement and calculations.

"Larry, where would the warheads be pulled off course to?" someone finally asked. Larry pondered for a moment, then drew a large X across the front page of a blue book he was holding and tossed it aside.

"Well then," said another, "suppose we orbit containers of spun filament nets that would be unfurled from geostationary supports to cover the entire troposphere of the Soviet Union, so they couldn't launch through it?"

By the end of the session Warren had learned another lesson of modern times: War is the extension of cost overruns by other means.

And by the end of the week he had quit again, which perhaps was just as well, because a letter had come announcing that the trial would begin in ten days. The pre-trial hearings moved excruciatingly slowly; Warren was never called on to speak, merely expected to be present to listen as the accusations mounted. His lawyer made attempts at plea bargains, but Warren would not accept them. Not, he told the lawyer, until I know whether I really am to blame, at which point the legal case would become irrelevant anyway. The lawyer always shook his head on that one.

Late one afternoon at the courthouse, Warren felt certain nothing more would happen that day. Not wanting to go back to his apartment, he wandered out across the lawn.

When built, the courthouse had occupied a prime location in the old downtown. Now the courthouse sat at the fulcrum of two elevated freeways constructed to get people over and past the area as rapidly as possible. Warren walked under one freeway in its shadow. Eight lanes thundered overhead, raised on steel stilts. He could almost feel the weight of the trucks and cars above him.

Beyond the freeway was a stretch of what had been important waterfront property back when the grain mills were operating and vast freighters chugging black smoke lined up like children to take their share. Farther down the waterfront, an abandoned factory of red firebrick had sat untended for years, its broken windows having lost their appeal even as targets for juvenile hell-raisers. The scene made Warren feel weary, as though his own life were near its end, or at least past the point where it held any interest for him.

Weariness of the heart comes too easily to the human animal, especially when events of youth overwhelm the mechanisms of unfinished spirits. Warren felt this weariness heavily. Nora was sure to have slipped away by now—into children, or a different lover, other habits and inclinations. Perhaps she too felt their fumbled chance meant no further love could enter her life, and had lost interest in the idea. Nature is inclined toward missed opportunity.

Near the waterfront stood a peeling drive-through hot dog stand. Most likely the spot had once been popular when mill workers were teeming back and forth along the local roads. Now it could hardly be reached except on foot. Warren bought a hot dog and a pineapple milkshake from a lone woman operating the stand. He sat down to consume them at a weathered picnic bench chained to a post.

In the distance a small boat appeared *put-putting* along, a hand-made vessel resembling a telephone booth nailed to a raft that looked like it had made a wrong turn on its way to the 1850s. The boatman cried out to the woman running the hot dog stand. Warren couldn't hear what he said because of all the machinery roaring above on the skyway. But he saw the woman run eagerly to help dock the boat. She was laughing and so was the boatman as they struggled through the task.

Neither face, though withered, looked anything like what Warren supposed the labor-bent and those past their time of promise should look like. Instead, both man and woman appeared serene and glad of each other's greeting, though Warren guessed they had greeted each other thousands of times before. In that moment he was shamed again, for he understood that love is so powerful it can make the old look forward to morning.

The night before the trial Warren's phone rang at 11:15 P.M. It was Max Rademacher downstairs, wanting to be let in.

"I know what you think of me so you don't have to say a word, okay?" Max said as he stepped out of the elevator. "And I'm a weakling. If you punch me you'll probably kill me. So please don't punch me." Max's tone was as frenetic as ever, but his appearance had been greatly refined. His shoes and eyeglasses were fashionable, and he wore a custom-tailored wool suit. The only exception to his otherwise polished appearance was dark smudges under his fingernails. He carried two small packages.

"Why on earth—" Warren started to spill out his confusion but realized that the situation called for him, as the aggrieved party, to sound livid and dangerous. "Talk," he said. "This better be good."

Max made no move to enter the apartment. Instead, he crumpled down into a chair that sat in the hall in front of the elevator, left there by a bumbling mover and never claimed. He withdrew an envelope from his suit. Inside the envelope was a cashier's check for $88,740.

"My profit-sharing and bonuses. We had an excellent year," said Max, holding up a hand for quiet. "Don't say you don't want it. Of course you don't want it. But you need it. I would have done this sooner but I had debts."

Warren fingered the check. Just holding it made him light-headed. He could get a car again, pay his bills—travel, if that still mattered. "I won't take this unless you tell me what happened," he said.

"I'm going to do more than that," Max said, looking down at his feet. His tone was cold.

"They gave me a choice. Cover for them; get a partnership. Come clean; get fired. Back out on the street, at my age." Max became animated. "I'm thinking, I've got them by the balls, now the tables are turned! They make me managing general partner in the deal. Look at this . . ." Max produced the new company brochure, which proclaimed "Kessey, Rademacher & Associates." On the cover was his picture, shaking hands with President Ford. Only now it appeared to be a private meeting between the President and Max. His former colleagues from Westinghouse had been neatly cropped out.

"I'm thinking, Finally I have a company by the balls." Max

spoke as though recalling the plot of an old movie. "Kessey can't touch me because of what I know. Bang, I would go to the police charging obstruction of justice. And final authority on all technical matters becomes mine. So I can guarantee only quality work. No more shortcuts."

"Shortcuts?" Warren was angry. "What *happened*?"

"All along I'm thinking, I can get it set right. Gifford will be exonerated, Hobard will pay, and I keep my partnership. Okay, so a little stress on my friend Gifford; I'll make it up to him privately. But the bastard Hobard, he keeps his files locked under separate key. Only key I don't have. So month after month I'm waiting, waiting for my chance. Never he slips."

Max turned to Warren with a look of childish anguish. "Don't you *see*?" he said. "I had to get the evidence on Hobard first."

"Max, explain yourself *immediately.*" Warren was indeed about to strike him.

Max motioned for them to step inside the apartment. There he opened one of the two packages and spread a series of documents on the floor. They were copies of correspondence between Hobard and Berns and Sons, the construction contractor, a company Warren hadn't wanted to use—too many mob connections—but that the mayor insisted on. Two weeks before work had been scheduled to begin, the letters showed, KD&H had sent Berns and Sons a package of change orders.

"Change orders?" Warren asked. "I never submitted any change orders."

"Right," Max said. "All signed by Hobard. Read."

A cover letter for one change order innocuously referred to the "reduction of redundant structural elements." Most concerned petty corner-cutting like substitution of lower-grade material. One stuck out. Instead of sinking pylons for the restraining wall moorings into bedrock, as Warren had specified, they would be anchored to a temporary base. New calculations showed the safety factor reduced from 100 percent of anticipated load to 15 percent. Later the newspapers would note that Berns and Sons desired this change because it would have had to subcontract the bedrock portion of the job, lowering its profit margin.

"Holy shit," said Warren slowly. "Didn't he realize—"

"Rained like the dickens the night before," Max said. "You were away, as I recall, so you didn't know. Poured the night long. Reservoirs rose to record levels."

According to the letters, Hobard had signed off on these changes himself, consulting no one. Around the firm Hobard was well known for his low opinion of the younger engineers. He was especially resentful of the long sessions of handwringing with citizens groups that accompanied even routine awards of government work. There was always some ecological self-promoter who would drone on about how pouring one more ton of concrete would melt the polar ice caps or disrupt vicuna molting cycles in the upper Andes. Hobard was also known for hitting the town with one of the many Berns sons. Around the time of the pump-generating project, Warren now recalled, he had run into Hobard exiting an expensive restaurant with a woman twenty years his junior on his arm.

"Proof, I needed the proof," Max said. "In my head I had this figured out, but nothing on paper. I was going to get the proof and send it to the district attorney anonymously. Then one day dragged into another, and into a week. It got harder and harder to turn back."

"For chrissakes. Why didn't you just call the police and have them bring a subpoena for the safe?"

"You're forgetting something. I had become an accessory to this crime."

Warren sat down, subdued. "How did you finally get them?"

"Blowtorch. Tonight, after work." Max laughed. "Wait till Hobard sees his office. Looks like it was attacked by the Green Berets. Cut open the safe. Burned up half the stuff on his walls doing it. Charred the shit out of his golf trophies.

"Tomorrow, first thing, I take these papers to the D.A. I figure I can bargain a suspended sentence for myself with them. And then, kaput for me. I'll never work again."

"Max—"

"Shh. I've deserved this for a long time." He picked up the

second package and began unraveling a heavy cord. "I see in your heart you have already begun to forgive me for doing this, Warren. You are a good person and it gives my life meaning to have known you. But this here, there is no forgiving."

From the package Max withdrew a metal-alloy cylinder about the size of a coffee can. The surface was smoother than a beam of light and glistened like revolving gold. It felt heavy and powerful in Warren's hand.

"Relief valve actuator for the secondary cooling system of a breeder reactor. See anything wrong with it?" Max asked.

"No. It's beautiful."

"You bet it's beautiful. Magnificent workmanship. Bench-tested and X-rayed five times. Molecular content analysis of the alloy. Cost more than a small house." Max took the valve back and tossed it into the wastebasket. "It's also the wrong size. Ninety microns too small. Would have popped in routine use."

"Your error?"

"No. From another department. Some numbers in a letter to a subcontractor were transposed by a typist. So obvious everyone missed it, except me. I was snooping through other people's folders as usual."

"Good thing you caught it."

"I caught it all right. But I didn't say anything. Six of these were installed in the test reactor."

It seemed very quiet in the apartment. Warren realized Max was whispering.

"The emergency feedwater system. I wanted so badly to see it run. I didn't say anything because I *wanted* the reactor to fail. Only if the primary and secondary systems broke down would mine ever be demonstrated. Fifteen seconds away from atomic explosion, Max Rademacher's pumps save the world. I would have been an important man after that day. A chair maybe at MIT. They don't know how lucky they were when they cancelled the program without a test."

"Good God, Max. Do you have any idea—"

"I do." He stood stiffly and walked out the door to the elevator, pressing the call button. Distant motors whirred. "I would have been in the control room. If my workmanship had been wrong, I would have paid."

Max stepped into the elevator as it opened. "We have all sinned and fallen short," he said. He was headed down.

The next morning at nine A.M. there was considerable turmoil in the courtroom. The D.A. opened his case by asking for a one-hour recess. Max was outside in the corridor. He and Warren looked at each other but did not speak; Max's head was bowed.

After consultations with the assistant D.A., Warren's lawyer signaled for him to reenter the courtroom. Motions went by at a swimming pace. Each side, in accordance with legal custom, was entering into the record a multitude of impossible demands on which it could later base technical appeals. Shortly before noon the name Warren Gifford began to pop out of the lingo. Warren's lawyer, the assistant D.A., and a half dozen other attorneys stepped forward. They spoke as fast and as comprehensibly as auctioneers. The judge rapped once and turned to take papers from a bailiff. Then a Berns and Sons attorney began moving on the stipulation of experts. Warren's lawyer motioned him back into the corridor.

"That's it?" Warren said. He had been dropped as a defendant in the criminal case and would be dropped from the civil actions later. After almost three years of wheel-spinning, it was over in the wink of an eye. Warren was amazed.

"I didn't even get to approach the bench," he protested. "I never even stood up." For a moment he wanted to take it all back, to stage a tense courtroom confrontation that years later he could tell exaggerated stories about.

The D.A. walked past. "Sorry it had to happen this way," he offered. Sorry? Why sorry? There was a strange expression on his face; Warren wondered if the D.A. had deliberately stalled prosecution, in order to keep the case hanging over the mayor as long as possible.

An awkward moment followed as Warren and the D.A. were

forced to stand together while the corridor cleared. "Did you see what His Honor announced yesterday?" the D.A. asked, indicating a morning newspaper discarded on the corridor bench. "All housing inspectors will be required to have sociology degrees. What a cheeseball." Then he disappeared in a flurry of aides.

Leaving the courthouse Warren went to his bank. He exchanged the check from Max for a certified check for $80,000 made out to cash, and put the remainder in his account—minus about a thousand in fifty-dollar bills that he would need for plane tickets, no longer having credit cards. On his way to the airport Warren mailed the $80,000 anonymously to Harriman Anzalone, Jr.'s widow. Forty-five thousand plus inflation works out to about eighty grand, Warren thought. Ford, I have passed it along.

Warren had no plan, or even any plan to make a plan. He only wanted to tell Nora of his innocence, explain his silence, and then depart from her life officially. After such a long absence Nora might hate him; at best, she'd consider him a crackpot. It would probably be a kindness to let her think the latter. Paying with cash just like a drug dealer, Warren bought a ticket for the next plane to Seattle.

In front of the house on Mercer Island, Nora's Toyota was nowhere to be seen. Two station wagons were parked in the driveway, both the same make and model. A big-wheels tricycle lay on its side in a row of flowers newly planted under the front window. The curtain that once hung there had been replaced by blinds. The house had been painted, too—a pale shade difficult to make out in the fading light. When Warren rang the front bell a middle-aged man in a cardigan sweater answered.

"We purchased this abode from the previous owners a considerable time ago," he said, dredging down into his larynx like a movie butler.

A female voice inside the house cried out shrilly, "If that's the Steinmarks they're early!"

Warren claimed to be an old neighbor who had been out of town, and requested the previous owners' new address.

"His or hers?" he was asked.

The woman inside cried, "Tell them they'll have to wait!"

"His or hers?" Warren echoed.

"His in Rochester or hers in Denver?" Seeing incomprehension on Warren's face, the man smiled with a self-superior curl of the lips. "My, my, you have been out of town," he said. "Your former neighbors have been divorced for two years."

16
WHY POINTLESSNESS DOESN'T MATTER

The morning of the trial, Warren had stuffed into his pocket the latest edition of the Azimuth newsletter. He tried to slip it out to read in court, but the bailiff wouldn't let him. Reading in a court of law is even more frowned upon than trying to make sense of the proceedings.

Instead, Warren read the issue on the plane to Denver. This edition came the way the first had, hand-typed on plain paper. Paragraphs had been cut out and stapled to different pages; lines were drawn through the entire first page, over which was written "see insert." Properly assembled, the newsletter said:

IF THE NIHILISTS ARE WRONG, THEN THERE'S NO POINT IN LISTENING TO THEM.

AND IF THEY'RE RIGHT, THEN THERE'S NO POINT IN LISTENING TO THEM.

Stylish pointlessness, intrinsic to most contemporary philosophy and to the minimalist forms of art, has it that the world is irredeemable; the observer can do naught but give voice to ambiguous anguish.

Big forces out there, beyond anyone's control, are pressing the dignity from life. Resistance is folly; the individual means nothing. Events are irrational, random; people are disconnected from each other and drifting. To speculate as to the reasons—much less suggest a solution!!!—is supreme folly. The knowing do not dare; artistic characters who dare are made to suffer greater miseries for their efforts, or are cut down by extreme cruelty.

The result is those movies where people stare without expression into the camera talking vaguely of unhappiness; those plays where characters float in a void; those short stories where passive people drift from one pointless experience to the next, or perhaps to an unexplained act of random violence when it's time for the story to end.

There is a distinction between using a gloomy technique and expressing a nihilist message. Some who do the former do not intend the latter. But contemporary forms almost by definition force art amd philosophy toward a pessimistic conclusion.

If the practitioners of stylish pointlessness actually believed their own doctrine, logically they could not practice it. The mere act of painting or thinking or engaging in any process intended to express despair implies that there *is* purpose, if nothing other than that people enlightened as to their own pointlessness are somehow more properly wretched than those unenlightened.

Even if the practice of art or philosophy is entirely self-centered—intended, say, to provide a modest teaching post or a modicum of money or self-respect to the practitioner—then we must posit that some physical comfort or consolation is better than none. Which forces us to posit that there are relative degrees in quality of life. And all of a sudden, we have established what you are, madam, and are simply dickering over the price.*

These comments are more than wordplay. If we are to accept that ideas have meaning, then we must be accountable for the content of the ideas.

Nihilism might be accurate in a metaphysical sense, but it cannot be a form of art or argument, for it is self-cancelling. Anyone who makes the effort to advance nihilistic views is, by definition, not a nihilist. If life is pointless, what possible purpose can interpretation of its pointlessness serve?

In its worst manifestation, stylish pointlessness embraces violence as a social statement. The drifter who beats a clerk to

---

*For readers who missed Volume 6, Number 11: A man meets a woman in a cocktail lounge and asks, "Would you sleep with me for $10,000?" The woman thinks it over and says yes. The man then asks, "Would you sleep with me for $10?" The woman cries out, "What do you think I am!" The man replies, "We have established what you are, madam. We are simply dickering over the price."

death in some Texas dust town can become, to the modernist who has never been to Texas, never been beaten, and never looked into the face of a human being in whom madness has been loosed, a sophisticated commentator on proletarian alienation—ripe for appointment to a tenured chair, if it weren't for that nagging worry he would ruin the sherry hour by stabbing his department head.

Artists and intellectuals who spring from the privileged classes often adulate criminal behavior and celebrate sadistic chic as "realism," a subject on which they may be inadequately schooled. The Metropolitan Museum of Art in Manhattan, for example, keeps stills from the Buñuel movie *Un Chien Andalou* in which the eye of a helpless (and gorgeous, of course) woman is casually slashed by a man with a straight razor: as though this were a great moment in creative self-expression.

Champions of stylish pointlessness eagerly seize on newspaper stories of roadside killings or farmer suicides as proof that contemporary life is horrible beyond words, rather than viewing such events as proof that *violence* is horrible, and that the social conditions which foster it must be changed—the view more often taken by intellectuals from the working class.

Here we come to the reason respectable forms of nihilism are popular in some circles.

If you suppose as a precondition of art that life is meaningless, then why bother trying to change it? Why trouble yourself proposing ideas that may only subject you to criticism if through some miracle they should actually be tried? In intellectual circles, depressing views are always least likely to be challenged. Stark portraits of a world gone mad are professionally safer—especially to the Campbell's Soup Can School of modernism—than theories about cures.

When the line of cant is set to read that artists can only chronicle despair, never intervening for good—kind of lets the artist off the hook, doesn't it? Pretty much the way lawyers are always exclaiming, Hey, we're not responsible for justice.

Some thinkers have always come to the conclusion that life is terrible, and some always will; perhaps, ultimately, they are right. Artists and intellectuals in general do have a special obligation to be negative, if only to balance out politicians and businessmen who can be counted on to deny that problems exist.

Stylish pointlessness, however, has come to dominate the presumptions of art and intellect so rigidly that other outlooks are often rejected by rote, not for being wrong, but for failing to conform.

In the classic historical sequence, modernism and minimalism were created as protests against existing rigid forms, such as florid art. Some practitioners used the new forms to achieve sublime expressions of those parts of life that are indeed disconnected or hopeless. Now, completing the cycle, the new forms have themselves become rigid, their advocates demanding that serious art conform to a style that imposes a preconceived conclusion—the reverse of what "creativity" is supposed to be about.

It may be that life is pointless. But if so, why say it? The only element of life we can be certain is pointless is pointlessness itself.

—17—

Pasted on the directory of a block of pseudo-Tudor apartments in Aurora, Colorado, just outside of Denver, was a sliver of paper on which was typed JOCELYN N. 207. The paper was smudged and difficult to read. To Warren it was a sennet of redemption.

He had arrived at mid-afternoon; no one had answered the buzzer. Warren had paced the length of the building, befuddled. For no clear reason he had tried to determine from the outside which apartment was 207. All around the building stood brand-new developments—townhomes, duplexes, and condominiums, their promotional banners flying. Construction mud flowed down the driveways of townhomes with exposed pink insulation fibers around doorsills, plastic draped over windows, and people already living in them. The mud flowed across sidewalks and lawns. Nora's complex was only half finished and already all the parking places were taken.

After waiting and feeling foolish, Warren had gotten back into his rented car and driven down a suburban boulevard where store after store beckoned. Beckoned floor tiles, Western wear, ski wear, pies, toys, guns, tacos, VCRs, 4-WDs, RVs, mountain gear, survival gear, "personal" computers, designer sheets, imported tires, lifetime wheel alignments, instant differential oil changes, self-storage, lumber, venetian blinds, video rentals, private security, homemade cookies, stain-it-yourself furniture, feline veterinary; beckoned drivers to come and join in the American experience of having exactly what you want.

Warren wanted a greeting card store. When he found one, he bought a jigsaw puzzle. Then he returned to Nora's apartment building and laid out the puzzle pieces on a concrete ledge by the entrance. People came and went, wrestling with their keys, paying no heed. Rain fell for a few minutes in the late afternoon, but puddles quickly vanished into the dry air. The clouds didn't last, either. Near dusk, Nora came around the corner and into view.

She looked older, underfed, and more sharply defined. She was dressed in a woman's business suit and carrying a flat leather pouch, the last step before a briefcase. Warren was too nervous to speak. He tried to glance up casually from his puzzle as though it were Central Park and he was sitting at his usual place.

Nora stopped when she saw him. Winds accompanying the rain had carried away that day's smog, turning the Colorado sky into a pearl of blue depth. After a long and empty pause Nora stepped forward, timorous, speechless. She mumbled hello or something like that and let herself into the building; Warren followed.

The walls in her apartment were made from what appeared to be injected fiberglass. The doors were hollow, so insubstantial they would have flapped in a stiff breeze. Every home appliance imaginable was present, however, including a dishwasher with digital temperature display, and a remote-control toaster. There was a single wineglass, unwashed for several days, on the coffee table. Clothes and magazines were strewn about carelessly, suggesting that the apartment rarely knew visitors.

They stood in the center of one room inspecting each other, Nora still holding her purse and bag. Finally she spoke very rapidly. "I think this development was put up by the Japanese. Took about four days start to finish. You can rent, lease, buy, time-share, co-op, or swingle. The townhouses across the street have enclosed yards about the size of a jail cell. That makes you a landholder. I almost bought over there because of the financing. Great place to grow one tomato. What in God's name kept you?"

Long explanations followed. His first, Nora accepting quietly, wincing during the legal parts. Then hers. She had told Ford shortly after Warren left Seattle, and divorce had come a few months later.

"Ford's feelings were hurt desperately," Nora said. "I was confident that in the course of time Ford would be happier with someone new. But I never would have guessed how much it could hurt. He's gotten so handsome in the last few years with his white collars and coats that fit. I tried to tell him he was going to have the time of his life, break all the girls' hearts. Stable men are in fashion now."

"Has he found someone?"

"Sent me a picture about a year ago. She's a respiratory therapist at Rochester Presbyterian. They looked very sweet together. He said the ceremony would be soon, but didn't give details. I guess he feels that's no longer any of my business. I wrote back to say, 'Where did you find such a pretty girl?' I'm sure that made him happy. Oh, and he got hired away by Kodak as a sales division manager. It's a big step up. He also sent me a picture of the house they bought, but I couldn't look at it. I threw it away immediately."

Nora explained that following the divorce she had lived for a while in Seattle with her friend Felicity. She had made some money when, through her public relations contacts in Los Angeles, she was asked to ghost-write a Brooke Shields about how Brooke longed for a normal life and privacy. Nora could have made more, but she declined to accompany Shields on a nationwide publicity tour to promote the book.

Using the money, Nora had moved to Denver and there found a temporary job writing press releases for an independent oil firm called Broken Arrow Petroleum. The owner had hired her full-time—her first real job—mainly to drive around the high rural sands of western Colorado talking to civic groups and planning commissions in the small towns where Broken Arrow did its drilling.

Nora reported excitedly that she was making $650 a week— small businesses, like newspaper publishers, tending to view employment on a weekly basis—and had bought a Saab with a heated driver's seat right off the lot, on the spur of the moment. She had an office on the sixteenth floor of a bank building in booming downtown Denver, where she could sit and watch the city blocks fill up.

"Why didn't you call me and tell me all this," Warren asked.

"You should talk," she answered. "I had my responsibilities, too. How could I be happy when Ford was unhappy? I wanted to wait till he found someone else and my conscience was clear. When so much time passed I grew accustomed to the idea of never hearing from you again and even got to liking it in a sense. I thought it meant that I had been right all along. If I was going to be lonely for the rest of my life, at least I'd have the consolation of knowing I had been right."

Nora produced the photograph of Ford and his new wife; the beaming couple made Warren feel old. "Where did they get the strength to start all over?" he asked. "From the beginning, learning a whole new person, new needs, new quirks. Explaining yourself all over again. It sounds overwhelming."

Nora took back the photo and put it aside. "Not if it's worth it," she said.

"People have a notion that only the first time counts. The first love, the first place, either works or there is doom. We flatter ourselves by believing we can get it right on the first try. Think of all the things we stop doing just as we get good at them. Parents spend their lives raising kids; just when they start to know what they're doing, the kids are grown. It might take many, many tries to get it right at something important like love."

They were holding each other now and they kissed. For them this kiss was just like the first.

Namely, incompetent. Don't be deceived by the Hollywood special-effects smooch. Genuine first kisses, even among sophisticates, have all the graceful poise of two freight trains colliding on a dark siding. But they lead to more. In its clumsiness and laughter it truly *was* their first kiss again. Soon Warren and Nora were slipping around each other the way the wind slips through the trees.

The following morning the sky was blue as when the world was new.

They decided that Warren would move to Denver. Then he went in to the office with Nora and met Ben Beamer—founder and owner of Broken Arrow Petroleum—an expansive, agitated man whose chair was covered with dozens of pink phone-message slips that fluttered when he sat. Hearing that Warren was an engineer, Beamer offered to hire him as a petroleum geologist.

"I know nothing about that field," Warren said.

"Good," Beamer replied. "No bad habits. All you need in petroleum geology is brains and a strong nose. More oil has been found by nose than by all the computers in the world combined. How do you think I beat the majors?"

Warren agreed to start in two weeks; he would have to make one last trip home to present testimony—now as a witness—in the trial, and put his affairs in order. That day he simply wandered through the downtown streets, waiting for Nora to finish work. About ten days later the D.A.'s office called and said he would be needed on the stand the following afternoon. By then he felt as though he had always been with Nora, that no other condition had ever existed or could ever be possible.

Nora drove him to the airport in her Saab with the windows rolled down and the heated seat turned up to high. "I was going to ask you once before," he said on the way, "and you were going to say no. Will another try work there, too?" She answered, "Yes." Warren called her from a pay phone as soon as he got off the plane, and they picked the date. It would be the day he returned.

When he at last arrived on the witness stand, Warren found legal proceedings even duller than expected. No tense courtroom confrontations; no suspects breaking down and confessing with a maniacal laugh. Mostly, Warren was asked to make formal statements of the obvious. Have you ever seen this memo? And this one? And this? Were you on this date employed by the company now called Kessey Engineering? Did you have occasion to observe a particular file? Did you later have occasion to compare that file with any other file? At one point Warren was asked if he recognized his own signature.

Just before court adjourned there was a furious duel of

procedural motions, the upshot of which was that Warren would
have to take the stand again, to repeat a single answer, in about
a week. In the corridor outside the D.A. explained, "I have to
give in to them on non-essentials so the jury will think I'm
magnanimous."

After what they'd been through one more week should have
seemed inconsequential, but Warren knew he could not wait that
long to see Nora again. He called and asked her to change their
plan: take a vacation week, come join me, then we'll go back to
Denver together. Get the first plane you can. Nora sounded
mildly displeased, but an hour later had called with a flight
number, Western 446, arriving early the following afternoon.
Warren then called Lil and Tommy to invite them over to celebrate a much-delayed happy ending.

Warren spent the evening packing some of the remaining
possessions in his apartment, his mind at peace for the first time
in as long as he could remember. One item he came across was
a folder thick with photocopies of old newspaper articles concerning the Spanish-American War; detritus from many days
spent in the university library, searching books and bibliothecas
from the early sixteenth and late nineteenth centuries for any
further reference he might recognize.

That his search had been fruitless, Warren found inconclusive.
Probably he had examined less than one percent of the printed
record from those periods, and the chance of any one person's
passing being included in the printed record of life was extremely slight to begin with. All the hearts that have been broken
and not a word left behind, Warren thought. All the acts of
heroism or common persistence that have gone unrecorded—
they must by now number in the millions—all the doers of good
deeds who died alone and bitter. Vanished from this earth.

Or had they? Besides being unjust, it didn't make sense. Warren could not imagine that the hardest polished stones of life—
courage, love, devotion, tolerance—simply crumbled into soil
that the next age stepped on. *Somehow* good had to be stored and
conserved for eventual liberation. *Somewhere.* Unless life really
was meaningless. Could there be a universe with exquisite physi-

cal law and not the slightest spiritual coherence? It doesn't seem logical, Warren thought, and he found immense comfort in the idea that logic rather than sentiment demanded that the world make sense. He tossed the folder of photocopies into the garbage.

The following morning Warren realized he had packed so much the night before that his apartment now looked bare. Wanting it homey for Nora's arrival, he began methodically unpacking the boxes he had just filled. Around noon, conscious of not being late for the airport, Warren turned on his clock radio—the stereo had been sold for cash months ago—which was set to an all-news station that announced the time frequently. There was a crack of static and then a sound that, from the service, Warren associated with disaster: the snick-snick-snick of helicopter rotors.

". . . like a locomotive. Or a tornado. Or a volcano," a garbled voice from the radio was saying, shouting over sirens and the snicking.

"The sound was like a locomotive?"

"Roared like a locomotive. Going past you."

"And you, sir, were you also able to see it?"

"Me? Talking to me?"

"Yes, sir. You're on the air."

"Smoke was coming from the left side. From the left engine nacelle. Then it flipped over. No warning. Been in this business thirty years and I've never seen anything like it. Less than five hundred yards out. They almost made it."

"And you saw it strike the ground."

"Do what?"

"You actually saw it strike the ground."

"No, no. I was behind—"

"We can't hear you, sir."

"What?"

"Could you speak louder?"

"Yes, it was very loud. No flame after the impact. Just black smoke."

"Gentlemen, thank you. You're listening to NewsFest 98,

where the talk never stops. We've been speaking live to two members of the El Paso County rescue squad in our continuing coverage of the tragic crash of Western Airlines flight 446, which turned over and struck the ground this morning while attempting an emergency landing at Peterson Field in Colorado Springs, Colorado, killing fifty-four passengers and a crew of five. In a moment we'll be switching to FAA headquarters in Washington, D.C. . . ."

Warren listened numbly to the stream of information. Flight number 446 developed engine trouble on takeoff from Denver's Stapleton Airport. Is believed an engine disintegrated and that flying remnants of the turbine fan severed control cables. Plane could not be turned. Was flying south. Pilot decided to continue flying in straight line to first field due south, Peterson Field. Hundreds of motorists along Valley Highway linking Denver to Colorado Springs reported seeing crippled craft as it struggled to keep above the mountains. Was in air for nineteen minutes. Fire trucks and ambulances from three counties lined field as crippled flight arrived. Seconds before crash pilot radioed that he expected successful landing. Then airliner flipped out of control, cause unknown. Tips of compressor blades in turbofan engines move at equivalent of three thousand miles an hour. Housings supposedly strong enough to contain flying shreds should fan disintegrate. Spokesman for McDonnell Douglas points out that company does not manufacture the engines used in its aircraft. It's a common misconception that we build airplanes, spokesman says. In fact what we build are *air frames.* Associated Press is reporting that last month the FAA issued a warning about faulty slat-disagreement interlocks on DC9s with the same serial numbers as one believed to be involved in today's mishap.

Mishap. The newscaster paused for a commercial, and when he came back on was preceded by a trill of space-age music and a deep voice announcing, "BOOKING TO OBLIVION: THE FLIGHT WESTERN 446." Already the station had put together an electronic lead-in to help it hype the story. When Warren could make himself move he turned the radio off.

* * *

Nineteen minutes. For the remainder of his time alive, Warren Gifford thought of little else.

Nineteen minutes of Nora sealed up in the most absolute loneliness. Terrified; sick from the violent dipping and shaking of the plane; maybe unable even to speak to the passenger next to her, lost in his own pit of fright, for a final human consolation.

Nora was a strong woman and if a flight attendant had come on the P.A. system to say they were going to die in nineteen minutes—perhaps reading an FAA-approved crash liability disclaimer—she would have accepted her fate. But to fall to death in uncertainty, not knowing whether it was going to be all right or end, having to cling to the tail of life instead of setting her mind to the next world. . . . Had she looked out the window, at the ground heaving up and down? Tried to focus on the seat back? Warren, having the time for reflection and proper gathering of thoughts, felt strangely guilty.

In a remote, almost detached way Warren called Nora's parents. He expected them to be hysterical but instead they hardly spoke. An airline vice president had called to make it official; the parish priest was there with them; they were leaving for the church. They had the preacher take the line because they could not stand to talk further. The preacher spoke of ashes and dust.

Warren put a few papers in order, signed and stamped a few brief letters. Friends and acquaintances would soon be hearing about the crash. Warren found he could not bear the thought of talking about what had happened, either. To avoid callers expressing sympathy he switched on his answering machine and turned the speaker off. Through the course of the afternoon the phone rang several times. In an idle way he wondered what would become of the messages.

Although he wasn't cold, Warren put on his old football jacket. The nylon crinkled as he moved; it felt good. He took the gun from its hiding place, a bracket under the desk, then took the clip from another bracket hidden across the room. He removed the blank round. There was no doubt in his mind. Even if there was only the slightest chance of meeting Nora again, he had to take it.

For a long time Warren sat fixing Nora's image in his mind as vividly as he could, wanting the final image of her to be so intense it would come along with him. Maybe he could find her again more easily that way. Or convince somebody he was sincere and deserved help.

After a while he could picture her so clearly in his thoughts that Nora actually seemed to be present—just out of sight in the next room, about to turn the corner. The feeling grew so strong that for an instant Warren became disoriented, thinking she really *was* there with him. When he came out of this trance he felt so alone he would have been afraid to watch snow fall. Warren knew it was the time. Had she been able to focus on him, too, just before that last moment?

A few hours later, when Lil and Tommy turned on the evening news, they heard about the plane. They came straight to Warren's building. Getting no response to his buzzer, they waited for a resident to come along and slipped in. When there was no reply to knocks Tommy tried the door, which he found unlocked. Then he blocked the entrance with his body so Lil wouldn't see.

By that time, depending on whom you believe, Warren and Nora had either ceased to exist, except as notations on some official forms; or were in each other's arms forever, and with their Father's blessing; or were wandering blind down an endless crystal hallway, looking for a door to step through in hopes of meeting again.

—18—
ONE STEP CLOSER

Unknown to Warren, an issue of the Azimuth newsletter had been delivered to his mailbox that last afternoon. Printed across the envelope was URGENT RUSH EDITION: OPEN BEFORE YOU DO ANYTHING ELSE! The letter had been mailed second class.

Had Warren seen the final newsletter, he would have read:

IS LOVE "REAL"?
THE TIME HAS COME. YOU MUST DECIDE.
To aid you in this trackless choice, let us consider how others have answered the same question. Let us consider the play *Romeo and Juliet,* written in 1591.

Its title characters believed love is real, and they wound up dead. Not much of a testimonial.

Yet to understand what love has meant to others who came before, we must recall how attitudes toward this encumbrance much sought have been altered by the course of time.

Today the action of *Romeo and Juliet* seems like carnival hokum. A 14-year-old girl pledges eternal troth to a boy to whom she has spoken twice, of whom she knows nothing. Five days after first sight they both commit suicide. While they woo the boy stands below her window making claims of veneration like:

> See, how she leans her cheek upon her hand!
> O, that I were a glove upon that hand,
> That I might touch that cheek!

Spoken by a character in a modern play, such delirium would cause the audience to guffaw. The words, however, have a social context that has been forgotten. When they were written, romantic love was disbelieved and close to forbidden.

Not in the Hollywood sense of "forbidden love"—She was a poor seamstress haunted by memories of the concentration camps! He was a wealthy playboy from the planet Xathnos!—but in the sense of opposed by political, civic, and religious convention.

Marriages in Elizabethan times were usually arranged, or took place between parties of only cursory acquaintance. Even if two potential lovers met outside the boundaries of social restrictions (unlikely enough), there were few accepted means by which they could begin to explore each other's character and inclinations. Dating, as we conceive it, meant about as much then as drive-through banking. Those who suffered the longings of romantic love were by and large considered mad—off their rockers in the clinical sense.

This social animosity to love was dictated to some extent by economics. As late as Shakespeare's day much of the population still lived in common rooms. Only the aristocratic class had access to physical privacy or the leisure by which to enjoy it. The economic structures necessary for widespread pursuit of romantic love simply did not exist, any more than economic structures existed for vacations in the Caribbean. Lovers who wished to spend their time locked away with each other—or worse, merely locked away, pining alone for their loves—were called crazy because economics demanded that such behavior be discouraged.

Post-Renaissance attitudes about romantic love took into account political expedience as well. Any breakdown of arranged marriage might begin the breakdown of an order premised on passive acceptance of class boundaries. This especially worried the ruling classes, who in asserting their claims to extraordinary privilege found it necessary to deny that nobles and commoners should even mingle, much less adore one another.

Love could likewise be a threat to state and crown. Should average people, through the force of romance, become loyal first to *other individuals*, not collectivities, their nationalist loyalties might fade. This may or may not be a good thing for humanity, but would unquestionably represent a disaster for government officials. German society grew so suspicious of the disruptive potential of love that its artists developed the notion of *liebestod,* meaning love-death—that when lovers entwined by passion rather than by sanction of parent or prince slept together for the first time, they would literally die of ecstasy. Presumably this discouraged curious pubescents.

The Catholic Church, which also held out against romantic love, had a parallel concern. Church administrators wanted their flock to love the hierarchy of priests, bishops, pope, and saints in lieu of loving God directly: if man made direct contact with God, the prelates would be out of jobs. Not that an outbreak of general religious rapture was exactly imminent, but the church felt it prudent to foreclose that possibility just in case.

Romeo and Juliet, then, were more than two teenagers making goo-goo eyes. They were a menace to the status quo. Their conclusion that love was real—that it took precedence over other claims on the individual, including claims of family, religion, and state—made them revolutionaries.

Arthur Brooke, on whose 1562 poem the play is based, saw fit to distance himself from the lovers by condemning them in a preface as "thralling themselves to unhonest desire" and "neglecting authority." Brooke consoled his readers by implying that such abnegation of civic duty could only transpire in heathen Verona, where the poem is set. Never in Mother England.

Friar Lawrence, who secretly marries Romeo and Juliet in his cell—in the *privacy* of his cell, for the lovers' private satisfaction alone—then hatches the baleful scheme to free Juliet from her parents by faking her death, today seems merely a gear in the plot. By the standards of the time he was a heretic: obedience to authority, even civil authority, being a far higher priority for the church than personal ardor. Shakespeare, believing in romantic love but also wanting to get his show performed, hedged on the politically charged issue of whether Friar Lawrence had done right. As the Prince of Verona appears in the denouement of *Romeo and Juliet* to restore social order, he leaves vague the question of whether the cleric will be "pardoned or punished."

When the first Shakespeare folios were placed in the Oxford University library in 1623, a single passage among them was read and read again, with reverence, by the brightest children of the realm. Read and reread until, in the words of one historian, "The margin of the page crumbled under the touch of countless fingers." That passage? The balcony scene from *Romeo and Juliet.* By today's standards, corn; by the standards of the time, a call for personal and political liberation.

Can anyone imagine students at the top schools of the present day pouring over a lyrical endorsement of romantic love? More likely to win their approval would be an adaptation in which Romeo is played as a gay mass murderer and Juliet is being held as a sex slave by the Capulet Corporation.

In a way, of course, this change is to be expected. The social barriers faced by lovers of the past have been torn down. Today just about anybody can steal away with just about anybody else just about anytime. Meanwhile, the "true" variant of love has become such a standard of schlock—used endlessly and indiscriminately in the media which surround us—that the idea is made to seem as improbable as the shows themselves. The worse a made-for-TV movie, the more likely it is to have "true" love oozing from its core. Actors whose lives the public knows to be successions of acrimonious divorce cases play naive lovebirds, while a sound track by some performer being sued for palimony in twelve jurisdictions croons on till you gag.

Given this, it would seem natural to conclude that the revolutionary potential of love was a pipe dream all along. Once, some droll medieval grad students dreamed that love would transform society. Now, love is sold on supermarket racks, and society remains a chilly cave.

Then again, should we abandon the quest for peace because we have so far failed to find it? Declare the very idea of peace a fraud because the word is invoked by those whose true intentions point elsewhere? That is the same as saying that since love has been a flop up till now, it won't work in the future. And a good conjunction of thoughts—because love, widely felt and practiced, would be as revolutionary as the abolition of war.

No doubt readers are now mentally calculating the odds of love becoming a major social force, and arriving at an integer followed by an impressive string of zeros. Fair enough; it would be absurd to pretend otherwise. Yet we face a world in which, by general agreement, some vital component is missing. What else might it be?

Name the other force, however distant, that could disarm the infantries of hatred, comfort the sad and too-wise heart, and give our material opulence meaning. Name the other force that could banish loneliness. Existing social mechanisms—law, charity, deterrence—seek only to manage the calamities of life. They offer no *solution*. Love does. And therefore is worth pursuing, the distance of the prospect notwithstanding.

To complete an earlier analogy, love is to humanity what gravity is to cosmology.

In individual cases, gravity is a trifle. The amount of gravity radiated by a baseball, for instance, is too meager to measure. Setting the baseball afire, on the other hand, would generate a decent amount of heat; splitting the baseball's atoms would produce enough power to destroy a small town; fusing those same atoms would flatten a medium-sized city; annihilating them with complementary particles of anti-matter would obliterate a metropolitan region.

When all the baseballs in the world are combined, however, with all the rocks and suns of the cosmos, gravity accumulates into a force surpassing every other in magnitude. Millions of nuclear bombs would not be sufficient to break the sun's gravitational grasp and move the earth from its orbit. Billions of nuclear bombs could not dislodge a solar system from its position in the galactic plane. The gravity singularities popularly called black holes have such majestic power they can swallow up the detonations of entire stars and not be damaged themselves. Some astronomers project that the cumulative effect of gravity will ultimately determine the fate of creation: the galaxies, for eons speeding away from our cosmic starting

point, will be drawn back by the pull of the places they thought
they left behind.

What if love turns out to be the same? Weak, minor, easily
abused on a small scale; overwhelming when accumulated.

If everyone believed love was real, then it would be—
wouldn't it? And then all other forces of human nature
combined would wither by comparison. To prosper, most
systems and theories require elaborate mechanisms of
implementation; a few require only faith. Ironically, though the
ones requiring faith have been most difficult to realize, it is they
alone over which the average man and woman can assert control.

None of this can be proven with facts. But what can facts
really "prove"? Argument from fact is invariably selective:
since the proponent cannot mention every item of information,
he mentions only those facts that support his case. His
opponent mentions only those that undermine. In a vast, diverse
society such as the United States, for each fact one side can cite
that appears to prove a point of view, the other can cite a fact
that appears to prove the opposite. This is why so many political
and intellectual disputes seem to go on forever.

And why, in the end, only what is believed is real. Beliefs can
be good or bad. Wrong beliefs have caused uncountable
sorrows; just beliefs have imbued life with purpose. But one
good belief is worth a million carefully verified facts: what a
person *knows* transcends anything he can prove.

Those who choose to believe that love is an impostor, or a
pettiness, will no doubt be pleased that so far the evidence is on
their side. Most human lives have passed, and continue to pass,
without the realization of love. Chance almost always sides with
failure, making it seem that nature herself opposes higher
emotions. And there's no way to "prove" this forlorn point of
view wrong.

Yet in so many lives a minor alteration of circumstance or
timing might have led to the attainment of love. Those who
despite the proof have faith that there is more—perhaps, much
more—will always believe that another outcome is possible.

At the end of the newsletter was a postscript written in Ned Stryker's hand. It said:

Warren,

Just did a computer simulation that shows there are more than 28,000 different possible outcomes to the average person's day depending solely on when he receives his first phone call.

The permutations caused by alterations of significant events, such as a change in travel plans, are too monumental to calculate.

Peace, love & muff,
Ned

—17—

Nora Jocelyn could scarcely grasp the evening headline: the flight she had been booked on had crashed.

It was chance she saw the headline at all. Her idled train was going to sit for at least another hour, according to what she could understand of the garbled public-address announcement—and with Amtrak an hour meant at least another two hours. So after trying once again to call Warren she had purchased a newspaper and sat down to read.

Nora had been too embarrassed the previous day when Warren called to admit that she, a grown woman, was terrified of getting on an airplane. What a thing to tell an engineer. Warren had not seemed to notice years before when she had left him standing in the art gallery so rudely with such bad news that she was leaving on a Saturday afternoon in order to get to Kansas City by a Monday morning; she was taking the train.

When Warren called about the trial delay Nora had decided to make an attempt to rise above her fears. Then, after she made reservations on the Western flight, Nora's courage deserted her. At about eleven P.M. she checked with Amtrak and learned there was an overnight train leaving at eleven-forty. Racing to meet it she had no time to stop and phone Warren. At each station since sunrise she had gotten off and tried to put through the call. But each time Nora had only been able to reach Warren's answering machine, a clunk followed by a strip of magnetized plastic imitating his voice.

When Nora first picked up the newspaper she had skipped right past the headline, as the eye is often repelled by insistent type and scans instead for word of events that offer the consolation of being taken lightly. Nora had slogged halfway to the end of a story about some federal cabinet official under pressure to resign—it was never exactly clear what the official had done, although the story went on for eighty column-inches—when she became aware that the gray pattern at the center of page one represented the remains of an airplane.

In the photo a fireman was standing next to a detached span of wing. The fireman wasn't doing anything, just posing as though with a trophy. A corner of the photograph, showing the fireman's face, was blown up into a box with colored borders at the top of the page, next to the teaser COLORADO CRASH CLAIMS 59. Other color-doused teaser boxes were lined up in a row. One said, PRESIDENT CALLS BASKETBALL COACH. Another, NOW: DESIGNER GLOVES FOR WEIGHT LIFTERS. A third, VANESSA WILLIAMS ISSUES PLEA FOR NUCLEAR DISARMAMENT.

Looking at the dotted little fireman, whose distorted countenance was unmistakable despite its image being no more than a quarter inch high, Nora wondered what would have been worse: to have been on the plane and killed, or to have been a rescuer arriving just in time to be useless.

The terror of the nineteen-minute cascade did not register with her. Had she been on the plane, she would have assumed herself dead from the first jolt. To Nora machines either worked with inexplicable sorcery or failed completely. She imagined that if a single fuse blew out an overhead light, or a single screw came loose in the galley, an aircraft would plummet to the ground instantly. For this reason Nora refused to use word processors, thinking that one erroneous keystroke would send her entire life's work into that phantom zone where electronic information goes and never comes back, floating forever with broken promises and the socks that disappear from clothes dryers.

Merely knowing mechanical principles was bad luck, Nora felt, whether the device at hand was a car, a computer, a furnace, or anything else. The more you knew the more likely something was to go wrong: the machine would sense your concern about its condition and fail on purpose, in order to get attention.

Shortly after reading the newspaper Nora began to worry that, because she had booked a reservation on Western 446, a computer somewhere was listing her among the dead. She called the airline. As soon as Nora identified herself the operator transferred her to a supervisor. Without so much as offering a pleasantry, the supervisor began reciting a prepared legal text about how passengers booked "but not personally present" on an aircraft that crashed were not entitled to compensation of any kind. Nora hung up and dialed her parents.

Both talking at once, they related how a neighbor had called around noon to tell them the news and sent the household into a panic. It was two hours before they could get confirmation from the airline that Nora had not boarded the plane. Meanwhile, another neighbor had called the local television station. By the time they found out nothing had happened to Nora, the police chief had arrived; the volunteer fire department had sent an ambulance; and three television vans had parked on their lawn, setting up antennas that looked like they were designed to make contact with the outer moons of Neptune.

"Dear, this makes the second time the media have been to this house," Nora's mother said. "People are starting to talk."

Her mother also said they had tried to call Warren to tell him there was nothing to worry about, but had been unable to get through. All they could get was his answering machine.

After talking to her parents Nora called Warren's number again. Again his machine answered. It was nine at night on the day she was due—where could he be?

Another garbled announcement emanated from the train station loudspeakers. The inverted-whorl anti-fenestration compensator on coach number four—or whatever the conductor said—had been fixed. After hours of listless delay the train was going to leave *right now,* all aboard *immediately.* Passengers who had been dozing on the station benches or pacing about absentmindedly began dashing and careening about madly.

The coaches themselves were not crowded. The train was a subsidy special, kept in operation thanks to the committee assignment of a congressman whose tiny hometown, which he had not visited in twenty years, happened to lie on the right-of-way.

Getting back on in haste like the rest, Nora discovered she had left her newspaper behind. She looked around. Just three other passengers in her coach: a man wearing what appeared to be half a dozen layers of clothing; a woman clutching her small valise to her lap though there were plenty of places to put it; and a young man in an Army jacket whose face was too rounded and smooth to be a veteran's. Nora had heard the young man hectoring a hapless Amtrak clerk during the layover—it was inexcusable, it was consumer fraud, did they know whom they were dealing with? As though he were the first person in the history of the world to be inconvenienced by delay.

Once the train was finally moving again, Nora relaxed. The rumble of forward progress lulled and pacified her. She tried not to think about where Warren might be or why he didn't answer the phone, since it had always been her policy not to worry about matters beyond her control. There had to be a rational explanation. The train cleared town and began to accelerate, rolling through the darkness. Drawn toward drowsiness, Nora thought again of the circumstances between her and Warren.

In Denver she had told him, "If the past has been stolen from us, whoever's got it can keep it." Nora felt little nostalgia or remorse over the passage of time, even though she knew this meant certain moments and sensations that had slipped by could never be recaptured. To her, looking back was a foolish exercise, particularly in light of the fact that the forebears over whom we now wax nostalgic spent their time looking ahead.

Had so much really changed? Nora was confident that anyone who had lived five hundred or even five thousand years before, teleported to our moment, would require surprisingly little time to adjust. Certainly no time to start complaining. The physical circumstances of life may have changed, and may change ever faster, but the point had not. Love; freedom; family; honor; comfort; money; pleasure; sex; a higher purpose: along the way there had been additions to the inventory of mankind's expectations, but few subtractions.

Nora found it significant that themes in writing from the past —whether Russian novels, Shakespeare, even ancient texts predating Rome—remained instantly recognizable to readers in the present. Modern audiences could appreciate *Antigone* without knowing the political or technological particulars of the period because they sense that variations on the mundane details that had obsessed the Greeks then, or the different types that obsess us today, are no more than curiosities in the larger scheme.

The new proton chip, the latest self-propelled telephone, the upcoming this or that—it made Nora's head swim. What mattered about all our marvelous machines was what people would say to each other after they were tired of playing with them, same as had mattered before.

In the fuzzy, unquestioning style of Americans, Nora believed in the future. One has, in a sense, no reasonable choice but to believe the future holds promise. Otherwise you'd go mad and your society would unravel. The countries that had fallen to pieces or become wicked were usually countries where people stopped believing tomorrow would be better than today. Thus Nora could not say whether choosing to believe in something she'd be nuts not to believe carried any moral authority. But believe she did.

There were those who said the promise of a better future was an opiate, and who predicted—sometimes, it seemed, impatiently—that everything was about to unravel. Surely, Nora thought, if the future were an opiate, people would have caught on to that by now: mankind having experienced thousands of years of the future from the perspective of our predecessors.

The future that captivated Nora's hopes did not have much to do with microchips or macroeconomics. Americans were said to be an optimistic genus because their material circumstances had steadily improved. For them food, warmth, and devices of extraordinary distinction had always been close at hand. Nora was bored with devices and gadgets, and that was one reason she felt optimistic for the future.

Someday—not tomorrow or the next day, but someday—the practical limits of devices and gadgets would be reached. What would come then? Even after mankind possessed every device it could reasonably possess, it would still need to grow. So, Nora thought, we would need a new assignment. It would have to be a challenging one, able to keep people occupied for thousands of years.

Nora had once heard Warren remark that he wondered what God's motivation was. Since no one could force God to be the sovereign, there would have to be something in it for Him, or He wouldn't bother. Perhaps, she thought, God has structured love in the form we see it sputtering among human creatures precisely because that is the love He seeks. *We are made in His image.* Why don't people take that simple phrase as meaning exactly what it says? Maybe God and man are not much different at all. If so then God must want what we want—family, company, comfort—must want us to find Him and ease His loneliness. I bet anything, Nora thought, God has a dog.

And if God is more like us, if "His image" works in both directions, then God would long to be told it's all right. To be set free from reproaching Himself for His mistakes. If He, like us, were afraid of dying, He would be anxious for assistance in the search for meaning. God would need us as much as we need Him: maybe more, if ever His good are to be crowned with brotherhood.

Parents, Nora reflected, go through several stages of affection toward their children. Children are loved first as creations, then as extraordinary pets, then as remembrances of the parents' own youth, and finally as complete beings in their own right. Each stage is transitory except for the last. In the end the parent takes advice from the child.

Nora felt her love for Warren well up and, in the flash that accompanies recognition of the obvious, beheld what was of lasting importance about these feelings. What matters about love, she saw, is that *anybody can do it.* She and Warren were affected by special circumstances but that was a bonus, not a requirement. After all, they still didn't know if they were reading from a new script or old, and they never would. *Anybody* could find love and offer it up to the heavens. Anybody who was willing to toss out the facts and believe.

Abruptly, the coach became bright again. The train was coming to a halt, brakes protesting. The underground station, in the manner of train stations, was dimly lit as though this would prevent travelers from noticing the dirt and disrepair. It was well past midnight. Groggy relatives and lovers, thinking ahead to how tired they would be at work in the morning, stood by to greet the arrivals.

Among them on the platform—in fact directly outside Nora's window, although the train had many windows to choose from —stood Warren Gifford. He wore the look of a man reading about a football game he'd already seen.

"I almost made a bad mistake today," Warren said as he helped Nora down from the train. He seemed blissfully composed. "But I was thinking about you, thinking very hard, and at the last moment I remembered something."

Nora regarded him quizzically. "At the last moment before what?" she asked.

He ignored her question. "I remembered," Warren continued, "there were no airplanes then. Lots of people were terrified of the sky."

Warren looked across the tracks at the barely illuminated station clock and smiled. "This train is really late," he said.